# The Vacant Seat

C.J. Toca

Saddle Ridge Publications, LLC—Madison, WI
ISBN:  979-8-9868996-2-6
eBook ISBN: 979-8-9868996-3-3
Library of Congress Control Number: 2022916375
Title: *The Vacant Seat*
Author: C.J. Toca
Digital distribution | 2023
Paperback | 2023

To my grandmother, devoted to the *Sanctae Romanae Ecclesiae*

Other books by C.J. Toca:


*The Secret Heir* published in 2022, the sequel to *The Vacant Seat,* and coming next *The Lost Painting,* the sequel to *The Secret Heir*

Visit www.cjtoca.com

# Chapter 1
*Rome, Italy, June 1*

Stefania cowered on the cobblestone pavement of a narrow Roman backstreet next to an idling black Maserati Quadroporte. Ringing permeated Stefania's head as explosions and gunshots surrounded her.

In seconds of life-shattering terror, the past day's events raced through her mind.

*I thought this Vatican story wouldn't lead to anything. Now I might not survive.*

"Stay down," Thomas instructed calmly in his English accent as he swiped his wavy blond hair to the side. His blue blazer, gold tie and khaki pants seemed oddly in place. Thomas' blue eyes evinced calm and safety, but terror gripped her.

"Thomas!" she yelled back.

Her heart pounding, tears poured down her cheeks, hands on her ears, she ducked next to the car in her now tattered full length black *hijab*. Bullets ricocheted off the Maserati, whistling through the air around her. Thomas stood, sprinted to the back of the Maserati and snatched an automatic rifle from the open trunk. Crouching down, he started returning gunfire in short bursts. Spent shell casings flew into the air, bouncing off the pavement like hailstones. Stefania took a panicked frightened breath. The acrid taste of gun smoke coated her mouth.

The haze of battle now obscured the bright late-day June sun like a fog rolling down the narrow street toward her. Everything moved in silent slow motion. Like rain, flaming debris fell all around her.

*Thomas don't leave me. Please don't leave me here,* she pled.

As if he read her mind, Thomas dropped the gun and grasped her forearm. Thomas yanked her from the pavement, put his arm around her waist, and led her down the street out of the maelstrom of destruction to safety beyond the killing zone. He had become her friend, her protector, and the one she loved but not yet her lover.

Six Days Earlier<br>Rome, Italy, May 24

Wearing a white terrycloth bathrobe and sitting on stool at eleven o'clock, Stefania looked at herself in the bathroom mirror and brushed her long jet black tresses. Late and unable to sleep, she placed the brush on the marble countertop and added some drops to her dry green eyes. Stefania examined her olive complexion, pulling her skin here and there. She liked her cute button of a nose, but maybe her lips should be fuller. Her first day as a journalist started tomorrow. Butterflies flew around in her empty stomach, which growled from hunger. Nerves kept Stefania from eating.

Her phone rang. She jumped.

*It's mama.*

"Hello mama," she answered.

"My darling daughter, I just called to wish you good luck at your first day at work tomorrow, and to tell you I miss you so much," said Fernanda in Portuguese.

"Thanks mama," replied Stefania.

Fernanda's soothing voice calmed Stefania's nerves.

"I so wish you hadn't left Rio. Your aunt, uncle and cousins miss you so very much."

"Mama, we've been over this many times," said Stefania.

"I know dear, but you can't blame your mother for caring. I'd hoped you'd maybe reconsider. You were doing so well in Brazil as a model, and helping me out with my design business, I think you'd be a great success in a year or two."

"I'm sorry, mama. I feel like I need to find myself, I need direction, a purpose in life, I want to make a difference. I have an empty feeling inside," lamented Stefania. "Thanks to papa, this journalism job may fit the bill."

"I don't know why you can't do that in Rio?" asked Fernanda. "You are twenty-seven, your whole life lies in front of you."

"That's the point," said Stefania. "I need a change of pace, a newness in my life. Moving to Rome will force me to break out on my own, experience new things, find that something, a feeling of

2

fulfillment that's eluded me. And it's not like I'm here alone, papa is here."

"Don't get me started with your father," replied Fernanda. "If he hadn't gotten you the job you'd never have moved."

"That's unfair," said Stefania. "If he didn't get me the job in Rome, I'd probably have moved in with one of my college friends in the states."

"Well my dear, I wish you the best for tomorrow, and please don't forget about us here in Brazil."

"You know that will never happen, mama. Good night and I love you."

"I love you too, my dear."

*Rome, Italy, May 25*

Stefania walked down the *Via Veneto* in the heart of Rome to the journal's offices, which were on the third floor of an old building with a marble facade, above a *ristorante*. After taking the elevator from the first floor lobby to the third floor, she stood in the reception area for a few moments, calculating whether this was a huge mistake as her mother had intimated. Other employees buzzed about, passing in and out of the reception area.

Not what Stefania expected, the offices were not new and sleek, but something she imagined from the 1950s. Hardwood doors, with glass windows, some frosted, some clear. The floors were worn white marble with black marble edging near the white plaster walls.

A short bespeckled gray haired woman in a blue dress emerged from a doorway behind the reception desk.

"Are you here for Rodolfo?" she asked.

"Yes, I have an appointment with *Dottore* D'Agostino," said Stefania.

"Follow me," the woman said.

She led Stefania through an outer office, where apparently the woman worked behind a small wooden desk, to another office.

"Rodolfo will be with you momentarily," the woman said. "Feel free to sit while you wait."

There was a black leather sofa against the far wall, and two black leather low-back chairs in front of a cluttered old oak desk. Stefania plopped herself in one of those chairs and waited.

3

She passed the time by fidgeting with odd and ends on Rodolfo's desk, files, books, papers piled about the messy space. Rodolfo, her new boss, hadn't arrived yet; another tortured delay in anticipation of her first day in a career she'd dreamt of since she chose her major in journalism at university. Perspiring from the lack of air conditioning on a warm May day, Stefania strained to keep cool. A little breeze came from the ceiling fan or from the open window. Car horns and exhaust and loud voices from the *Via Veneto* three floors below echoed through the cluttered office.

Stefania's dark mane hung over her shoulders to just above her modest pert breasts. She fiddled with her hair, a nervous habit of hers. Her green eyes took stock of the messy office. She crossed and re-crossed her olive toned athletic legs several times, readjusting her knee length white skirt every time. She then turned attention to her floral print blouse. She didn't have much cleavage given her slim figure, but she didn't want to show too much. Various *bric-à-brac* covered the shelves of a wooden bookcase on the wall behind the desk.

*I should have worked out some of this energy. Yoga or Pilates this morning would have done some good*, she thought.

The musty room combined with a tinge of car exhaust gave her the sniffles. Stefania's mind started drifting. All of a sudden with a creak and a thud, a door opened and closed. She turned, and there stood a short, thin bespectacled Italian gentleman with a full tuft of gray hair, wearing a rumpled blue suit, white shirt, and orange and blue tie, slightly loosened around the neck.

Hired on recommendation from her father, a university professor in Rome, she had never met her new boss. He sidled behind his desk and sat.

"Well, you must be Stefania," he bellowed with a slight smirk.

"Yes, sir," she replied.

"As you may have surmised, I'm Rodolfo D'Agostino. You're ready for your first assignment, eh?" he queried, as if her response was going to be anything but *yes*.

He scratched his head with his left hand.

"I understand you've been out of university in America for a few years, you're twenty-seven, young and enthusiastic, I hope. What did you do between university and today?" Rodolfo asked.

Brushing the strands of her hair from her eyes, Stefania considered her response.

"I traveled some in Europe and South America," she answered. "I lived with my mother in Rio for a while, helped her with her fashion design business, did some modeling but wanted to pursue a writing career. My father lives here in Rome, so I moved back to Rome and here I am."

"I know your father, naturally, which is why you're here. He and I have worked on some historical projects together over the years. I must say, I don't see the family resemblance; maybe your nose. It looks Italian."

"Everyone says I most resemble my mama, who's Brazilian. My complexion is more Brazilian than Italian."

"Anyway, how much do you know about church history?" he asked.

Stefania, sweating anew, played with her hair again.

*Which church? What religion?* She thought.

"Well?" Rodolfo asked again in a slightly more forceful tone. "What do you know about church history? Has the cat got your tongue?"

Clearing the mucky phlegm that suddenly clogged her throat, she sheepishly managed a response.

"Sir, ah, which church's history?"

"Miss," Rodolfo replied, "well, of course I'm speaking about the Catholic church, the Roman Catholic Church, the universal church. Do you understand me? When in Rome and one speaks of the Church, there's only one church."

"I'm sorry." Stefania quickly concocted an excuse. "I didn't understand your question fully. I apologize."

"Well, do you have a decent knowledge of church history or not?" Rodolfo persisted.

"I took a class in church history in college so I have knowledge of church matters," she stated with feigned confidence.

"Hmm, and you can read and write in Italian and Latin, yes?" he asked.

*That's a question I can at least answer truthfully and proudly.*

"Yes, I can read and write in Italian, Latin, French, Spanish, Portuguese, and American English."

"Very good. You're perfect for this assignment. Outside of church circles it's difficult to find someone who reads and writes Italian and Latin well, especially among journalists. Of course, Italian and Latin are the official languages of the Vatican City State, so the materials you'll be reviewing will be either in Latin or Italian."

"Naturally," Stefania replied meekly, "of course."

"Due to my connections with the Vatican, as the editor of the *Journal,* being a scholarly periodical, I'm accredited with the Vatican Secret Archives, which is a difficult accreditation to obtain. I've taken the liberty and had you accredited as my assistant."

"Thank you, sir. What materials will I be reviewing?"

"Only papal materials prior to the pope's death in October, 1958 are available for outside review by the few accredited researchers and organizations. All materials after that remain secret unless ordered by the pope. I've asked for materials from 1918 to be pulled for review in connection with the pope's efforts to resolve the First World War and the peace process leading to the war's conclusion. I've been desirous of publishing an article on this subject for some time now. You are to review the documents and hopefully develop a story line. The archival materials will be made available beginning tomorrow. Do you understand what I'm saying?"

"I think so," Stefania replied somberly with dejection. "But other than a short visit to Saint Peter's Basilica and Vatican museums years ago, I've never been to Vatican City, and certainly not to the non-public areas."

"No matter. There's a first time for everything," Rodolfo retorted.

*Who cares what happened in 1918? What about the great problems of today? The northern Italian regions who want to separate from Italy, terrorism, the Middle East, the war in the Ukraine, the immigration crisis in Italy?*

Deep in her heart Stefania knew she'd have to start somewhere, and that somewhere appeared to be at the Vatican Secret Archives.

"If you need assistance, I'll be available, and you should expect that I will co-author the article. Understood?" Rodolfo queried.

Stefania nodded.

"Depending on what you find, I'll give you great latitude as to what direction to go with the article. Go tomorrow to the archives, see what you find. Use as much time as you require and report back to me. We'll discuss a tact going forward. Here are the instructions for entry to the archives, your accreditation, and other necessary paperwork."

Rodolfo, now smiling, handed Stefania some documents.

Stefania took the documents.

"Thank you, sir. I'll report back after my initial review," Stefania replied in a monotone.

Traipsing out onto the *Via Veneto,* she gazed up at the clear blue sky.

*Aces! What an awful start. Now I'll have to spend my night researching the Catholic Church as well as the First World War.*

*The Vatican City State, May 26*

Walking past the mile long rope of humanity waiting for entry to the Vatican museums which wound around the ancient walls of Vatican City, Stefania arrived at the Vatican Library entryway on the *Via di Porta Angelica* at nine o'clock. She struggled the entire time to suppress nausea, the kind she got before a first date.

*Will my lack of knowledge be my downfall? Will I be able to sift through the materials here and intelligently report back to Rodolfo?*

Arriving at a huge arched portal known as the *Porta di Santa Anna*, Stefania proceeded through to a guard station.

She expected the chaos typical of the entrance to the Vatican museums, queues of people, noisy, a din of activity. Instead, she found a quiet glass-enclosed guard station with an x-ray machine, a metal detector, desk, and a smartly uniformed gendarme at the desk and another behind a glass partition.

"Credentials?" the guard at the desk demanded.

Stefania, sniffling, rubbed her nose. An odd combination of sanitary cleaner used on floors and the cologne of the gendarme hung in the air. Stefania presented the papers given to her by Rodolfo, sizing the gendarme up.

The officer, in a crisp blue uniform, made eye contact with Stefania.

"Your name is on the list," he quipped, checking her name off.

Stefania placed her ever present large black leather shoulder bag onto the conveyor belt for x-ray viewing, and then proceeded through the metal detector.

The guard rifled through the contents of her bag.

"You'll have to check any phone or camera here," the guard declared. "No electronic devices other than laptops are permitted and no photos permitted beyond this point. You can only make written notes in pencil or laptop. No pen, food, or drink is permitted."

The guard looked over her things.

"No laptop?" he asked.

"No," responded Stefania sheepishly. "I didn't think to bring it, just pad, paper and pencils."

Before she could remove her phone from her coat pocket, she heard loud voices and a commotion down the hallway. A man yelled in Italian, with the gendarme bolting off down the hall and another appearing from behind a partition, staring down the hall from where the voices were coming from.

"It must stay, it must stay," the gendarmes in the hallway ordered. "Get him out!"

The new guard, appearing to be preoccupied with the events unfolding in the corridor gave the bag back and didn't bother searching Stefania's coat.

"Ride the elevator to the basement reading room level. I'll let the archivist know you're on the way, and she'll meet you at the elevator," he hurriedly said.

Stefania met the archivist as instructed. The archivist turned out to be a peaked fiftyish skeleton of a woman with gray hair, garlic breath, a huge mole on her cheek, thick eyeglasses, and a pencil sticking out of a bun in her hair.

*Not a forgettable person*, thought Stefania.

"Follow me, miss," the archivist directed, escorting Stefania through this strange space in the depths of the Vatican. Sweat beaded on her forehead. Perspiration soaked her red blouse.

Dull and flickering fluorescent lighting lit the way through the long narrow cave-like passageway, which consisted of drab gray ceilings barely two meters in height with bookcases and shelves on both sides. Fearful of enclosed spaces, she desperately hoped that she would end up in a less confined spot. Finally, through a doorway, a larger, brightly illuminated reading room furnished with long tables and chairs. Surrounding the tables, bookshelves filled with materials. Despite several other desks in the reading room, Stefania had the place to herself.

"Here are the materials *dottore* D'Agostino requested for your review," whispered the archivist, pointing to one of the bookshelves with slipcases with "1918" handwritten on the spines.

"They're not digitalized?" asked Stefania.

"No, miss."

"Aces."

Stefania, catching her breath, calmed herself and now hoped she could get through her initial review quickly.

"You must wear these gloves when reviewing the archival material," the archivist directed. "Report to me when you've concluded; you saw my office on the way in. You have until 1700. If I don't hear from you before then, I shall come to collect you. The materials will stay on these shelves here until we're informed that your research has concluded."

Except for the sound of the air conditioning from the vent overhead, muffled voices, and occasional distant footsteps, silence drenched the room. Stefania, now completely alone in this deserted place, began perspiring again. On the shelves in front of her stood stacks of off-white slipcases with writing on the spine indicating the year and volume. She noticed a camera above the entry door. Someone, somewhere, watched her every move.

*What am I doing here? Why can't I be interviewing a major political figure of the day, the mayor of Rome, a minister of state? I suppose one has to start somewhere. But the Catholic Church? A subject that's about as far from my interests as football.*

Stefania lamented her lack of a love life. She had gone on a date with a Spaniard banker named Andres the week before in Rome. He ghosted her.

Taking out her notebook, pencil, and slipping on the white gloves given to her, she removed materials from the first case.

*This must be a mistake. All of this stuff is schedules of meetings and agendas for a pope in 1978.*

The night before when she discussed her assignment with her father he mentioned a pope who held the papacy for only a month or so in 1978 and died unexpectedly. She thought Rodolfo said that materials after 1958 couldn't be released.

Examining the slipcase, the year "1978" was sloppily written on the side by what looked like fountain pen, but the seven could easily have been mistaken for a one.

*This must have been misfiled,* she concluded. *It probably isn't even ready for release, given the fact that the date on the slipcase was handwritten.*

Holding the slipcase in her hands, she stared at it for a minute or two.

*This mistake could be an opportunity to find something interesting not available to the public.*

Stefania went through the materials meticulously and with great detail. She took notes regarding correspondences with world leaders, congratulatory notes from such persons, from members of the clergy and nobility. She examined a ledger of those who met with the pope during his brief pontificate. She copied down this copiously. The material contained little information on the pope's death, only a death certificate listing the cause of death as a heart attack.

Stefania, skipping lunch, continued reviewing the documents from 1978, not wanting to go through the bother of leaving for lunch, then returning through security and the claustrophobic passageway.

*This is depressing. I thought the archivist's error could lead to something exciting. This is all drivel, probably worse than reviewing the actual 1918 stuff. I should complete reviewing the 1978 stuff in case they discover the error.*

Having been at the archives now for almost eight hours, Stefania yawned, stood, and stretched. She instinctively reached into her shoulder bag for her phone to check messages but caught herself before she pulled her phone out.

*The camera above the door; someone would see the phone. The guard must have forgotten to collect the phone due to the commotion in the hallway.*

Having finished reviewing the last volume, she lifted and placed it on the shelf when she dropped the slipcase and it fell to the floor with a loud smack. Startled, she jumped.

Picking up the volume, she noticed that the binding cracked and a folded paper fell out. She must have missed this paper before because the document apparently had been stuck between the binding and the slipcase volume cover.

She quickly read it, translating the Latin in her mind.

*Hmm, an invitation to cardinals to attend a meeting in Vatican City in 1970. Interesting, but this is well before the pope was even elected. Another mistake. It's almost 1700, too late to transcribe the particulars of this by hand. I'll take a quick photo of it.*

She laid the document flat on her open bag which sat on the chair next to her, with her jacket draped across the armrest. Turning her back to the camera, and with her bag in front of her on the chair, she took out her phone and photographed the document. She opened her blouse and slid the phone into her bra, concealed by her loose fitting frock. She placed the document back into the slipcase, and shoved it back onto the shelf.

*I'm pretty sure I got the photo out of view of the camera.*

Footsteps proceeded toward the room; someone approached. The archivist with the mole appeared at the doorway.

"Oh, you surprised me!" Stefania exclaimed.

"It's time for you to go," the archivist announced.

Slipping on her coat, Stefania took care to conceal the phone she hid in her bra.

The archivist quickly glanced at the slipcases on the shelves and wrote something on a piece of paper.

"Give this to the gendarme on your way out," she said.

Stefania began sweating again.

The archivist led Stefania to the elevators. Stefania proceeded back to the guard station and presented the paper to the gendarme.

"Thank you, but I must still inspect your bag and coat," the man declared.

Handing over her bag, the officer rifled through it. Appearing satisfied, he gave it back to her.

"May I have your coat?" he asked.

Stefania handed over her coat. The guard looked through the pockets and sleeves and handed it back. He paged through papers on his clipboard for a time bending minute.

Over the guard's shoulder she saw the black and white video screen of the room she just left. The hair on the back of her neck stood on end.

"Says here you didn't check any phone, tablet, or camera?" he inquired.

"Correct," she answered.

All of the muscles in her body tightened.

"Good evening, miss. You're free to go," the guard said with a nod and a smile.

"Good evening," she replied, letting out a breath of relief.

*Whew, fortunately the gendarme didn't search my person, and I didn't have to go through the metal detector on the way out. I've got to get out of here quickly.*

Dashing down the hallway out of the archives, she rushed up the white marble staircase to the main entry area. Turning the corner of the stairwell landing, she ran straight into a tall young man in a tan suit and yellow striped tie, dropping her large shoulder bag and its contents onto the floor at his feet. A cleric accompanied the man.

"I'm so sorry," she said apologetically in Italian.

"Do please let me help you," the man replied with an English accent, his right hand swiping his blond hair off his forehead.

His blue eyes made contact with hers.

"That's alright, I've got it," she replied in English, starting to gather all that fell onto the floor and repacking her bag.

"Right," he replied with a smile, still gathering the flotsam from her bag which littered the marble floor.

"Thank you," she responded, brushing herself off.

"I'm Thomas; Thomas Houghton," he said, introducing himself as they both crouched down picking up the various sundries, pencils, a pad, makeup, lip gloss, a spare tampon, other odds and ends, which had fallen out of Stefania's large shoulder bag.

"I'm Stefania," she retorted, blushing.

*This Thomas is thin, tall and athletic build, and crazy blue eyes, and that accent. Whew! A complete package.*

"What brings you here?" Thomas inquired.

Thomas now stood with her pencil and pad in his hands. Stefania pulled herself off of the floor with her bag and what she had gathered.

The cleric who accompanied Thomas stood by with a look of impatience on his face.

"I'm reviewing materials at the archives."

"Oh, that's interesting," Thomas said with a stammer.

"And you?" Stefania replied, now curious about this Thomas.

"Pardon?" Thomas appeared confused.

"And you; what are you doing here?"

"Well, I have business here at the Vatican," Thomas answered, again stuttering as he placed what he had of Stefania's flotsam back into her bag.

Stefania, seeing two uniformed gendarmes approaching the group from behind Thomas, decided to make a quick departure, as much as she desired to stay and speak with this handsome Englishman.

"I have matters to attend to. I shall be in touch with your grace regarding today's meetings with the secretariat of state," declared the cleric standing next to Thomas.

"Yes, thank you, monsignor," Thomas replied.

Stefania, taking advantage of the interruption, trotted across the busy vestibule and sped out of the archives' entrance, picking up the pace as she strode down the *Via Sant'Anna* to the exit of the Vatican City State at the *Via di Porta Angelica*. Her heart rate quickened, pounding against her ribcage, and she started to perspire. After having been waved through the exit, she exhaled a sigh of relief, calming down as she walked up the *Via di Porta Angelica*.

*Once again I missed a terrific opportunity; it would have been nice to get to know him. I'm famished. I can't believe I spent the whole day buried in there without having eaten a thing.*

Stefania crossed the *Via de Porta Angelica* to a small *trattoria* crowded with people having a drink or espresso after work. She got the last seat left outside at a sidewalk table for four.

"Miss, if we have other customers, you'll have to share the table," the *cameriere* warned.

"Yes, I understand," Stefania responded as she began looking at the menu. "I'll have a bottle of flat water and a glass of the house red wine, thank you."

"Certainly," the *cameriere* responded.

Having been served her water and wine, she declared, "I'll have fried artichoke hearts, *prosciutto de Parma* with buffalo *mozzarella*, and fresh strawberries for dessert."

"Yes, miss," the waiter responded.

Stefania scrolled through her texts and e-mails on her phone, having accumulated a full eight plus hours of messages from the early hours of the day. Engrossed in her phone, she hardly noticed when the *cameriere* sat another customer diagonally across on the other side of the table.

"Stefania?" someone said.

Hearing her name, she looked up and noticed Thomas, the Englishman from the Vatican.

"Ah, hello," she responded.

"I hope you don't mind if I join you. I typically come here for a glass of wine or espresso late in the day after business in the Vatican, and this is the only seat available here," Thomas explained.

*This may be my second chance with Thomas.*

"Yes, of course. I don't mind at all."

*I'm extremely curious about this guy.*

"So you're a researcher?" Thomas inquired.

"Sort of. I'm a writer for an Italian scholarly periodical called the *Italian Monthly Journal*. I was in the Vatican on assignment; my first assignment actually," she responded.

"I've heard of that journal. So you're doing historical research then?" Thomas pressed.

"Yes," Stefania replied.

"You sound ambitious. That's admirable," Thomas observed.

"I've been called that, yes," Stefania answered.

*I don't like talking about myself. I'll change the subject.*

"Well, what were you doing at the Vatican?"

"I was there to introduce my friend, one of the Anglo Catholic clergy, to the secretary of state of the Holy See. I'm acting as a sort of facilitator," Thomas replied.

"But you're not clergy?"

Thomas laughed, taking a sip of his now served house wine.

"No, I'm not clergy. My family has been involved over the years in church matters, so you could say I'm involved in church affairs," he clarified.

"Why did that man refer to you as 'your grace?'"

"My family is prominent in church circles," explained Thomas.

*An evasive answer*, she thought.

The *cameriere* served her food.

"You don't mind if I eat, do you?" she politely inquired of Thomas.

"Not at all," Thomas replied. "I'm the interloper here."

"Would you like a fried artichoke heart or two and some of my *prosciutto* and *mozzarella*?" she offered. "I won't finish it all."

"If it's no bother," Thomas replied.

"Not at all."

Stefania placed some of the artichoke hearts and ham and cheese onto Thomas' bread plate.

*Don't lose control of the conversation, Stefania. Keep the questions flying*, she thought.

"So you live in Rome?"

"No, I live in the UK; to be exact, near a village called Houghton-St. Giles at my family's residence there."

"So you live with your parents then?"

"My parents are deceased. They died in a car accident when I was but three years. I was raised by my grandmother, my father's mother, and also by my Aunt Josephine, but mostly by my grandmother, and of course a governess. I'm an only child."

"I'm so sorry to hear that."

"It's fine really. I have no recollection of my parents. My grandmother is the only mother I've ever known. What about you? You're Italian?"

*This guy is charming and easy to speak to. His good looks and sophistication are a bonus. I'll open up a little.*

"My papa is Italian, and my mama is Brazilian. My papa lives in Rome. He's a university professor here, and my mama lives in Rio. She's a fashion designer. They're divorced, and I'm also an only child. That's about it."

"So where do you think of as home, Rome or Rio?"

"Neither. I went off to university in the states. I lived in Rio with my mama but spent winters, I mean your European summers, with my papa in Rome. When at university, I would spend most holidays with my mama and her family in Rio, then summers in Rome with papa."

"Well where do you prefer, Brazil or Rome?" he asked.

"I'm not really wedded to either place, Rome for now I suppose."

"What did you do following university?" Thomas asked.

"After university, I worked for my mama's designer business in Brazil, wrote press releases and descriptions for her website, and did some modeling. Then I decided I wanted to become an author, so my papa helped obtain a position for me with the *Italian Monthly Journal*. He knows my boss, Rodolfo D'Agostino."

*It's nice he's interested in my background.*

"So you speak Italian and Portuguese?" Thomas asked in choppy heavily English-accented Portuguese.

"Yes. You speak Portuguese?" Stefania excitedly asked.

"Yes. Italian, French, Spanish as well, and a pinch of Scott's Gaelic," Thomas admitted.

"I speak all of those, as well as Latin; except Gaelic, of course," Stefania replied in Portuguese.

"Unfortunately I never quite mastered Latin, I do know a little here and there," Thomas, switching to Tuscan Italian, acknowledged. "Bits and pieces, church Latin mostly, despite my grandma's insistence that I master it. So what are your favorite places in Italy?"

"There's this small little town in Tuscany, takes seemingly forever to get to from Florence, on top of a mountain," Stefania replied also in Italian. "It's called Volterra. The people there specialize in alabaster carvings and statuary. It's off the beaten track. Although it's getting on the radar, still few tourists, and the views. . ."

". . . and the views from the wall along the main mountain road up to the town are incredible!" Thomas finished Stefania's sentence. "Those views must go miles and miles over the countryside. I've been there myself. There's an ancient Roman amphitheater there, narrow cobbled streets, and the town has a small *duomo*, ancient baptistery, as well as a small civic museum with some wonderful works of art."

"That's so funny that we've both been to this place. I've been to the museum too. Unlike the rest of Tuscany, you have Volterra to yourself even during tourist season."

"Yes, yes, similar to Montalcino in that respect," Thomas noted.

"I love Montalcino as well," Stefania replied. "I think I was there during the high tourist season with my papa, and it seemed like we had the place to ourselves, at least in the morning."

"Ah yes, and the nearby monastery of San'Atimo is a great place to visit, and for a picnic lunch," Thomas observed. "Too bad no one tells you about the mosquitoes in Tuscany. My God, they must be the state bird."

"That's so true," Stefania agreed. "I was with my papa at a tree nursery near Cantagrillo and we almost got eaten alive! Another great little mountain town is Coreglia Antelminelli, secreted up the Serchio Valley in Tuscany. Not a touristy place but delightful panoramic views."

"Yes," Thomas responded excitedly. "I know the place. I've been there too. It's known for its plaster figurines. There's also a wonderful painting of *Our Lady of the Rosary* by Pietro Sorri in the Church of San Martino off the main *piazza*."

"I've been to the town, but not to the church. It's coincidental you and I have been to these same places in Tuscany, especially since I only travelled with my papa in the summers when I'm in Rome," Stefania replied.

*Wow, we have some things in common.*

"So you never answered what was the specific reason you were at the Vatican anyway?" Thomas asked in French this time.

"Well, it requires some explanation," she responded in French. "As I said, I'm on my first literary assignment for the *Journal*. I was reviewing materials at the archives today, all of which dealt with the brief pontificate in 1978. The most frequent visitor to the pope during 1978 was an imam, Sheikh Ali Salah el-Amin. Based on materials I read in the archives, I think this Sheikh lives somewhere here in Rome," she said with a shrug and paused.

"How do you know the most frequent visitor to the pope in 1978 was this Sheikh?" Thomas queried with a cocked head.

"I reviewed those materials at the Vatican archives today. You know, that's where I was coming from when you and I first met," she responded without much thought.

"But," Thomas began to say, scratching his head with his right hand, but seemed to catch himself, "I didn't know those materials had been released?"

"Well, I saw them," she off-handedly responded, recognizing belatedly that she let the cat out of the bag so to speak.

"Hmm, matters involving the brief pontificate in 1978 interest me very much," Thomas explained, rubbing his chin with his right hand. "Mostly due to my Aunt Josephine, Sister Josephine actually. She's a nun, retired of course. She was one of the pope's attendants in those days, but she rarely discusses her experiences then. I assumed because the pontificate was so short. Members of the family stopped inquiring because it would get her out of sorts. No one has raised it for years."

Taking out her notebook, which Stefania kept in her ever-present shoulder bag, she flipped through a few pages.

"My notes indicate there was a Sister Josephine who was one of the pope's attendants in 1978 and served him regularly. You're telling me that's your aunt, your grandmother's sister?"

"Not quite. She's my grandfather's sister, but she lives with my grandmother," Thomas explained.

"Again, I'm sorry. I thought your grandmother was deceased. She's still with you?"

"Oh yes, quite. She's in her early nineties and a spitfire. She's sharp as a knife. She and my aunt live together, sometimes with me at Haverford and sometimes at my great uncle's lodge in Scotland."

"If my editor wants to pursue this, can I call your aunt for an interview?" Stefania interjected.

"I don't think that's a good idea. She's not particularly ambulatory, has some difficulty hearing over the phone, and frankly, if you have any luck at all with her, it will be in person," Thomas replied with apparent apprehension. "She's refused to speak of her time at the Vatican, of which I'm extremely curious."

"That's unfortunate. If my editor lets me change the direction of this project, an interview might be the next step," Stefania interrupted.

"Well," Thomas continued, "Aunt Josephine is now well in her eighties, not in particularly good health and maybe, just maybe, she might be willing to speak about it now, especially if you spoke to her in Tuscan Italian, a language she loves to hear. You may be the catalyst to get her to spill the proverbial beans about her experience in 1978. I frankly would love to hear what she has to say about it. I've wondered about it desperately for years, but she's refused my enquiries, and I'm not as conversant in Italian as you. She hasn't long to live after all."

"This is quite coincidental, me reviewing these archival documents where your aunt is mentioned and meeting you," Stefania remarked with a smile.

Thomas smiled back.

"There are no such things as coincidences," he observed. "Coincidences are when God is winking at us. There's a local saint in Norfolk, Saint Julian of Norwich. She was an important mystic of her time. She documented her mystical visions. In her missive called *Revelations of Divine Love*, of coincidences, she wrote 'And I saw that truly nothing happens by accident or luck but everything by God's wise providence.'"

"I'm not sure I *buy that* explanation, but why does the 1978 pontificate interest you so?" Stefania queried.

*Interesting, normally I'd think this guy's historical digression boorish, but it's a pleasing quirk about him.*

"There were rumours the pope's death wasn't by natural causes, but they were only rumours. I was always curious about it. If anyone would know details, it would be my aunt," Thomas replied.

Stefania toyed with the leftover food on her plate with a fork.

"I see you've finished your wine. Would you like some more?" asked Thomas.

"Yes, thank you."

Thomas poured some wine from the decanter into Stefania's glass, which she eagerly sipped.

"I saw the death certificate. It listed a heart issue as the cause of death," Stefania recalled.

*If Rodolfo had me follow-up on the 1978 archival material, he'd want me to speak to Sister Josephine. If I could go back to Rodolfo with at least that option, I might be relieved of reviewing the 1918 material which was bound to be skull drudgery.*

"An interview with your aunt would make sense if my editor wants me to pursue a story in connection with the 1978 materials. My original assignment was to review the 1918 archival materials," she continued.

"That would make sense, if your editor modifies the scope of your project," replied Thomas.

"Initially I wasn't too enthused about this project. I'm not religious, don't know much about religion, and personally think a lot of this stuff is mumbo jumbo. It's a crutch for the weak to justify why things happen. Didn't Karl Marx theorize that religion is the opiate of the masses," she said.

"Actually I'm not sure that's precisely it, but he did ponder some such thing. I'm religious and deeply spiritual and believe in these things. Many people do. Spirituality is not a crutch. In my view it's a natural and important part of humanity," Thomas, clearly insulted, replying in English and changing his tone from the casual to the serious, said with a tremor in his voice.

Her heart skipped a beat.

"I'm sorry if I offended you. I wasn't brought up in a religious household, and frankly, at university in New England, my education was secular. 'Religion' and 'spirituality' were bad words there, especially regarding Christianity. The elites in America are hostile to religion in general."

"Yes," Thomas agreed, "the church of the masses has become the church of the very few and devout."

Stefania nervously fidgeted with her hair.

Thomas abruptly got up from his chair to leave.

"I'll pay the tab. Consider it my treat," he said politely with a half-smile.

Stefania didn't resist. Having lost track of time, she checked her phone for the first time.

"Thank you.  My, I must be going too. I'm supposed to meet a friend in a half hour. If I'm authorized, when can we arrange for me to speak with your aunt?"

"Give me your mobile number, and I'll text or phone you regarding meeting her," Thomas asked. "I'm flying back home this evening, and I'll see what I can do. I'll be in touch."

"Give me your number and I'll text you so you have my number," retorted Stefania, not wanting to lose the potential contact with Thomas.

The two exchanged numbers by text.

"It was nice meeting you, Stefania. As I said, I'll be in touch if I can arrange something. Good evening."

Thomas got up and departed, fading into the crowds on the *Via di Porta Angelica.*

*Aces. I probably torpedoed any opportunity to interview his aunt through my stupid statement about his religious beliefs. I hope I hear from him.*

# Chapter 2
*Yasenevo, Russia, May 27*

Quite contented and in-charge, Svetlana Greschenko sat behind a sleek new Scandinavian style birch-wood desk in her expansive air conditioned offices at the modern headquarters of the Russian Foreign Intelligence Service, the SVR, in suburban Yasenevo. Tinted windows wrapped around the outside walls of her corner office, with light wood parquet floors, accented by a beige throw rug and matching beige walls.

A career operative, and physical fitness junkie, the thirty-six year old Greschenko pulled her shoulder length brown locks back in a pony tail for comfort. Always stylishly dressed, this day Greschenko wore a loose fitting black blouse and a short tight fitting black and white striped skirt. Her bare toned legs telegraphed her incredible physique.

The office door opened; an expected face walked in.

*It's Vledev.*

"Good morning Boris Androvich," said Greschenko. "I appreciate this final visit on your last day. I understand I have large shoes to fill, but you and Vasily taught me well. I'll hit the ground running, so to speak," Greschenko continued.

"Yes, Svetlana Sergeyevna, I suppose you're quite prepared. May I sit?" Vledev asked in his baritone voice. Vledev wore a baggy gray suit with a gray tie and white shirt. Heavy and in his seventies, with loose strands of gray hair swept across his jowly head, Vledev looked the part of a retiring senior spy.

"Certainly," she responded as she also sat down. "I'm sorry I couldn't see you earlier, but I took my morning swim and exercised."

"Yes, Svetlana Sergeyevna, the whole directorate is well aware of your fitness regimen. Every man, and some of the women, in the directorate give you a look over in the gym, if you know what I mean."

"Thank you, Boris Androvich. I appreciate the compliment, I think."

"I don't have to remind you, of course, that at thirty-six you're the youngest head of Directorate KR. But there are some things you don't know, and much yet to learn. Naturally, your succession to my position indicates that our superiors see you as dedicated to the Russian Federation. Your ambition is legendary," commented Vledev.

"Again, I thank you, Vledev. Although I cannot imagine anything I don't know," responded Greschenko confidently, putting on her black-framed eyeglasses.

At six feet tall, Svetlana Greschenko knew she had the looks and build of an athlete. Her position, however, made her much more dangerous than an Olympian.

"I'm afraid I'm in good spirits this day, Boris. There's little you can do to quell my good mood."

"Before I get to the task at hand, may I offer you some advice?" asked Vledev.

"Certainly," responded Greschenko.

"You may not wish to hear these things, but I offer you thoughts as a colleague who only wishes for your continued success," noted Vledev.

"Boris Androvich, this is quite unlike you. Well, what advice do you have?" queried Stefania with a dismissive huff, taking her glasses off and tossing them onto her immaculate desktop.

"It is about your reputation."

"My reputation?"

"The entire directorate knows you are incredibly ambitious. Ambition has its downfalls. Toes may be stepped upon. Those toes have friends, and their friends have friends," said Vledev.

"I don't understand," remarked Greschenko.

"Oh, I think you do," replied Vledev. "Some see you as a back-stabber, an operative who will do everything and anything to rise to the top. There are rumours you slept with superiors to obtain your promotion to deputy director, whether true or not, I know not. Many don't trust you."

Ire churned through Greschenko's gut, and her fists clenched.

"I have worked hard for everything I've obtained," she shot back, slamming her right fist on the desktop.

"I know that, but others do not. You've left debris in your wake," said Vledev. "Debris equates to enemies. Everyone has enemies, but in our business it is better that the enemies are from other countries, as opposed to our own."

"I know I've enemies Boris, but I'm dedicated to the Russian Federation," responded Greschenko. "No one can challenge my loyalty. I intend to be director one day. That's my objective, and I don't care how I obtain the directorship."

"You were protected Svetlana Sergeyevna, first by Vasily, then by me because I promised Vasily I would look after you. The president likes you, but His Excellency will not be around forever. He can be persuaded by others with power. He feeds on power like a shark feeds on flesh. Then there is the issue of how you dress, what you wear, your bags, shoes, hats."

"So I like nice things, so what?" Greschenko asked.

"It raises eyebrows," said Vledev. "The best way to defuse your enemies is to take their ammunition away."

Resentful of Vledev's comments, Svetlana's blood was boiling.

"Do you choose to be unattached?" he asked softly.

"No," responded Greschenko defiantly. "Love has not found me and frankly I don't know if I've time for it. Love is a liability in our business."

"I see," murmured Vledev. "It is easy in this business to fly solo. Is it convenient? Yes. Is it ideal? Perhaps. Is it practical? No. I would never have maintained my sanity over the years without my dearest Anastasya who will accompany me in my retirement. Life is easier with a companion, a human companion, not a house cat. These are some thoughts for you to consider in your new role."

"Is that *all* Boris Androvich?" she asked somewhat curtly.

"There are also rumours about your sexual preferences," Vledev stated with a raised brow. "Being bisexual is frowned upon."

"Rumours Vledev," snapped Greschenko. "Rumours meant to harass me."

"More than harassment will befall you if these rumours are in fact true," Vledev replied calmly.

Greschenko scoffed.

"There is one more thing Svetlana Sergeyevna. You're aware of almost everything you'll need to know. You're aware of all active matters already, but there is one dormant matter of which you haven't been made aware of which you should be briefed," said Vledev.

"You have a sense of humor after all, Vledev," responded Greschenko, chuckling.

Greschenko assumed Vledev joked, except she knew that, like her, he didn't engage in frivolous banter.

"Vledev, are you serious? There's virtually nothing which has gone on in SVR in the last fifteen years or so that I'm not aware of."

"Unlike your prior position as my vice deputy, your promotion comes with a government car driven by a bodyguard, a government jet, and some unfortunate and extraordinary responsibilities. I'm serious, deadly so. The only persons who were aware of this particular operation were me, Vasily as the chief of the First Directorate KGB, the general secretary of the CPSU, and later the president of the Russian Federation," continued Vledev.

"So this pre-dates the Russian Federation then? Why should we care after all these years? I don't want to be saddled with someone else's problems."

Greschenko smelled trouble, and her instincts tended to be uncannily accurate.

"Let me state first off that this was Vasily's brainchild. Second, I think I'm the only one other than the president who's able to provide you with the necessary introduction, most of it anecdotally. As the successor to the First Directorate KGB, Directorate KR is responsible for this matter. It comes with the office. You have little choice. As my successor, this operational file comes with the job."

Silence filled the room. As his protégé, Vasily took Greschenko under his wing. He had no family, and Greschenko was his legacy. Greschenko knew Vasily thought of her as a grandchild. Other than her sister and brother, nephews and nieces, Greschenko loved no one except her cat. The one exception-her loyalty to Vasily. He was the closest she had to family in Moscow before he died of lung cancer.

"What do you mean it was Vasily's?" she queried. "When you assumed Vasily's position upon his death, then I took your spot as deputy, I assumed I wasn't kept in the dark on any matter."

"This operation was conceived and handled solely by Vasily from the early 1950s to 1981. Not even the chairman of the KGB was aware of the project, at least up to the point he became general secretary in the case of Comrade Andropov."

Vledev removed a large manila file from his briefcase held together by two brown ribbons tied together.

"What have you there?" Greschenko inquired.

"None of the Archangel files were ever digitalized, nor should they ever be. There are two paper files, one in the possession of the president and one in the possession of the deputy director SVR Directorate KR. This is Vasily's paper file which he kept in his document safe, and which I inherited from him. Now you inherit it from me. May I finally explain?"

"Certainly, yes," assented Greschenko, recognizing that this truly may be an important matter, and likewise cognizant of Vledev's impatience.

"The operation was called Operation Archangel," began Vledev. "It was conceived by Vasily in the early 1950s as a plan to infiltrate the Vatican to manipulate events so it wouldn't be confrontational with the USSR, and so that it wouldn't be a continuing threat or obstacle to the USSR and Warsaw Pact allies with significant Catholic populations, such as Poland, Hungary, and Czechoslovakia, and wouldn't interfere with the spread of the socialist revolution in Cuba and in central and south America, also where Catholicism is prevalent. There's also a prophecy involving the dedication of Russia to the Holy Mother by the pope which the USSR didn't want to come to pass due to its propaganda value."

"This interests me, Vledev. As you know, my mother was Russian and my father Ukrainian. At the urging of his mother I was secretly baptized as a Ukrainian Greek Catholic. I've never practiced and it's not part of my *persona*, but my brother and sister are devout Catholics. When I served as the SVR resident in Rome I actually visited the Vatican with the president and brought back rosaries blessed by the pope for my sister and brother. Tell me more, Vledev. Was this Operation Archangel successful?"

"Yes," Vledev admitted with discomfort in his voice. "In fact, it proceeded extraordinarily well for twenty years. Archangel went dark in 1981 when the attempted assassination of the pope failed. Because of the incredible secrecy, nothing substantive regarding

Archangel is to be placed in electronic files, and any and all communications with others regarding Archangel, should there be the need, are to be in person and not by phone or electronic means, and away from prying eyes."

"Well shouldn't the director of SVR know the details? Why should this be my concern?" Greschenko asked.

"The director of SVR isn't aware of this operation and is not to be made aware of it. You must understand that, given the Russian Federation's foreign policy objectives, its current relationship with the Vatican, and the Moscow Patriarchate's relationship with the Vatican, nothing regarding this operation may ever come to light, and Russia must never be associated with it. To my knowledge, we've been lucky thus far."

"To say the least," snipped Greschenko.

"Well, it's all in the file here." Vledev tapped the folder with his right hand. "It's now a dead operation," he declared.

Greschenko, now intensely curious, stared at the folder on Vledev's lap.

"Do you comprehend the repercussions?" asked Vledev softly.

"Certainly," she responded. "I can only imagine the consequences. Even now the Vatican is acting as an important intermediary with Russia and the western powers to resolve the conflict in the Ukraine, as well as sanctions imposed by the UK. A summit meeting between the pope, the prime minister of the UK, and the president is scheduled for July first, and I plan on being there, ostensibly as a diplomat."

"Russia is no longer an atheist state, Svetlana Sergeyevna," Vledev emphasized. "As you know, the president is ostensibly devout and has close connections with the Orthodox Church. It's imperative that Archangel, and the fact that it ever existed and was implemented, never sees the light of the day. You're a minder of Archangel, so to speak. You must make sure that the details of the Archangel plan are never made public. All persons with potential knowledge have been flagged in SVR's database. If any leaks occur, you must plug them, if you know what I'm saying."

"Yes, I understand completely," replied Greschenko, now eager to review the file, which would be nostalgic given Vasily's involvement. "Plug them with wet operations."

"Very wet.  I strongly suggest you keep the Archangel file in your document safe. Now if you don't mind, I'll take my leave. My last flight on my government plane will be to Sochi, and it's fully fueled and waiting for me with Anastasya at Kubinka."

Greschenko stood and shook hands with Vledev.

"Good luck, Boris Androvich," she said as they parted.

"Thank you, Svetlana Sergeyevna, but you're the one who's going to need the luck," he responded with a slight frown as he hurried out of the office.

After Vledev left, Greschenko snatched up the Archangel file and went over to her eclectic birch conference table next to the tinted window overlooking lush and leafy Bitsevsky Park and sat down. She untied the ribbons securing the folder and began leafing through the paperwork.

The Archangel documents had Vasily's name and writing all over them. She pored over the file, filled with a treasure trove of Cold War documents, communiqués, identities of double agents, and dossiers on the subject of blackmail, as well as photographs and other intelligence. Transfixed, Greschenko hadn't the time but skipped lunch and spent the entire day reading the complete file anyway.

*This is remarkable. Vasily, you were truly exceptional. Those were incredible times. What an ingenious plan. I wish I were with you then during those heady days when you conceived and implemented this operation. I can only imagine the excitement then. However, I trust my old friend that I'll never have to deal with this.*

# Chapter 3
*Rome, Italy, May 27*

Stefania set out from her father's flat where she lived to Rodolfo's offices on the *Via Veneto*. Taking a deep breath of the humid May Roman air, her nose filled with the sweet aroma of citrus blossoms from nearby rooftop lemon trees. A sunny day, Stefania walked down the hill on the *Via Veneto* from the *Porta Pinciana* evaluating her predicament.

*Maybe what I've found may provide an excuse to either follow-up a new lead with Thomas' aunt or result in a different assignment altogether.*

Checking her phone as she walked up the stairs to Rodolfo's office at the *Journal*, she saw no text from the Spanish banker she went on a date with last week.

"Ugh," she said.

*Am I ever going to meet someone? Maybe something with this Thomas might pan out, but there's no text from him either. I should have stalked him on the internet last night.*

She strode into Rodolfo's office, where he sat at his desk.

"Good day. You're back; that was quick. I expected it would take you a few days or a week for your initial review the material," Rodolfo snapped as Stefania entered his office. "Well then, what have you found?"

After sitting down, she cleared her throat.

*I'll make the best impression possible, and I've got to shake this downcast mood.*

"Well, I didn't yet review the 1918 archival material," she said.

"Why not?" Rodolfo asked in an irritated tone.

"They gave me material for 1978 in addition to the 1918 material. It must have been a mistake. I noticed the '1978' sloppily written on the spine of the slipcase looked like '1918' and it was probably misfiled. I know you said that the archives hadn't released any material after 1958, so I thought it was worth reviewing the 1978 material before the error was discovered."

"What?" exclaimed Rodolfo. "This is the first time I've heard of the archives making such a grievous error. Are you positive?"

*I'll be assertive and confident this time. I was less than self-assured, almost meek, when I first met Rodolfo.*

"Yes, I spent the entire day reviewing the 1978 material. The mistake was likely caused by the conflation of the seven and the one on the dates. Both spines were poorly handwritten in fountain pen with similar ink and looked virtually the same. I hope you're not offended that I reviewed material which shouldn't have been released."

"Of course not," Rodolfo gleefully countered. "It's the Vatican's transgression, not yours. As journalists, we must accept the opportunities that present themselves. I commend you for taking the initiative. The 1918 material will always be available. Once they discover the mistake, the 1978 material might not be available until 2048 at the earliest. So what was in the 1978 material?"

"It was only the material regarding the pope's short reign in 1978. Because the 1978 pontificate was short, there wasn't much there except scheduling, some correspondence, and the like, as far as I could see. Nothing significant on his death of interest, other than the death certificate saying the cause of death was a heart attack, which my subsequent research indicated had already been made public."

Picking up her notes, she showed them to Rodolfo.

"There were also papers regarding the *sede vacante*. I may have to go back a few more times. But the pope had many contacts, many of whom are deceased. He was particularly good friends with a certain Sheikh, the former Grand Mufti of Alexandria, Ali Salah el-Amin. Apparently they were involved in some kind of ecumenical discussions."

"I know of this Sheikh," Rodolfo observed, edging up on his seat. "I'm sorry, Stefania. Please continue."

"Well, the Sheikh met with the pope four times during the thirty-three days when he was pope, which was the most of any person outside of the Vatican. In fact, he met with the pope hours before he died, the last person outside the Vatican to have done so. Based on my research, he's still alive apparently, in his eighties, and believe it or not, lives here in Rome, but he never sees visitors, and the most I could determine was that he lives here, but I don't know where, and I have no way to contact him. Perhaps he could provide insight on the pope, his relationship with him, maybe his state of mind before he died?"

"Hmm, you raise an interesting angle," he replied. "This Sheikh was before your time, but he was controversial in his native Egypt years ago. He lives in exile."

"Why was he controversial?" asked Stefania.

"He was in Egypt when Nasser was in power. There were rumours that he was an agent of the CIA or MI6. Nasser was a socialist and close with the Soviets. There were death threats against the Sheikh; there's still a mark on his head to this day. I tried to get an interview with him years ago, but although I spoke to his assistant, he would never see me. Keep in mind there were rumours that the pope's death in 1978 was not by natural causes as claimed by the Vatican. Did you see anything else in the event this Sheikh becomes a dead end?"

"Merely a document on a meeting which occurred well before his pontificate, and a list of the pope's household," Stefania replied with a shrug.

The arrival of Rodolfo's wife interrupted their conversation.

"This is my wife Sofia," Rodolfo introduced the two. "She stops by occasionally to keep an eye on me," he said followed by a laugh.

Sofia appeared about Rodolfo's age, a short graying mousy brunette with shoulder length hair but much lighter skin, plainly dressed in a white blouse and black pleated skirt.

"Sofia completed me," Rodolfo continued. "I was walking in the wilderness, and then I met Sofia."

"How did you meet?" Stefania inquired, always interested in how people fell in love and got married, hoping one day happenstance would grace her with love.

"I was covering the pope's pastoral visit to England in 1982 when I met Sofia at Westminster Cathedral," he explained.

"I'm from the UK. My name is actually Sophie," Sofia interjected.

"Anyway, it was love at first sight, and Sofia brought me back to the church!"

"I'm an Anglican convert to Catholicism," Sofia explained.

"That's so funny," Stefania followed. "So while I was in the Vatican I met this Englishman. I met him again at a local *trattoria.*

We got to talking and it turns out his aunt, a nun, was one of the pope's attendants in 1978. She's still alive, and I asked if I could interview her. He said he would get back to me, although I'm not sure if he really meant it or if he was being nice."

"That's fascinating. What was this Englishman's name?" Rodolfo asked.

"Thomas," Stefania answered. "I recall he said his name was Thomas Holland, err, no, let me check my phone."

Stefania scrolled through her phone contacts.

"It was Thomas Houghton. I was going to check him out on the internet, but frankly I ended up researching the pope's death in 1978 last night. Checking out Thomas slipped my mind, and I kind of forgot his last name until now. I have his mobile number, though."

"What did you say his name? Thomas Houghton? Why do I know that name?" asked Rodolfo.

His hands on his head, clearly thinking deeply, Rodolfo now seemed curious.

"Describe this Thomas Houghton to me," Sofia interrupted, "and Rodolfo, do a quick search for Duke of Radcliffe on the internet, *pronto*!"

"Less than two meters in height, brown hair, piercing blue eyes. He was wearing a tan suit."

"How old, how old?" Sofia demanded with a raised voice.

"I think he's in his early thirties. Why all the questions?"

"He lives where?" Sofia yelled back.

"I think he said he lives near someplace called Houghton-St. Giles," Stefania curtly responded with a tip of the head.

Stefania looked down at the notes on her phone.

"Yes, that's it."

"I found it," Rodolfo said excitedly. "Look at my computer screen."

"Right!" Sophie countered. "This is exactly what I thought."

"What, what, what?" Stefania desperately wanted to know the answer. "Is he a bad man?"

Sophie paused for a moment.

"No, quite the contrary. His photo is on the internet and his biography, see here? If it's the same man, you were speaking with Thomas Pole-Houghton, the sixteenth Duke of Radcliffe, an incredibly wealthy and influential man and perhaps the most eligible bachelor in England."

Stefania looked at the photo.

"Oh, Madonna, that's him alright."

"His family is one of the most prominent Catholic families in England," Sofia continued, "and certainly one of the most influential Catholic nobility. His title is in the peerage of England and he sits in the Lords.  His mother was the queen's cousin. If he weren't Catholic, he'd be in the line of succession to the crown. His family seat is Haverford Hall near Houghton-St. Giles. If you're single, not a bad prospect."

"The priest he was with at the Vatican referred to him as 'your grace.' What do they say when one speaks to a duke?" Stefania asked.

"'Your grace.' He's either a duke or a bishop!" Sofia responded.

"I'm intrigued with the potential of a story regarding the death of the pope in 1978. The review of the 1918 archival material can wait," Rodolfo insisted. "The 1978 archival material hasn't been released. As you said, most members of the pope's household from 1978 are deceased. If you could score an interview with this duke's aunt, combined with your review of the 1978 archival materials, it could shed some significant light on what went on in the papal household before the pope's untimely death. That could be a good angle for a story, sort of an hour by hour of what happened before the pope died."

"Yes perhaps," Stefania grumbled.

"Then, of course, there's the issue of the Sheikh as well. Since the archival material officially hasn't been released, I'll bet few people know that he visited the pope just before he died. You say he was the last person outside the Vatican to see the pope alive?" Rodolfo continued.

"Yes, that's correct. He was the last person on the ledger kept by the Vatican Gendarmerie," Stefania affirmed.

"I must be going. I *am* interested as to whether you hear from the duke. He keeps a low profile but is prominent in the UK," Sofia commented while kissing Rodolfo on the forehead, then left the office.

Rodolfo, now paying little attention to Stefania, shuffled through the documents on his desk and credenza, went through piles of papers and shelves, moved folders around, opened drawers, and reorganized files. After what seemed like an hour of sitting watching Rodolfo turning his office upside-down, although only a few minutes, Stefania started to get impatient.

*Despite Rodolfo's shift to the 1978 angle, I still don't like this project. Maybe Rodolfo will see it as a waste of time and give me something more interesting.*

Just when she developed the courage to vocalize that very suggestion, Rodolfo stood.

"Ahhh! I found it! I found it!" he yelped.

"Found what?" she inquired.

"Sheikh Ali's phone number, that's what, or at least his assistant's phone number from maybe five, six years ago. Maybe it's still good, maybe not," he continued, all the while gesturing wildly in the air, waving the small piece of yellowed paper in his right hand. "Let's see if it still works," he said excitedly with a wide grin.

*Wouldn't it be my luck*, she thought, somewhat astonished. *He found the phone number of a guy who's probably senile, who should be dead. Maybe it will be the wrong number.*

Sitting behind his desk, Rodolfo picked up the phone and dialed the number. Stefania listened.

"Hello? Yes, who, yes, Rodolfo D'Agostino, from the *Italian Monthly Journal*. Yes, what? Of course, yes. Is the Grand Mufti available for an interview? Okay, can you get him a message from me? Yes, ask him if he would mind if we interviewed him regarding his meetings with the pope in 1978, yes. How did I get this number? I've had it for years, I suppose. You can call me back at my office at this number."

Stefania, starting to daydream, checked her text messages as Rodolfo concluded the conversation.

"Yes, good afternoon," he finished.

"Well, we'll have to wait for a call back. It may never come, or who knows?" he said, laughing. "In the meantime, reach out for this English duke. Let me know as soon as you make contact with him. We mustn't let this slip through the cracks. Maybe his aunt will have some insight as to his Holiness's meetings with this Sheikh."

"So you wish me to pursue this new angle regarding the 1978 material?" Stefania asked.

Rodolfo stood and looked at Stefania.

"Yes, I think it more pertinent, especially if you're able to interview this duke's aunt and the Sheikh. Why?"

*While I'd like to meet this Thomas again, I doubt my ability to handle this assignment.*

Stefania got up from her chair.

"Sir, I'm not sure I'm the best one for this assignment," she announced. "I know little of the church or religion and am not religious or spiritual myself. I'm uncomfortable with this subject matter and don't believe I'll do it justice."

Stefania deliberately understated her view. She considered herself a borderline atheist. Her studies at the small liberal arts college in New England made her hostile to religion in general, and to Christianity in particular.

"I'm not sure frankly whether I can be impartial. Also, this duke said his aunt hasn't spoken of her time in the Vatican for decades. She's old and infirm. Who knows, maybe she can't remember, has dementia. Perhaps someone who understands these things better."

Rodolfo sat back down behind his desk and sighed.

"Stefania, please sit down."

"All right," she acceded as she settled in an office chair facing his desk.

"Let me tell you my story," Rodolfo began. "When I was young, I was like you. I wasn't spiritual, not religious, but being a native of Rome was well aware of the church, and I of course I reported, critically, I might add, on church matters for the *Journal*. I was on an assignment in London covering the pope's visit there for the *Journal* when I met Sofia. It wasn't till I met my wife Sofia that a spiritual fire lit up inside me. Sofia's love, support, and spirituality got me to where I am today."

"I'm not following you," Stefania replied.

"Listen, I'm not saying you have to be religious to accept this assignment. But you should keep an open mind about things. If I hadn't had an open mind, I would never have met, understood, and married Sofia, the love of my life. As a journalist, you'll be exposed to a great many things that are outside of your comfort zone."

"But—" Stefania attempted to interrupt.

Rodolfo raised his palm.

"I can have someone else follow-up on these leads, or I can make you do it under threat of discharge, but I strongly suggest you undertake it voluntarily. What do you have to lose?"

"But—" she again interrupted.

"Just keep an open mind. You have to start somewhere, and the *Journal* will pay your travel expenses. Plus, you have the connection with this duke and have the language skills needed. He may not extend the interview offer to another reporter he doesn't know."

Stefania sat in the chair for a moment, mulling it over.

*A trip to the UK, in the big scheme of things, would be slightly inconvenient. I'm not convinced anything will come of it anyway. It would be a trip with no purpose other than to perhaps meet Thomas again. I'd like to see him again, so I might as well do it. Plus it will get me off the 1918 angle.*

"If I hear from this duke I'll go to the UK," Stefania reluctantly agreed.

"That's good. I'm positive that this will lead to something," Rodolfo replied. "If you don't hear from him today, please reach out to him. If you get no response, let me know. I'm sure I have a mutual contact somewhere who may be able to force the reintroduction."

"Yes," Stefania again murmured softly. "I understand."

# Chapter 4
### *Near Houghton St. Giles, England, UK, May 28*

Thomas sat in his cavernous oak paneled library observing through the French door windows the early morning mist rise from the acres of lawns and park that were part of the Georgian style Haverford Hall, his family's ancestral estate. Contemplating the upcoming day's activities, Thomas scrolled through the contacts on his phone to his Cousin James and pressed the call button.

"Thomas, good to hear from you," James answered the call.

"Yes, enough of the pleasantries James, let's get down to brass tacks. Are we still on for a little riding this morning at Haverford?"

While talking, Thomas took stock of the oak-paneled room lined with scores of books and volumes, accumulated for hundreds of years by his ancestors.

*I'm so at home at this place. It's a part of me, heart and soul.*

"You really love your horses, Thomas," responded James, laughing. "How was Rome?"

"Rome is always delightful. One odd thing happened, though. I met the most interesting woman. Well, I suppose I can't say that I met her as much as she almost trampled over me. She's insanely beautiful."

"Good for you, Thomas. How often have you seen her since?" James asked.

"Well, after I met her initially, I then saw her sitting alone at a *trattoria* outside the Vatican, and I sort of imposed myself on her, accidentally on purpose, I suppose. She's a journalist and is actually working on something that interests me; very much so. I have to see if I can finagle something with grandmamma and Aunt Josephine."

"So does this vixen have a name, and what does she look like?"

"Her name is Stefania, and she was about five and a half feet tall, green eyes, olive skin, and an incredible mane of jet black hair. She's half-Brazilian and half-Italian."

"Sounds fit, but if you met her in the Vatican, old chap, you'd better be sure she isn't a nun before you chat her up," James joked.

"Hilarious, James. Coincidently, she initially thought I was a vicar. Frankly, she insulted my religious beliefs, so I'm not sure there's anything amorous that will come out of it."

"If you only dated women who bought into your religious beliefs you'd be forever single," said James.

"Well, I was also a bit put off by her personality. She studied in the states, and she may have that Yank sharpness I despise. You know how I detest the impolitic of Americans. I'm now somewhat regretting that I told her I would try to obtain an interview with Aunt Josephine. Nevertheless, if she can get Aunt Josephine to finally speak about her time at the Vatican it would be well worth the effort, even if there is no relationship potential."

"Hmm, insulting and attractive, and hates Catholics. Sounds like the wives of most of the local gentry 'round here," James replied. "She'd fit right in."

"You're quite the card today, James. It's intriguing, she spoke of a mysterious Sheikh I've actually heard about. Also, the fact that Stefania saw 1978 material from the Vatican secret archives is also incredible. That material won't be released for decades. I've always been convinced there was much more to the story of the pope's death than the official Vatican pronouncement that he died of natural causes. This suspicion has been exacerbated by Aunt Josephine's odd but deliberate silence over the years. I'm also naturally suspicious of Stefania. I hope she's not some tabloid reporter."

"I'm not sure what all that means, but if you're concerned, call Harry and have her checked out. I did that with Caterina. He gave me a full report. Harry can find out anything about anyone."

"I wish I could only be as lucky as you. Caterina is a delightful woman. You should thank God grandmamma found her for you. Too bad I was preoccupied at the time. Otherwise you'd still be single or worse off. Anyway, will I see you in an hour?"

"Certainly. It's a perfect day for riding. The sun is shining and the ground isn't too soggy," James affirmed.

"Splendid. See you in an hour. I'm looking forward to it, and please, no word to granny about Stefania."

Thomas hung up, now eager to visit with his grandmother, the dowager duchess. As was her custom in the mornings after mass and breakfast, she meditated in the drawing room.

#

Elizabeth patiently sat in the drawing room, reading her prayer book, waiting for Thomas to greet her. A black lace dress draped over her boney ninety year-old frame. Her rosy cheeks set off her otherwise pale complexion. The vast room's mustard yellow hewn walls covered with paintings of Houghton ancestors had a calming effect on the duchess.

"Good morning, grandmamma," Thomas bellowed, sauntering into the drawing room in his riding clothes, the sun shining through the large French doors from the portico overlooking the grounds of Haverford Hall, his black flat coated retriever dog Connie in tow.

"I've always thought this room was the smartest in the hall. It has the best view of the park looking southeast, over the great lawn down to the lane," he said.

She took her reading glasses off. The glasses fell to her chest, held in place by an ornate silver neck chain.

"Thomas, it's so good to see you, my dear boy. Will this be a long visit or one of your brief stopovers?"

Elizabeth got a kiss on the cheek from Thomas.

She recalled at that moment how she had raised him on her own since age three when his parents, the fifteenth duke and duchess, the queen's distant cousin, died in an auto accident. How she acted as much more than a grandmother to Thomas; she played the part of a mother, mentor, and counselor. A widow since before Thomas's birth, Thomas was now the duchess's *raison d'être*.

Thomas sat in the sofa across from his grandmother.

"Ah, grandmamma, I've returned from the Vatican where I attended a series of impromptu meetings with the secretary of state, Monsignor Pennington, and others. I was planning on hosting a dinner here for Pilgrimage Day on May thirty-first for a few of the prominent Anglo-Catholic Walsingham pilgrims. You're welcomed to stay, of course."

"I'm so proud of you, Thomas. This is what I had intended for you, to continue the family tradition of wealth, privilege, and faith. Your father would also be proud," the duchess commented with pride.

"Grandmamma, you know I've done my best to meet your expectations, but you *will* stay for the pilgrimage *fête*, won't you?" Thomas inquired.

"Thank you, but I must regrettably decline. As you know, dear, I was planning to leave for Scotland today on the jet with Josephine for the season. Josephine is in ill health, and I think the salt air from the Irish Sea may do her some good. We're prepared to leave this afternoon after luncheon. I have to let Malcolm know when we'll be arriving."

"Certainly, granny, I confirm the travel arrangements for this afternoon. How is Aunt Josephine?"

"Like all of our generation, she has good days and bad. She's had many bad days of late. I think she is up for the trip, though. How was Rome?"

"Delightful. When I was there, I visited some old classmates from Sandhurst stationed in Italy with whom I served in the SAS," Thomas said with a deliberately mischievous look.

"All I can say is good riddance to the service. You taunt me, Thomas. I thank God every day you came out of it alive and in one piece. I was against Sandhurst from day one, as well as your service with the SAS. I know you wanted to follow your father's footsteps, but it grieved me to know you were in harm's way in Afghanistan. I'll only ever be satisfied when you're out of the reserves. Frankly, a phone call here and there and I could make a discharge happen."

"Now, granny, that won't be necessary," Thomas replied with a faint smile. "I'm quite contented doing what I'm doing, looking after you, Aunt Josephine, Uncle Robert, our business ventures, politics, and, of course, church matters. As much as I loved the service, I can't imagine that I'll be called to serve again."

"Yes, all that is well and good, Thomas, but have you any female friends? Are there any prospects? I pray every day that you'll meet someone suitable. You're thirty-two and I'm ninety; time is not on my side. You need an heir or two or three. How did your date with Lady Annabelle go last week?"

"Since I didn't tell you about that liaison, I can only assume you learned of it through your usual sources. I found Lady Annabelle pleasant enough, but her interests lie in status, money, prestige, and partying. Not my type. I like to think I have more to offer than money, prestige, and a title."

The duchess leaned onto the silver handle which topped her black cane, all the while nodding enthusiastically in agreement.

"You must be careful of fortune hunters, Thomas. Also, Lady Annabelle is not Catholic. She would have to convert, which, knowing her parents, I doubt she would do, and as you know, I'm leery of converts. Unfortunately, there's a significant lack of available Catholic royals on the continent of your age. All of the former Italian nobility are men! And the Grimaldis are not up to my standards."

"I'm well aware of that," Thomas somewhat sarcastically replied. "As you've reminded me time and again, despite the fact that you think I'm doing nothing to find someone, I've been doing the best I can. I've not met anyone with whom I have chemistry. Then, of course, they have to meet your laundry list of requirements."

"Always best not to settle, Thomas," reminded the duchess.

"Listen, grandmamma, I'd like to come up to visit with you and Aunt Josephine in Scotland. I have an Italian friend who wishes to speak with Aunt Josephine regarding her days at the Vatican in 1978. Do you think that's possible?" Thomas inquired.

She started to speak and paused, leaning forward on her cane.

"Candidly, Thomas, I'm not sure. I'm not keen on the idea, but you know Josephine may consent if it's your request. Whether she's willing to be cooperative, well, your best bet is not to give her too much advance warning."

"How should I approach it then?" Thomas asked.

"My guess is that if you show up with your friend and ask to see her, she'll be compelled to grant the audience. I won't let on until you arrive. Please let Malcolm know when we can expect you, dear. I'm overjoyed you'll visit us in Scotland. The purpose is immaterial," she said, nodding approvingly.

Thomas grinned back at her.

"The horses should be ready. James is coming over, and he and I are going on a ride throughout the park. I'll be back in time for luncheon. Will you join James and me for luncheon before you take your leave?"

"Most certainly. I should enjoy luncheon with you and my dear James," the duchess replied with a smile.

Thomas stood and kissed the duchess on the forehead.

"Have a pleasant ride then," she said with a whimper, turning toward the great windows. "I'll see you and the ninth Earl Layton at luncheon. It should be nice to see my godson," she said in a raised voice as Thomas walked toward the door, now alone in the big empty room.

*With my only friend Josephine frail and bedridden, I live only for Thomas. My life and legacy has just walked out the door.*

The duchess finished reading her daily prayer book and contemplated scripture. She meditated, got up, and walked over to the French doors overlooking the vast park. Thomas and James, on their horses, cantered up the far hill toward the forest bridle path.

*I pray for you every day, my child, that you're safe, that you're sound, and that you find an everlasting and wonderful love like I found with your grandfather. You're one of the most eligible and wealthiest bachelors in all of England; you just need a little luck and maybe a directing hand.*

*Love is all about timing*, she thought. *May God grant you the right timing.*

#

After luncheon with his grandmother and Cousin James concluded, Thomas saw them both out; James to his car for the short drive home and the duchess and Aunt Josephine to his SUV for the drive to Norwich, where they would fly to Scotland.

Thomas went to his library and checked his phone. Stefania had texted him:

HELLO MY EDITOR HAS APPROVED MY ABILITY TO INTERVIEW YOUR AUNT WHAT IS HER STATUS?

Thomas held the phone in his hand for a few moments and considered the matter.

*This Stefania had virtually no social media presence.*

He scrolled through the contacts on his phone and pressed the number for Harry Foster.

"Harry, this is Thomas. I apologize for calling you off the cuff. How are you?"

"Fine, Thomas. Who is it this time?" Harry asked in his characteristic Australian accent.

"Hah! Harry, you make me laugh, you mind reader!"

"No mind reader, I spoke to James earlier," Harry replied.

"Ah. This one might be difficult. Stefania Maria DiMaggio, that's her name. She resides in Rome and her father is a professor or some such thing. She said she works for the *Italian Monthly Journal* as a writer or reporter, and she was schooled in the states. Her mother is Brazilian and lives in Rio. She speaks several languages. That's about all I know substantively, other than her travels here and there. Please check her out."

"How'd you meet her?"

"How'd I meet her? Well, I first met her at the Vatican, and we introduced ourselves. Later I had a glass of wine with her at a café in Rome. I'm not sure if I even like her much. We don't seem to have much chemistry, at least initially. I'm interested in a project she's working on and am prepared to help her for my own purposes at this juncture, but I don't want to take any risks."

"Is this bird fit, and have you snogged yet?" Harry says, laughing.

"Yes, she's comely. No, we've not snogged, you old dog! Call me on my mobile or send me a text. Under no circumstances are you to mention this to the duchess. As usual, be discrete. I don't want Stefania or her publication to find out I had her checked out."

"Do you have a deadline for this information, mate?" Harry asked.

"As soon as practicable. I told her I needed the night to arrange a visit with my aunt, but I'm going to tell granny that I'm coming up tomorrow with a friend. If she turns out to be a problem, or worse a fraud, I'll tell her that my aunt isn't receiving visitors. Also, please get me all you can find on an imam. His name is Sheikh Ali Salah el-Amin."

"A Sheikh. Any idea where he might be? That would help, Thomas."

"I recall he was last in Rome. There's nothing recent about him on the web. Please bill me the usual fee plus any incidentals. Many thanks, Harry."

Thomas pressed the button on his phone, ending the call, tossing it back onto his desk. The phone skipped across some papers.

Thomas figured that if anyone could assist, it would be Harry, an old family friend in London who had done work for Thomas' father and the duchess, Harry being sort of a master of all trades, a "fixer."

When Thomas first asked Harry what he did for a living, the bald beefy sixtyish confirmed bachelor said, "I'm a problem solver."

Thomas believed that Harry, an army veteran and ex-MI5, could work miracles. He knew that the duchess had used Harry over the years. Thomas never asked questions but Harry's discretion was bought and paid for.

Thomas snatched up the mobile and quickly texted his assistant:

EMMA HAVE PLANE RETURN AFTER GRANNY GETS TO SCOTLAND. HAVE READIED TO FLY ME TO GLASGOW TOMORROW AND HAVE CAR MEET ME IN GLASGOW AIRPORT TO TRANSPORT ME AND GUEST TO GRANNY'S CALL OR TEXT ME WHEN ALL IS CONFIRMED

He then phoned Stefania.

"Hello. Yes, Stefania, can you fly up to see my aunt tomorrow?"

"So she's well enough to see me?" Stefania asked.

"Hopefully, yes, tomorrow. We'll have to see for sure when we get up there. There are no guarantees. You'll have to get to Glasgow Airport. I'll meet you and we'll drive to my great uncle's lodge. My grandmother and Aunt Josephine are there. Text me your flight information. I'll collect you at the arrivals terminal," Thomas answered.

"That works. Thank you very much," she retorted.

"Don't thank me until after we've reached Seil and you've met my auntie and granny. I'm afraid, due to its rather remote location, you'll have to stay the night there. There are no inns nearby. The accommodations are pleasant enough. You'll have your own room. I understand if you have discomfort with this."

"Okay, I'll have to make my editor aware of these plans, assuming he agrees to the flight costs," Stefania replied.

"Naturally," replied Thomas, now eager to end the call. "Hopefully I'll see you tomorrow. I'll wait for your text."

"Okay, see you tomorrow," Stefania responded as Thomas hung up.

*Hmm,* Thomas said to himself.

He then phoned his grandmother's residence, and Malcolm, her butler, answered the line.

"Malcolm, this is Thomas."

"Yes, your grace," replied the old Scottish butler.

"Please inform the duchess when she arrives that I'll be coming up tomorrow for an impromptu visit. I'll have a friend with me to see Aunt Josephine. She's aware of this possibility. I'm not sure when I'll get there, but you should assume I'll arrive in time for dinner. I'll call when we leave Glasgow. My guest and I will be staying a night or two; separate rooms obviously."

"Very good, your grace. I'll inform the duchess," replied Malcolm.

"Excellent. Thank you, Malcolm."

Thomas knew when he mentioned "a friend" the duchess would assume a male friend. She usually knew in advance about female friends, but he didn't want to answer any of granny's questions about Stefania just yet. Thomas considered what he told Stefania; technically correct but for the fact that his aunt and grandmother were staying in a remote Scottish location, and the lodge was a castle located on an island. Thomas went over what he had set in motion. Still not sure whether he liked Stefania, if she could get Aunt Josephine to recount her time in the Vatican, the meeting he orchestrated might be well worth the effort.

# Chapter 5

*Glasgow to Seil Island, Scotland, UK, May 29*

Thomas arrived at Glasgow airport early and waited for Stefania's plane to arrive about noon. Checking his phone, he realized he missed a call from Harry. Thomas walked to a quiet spot in the airport and phoned Harry.

"Yes, Harry?"

"Can you talk?" Harry replied.

"Yes, I'm alone right now, but I don't have much time. What have you found?"

"Well, mate, she pretty much checks out. She works for the *Italian Monthly Journal*, she started literally days ago. Her father is a university professor in Rome. Her mother is a fashion designer from an upper class Brazilian family. Her grandfather was a doctor there. She was born out of wedlock. Her mother and father met, they shagged, and she was the result. They then married and now are divorced. Her story about studying in the states checks out," reported Harry.

"Yes, I'm sure she's well educated, but like most who graduate from American universities, she's smart but doesn't know much," countered Thomas. "What about her personal life? Any leads there?" Thomas inquired.

"As far as I can tell she wasn't a saint in college, but she wasn't a tom either. She's likely been with a few men, two for sure, maybe one more, none of note. No significant others either. Her last boyfriend was in Brazil, but at least according to her social media accounts they don't keep in touch. She did a modeling gig in Brazil and now lives with her father in Rome. She has two close girlfriends there. It appears that she did do some European traveling with her girlfriends while in school and after she graduated. Of all the women I've looked at for you, she's the best looking and the least damaged."

"Thanks, Harry, that's helpful—" Thomas noted, intending to end the call.

"Oh," Harry interrupted, "and I almost forgot, I couldn't find any baptism or confirmation records for her. That doesn't mean she hasn't been baptized or confirmed, but I can't determine that. Those records are difficult to come by unless I know what particular parish to look to. Her family doesn't appear to be religious, though. That might be a problem with the duchess."

"Hmm. I'm aware of the religion issue and realize that *will* be a problem with granny. Let's hope it doesn't come up. I've thought about it ahead of time, and I'm prepared to engage in some preemptive measures. Many thanks, Harry. Oh, anything on the Sheikh?"

"Still working on that one, mate. Sounded like this Stefania was more urgent."

"Yes, Harry, thanks," Thomas replied.

Immediately after he hung up the phone Stefania appeared out of the departure area with an overnight bag and her ever present oversized black leather shoulder bag.

#

The couple relaxed in the soft leather back seat of the chauffeur-driven hunter green Range Rover and began the three hour drive from Glasgow to Seil.

"So you say your great uncle has a lodge in Scotland. Is that where he lives?"

"Not exactly. My uncle is in his early nineties, two years older than grandmamma, and he's kind of lost it, unfortunately. He's in an institutional residence in Glasgow and not in good health. Granny visits him when she can, but he doesn't recognize any of us. Very sad. Granny is his heir, so she manages all of his properties and finances."

"What do you mean, she's his heir?"

"Well." He paused. "Uncle Robert is a Scottish lord."

"And what does that mean?"

"Well, my uncle's Scottish lordship is a feudal barony, which dates from antiquity. They're based on familial locations, and unlike English peerages, such as my title, they're not granted through letters patent by the crown. So his title is Baron or Lord of Saoil. Also, again unlike most English peerages, a feudal barony can pass on to female family members, and it used to be the case that they were transferred, bought, and sold. The lordship, or laird, has been in my grandmother's family since before the reformation, and they were one of the few who refused to convert. The castle even has a priest's nook."

"What happens to the title when your uncle dies?" Stefania asked.

"My uncle never wed, has no children, and therefore, my grandmother will inherit the title upon his death, if she survives him. If not, I'll inherit the title and all of his lands, more or less by accident," Thomas explained.

"I think I understand," Stefania responded. "What is a priest's nook?"

"My, you're inquisitive."

"Yes, I hope you don't mind."

"Not at all. Quite refreshing actually. A priest's nook was a hiding place for Catholic priests during the reformation. Cromwell's men would search the estates of recusants for priests, and if found, the family would lose their assets, perhaps their lives, and the priest would be taken away, probably tortured and brutally executed."

"Oh," Stefania replied. "So is all his money inherited, or did he have a job or company?"

"Well, like much of the landed gentry, his family was land rich, money poor, but during prohibition in the states the Italian mafia contracted with a scotch distillery, which his family owned, to distill spirits for import into the states through Canada, illegally of course, which made the family a small fortune until prohibition ended. The distillery is still in the family to this day."

"I see, all very interesting, so your uncle is 'connected' as the American's would say?"

"I'm not so sure about that. Now, Stefania," Thomas stuttered, "I don't want to be impertinent, and not that it matters to me particularly; well, actually it does, but it will matter more to granny and my aunt a great deal. What I'm saying is, I've assumed all along, despite your antipathy toward religion, that you're a Catholic. I mean, you are half Brazilian and half Italian, right?"

"What difference does it make?" Stefania shot back defensively.

"The difference it makes," Thomas responded sarcastically, "is that my family is religious. You're going to be interviewing my aunt, a retired nun, about a religious topic. If they conclude you're atheist or agnostic, she'll not talk to you, and my grandmother may very well throw you out of the house. Do you want this story or not?"

"Yes," she replied. "At least my editor wants the story."

"You *have* received all of the initiation sacraments?"

Stefania hesitated.

"Yes, but my family isn't particularly devout," she added. "My momma and papa are both Catholic but not practicing; they are divorced."

"If the issue arises, it's important that you're Catholic. However, my grandmother and aunt should perceive that you're more devout than you are. Will that be a problem?"

"Of course it's a problem," she retorted.

"Then you'll not get your story, I'm afraid," Thomas, obviously perturbed, shot back. "We might as well turn around. You came all this way for nothing."

"Okay, okay, it's not a problem, I suppose, for the sake of getting the story," she responded.

"If the subject of your parents comes up, say that they received an annulment, alright? No mention of divorce. This should keep any questions from granny about it to a minimum."

"I'm not comfortable lying, but if it will get me the story, I'll consider it," she replied.

"To be completely in character, you should wear this during your visit. Consider it on loan."

Thomas presented Stefania with a green emerald silver cross necklace.

"Also, you'll be expected to go to mass."

"Aces. Let me put it this way, I'll think about it. The necklace is one thing; going to mass is completely another," Stefania curtly responded, her mood clearly turning for the worse.

She took the necklace from Thomas, huffed, and put it in her shoulder bag.

Thomas rolled his eyes.

"You're making this unnecessarily difficult. If my aunt is going to talk about 1978, it will be to you. She's said nothing to the rest of us for decades. The information you have from a review of the archives may prod her along. You have to make some compromises."

"I said I'll think it over," she responded curtly, her green eyes staring directly at Thomas's with an air of irritation. She then turned away.

Stefania's eyes were now glued to the car window as the scenic hills and lakes of the southern highlands flew by.

Her mood lightened, the guilt about her bold faced lie to Thomas regarding having been confirmed in the church now tempered by her enchantment with the vistas.

"I've told the driver to go the scenic route through Queen Elizabeth Forest Park, and I've informed granny that we'll be a little late for dinner. Ah, we're at Loch Ard. Let's step out to stretch," said Thomas.

"What an incredible view, with the loch and purple flower-covered craggy mountains beyond," gushed Stefania.

"Yes, the contrast between the green Scots pines and the heather is delightful," Thomas proudly responded.

Stefania shivered from the cool breeze blowing off the loch. The wind whistled through the pine needles as the Scots pines swayed in the breeze. White caps covered the loch from end to end. Not warm enough in her short dress and sweater, she trembled with chills, goose bumps running up and down her arms and legs.

Thomas took off his wool jacket and draped it over her shoulders.

"Let's go. Next stop is Loch Katrine," said Thomas.

They drove on. At Loch Katrine the sun shone off the gray waters of the loch and illuminated the rocky hills beyond as the puffy clouds flew by, creating a patchwork quilt of dark and light throughout the landscape. From her vantage point there appeared a veil of a rain shower falling on the hills beyond the loch, then a sunburst following through the passing clouds.

"How terrific is this!" exclaimed Stefania as she took photos of the loch.

The two posed for a photo taken by the driver. Stefania's irritation with Thomas ebbed and her guilt cast aside for the time being. Thomas' company began to grow on her.

"I hate to be a spoil sport, but we must be getting on. It's late. We can pass through again on the way back when we'll have more time if you wish," Thomas softly said.

Stefania nodded, smiling at Thomas as they jumped into the Range Rover. She gazed back at the stupendous viewshed as they drove off. The ice of their earlier conversation seemed to have been broken by the wilds and wonders of the north country.

In the lingering daylight of the long May days, the Range Rover flew past a road sign indicating that they were approaching Seil. The SUV slowly drove across a stone arched bridge.

"This is the 'bridge over the Atlantic,'" Thomas said as the SUV crossed the stone bridge. "We now cross from the mainland to Seil Island."

"Where is your uncle's residence?" Stefania inquired.

"A bit farther on," answered Thomas. "It's known locally as *Caisteil Saoil*, which is Scot's Gaelic for Castle Seil, and has been in my grandmother's family since at least the early 1300s. The foundations date from the early Middle Ages, but the vast majority was constructed in the late Middle Ages, and refurbished over the years. It's been converted to a manor house. On the grounds is a small chapel dedicated to Saint Columba. Local legend has it that Saint Columba's relics were initially stored here after the Vikings sacked the abbey in Iona."

Always eager to learn new things, Stefania enjoyed Thomas' little history lessons as she watched the scenery fly by.

"Why does your grandmother come up here?" she queried.

"To my grandmother, the castle was home, as it's where she was raised. After she married my grandfather, she became accustomed to living at Haverford Hall, but my grandfather knew of her love for the castle, and with my uncle's standing invitation, the family would often summer here. She now splits her time between the castle and Haverford."

The SUV drove over a stone bridge spanning a dry moat. Sitting on the top of a windswept cliff on a barren grassy bluff with rocky outcroppings, like sentinel standing guard, the gray field stone manor house overlooked the sea. Next to it sat a small simple stone chapel. As the late spring sun set over the western sea view, it created a spectacular ochre sky.

"Also, my grandmamma may speak to me in Gaelic if she doesn't want you to understand what she's saying," noted Thomas.

"I see," Stefania replied.

After the SUV stopped in front on the pea gravel driveway, Thomas led her to two huge wooden front doors with iron fittings. Thomas opened the doors, and the butler with a closely cropped gray beard and a tartan kilt greeted them.

"*Feashar math*, your grace. I'll have your things brought to your rooms. The duchess has held off dinner up to your arrival," the butler said in a virtually unintelligible Scottish brogue.

"*Tapadh leibh*, Malcolm," said Thomas.

The castle interior consisted of plastered over stone or pine panel with trim. A small fire burned in the huge stone foyer fireplace behind ornate brass andirons to drain the chill from the early June evening air. Deer antlers and taxiderms peppered the walls of the great hall.

Malcolm ushered the couple through the great hall to the simply furnished drawing room with an intricate red Persian carpet covering the pine plank floor, all illuminated by the flickering flames of a small fire in an ornate white marble fireplace.

"I'm lost of energy and about to fall over from exhaustion," Stefania said and let out a long deep yawn. "Perhaps I should turn in. I don't think I'm going to be too entertaining this evening."

An irritable frown graced Thomas' face.

"Look, if you're going to have any luck with Aunt Josephine," Thomas sternly responded, "we'll need Granny's assistance. You're going to have to muddle through dinner. Do you want some coffee or tea to keep you awake?"

"Oh my God, if you insist, I'll have dinner," Stefania sniped.

"I thought God wasn't in your vocabulary," Thomas shot back with a grin. "Oh, and I almost forgot. You should refer to her as duchess, unless she tells you otherwise. She's still much a stickler for convention and tradition. She'll be announced as such by Malcolm. Also, as I told you earlier, it's likely she'll expect us at mass tomorrow morning at 8 o'clock in the chapel, before breakfast. She's a daily communicant, and it will be a low mass in Latin, which was the most common form of mass before 1969. And there will be grace before dinner."

"Seriously?" Stefania replied somewhat facetiously. "You're lucky I agreed to wear this necklace."

"Yes, I'm serious. If you don't participate, you'll have to concoct an excuse. Would you like a drink? I can pour some wine, or liquor if you like? Maybe it'll calm you down a bit. You seem on edge," Thomas asked snidely.

"Some red wine, whatever you have, would be nice," she replied, standing, rubbing her hands together, warming herself near the fire, yawning repeatedly. "Latin is a language I at least understand!" she exclaimed, then yawned.

The brisk wind howling off the Irish Sea could be heard through the fireplace flue. Stefania's nose twitched, and she sneezed due to the slight odor of a dank basement with a touch of smoke.

"Bless you," said Thomas. "We have some red wine that's been decanted here. Will that do?" Thomas asked as he poured himself what looked like scotch with some ice.

"That sounds fine. I'm not much of a connoisseur. I typically drink the red house wines at the restaurants in Rome." Stefania took a sip, commenting, "This is excellent wine. Thank you."

Thomas laughed.

"I should hope so. It's from Uncle Robert's private collection. I would hazard a guess it's an excellent vintage."

"So what other traditions is your grandmother into?" asked Stefania.

"Well," replied Thomas, rubbing his chin, "when she's in residence either here or at Haverford there is afternoon tea at 4 o'clock, cocktails at 7 o'clock, a formal dinner at 8 o'clock, and after dinner drinks in the salon, just like when she was growing up in the 1930s and 40s."

"Hmm," said Stefania, "not the worst traditions I suppose."

"They used to be more populated affairs, but unfortunately all of her friends and kin have predeceased her, save me. Typically now it's me, when I'm around, granny and Aunt Josephine, sometimes a guest or two," explained Thomas.

The butler Malcolm opened the door to the drawing room.

"Her grace, the dowager duchess of Radcliffe, dowager countess of Haverford, dame of Malta," he announced.

The hunched, elderly, thin, and somewhat gaunt duchess walked in slowly with the aid of an elaborately carved silver-topped dark wooden cane. Wearing a black dress with black lace sleeves, apparently still in mourning due to the long ago deaths of her husband and her son, she clearly noticed Stefania but held back her acknowledgement at first.

Thomas kissed her on the cheek. The duchess, smiling from the side of her mouth, grabbed his right hand with hers enthusiastically.

"*Madainn mhath.* Thomas, my boy, it *is* so good to see you, *tha mi gad ionndrainn.*"

"Granny, there's someone I should like you to meet."

"Yes, you said you would have a companion," the duchess noted, turning to Stefania.

"This is my friend Stefania."

The duchess held out her hand.

"Well, Stefania, it's a pleasure to meet you, and I'm glad you could visit with us. Any friend of Thomas' is welcomed here. That's a delightful necklace you have there. Is it a family heirloom?"

Before Stefania could speak, Thomas interrupted.

"Stefania and I met at the Vatican last week. She's writing a story on the short pontificate and the pope's death in 1978, and she asked to interview Aunt Josephine. I thought—"

"Yes, I know, you *thought* that Stefania could speak to your aunt," the duchess remarked, shaking her finger at Thomas. "Well, we'll see if she'll have of it. I've spoken to her. She doesn't like to speak about those days, but she may discuss the matter, which is better than her previous response to such queries. She wants to meet your friend, as she's eager to converse in Italian. On the morrow perhaps, Sister Josephine is already asleep. She's not at all well."

Thomas poured the duchess a glass of wine, and she sat on the sofa by the fire.

"Please do sit down, here next to me," she asked Stefania.

The duchess then proceeded to politely interrogate her about her background, her work, her family. Stefania reluctantly stuck to the script. She was Catholic, her parents' marriage annulled.

"Where were you baptized and confirmed?" the duchess asked.

Stefania was stumped.

"*Santa Maria della Concezione dei Cappuccini* in Rome."

*I had to lie, I had no choice,* Stefania thought. *I lied to Thomas as well, again no choice. The lies get me the interview and also keeps Thomas interested.*

After dinner, Malcolm showed Stefania to her large bedroom. A red and blue Persian carpet adorned the floor, and an old king size four post bed waited. A small fire flickered in the fireplace.

Stefania peered out the leaded glass window overlooking the sea, lit by a bright full moon surrounded by a brilliant halo.

"What a wonderful view," she exclaimed.

"Your room overlooks the Firth of Lorn," he noted.

A breeze whistled through the old window frame. Stefania changed to pink pajamas and settled in for the night under a thick wool blanket. Picking up her phone, she texted the photo of herself with Thomas to one of her girlfriends in Rome:

IN SCOTLAND WITH WONDERFUL SCENERY

Her friend texted back:

WHOS THE GUY

She responded:

DUKE THOMAS HAUGHTON I'M WITH HIM ON ASSIGNMENT FOR WORK

She placed the phone on her night stand, turned off the lamp, and quickly fell asleep to the fading glow of the fire.

#

Closing the doors to the salon quietly behind him, Thomas immediately phoned Harry.

"I wondered when you were going to call, mate," Harry answered.

"Granny called?" Thomas whispered.

"Yes, just. I told her nothing. Now what do you want me to tell her?"

"Tell her what you told me, except tell her that Stefania has been baptized at a church in Rome called *Santa Maria della Concezione dei Cappuccini*. If she asks about the annulment of her parents' marriage, you haven't been able to determine that one way or the other," he continued in a low voice.

"I've never pulled one over on your grandmother, but I suppose at some point it's bound to happen. You must really like this Stefania?"

"Not really, or not yet anyway, as much as putting up with her for the time being. She's sort of a means to an end. Catching her in a lie would be a death knell to any prospect she might have of getting Aunt Josephine to cough up secrets. I'm dying to see if she can get Aunt Josephine to open up about her time at the Vatican in 1978," Thomas said, smiling. "She's interesting, gorgeous, and seems genuine, but her personality is a bit sharp; however, beauty, like new paint on a dirty wall, often compensates for a multitude of sins."

"You're right on that. Well, I suppose we all have our reasons. I'll be in touch, mate," Harry said as he hung up.

# Chapter 6
*Seil Island, Scotland, UK, May 30*

Stefania, still groggy from the night before, woke to her phone alarm as raindrops pelted the window. Sheets of rain fell like a curtain of gloom over the Irish Sea. Sinister clouds came from the southwest as a gale blew in across the green foaming waters. The fireplace flue now damp from the heavy rain, filled the room with a smoky aroma. Dressed in a long wool sweater and her black skirt, Stefania met Thomas in the chapel, sniffling the whole time from the smoky smell.

In the cool simple chapel sat the duchess, Thomas, and some members of the household staff. Old stone walls held up a roof of wood timbers. On the few old wooden pews sat the assembled group. Stefania stayed in her pew while the priest dispensed communion. Stefania understood the Latin verbatim.

*This is mystical and inherently spiritual,* she thought.

Something stirred inside her; something she hadn't experienced before.

Thomas sat next to her. Out of the corner of her eye she looked him over.

*I initially saw Thomas as charming but stuffy. The more time I spend with him, the more down to earth he is.*

In these new unfamiliar surroundings, Thomas reminded her of a security blanket she slept with as a child and kept close for comfort.

After mass, Stefania met Thomas and the duchess for breakfast. Stefania took stock of the large dining room adjacent to the salon. The three sat at one end of the large dark wood table and served themselves from a buffet set up on a table along the wall at the end of the wood paneled room. A wall of windows looked down on the violent frothy sea below the cliffs. Stefania could see her reflection in the fine bone china and in the silver service.

"My child, why did you not commune?" the duchess inquired.

"I apologize, duchess. I was hungry and broke the fast prior to taking communion. I didn't want to insult you by taking communion under the circumstances."

It was the best excuse Stefania could come up with, knowing full well from her internet research there no longer existed a requirement of fasting before communion.

"I see," the duchess responded in a skeptical tone.

"Where is your aunt?" Stefania mumbled to Thomas.

"She isn't well, in bed still. The priest is with her now, and we'll see her after breakfast. Awful excuse, by the way," he whispered back.

"Aces," Stefania murmured back.

Thomas carried most of the conversation, the duchess not being particularly loquacious.

The butler entered and whispered into the duchess' ear.

"*Gabh mo leigeul*, I have a phone call I must attend to," the duchess declared and left the room.

She rejoined them again after a few minutes.

"Josephine is up to seeing us all after breakfast, in her room, naturally," she announced.

All three climbed the stairs to Sister Josephine's room. Considerably larger than Stefania's, red paint covered the room's walls and an elaborate beige Persian carpet the pine plank floor. A large blaze in the black marble fireplace opposite the bed warmed the room and the undrawn drapes let the light in through the leaded windows.

Sister Josephine, although obviously old, infirm, and ill, appeared worse than Stefania had expected. With rosy red cheeks she managed a slight smile. The old nun's gray stained teeth had seen better days. A messy bun held her curly gray hair together. A gold cross and chain hung around her neck over her white bed clothes. She appeared to be in the middle of praying the rosary.

Immediately Sister Josephine, speaking in a low raspy voice grizzled by age, greeted Stefania in Italian.

"Good morning, miss. I understand you speak Italian?" Josephine asked, all the while coughing, gurgling and spitting phlegm in a tissue.

"Yes, Sister, I do, and you speak it very well," Stefania replied in Italian.

Stefania noticed an irritated look on the duchess' face. She clearly didn't understand the conversation.

"I hear you've come to ask about my time in the Vatican in 1978?" Sister Josephine continued in Italian.

The old woman seemed oddly eager to speak about her experiences.

"Yes," Stefania admitted, pausing while clearing her throat and blowing her nose. "I have. I noticed a certain Sheikh had visited the pope quite a few times during his pontificate, including the day before his death."

"Yes, he and the Holy Father were great friends. He was one of the last people to have visited the Holy Father the day before he died. The Holy Father always met with the Sheikh alone, as well as a certain bishop from South or Central America. In fact, that bishop had met with the Holy Father earlier in the day, then the Sheikh came, but he wasn't supposed to be coming that day. It was sort of spur of the moment. Thomas, Thomas?" the old nun called, coughing.

"What did she say? What did she say? I can't understand," said the duchess.

"Yes, Aunt Josephine?" Thomas responded in English, ignoring the duchess.

"In the top dresser drawer there's a wooden box. Please get it for me."

Thomas pulled a book-size mahogany box from the drawer.

"I haven't long to live. I'm fading as we speak," she continued in Italian. "I didn't want to leave this world without my dear Thomas at my side. Now that he is here, I am prepared to go, but not before—"

Thomas placed the mahogany box on her lap.

"It may be a sin that I haven't spoken of this before, but now it is time. After the Holy Father died, there were two documents found in his apartments, as well as a death certificate issued by the Camerlengo."

"I know of this, Sister. I've seen the death certificate in the archives," remarked Stefania.

"No, you have not," the old nun insisted, raising her voice ever so slightly. She started coughing and continued in Italian, speaking slowly.

"What you've seen is a forgery. After the original death certificate was issued, the Camerlengo had second thoughts. He gave it to me and instructed me to shred it. I grabbed another document in the anteroom to his offices and shredded it instead. I put the death certificate in my habit and have kept it ever since, thinking one day the truth should be known. Perhaps this is the time. I can't go to the Lord with this burden in my heart."

*"Ma's e do thoil e, gabh mo leisgeul! Han eil mi 'tuisginn?"* the duchess animatedly asked Thomas.

*"Bi samhach,"* he whispered.

"What's she saying? What's she saying?" she interrupted again, this time in English.

Sister Josephine opened the mahogany box and removed an official document with a seal which had been folded in fours. She grasped the document between her trembling fingers, and handed it to Stefania. Stefania examined the document.

"It's in Latin. Ah yes, this is the death certificate issued by the Vatican City State on September 29, 1978 for the pope," said Stefania. "It's identical to the death certificate I reviewed in the Vatican archives, except it lists the cause of death as an overdose of pentobarbital. It's signed by the Camerlengo of the Holy Roman Church. Oh Madonna!" Stefania exclaimed. "The death certificate I saw in the archives listed the cause of death as a heart attack!"

"His Holiness had mild seizures and insomnia which is why he took pentobarbital. There's no way he could have ingested enough to kill him because I gave him the pills. The pill bottle was in the papal apartments. He could have swallowed more than his dose on his own, or someone could have given him more than the proper dosage. I've gone over that evening my entire life. Did I give him too many pills? But I didn't. But the pill bottle was almost empty when the Camerlengo found it, or at least he said it was almost empty."

"So you think he either committed suicide or someone killed him?" Stefania asked.

"I've never spoken of it prior to today. They kept it a secret. They wanted it kept secret. I was afraid of them. I'm going to the Lord in heaven today, God willing, so my fear is gone. There were also two other documents which the Camerlengo gave to Father LaCroix, one of his assistants, to destroy. He was supposed to shred those too, but he did like I did. He kept them."

"What are they talking about? What did she give her? What does it say?" the duchess inquired, obviously irritated.

Thomas motioned for the duchess to stifle.

"What is a Camerlengo?" Stefania asked.

"More like who," Thomas interjected. "The Camerlengo is a cardinal. He acts sort of as the chancellor of the Holy See. He effectively runs the papal household. Other than the pope and the secretary of state of the Holy See, it's probably the most powerful position in the church. He's the acting head of state during the *sede vacante* and acts as the acting head of state until the time a future pope is chosen. As I recall, he's also responsible for the determination of the death of the pope—"

"The Camerlengo is dead," remarked Sister Josephine. "One of his former assistants is still alive. He's Monsignor Francois LaCroix. I've kept in touch with him over the years."

To Stefania's surprise, Sister Josephine, straining with a great deal of effort, picked up her tablet from the nightstand and looked up LaCroix on social media.

"He apparently is on the Camino."

"What's the Camino?" Stefania, again confused, asked.

Thomas answered before Sister Josephine could.

"The Camino is short for the Camino Santiago, the way of Saint James. It's an ancient pilgrimage route from France to Santiago de Compostela, Spain."

"Says here he's presently in Spain," said Josephine, referring to her tablet with exhaustion in her voice. "He can't be reached because he's on the Camino but should make it to Santiago tomorrow. Here's his photo and social media feed," continued Josephine, handing Stefania the tablet with LaCroix's photograph, coughing again.

"How old is this guy?" Stefania blurted, still in Italian.

"Oh he's young," replied Josephine, coughing. "Sixty-five, sixty-six. He was about twenty-six or twenty-seven as a young priest working for the Camerlengo in 1978."

Stefania pulled her notebook from her shoulder bag and reviewed the notes she took of her inspection of the archives.

"My notes from the archives indicate a Bishop Gonzalvo from Brazil had visited the pope, as did the Camerlengo and two assistants, one named LaCroix. Was the bishop from South or

Central America named Gonzalvo? Only he and the Sheikh saw the pope the day before he died, correct?" Stefania asked.

"I don't really remember. Maybe. He saw the Holy Father perhaps twice," replied the old nun, clearly straining to remember.

Stefania continued to flip through the pages of her notebook.

"My notes indicate that he formally met the pope once, the day before he died. That's it. You say there was another time?"

Sister Josephine propped herself up in her bed as best she could.

"My memory is old and fading, but I'm sure I saw this same bishop with the Holy Father at least twice. Maybe his visit wasn't recorded. In addition to LaCroix, the Camerlengo had another assistant, an Armenian priest, but I don't remember his name. He left the Vatican after the pope's death. I don't know what became of him."

The sister seemed to be steadily weakening. The discussion had taken its toll. She started wheezing and coughing uncontrollably.

"How many people could have access to the papal apartments the day or night before he died?" Stefania quickly asked.

The sister paused.

"The household staff, myself, and two other sisters who are deceased, the Camerlengo, and his two assistants, and maybe one or two cardinals, and the pope's secretary," she replied.

"The official Vatican version was that the pope was found by a sister at about 0530 on September 29, 1978 in his bed, with a book next to him on his bed. Is that correct?" Stefania asked.

"Yes. Sister Anna came out of the papal apartments in distress," the old nun, now hoarse and laboring to speak, replied. "Then I accompanied her back to the pope's bedroom. We then informed the Camerlengo, who came to the papal apartments with his two assistants and went through the pope's papers. He carried numerous documents out of the apartments. After the pope's body was removed, the apartments were sealed with a ribbon and the wax seal of the Camerlengo."

"This is all incredible. This document, if genuine, is fantastic," Stefania theorized. "The next step would be to see this Father LaCroix, I would think. The other documents; I wonder what they could be?"

"My child, I have no knowledge of what the other documents were," Sister Josephine softly responded.

Thomas, heretofore silent, finally spoke up in Italian.

"Aunt Josephine, what you've stated and provided is truly disturbing. It correlates with the theory that the pope's death wasn't an accident as originally reported. This is serious. Are you absolutely positive of what you're saying?"

"If I'm incorrect," the old nun, clearly straining now, her eyes watering, shot back in Italian between coughs, "then the only other alternative is that I killed the Holy Father with an overdose of his medication. I didn't do so. It's weighed on my conscience for decades, Thomas. Do you not believe me?"

"I believe you, Aunt Josephine. I don't have an alternative but to do so. That means the Vatican has been perpetuating a fraud for forty years. If the pope committed suicide, the big question is why? If he was killed, that raises even more questions. Either way, these are explosive developments which could shake the church to the core."

"I know what I know," the old nun murmured, clearly fading and slumping back in her bed, sighing, placing her right hand on her chest and her left over her forehead.

Thomas then took the opportunity to explain to the duchess in English what had transpired.

The aging duchess stood, leaning on her cane.

"*Tha mi 'tuigsinn!* For the love of God and all that's holy," she blurted in as stern a voice as she could muster, "Josephine, how could you! This will result in scandal and harm to my church, and to the family. I won't have it. I won't stand for it. Thomas, you shall not permit this to happen. You shall prevent this from becoming known. If the family is connected to this, I can't even imagine the repercussions!"

"I can't go to my death knowing that others have perpetuated a lie upon the world for forty years," she replied ever so softly. "I loved the Holy Father. He was a good and decent man. He would have wanted the truth to be known. I want to go to the Lord with a clear conscience. It's in God's hands if I'm judged badly for what I've done. I've confessed my sins. I asked for absolution during the jubilee year of mercy. Now all I desire is to be anointed and to go with God," she said softy as she slowly struggled to make the sign of the cross.

"I can't let this get out, I will not!" the duchess shouted as she stood there trembling. "I've never been so vexed!"

Other than the duchess's outburst, no one made a sound.

*The next step is to find Father LaCroix,* Stefania thought during the silent interlude.

Stefania grasped the sister's hand while Thomas and the duchess continued to argue in hushed tones in Gaelic and English. The priest who said mass entered the room, now rid of his vestments, dressed in a simple black cassock.

"Sister, you've given your penance earlier. Are you prepared to receive the last rites of the Holy Roman Church, the extreme unction, and the *viaticum*?"

"I am. I've confessed my sins, and my conscience is clear."

In a sight Stefania had never witnessed before, the priest blessed the sister in Latin, "*In nomine patris, e file, e spiritus sancti.* Amen."

Thomas leaned over and in a soft voice explained the process as it occurred, although Stefania understood the Latin.

"They're reciting the apostle's creed, the litany of saints, and renewal of her baptismal promises. This must be the pre-Vatican Two last rites. Whatever it is, the procedure is quite unusual," Thomas murmured. "Perhaps this is how Josephine wanted it to go. He's now anointing her with the Easter chrism oil, and they're chanting the Lord's Prayer."

"May the body of Christ bring you to everlasting life," the priest said softly.

The priest placed a communion wafer on her tongue, she took it and muttered a hardly audible "Amen."

"May the Lord Jesus Christ protect you and lead you to eternal life," the priest whispered to her.

The sister's voice got softer and quieter as she and the priest together said, "*Si ambulem in medio umbrae mortis, non timebo mala: quoniam tu mecum es Domine. Virga tua, et baculus tuus, ipsa me consolata sunt. Alleluia, Alleluia,*" which Stefania understood to mean "Though I should walk in the midst of the shadow of death, I will fear no evils, for Thou art with me, O Lord. Thy rod and Thy staff, they have comforted me. Alleluia, alleluia."

"They just recited *The Gradual* from the *Twenty-Second Psalm,*" Thomas noted.

The old nun, clearly intending to die on her own terms, turned to Stefania, looked at her, smiled slightly, closed her eyes, and settled back onto the bed. Her breathing became labored. A single tear slid down from the corner of her eye, down her temple and onto her pillow. Still holding Stefania's hand, she clenched it tightly, then let go.

Stefania's stomach sank. Her eyes welled with tears which filed down her cheeks, slid down the side of her nose, and lingered on her lips.

The fire seemed to die out at that very moment, and a chill came over Stefania from head to foot. A sudden wind gust could be heard slamming the leaded window with raindrops, and a clap of thunder shook the room.

The duchess finally sat down. Whimpering, she wiped her eyes with a handkerchief from her dress pocket. She held Thomas' hand, her ancient watery pale blue eyes gazed forlornly up at him.

"Josephine will be interred in my family's crypt here on the morrow," the duchess declared after composing herself. "We have no undertaker here, so she must be interred quickly. She was my dearest friend, and I want her close to me always. The requiem mass will be held tomorrow in the chapel. You, Thomas, are her closest blood relative. You'll deliver the eulogy. I won't countenance any objections."

"Certainly, grandmamma, that's how it will happen," replied Thomas.

*Seil Island, Scotland, UK, May 31*

The rain had gone, but fog covered the cliffside chapel like a blanket, creating a somber atmosphere for the funeral. Following the mass the duchess approached Thomas on the lawn outside of the chapel. Stefania stood on the other side of the chapel lawn apparently scrolling through messages on her phone.

"I assure you, grandmamma, I'll distance the family as much as possible from Aunt Josephine's revelation. Stefania or her publication could accept the credit of finding the information. I have no intention of letting any of this come to pass if it will harm the church. Therefore, I *must* interject myself within this investigation," implored Thomas.

"I don't like lying, I don't like your plan, and I'm starting not to like Stefania. If the story comes to light, Stefania would be connected to you. Why would you even consider pursuing such a matter?"

"Curiosity, I suppose," Thomas responded. "Also, what better way for me to determine where this leads other than being involved with it? Aren't you interested in where this will go?"

"I'm not convinced. I'll wager you have affection for this Stefania," she noted prophetically, pointing her index finger at Thomas, sticking it right in his chest. "And remember, Thomas, it was curiosity that killed the cat."

"You must see this is the best way," Thomas insisted.

"Yet I want you to be happy." The duchess' tone now softer, she lamented to Thomas, grasping his hands, "I want a great-grandchild before I die and an heir to carry on the family tradition and faith. All of this will unnecessarily complicate our lives."

"I'm sorry, grandmamma. The matter is settled. I've discussed this with Stefania, and we're flying to Santiago de Compostela tomorrow to attempt to find this Father LaCroix. I want to be with Stefania. I think I should be involved in this to keep track as to where it's all going," Thomas replied as if asking a question.

The duchess offered no response.

*I'm not going to have the family's reputation, or that of my church, tarnished by some meddling upstart,* she thought.

Torn between her faith and her grandson, she recalled the great lengths, devious sinful depths in the distant past to which she went to assure the continued devotion and adherence of the Houghtons to the Catholic faith.

*In the Distant Past*
*Near Houghton St. Giles, England, UK, June 15, 30 Years Earlier*

"I don't like it, I don't like it one iota. The hell with it; I won't have it!" the dowager duchess curtly noted in a bitter tone to her sister-in-law Josephine. "I should be in a fine mood, but I'm vexed by this," she said, her voice cracking with anger. Her sixty-year-old hands shook nervously.

"My dear, it can't be as bad as all that, can it?" Josephine responded. "It's a wonderful day. Let us enjoy the sunshine and the sweet smell of spring in the air. I have to go back to the heat in Rome in a few days.”

The dowager duchess enjoyed spending time with her fifty-nine-year-old sister-in-law. The duchess and Josephine, wearing her white summer habit on holiday from her work in the Vatican, sat around an antique oak tea table on the grand south lawn of Haverford Hall. With them, a young nursemaid attended to three-year-old Thomas. A bright sunny day, whipped cream clouds flew by under the canopy of a clear blue sky.

“Josephine, as a nun, you always see the best in people. If my son’s wife; that’s right, I call her not the duchess, but his *wife*, who has raised the issue of converting, what in bloody hell has this family been doing for the last five-hundred years!”

“Elizabeth dearest, don’t you think you are being overly dramatic?” Josephine asked.

“I’m sorry, we’ve kept the faith through thick and thin. My husband’s ancestors didn’t risk life and limb during the reformation, serve as secret liaisons to the Vatican for the crown for centuries, and build their wealth and reputation simply because Sarah thinks it’s not prestigious enough being married to the fifteenth Duke of Radcliffe. Now she wants herself, my son, and grandson back in the line of succession. I should never have consented to the marriage in the first place, and I wish her majesty had never sanctioned the match.”

“Please Elizabeth,” Josephine interrupted.

“I’ve allowed the contamination of my husband’s Plantagenet blood. I should have known that she converted only for the money and the title. Common rabble.”

“I *do* prefer to see the best in people. You don’t know that they definitely want to convert, do you? I mean, it was only something you thought you overheard. Plus, Sarah is the mother of your grandchild. You should be more forgiving,” observed Josephine.

Elizabeth sat in silence, preferring not to respond to Josephine.

“Elizabeth, you’re still fighting the reformation, but we’re now five-hundred years on. It’s time to let it pass,” Josephine continued.

Elizabeth continued glancing at the phone on the tea table, a cord strung from the nearby gazebo, waiting for it to ring. The chirping of birds, the rustling of leaves in the wind, and the distant bleating of sheep in the nearby fields resounded in the mid-afternoon air.

"I'll forgive her in purgatory when we're all dead and buried," she shot back.

"You can't possibly mean that," Josephine responded in apparent disbelief. "Would you like more Earl Grey?" Josephine inquired as she poured herself another cup of tea. The duchess didn't answer.

"Look at Thomas on the blanket. Think of how blessed we all are. What a handsome child, my nephew."

The phone rang, and Elizabeth snatched the phone off the table and walked toward the gazebo out of earshot of Josephine, dragging the phone line with her. Expecting the call, the dowager duchess intended to act, depending upon the information she received.

"Yes?" she inquired.

"They were at Lambeth Palace for a couple of hours meeting with the archbishop," the man on the line said. "They're on their way back to Haverford now."

Pausing for several moments, she held the phone down close her waist. Her stomach sunk. Anger filled every corner of her being.

Trembling, she put the receiver back up to her ear and replied, "Lambeth Palace, you say. Well, we know *why* they were there. You know what to do."

"Understood," replied the man on the other end of the call.

Hanging up the receiver, she walked back to Josephine and Thomas with the phone and placed it back on the table.

"Who was that?" Josephine asked.

"My solicitor; nothing important," she replied.

The wind picked up, tossing Elizabeth's gray hair in the air, and blowing Josephine's white summer habit about. The duchess wore her typical black dress; she had kept in mourning since the untimely death of her husband, the fourteenth duke, a few years earlier from cancer.

"We were meant for each other, you know. We're all descended from recusants. We were passionately in love. I can't believe I'm without him. I miss him incredibly so," she said aloud but not meant for Josephine.

Josephine, looking over, smiled to offer comfort and held the duchess's hand.

*Without the faith, the Radcliffe title and its position would be worthless; the Houghtons would be no different than the scores of*

*English aristocrats with grand estates, spoiled children, and bad reputations. Now my son slips away.*

"Elizabeth, conversion can't be a realistic option. It seems so farfetched," Josephine queried. "I mean, if Charles and Sarah convert, Sarah and Thomas will be in line of succession, but what would it be, 40th, 41st in line? Sarah is her majesty's cousin, but there are many more before her and Thomas in line. Charles is even further behind. He would give up the prestige and position of the family with the church for an infinitesimal chance of succession?"

The duchess scowled.

"I know what I heard. The wife wants it. It vexes me," she snapped.

The duchess, now convinced of her son's intention to convert, didn't doubt the certitude of what she heard. She decided to choose her faith over her son.

"I won't let it happen," she blurted.

"That's what you think you heard," countered Josephine. "You may have misunderstood."

The two women drank more Earl Grey and played with Thomas. The duchess's old pale blue eyes looked into Thomas' deep blue ones. She loved Thomas more than anything, even more than her son. After an hour or so the three were interrupted by the tall old butler who came down from the main house.

"Your grace, the local constable and Father Michael are here to see you. They're coming down now."

The duchess gazed up the lawn as the portly local constable in his uniform and custodian's helmet, and the similarly portly local priest, Father Michael in his black cassock with bible in hand, bounded down the lawn. They both looked deadly serious.

*Given their presence, everything probably went to plan,* she thought.

Approaching the women, Father Michael took his black biretta off and spoke first, wiping beads of sweat off his forehead with his white handkerchief, stuttering initially.

"Your grace, we have some horrible news. It seems; well, it seems that the duke and duchess were killed in a car accident this afternoon. They were on their way back to Haverford Hall, it appears, and their car—"

"My God!" the duchess screamed theatrically on cue. Standing, she threw up her arms, still screaming, "Sarah and Charles gone? How?"

"Their car went off the cartway into a ditch," the constable abruptly interjected with little emotion. "It hit a tree and tossed over. It was a convertible, as you know. They were both killed in the accident. There were no witnesses. It appears they might have been hit by a lorry or another vehicle, but that's only a guess. Someone came upon the scene fifteen minutes after it happened, maybe more, and phoned the constabulary from a nearby farmhouse. We think they likely died instantly, if that's any consolation."

"How could this have happened?" the duchess asked, feigning denial and confusion. Looking at Josephine, she exclaimed, "Josephine, what are we to do?"

Josephine appeared in shock at the loss of her only nephew and said nothing.

The duchess grasped her hand and the hand of Father Michael.

"Father, please lead us in a prayer to the Holy Mother for the souls of Charles and Sarah."

Father Michael sat down and obliged. The constable left the group to pray in solitude. The duchess stared adoringly at the toddler Thomas.

Following the prayer, the duchess picked up Thomas and whispered into his ear, "May God bless you, my child. You're now the sixteenth Duke of Radcliffe, will succeed your father as heir to his vast fortune and holdings, his subsidiary titles, his position as an English peer, and as keeper of our faith which has survived centuries in a hostile land. With my guidance you'll serve your church, your government, and your sovereign well, my lad. You are the Radcliffe legacy."

# Chapter 7

*41,000 feet over the Bay of Biscay, May 31*

As they flew from Glasgow to Santiago de Compostela on Thomas' Falcon 8X, Stefania connected to the plane's Wi-Fi and texted to Rodolfo,

A LEAD BRINGS US TO SPAIN

WHAT LEAD? WHERE IN SPAIN? Rodolfo demanded in response.

*I don't want to reveal the death certificate from Sister Josephine just yet,* she thought.

Stefania texted back,

TRYING TO TRACK DOWN AN OLD PRIEST IN SANTIAGO WHO WAS AN ASSISTANT TO THE CAMERLENGO IN 1978

Rodolfo seemed assuaged for the moment and responded, OK.

While texting, Stefania noticed Thomas glance at her. Their eyes met briefly; Thomas smiled back as he spoke on the plane's satphone.

"I initially hated this project, but you've somehow made it more bearable. I'm actually becoming invested in this story," Stefania remarked to Thomas.

*Boy, that's an understatement. The old nun's dying confession lit a fire in me to see this assignment through, as if her life energy somehow transferred to me, and then there's you,* she continued the thought whilst carefully watching Thomas talk on the phone, dissecting his every word and movement.

*What makes this Thomas tick? I wonder. He's an interesting guy, but there's something about him. I can't quite put my finger on it. I'm curious about him. He intrigues me.*

Thomas, still on his call, didn't respond, but Stefania didn't necessarily expect him to.

Stefania turned back to her tablet and researched Monsignor Francois LaCroix on the internet. In addition to LaCroix's social media feed, the websites of various sedevacantist groups mentioned him. Thomas' phone call ended.

"This jet of yours is fantastic," Stefania noted.

"Yes, it seats about eight or so, has a range of in excess of six-thousand miles, so it can take me almost anywhere I want to go without stopping to refuel, and we can cruise at about 50,000 feet, above 99% of all turbulence."

"That's sweet."

"Yes, it's a luxury, but given the fact that I travel so often it's worth it. I also used it to ferry granny and Aunt Josephine back and forth to Scotland. I try to offset the carbon footprint with three football pitches worth of solar panels at Haverford."

"It seems our priest in Spain at some point in the late 1970s became affiliated with sedevacantist groups. He's a somewhat prominent advocate on their behalf. What does that mean?" Stefania asked.

Thomas paused for a moment, apparently giving the question some thought.

"Sedevacantists are Catholics, some still in communion with the Roman Catholic Church, some not, who believe that the seat of Saint Peter as Bishop of Rome, that is the pope's seat as Saint Peter's successor, is vacant, in a perpetual state of *sede vacante*, and that the current pope is not the true pope."

"The word must come from the Latin *sede vacante* means the seat or chair is vacant," Stefania interjected.

"Correct. Some believe that it started with the election of Pope John XXIII, others with the election of Pope Paul VI, or the final implementation of the Second Vatican Council in 1969. They believe alternatively that either John XXIII or Paul VI were heretics, mostly due to Vatican Two. Many subscribe to the view that only popes, bishops, and priests consecrated under the pre-Vatican Two rites of the church are canonically valid. All others are apostates. The largest of these groups have some canonical status within the church, the smaller ones don't. Some leaders of these groups have been excommunicated by the pope. Does it say which group LaCroix is associated with? There are several."

"No, it only says he's been associated with various sedevacantist groups in France, Spain, and Switzerland mostly. Does this mean that he'll be more likely or less likely to talk about the papers he was given?"

"Excellent question. You are a quick study," Thomas stated. "It could be either, really. Does his social media feed indicate where he is presently?"

"It says he expects to complete the Camino today and attend the pilgrim's mass at the Cathedral of Santiago de Compostela at 1630."

"That certainly makes sense. We should be in Galicia well before half-past four," said Thomas, checking his watch.

"What happens if they're correct?" she asked.

"Who?"

"What if the sedevacantists are right? What if the pope isn't the pope?" Stefania clarified.

"Well," Thomas replied, thinking for a moment, "chaos; theological chaos for one billion faithful. Such a revelation would convulse the church, fracture it probably beyond repair."

"The sedevacantists seem to be getting along alright. Who would care?" she asked.

"The sedevacantists are a small minority," Thomas replied, raising his voice slightly. "Jesus bequeathed his ministry to his apostles, and in particular he directed that Peter was the rock upon which the church was to be founded. The Catholic popes trace their uninterrupted history to the Apostle Simon Peter, the first pope. The current pope is the two-hundred sixty-seventh successor to Saint Peter. The pope is the glue that holds the church together and the absolute monarch of the Vatican City State, infallible on issues of faith. If there is no pope, there ceases to be a church; no universal church anyway, don't you see?"

"I suppose I understand now, yes," Stefania, not being in a position to argue with Thomas, responded nonchalantly.

Thomas' eyes seemed to well with tears during his answer to Stefania's inquiry.

"I see," Stefania blurted softly.

*Thomas' dissertation adds emotion, warmth and intensity to him, an interesting dimension,* she thought.

"One last question. I researched the Second Vatican Council, I guess I mean Vatican Two, and don't understand why the sedevacantists think it signaled the end of the papacy?"

Thomas composed himself.

"Vatican Two changed the holy mass, which in the Catholic and Orthodox tradition is much more than a service; it's communing with God. From the time of the Council of Trent in the 1500s through the final implementation of the *Novus Ordo*, the mass of Paul VI, in 1969, the mass in the ordinary form was said in Latin. It was the same mass said in every Catholic Church, in virtually every country, for about five-hundred years. After Vatican Two, the order of the mass was changed, and it was said in the vernacular, rather than in the language of the church, which was Latin. The sedevacantists believed that the changes made by the Second Vatican Council were heresy."

"I appreciate you putting it in context," Stefania responded softly, recognizing that the subject matter of the conversation had either depressed Thomas or caused him to be introspective.

"So, what do you like to do in your spare time?" Stefania asked, piercing the somewhat odd desert of silence that had enveloped the cabin.

"What, I'm sorry?" responded Thomas, seemingly lost in a daze.

"Well, what do you like to do? What are your hobbies?"

"I suppose..." Thomas again paused while thinking, his hand to his chin. "I like to see new places, particularly those areas with raw natural beauty. I'm a foodie. I enjoy riding. But sometimes I'd just as soon find myself on the Italian Riviera or Bermuda away from it all, reading a book. So much of my time is spent on my various business ventures, dealing with solicitors, my political role in the Lords, church matters, taking care of granny, Aunt Josephine, and Uncle Robert. Sometimes I suppose I forget to slow down and smell the roses. I like popular, classical, liturgical, and operatic music that's intense and impactful."

"My father took me to the opera whenever I stayed with him. What opera is your favorite?" she asked.

"I prefer moving opera." Thomas rubbed his chin with his right hand. "So I suppose I'm gravitated to Puccini in that respect. I saw *Tosca* at the Royal Opera, and I'd have to say my favorite of all time is the *Te Deum* at the end of Act 1 of *Tosca*. I also enjoy Wagnerian opera."

"That's funny," Stefania replied excitedly. "I saw *Tosca* with my papa at the *Arena di Verona*. My favorite part was the killing of

Scarpia in Act 2. Tosca, rather than surrender herself to Scarpia, kills him; extraordinarily moving and symbolic."

Thomas nodded.

"I see your point. I still prefer the *Te Deum*, but in terms of emotional impact, the killing of Scarpia is quite intense. Another of my particularly favorite pieces is Orff's sung version of the *Carmina Burana* poems. The *O Fortuna* is one of my favorite movements."

It seemed like Thomas had more to say but became lost in introspection.

"I'm a bit of an old soul, I suppose. Because I was raised by grandmamma, I was brought up in a different generation, in her generation, rather than in the present. Granny laments that I'm not attached, but she relishes the fact I have my hands in so many things, particularly the church, so she can't complain."

Thomas stopped talking again, looked up at the cabin ceiling shaking his head, and continued.

"Hah, she can't complain because almost everyone I date isn't good enough, isn't Catholic enough, is a gold-digger, a party girl. There's a laundry list. Christ!"

"Sorry to upset you," Stefania replied.

"What about you, Stefania? What moves you?"

"I'm also a foodie; I love trying different cuisines," Stefania eagerly responded. "I also like to travel, although thus far my traveling has been limited to Western Europe, Brazil, and the United States, and one of my favorite things to do is to hit Ipanema Beach, sunbathe, and read a book. I like non-fiction mostly, biographies, some history, human interest stories, some fictional period pieces, that type of thing. I learned *capoeira* in Brazil and am quite good at it; I suppose you could say I'm a *capoeirista*. I used to model some for my mama's design company in Rio. I started writing press releases and descriptions on her website, so I decided I wanted to be an author. At this point I really want to make a go of it. Maybe then consider fiction writing."

"Well, your first story is certainly pithy so far. We'll see what this LaCroix has to say. What about music?"

"What about it?" she replied.

"Your taste in music Stefania," Thomas said in a sarcastic tone, tilting his head toward her.

"I like American artists, my favorite is Indie style rock."

"Heavy stuff, that means you have depth," said Thomas. "You must know you're incredibly beautiful. Who is your boyfriend? "

Blood rushed through Stefania's cheeks. She blushed.

*What a direct and impetuous question, but I'm glad he asked.*

"Most of the men I've met are immature, superficial, or narcissistic," she explained. "They're interested in me as someone to hang on their arm but don't like me for me, if that makes any sense. Once they realize I have a strong personality and they aren't going to get into my panties easily, they move on."

*I must provide an excuse for not being attached.*

"I'm unattached at the moment mostly because I'm getting settled in Rome."

"Makes total sense," Thomas retorted. "I know the type, believe me, like all these English 'ladies,' daughters of dukes and earls, gentlemen all, who are interested in money, lifestyle, parties, and superficiality. But you must admit, Stefania, you're a bit tempestuous."

"If by that you mean I'm pushy, show me an Italian or Brazilian woman who isn't. You won't find one. It's a thousand years of genetics. I'm the daughter of a strong woman, and my mother, grandmothers on both sides, are as tough as nails. At least I admit it. There are so many women who refuse to admit they're bitchy."

*Thomas is so easy to talk to.*

"Ah, my experience with strong women is legion," Thomas replied with a laugh. "You've met granny and Aunt Josephine, backbones of steel, both of them. Sometimes I consider if I didn't go in the direction granny wanted, she'd have me brushed off."

Thomas again stopped talking for a second.

"I do wish I had known my mum. Everyone says she was tough too but in a gentile English kind of way. They say she marched to her own drummer, which is what my father loved about her. I gather granny and my mum didn't get on. Before she died they had some sort of row."

"I, for one, admire your devotion to your grandmother, aunt, and uncle."

Stefania found Thomas' paternalistic side appealing, not ever really having a father figure in her life. She visited her father a few months of the year, and the rest he was in another hemisphere. Thomas, despite his worldliness, wealth, and position, didn't appear a self-centered jerk, like so many of the men she attracted. His sensitive and spiritual attributes made him interesting, different, and stable.

*Stability; imagine that,* she thought. *Hmm, Thomas could be both a best friend and a protector, a stable column to lean on.*

"*Capoeira*, the Brazilian martial art; Stefania, remind me not to get on your bad side," Thomas quipped animatedly with a laugh.

"No need to worry. I'm careful not to break bones or necks."

The jet started bouncing about and Stefania jumped. Thomas put his hand on her knee.

*That's nice,* she thought.

"We're descending to Santiago," Thomas observed.

"Aces," she replied.

"Only a few clouds, you feel turbulence much more in these smaller jets than when you fly commercial."

She settled back in her seat and looked out the window at the Spanish countryside below as the clouds flew by, her spine still tingling from that ever so subtle touch of Thomas's hand to her knee.

*Santiago de Compostela, Galicia, Spain, May 31*

Crammed in the backseat of a taxi, the two headed from the airport toward the Santiago city center.

Stefania's eyes cut to Thomas. "I'm excited at the prospect of visiting Spain. I've never been here before. I forgot to ask you about the arrangements. Where we will be staying?"

"I've had Emma book a suite at a hotel," Thomas reported. "It's a short walk from the cathedral across the *Praza do Obradoiro*. There will be two rooms, one for each of us, but connected to a common living area. We can settle in our rooms, catch a bite to eat, and make the short walk to the cathedral for mass at half-past four."

"That sounds like a plan. Thank you for the plane, the car, the room. I'm not sure what I can do to repay you," Stefania replied.

Thomas countered with a grin. "I also am now very interested in your assignment and the outcome. Despite Aunt Josephine's passing, which we all knew was coming, so far our acquaintanceship has been well worth the investment."

Stefania stammered for a moment. "Yes, well, I suggest we pull up LaCroix's photo on our phones so we'll know him when we see him. We can assume that Father LaCroix speaks French and Spanish, and maybe English too."

"That shouldn't be a problem. You and I speak all three," replied Thomas.

#

Walking through the crowds in the sun-bleached *Praza do Obradoiro*, the couple proceeded toward the western facade of the Cathedral of Santiago de Compostela. The tolling of the tower bells reverberated through the square in advance of the pilgrim's mass. The immense Romanesque cathedral rose from the square in front of them.

"The cathedral itself is one of the oldest in Catholic Europe," Thomas explained. "Construction commenced in 1060 and was completed in 1210 or so. Its significant attraction is the tomb of the Apostle Saint James the Greater."

They walked through the western facade of the cathedral and both marveled at its beauty. Like a chasm, the nave continued forever to the high altar with the *botafumeiro* hanging in front of it, the late day sun making the interior glow hues of red and blue through the stained glass windows.

"This huge thurible," Thomas whispered, pointing at the *botafumeiro,* "is filled with incense on feast days and swung by red-robed *tiraboleiros* back and forth across the transept by way of a pulley mechanism dispensing clouds of sweet smoke throughout the cathedral. The incense symbolizes the prayers of the faithful rising to heaven. The pilgrims will have their pilgrimage passports stamped and then file in for the pilgrimage mass; we should look out for Father LaCroix."

"This is an incredible place," whispered Stefania.

"I know," Thomas whispered back.

As the mass progressed, the choir seemed to be singing at the top of their lungs as the huge thurible swung back and forth through the grand cathedral's transept, incense wafting high up to the rafters. The sweetness of the smoke tickled Stefania's nose.

To her own surprise, Stefania sang along with the choir in Spanish.

*I don't know why, but this is intense.*

Later, as the choir sang the recessional hymn, a lone tear slid down Stefania's smooth olive cheek and paused in the side of her lips before she took out a tissue from her bag and patted dry her green eyes and cheek.

Stefania noticed a glance from Thomas.

"I don't see LaCroix," she said.

"Neither do I," responded Thomas.

With the mass almost over, Thomas tapped Stefania's shoulder, motioning toward a slim man wearing worn khaki pants, white shirt, with a gray beard and gray hair walking toward a side exit with a backpack and walking stick.

Stefania followed Thomas as he left the cathedral, catching up to him in front of the cathedral's museum. Now about twenty feet behind LaCroix, Stefania took Thomas by the hand, and they ran up to the priest.

"Father," Stefania called in French. "Father LaCroix?"

"Yes?" he responded. "Who are you? How do you know me?"

"I'm Thomas Houghton," Thomas, panting after catching his breath, blurted out. "You knew my Aunt Josephine when she was at the Vatican in the late 1970s."

"Yes, I knew Sister Josephine." LaCroix, looking perplexed, acknowledged. "So you must be the duke then?"

"Yes, but my Aunt Josephine died a few days ago and she asked us, literally on her deathbed, to seek you out. Do you have a few moments to chat privately?" he asked.

"I'm sorry to hear about Josephine. I'd love to talk with you, but I'm fatigued. I probably walked fifteen kilometers today."

The priest appeared fit and in shape for his sixty odd years. Tall, thin, and balding with a few gray hairs sprouting from his scalp, he looked like a miniature version of Charles de Gaulle.

"Where are you staying?" Stefania asked.

"I have reservations at a Catholic guest house here in Santiago, but of course I haven't gotten there yet. Why do you ask?"

"Would you like to come to our hotel? You can wash up and we can get you something to eat, then we can chat?" Stefania offered.

"Yes, you can come to my room, clean up, and we can order you room service. Whatever you like," Thomas chimed in pointing to the hotel across the square.

"Well," the priest said, looking the two up and down, "you're too finely dressed to be criminals. It's a safe bet you are who you say you are. I appreciate your kindness and generosity, but how did you know how to find me?"

Stefania, picking her phone out from her shoulder bag, showed him his own social media feed.

"Can I see your identification so I know you are who you say you are?" he inquired.

Thomas pulled out his passport and showed it to the priest.

"And who are you then?" LaCroix asked, looking at Stefania.

"She's Stefania, my girlfriend," Thomas answered before Stefania could respond.

Stefania blushed.

LaCroix seemed convinced, switching to English.

"That sounds fine, but I'd like to get back to the guest house by dark. I'm exhausted."

"We'll see to it," assured Thomas.

#

After arriving at the room, Father LaCroix showered and Thomas ordered room service to have dinner brought up for him. Stefania and Thomas decided Thomas would take the lead with LaCroix after they got him seated and eating. By the time LaCroix finished showering, shaved, and dressed, the food arrived, and had been set out on a table for him. He sat down to a hearty salt pork stew with fava beans, fresh crusty bread, and a bottle of Malbec. Fortunately the French priest started with the Malbec after he said grace.

"Before my aunt passed away she made a confession of sorts to Stefania and I, and your name came up, which is why we sought you out. She told us that there were two documents that you were given by the Camerlengo in 1978, which were supposed to be destroyed but which you kept. There was a third document which she was supposed to destroy but didn't, and she kept it until her dying moments. You see, it was her dying wish that we find out what these other two documents were."

The priest kept on eating as if he hadn't heard a word.

79

"You understand that we mean you no harm. My family is, of course, prominent and devout, but this mystery has been haunting us since my aunt passed," Thomas continued.

The priest, wiping his mouth with the fine linen napkin, finished chewing what looked like a particularly tough chunk of salt pork from the stew.

"Your aunt was one of us," he said.

"I'm sorry?" Thomas inquired.

"Your aunt was one of us. After the Holy Father's death she became disillusioned. She never broke with Rome, but her heart was with those of us who wanted to worship as we had before 1969. I know that to be true. Was the document she had the original death certificate?"

"Yes, it was," Stefania interjected. "What were the documents you took?"

"I know what the death certificate said because I saw it. The documents I have make the death certificate seem inconsequential," admitted LaCroix.

"What? Why is that?" pressed Stefania.

"Early on I assumed one day someone would come calling about this, but years have gone by and I thought it was long forgotten, the world had moved on. That was four popes ago, although they weren't my popes. I'll tell you, not because I have to, but because Josephine unearthed this again, and God works in mysterious ways. She was carrying this awful truth weighing heavy on her heart for so many years, as have I. It therefore must be time," replied LaCroix, pausing for a moment.

He looked up at the ceiling.

"If this is not what I'm to do, forgive me," he said. "The first document is signed by the Holy Father consecrating Russia to the immaculate heart of the Holy Mother, in fulfillment of the second prophecy of Fatima. Neither of the prior two popes would take that step for fear of offending, at the time, the Soviets, and incurring their retribution. So the pope did it in secret in 1978. The second document was the remaining portion of the third secret of Fatima."

"I don't understand," Thomas inquired in a harsh tone. "All three secrets of Fatima were revealed, all of the prophecies were made known by the Vatican. What do you mean by 'remaining portion'?"

*Now I'm confused. What the hell are they talking about?* thought Stefania.

"Okay, now what are the secrets or prophecies of Fatima you're talking about?" she asked.

LaCroix seemed content in finishing his meal.

"Right," Thomas began. "So in the spring, summer, and fall of 1917 three Portuguese shepherd children witnessed a series of apparitions of the Virgin Mary near Fatima in Portugal. Some of the apparitions were witnessed by tens of thousands of other people. The Virgin Mary disclosed three prophetic secrets to the three children. Sister Lucia, one of the seers, wrote the prophecies down in the 1940s. Those secrets were given to the church, and all three, as far as I know, were revealed."

"I'm not interested in arguing the issue with you," said LaCroix, clearly becoming impatient. "The church didn't release all of the third secret. It held a portion of the third secret back. The unrevealed portion of the third secret stated that there would be a pretender to the papacy, a pope who wasn't truly the pope, a false pope. The document consisted of the last page of the letter written in Portuguese by Sister Lucia herself. I was told by the Camerlengo to destroy Sister Lucia's writing and the pope's consecration of Russia, which I didn't do. Sister Josephine ran other worthless papers through the shredder while I hid the documents in my cassock. As far as I know, Sister Josephine and I are the only two persons who knew these documents weren't destroyed and still exist."

"I thought the papal apartments were sealed after the pope's death?" asked Thomas.

Following several minutes of sipping wine, LaCroix continued.

"The Camerlengo went through the pope's private papers before the apartments were sealed. The pope also created a cardinal *in pectore*; in other words, the pope created only one cardinal during his pontificate, and that cardinal's identity is not known. His identity remains secret to this day. The document creating the cardinal was nowhere to be found after his death, but I saw it several days before the pope passed away, then it went missing. If it was still in the papal apartments after his death, it would have been given to me or to Sister Josephine, or the Camerlengo, or his other assistant, to destroy. To my knowledge that wasn't done."

"Fascinating," posited Thomas.

Stefania busily pecked on the keyboard of her laptop, transcribing notes of the conversation.

"Moreover, the pope was going to roll back many of the reforms of the Second Vatican Council. That was his plan, anyway. If he had his way, holy mass would have been offered in both Latin in the Tridentine form and in the vernacular *Novus Ordo Missae*, starting in 1979 as a compromise between traditionalist Catholics and progressives—" LaCroix added.

"So where are the two documents that you kept?" Stefania asked.

LaCroix got up, walked over to his backpack on the other side of the hotel suite, opened it, took out a sealed plastic packet, and handed it to Stefania.

"These documents were too valuable to leave unattended. I've carried them on my person since 1978. You may have them. I've cleared my conscience, as Sister Josephine cleared hers. Well, I must be going. Thank you for your hospitality."

"Wait." Stefania stood and asked, "You know what the death certificate says. Do you think the pope was murdered? Who was the pope's private secretary, and would he know anything?"

LaCroix stood by the door with his backpack in hand.

"I can't say. The pope's private secretary was a bishop, who is long dead. I think he was oblivious to everything."

"Well, there must have been circumstances which led you to question the official cause of death since you knew it was untrue," said Stefania.

"I will say that maybe a day or two before his death the Camerlengo went to see the pope with his other assistant, Father Zerkorian. After that meeting, the pope's demeanor changed substantially. We all noticed it. He seemed depressed, almost manic."

"Did he do anything suspicious after that meeting?" asked Stefania.

"After that he cancelled his usual schedule, saw a few special appointments, then, well, died. I know that when the Camerlengo and Father Zerkorian went to see the pope, Father Zerkorian was carrying a blue envelope with some other papers. Neither had the envelope when he and the Camerlengo left the papal apartments, so he must have left it with the pope."

"Did those documents turn up after the pope died?" queried Stefania.

"I know the Camerlengo scoured the papal apartments for documents before the apartments were sealed, but I'm pretty confident that whatever Father Zerkorian gave the pope wasn't in the apartments when he died. The Camerlengo insinuated that he didn't find all of the documents he was looking for. What those documents were, I don't know, but after they were brought to him, the Holy Father was affected."

"Who was this Father Zerkorian?" she asked.

"He was the Camerlengo's other assistant. An Armenian. Emil was his first name. Like myself, he left the Vatican after the pope's death, and I haven't heard from him since. I tried to look him up on the internet, and he sort of dropped off the face of the earth."

"How old was he then?" Stefania inquired.

"He was about my age then, I don't know for sure. So he's probably in his mid to late sixties today, if he's alive. Now I must be going." He turned to Thomas. "Can you please accompany me down to the lobby?"

Thomas left with LaCroix. Stefania took advantage of the interlude to feverishly go through her notes. She also examined the documents provided by LaCroix.

When Thomas returned, she looked up at him, holding LaCroix's papers.

"These appear to be genuine," she noted. "One is an old note written longhand in Portuguese, clearly by a woman, dated 3, January, 1944 and indicates it's the fourth page of a four page document. The other is an official pronouncement in Latin, dated 26, September, 1978, signed by the pope consecrating Russia to the Immaculate Heart of the Madonna. That would have been two days before his death, which is probably why the document was never made public."

"Do your notes from your review of the archives provide any confirmation to LaCroix's account?" Thomas asked.

"According to the records in the archives, the Camerlengo and an assistant, no name is mentioned, but it must have been Zerkorian, met with the pope on September 25, 1978. Between that day and the night he died, he met with the Camerlengo again each day with LaCroix. The day before he died he met with a Cardinal Siri, as well as with this Bishop Gonzalvo and later with the Sheikh, both on the day he died. Damn, I should have asked LaCroix about this Bishop Gonzalvo."

Thomas rubbed his hand on his chin.

"Look him up," he instructed.

"What's that?" Stefania asked.

"Look him up," Thomas clarified. "If Gonzalvo was a bishop in the Catholic Church, he's bound to have a biography online."

Stefania typed his name on her laptop keyboard.

"Yes, there is a Bishop Affonso Gonzalvo. Says here he's in his eighties, is retired, and resides in Aparecida in Brazil. He had a translator's position in the Vatican secretary of state's office in the early 1970s, he was then appointed the provincial superior for the Jesuits in Brazil. Hmm, Aparecida is about three hours from Rio by car as I recall. I've never been there."

"Well, I've actually been there once," Thomas offered.

Puzzled, Stefania raised her eyebrows a hair, and frowned slightly.

"*What* were you doing in Aparecida, Brazil?" she asked.

Thomas grinned.

"I think you're going to chuckle, but Aparecida is a major pilgrimage site in South America. It's the location of the largest basilica dedicated to the Virgin Mary in the world, and the church there is only second in size to Saint Peter's in Vatican City. Granny, Aunt Josephine, and I went there once, maybe five, six years ago, on pilgrimage."

Thomas swept his hair to the side with his right hand.

"You know there was always suspicion that the church didn't release the entirety of the third secret of Fatima. I seem to recall some controversy that the original letter of Sister Lucia was four pages, but the document released by the Vatican was two or three pages. Quite disconcerting. Well, do you want to go to Brazil? It would be kind of a homecoming of sorts for you."

"Not right away. I'd like to go back to the Vatican and see if the death certificate your aunt gave us is authentic. I also want to see if I can determine the authenticity of the pope's document given to us by LaCroix. I don't know how we can check whether this letter from 1944 is genuine. I'd like to meet this Sheikh. Then perhaps Aparecida. Are you game?"

"Of course I'm up for it," Thomas enthusiastically responded.

Stefania's phone rang.

"*Pronto.* Good evening, Rodolfo," she answered.

"I'm eager to know what you found," he countered.

"What have I found? We've found some leads, and I think we'll be back in Rome tomorrow. I'll need to go back to the Vatican archives. Where do things stand with an appointment with the Sheikh?" she asked.

"I've heard back from his assistant, and he's willing to meet with you under certain conditions which shouldn't be a problem. I'll explain further when you arrive in Rome," Rodolfo responded.

"Good. I'll text or e-mail you when we leave. Thank you, good evening, and until tomorrow," concluded Stefania.

#

Thomas' phone rang.

"Stefania, please excuse me for a moment; business," Thomas said.

He went to his bedroom and shut the door.

"Yes, Harry."

"No word from your grandmother, but she sidestepped me and hired her own investigator," reported Harry.

"Who did she hire?"

"I don't know for certain. My sources indicate that she was speaking with one of your father's old MI5 chaps. If that's the case, he's probably someone good but not as good as yours truly. I understand that whomever she hired may have associates. You should take care."

"Right. Thanks for the tip. Try to find out whom. Also, I need you to check out an Armenian priest, or former Armenian priest, named Emil Zerkorian. He worked at the Vatican as an aid to the Camerlengo in 1978. Don't ask why, but I'd like to know if he's still alive and where he is. My guess is he's in his sixties. Maybe you can use one of your MI5 or MI6 contacts to find him. You can drop my name if need be."

"I'll get on it straight away. I haven't found anything of note on your Sheikh. I've got an old mate from the army at MI6. That bloke owes me a dozen favors, and dropping your name always helps. I'll

85

see if he can assist on the Zerkorian and Sheikh angles. Also, you may want to look at the London tabloids' gossip pages."

"What for?"

"You'll see."

"Right. Thanks again, Harry."

Thomas walked out of the bedroom.

"Stefania, can you please pull up the gossip page for any of the London tabloids?"

Stefania pecked a few keys on the keyboard of her laptop. "Oh, oh my," she declared.

The headline read "Bachelor Duke Brings Mystery Brazilian to Scotland to Meet the Family." A photo of Thomas and Stefania in Scotland made it into the tabloids.

Stefania turned to Thomas.

"I'm so sorry I texted the Scotland photo to my friend in Rome. She must have posted it."

Thomas put his index finger on her lips.

"The tabloids gave up on me long ago," he said softly. "But they were bound to come back. The good thing is, at least for the time being, granny doesn't know. She's the one who would be upset. Fortunately, as far as I know she doesn't use the internet, and she only reads the *Times*."

"Thank you for your understanding," Stefania replied.

Thomas smiled.

"Don't bother yourself. It's fine. I'll have the jet readied and we'll fly to Rome tomorrow."

*Whomever granny hired might find out the truth behind Stefania's alleged religiosity, or worse, the paparazzi could dig up dirt and it could be in the tabloids. The London tabloids likely will now be following us. If granny finds out the truth, there will be hell to pay,* thought Thomas.

Thomas smiled and sat back going through his messages on his phone.

# Chapter 8
*Yasenevo, Russia, May 31*

Running late because she had to take her cat to the veterinary, Greschenko missed her morning swim as well as her down time when she had her black tea and *kasha* and went through the morning news on her office computer. She hardly got her coat off when her assistant intelligence officer, Anatoly, entered for the usual and relatively mundane daily intelligence briefing.

Slim and tall, the twentyish Anatoly, in his crisp dark suit and thin grey tie and white shirt, sat down with some files and a tablet at the conference table in Greschenko's office.

Anatoly went through the list of ongoing matters and provided updates. About to conclude, he stated, "Last is something new to report and quite unusual."

"Well, what's the nature of the report?" Greschenko asked.

"Apparently yesterday signals intercepted and translated an unencrypted phone call between MI6's Rome station chief and someone named Harry in London. The conversation mentioned an Armenian, Emil Zerkorian, as well as an imam, Sheikh Salah el-Amin. The only reason I'm bringing this to your attention is that Zerkorian was an agent of the Bulgarian committee for state security in Rome in the 1970s and was involved in something called Operation Archangel, which was flagged. His last known address was in Azerbaijan. Zerkorian is one of his many aliases in our database. The Sheikh was a propaganda problem for us in Chechnya during the Second Chechen War. There was a sanction order on him, but he fell off the earth and hasn't been heard from since. As far as I can tell the sanction order was never carried out."

"Did you turn up anything on this Operation Archangel?" she asked with a raised brow.

"Interestingly, there's virtually nothing. A search of the operations files didn't turn-up an active Operation Archangel, other than that it *was* a KGB-funded black operation. There are no computer files on it, probably because the operation is so old. If Zerkorian and the Sheik hadn't been mentioned, I wouldn't have felt the need to report it to you. Also identified in the phone conversation was the Duke of Radcliffe, a Britisher nobleman. If you want me to go through the archives for more on this, I can."

"That's not necessary. Seems odd that MI6 is now interested in this Bulgarian agent from the 1970s," said Greschenko.

"Also, this imam, Sheikh Salah el-Amin, an Egyptian, was also flagged in connection with this Operation Archangel, but nothing more is in the file on why. Last information we have on him is that he lives in Rome. The full transcript of the phone conversation is in the file here for your review. The most recent photographs of this Britisher nobleman are also in the file, as is our file on him, as well as our file on the Sheikh."

"You say there's an outstanding sanction order on this Sheikh?"

"Yes."

"Thank you, Anatoly. I have a headache and other pressing matters to attend to as I arrived late today. You're dismissed. This Zerkorian and Archangel are old news, nothing to be concerned about. Just keep me informed in the event anything else pops up regarding these individuals or Archangel."

"Certainly, Deputy Director. I was finished in any event," replied Anatoly as he left the office.

Greschenko picked up the photos and file and sifted through them. She turned around, opened her office safe behind the Russian flag, and pulled out an ancient file folder labeled "Archangel."

*Vasily, my old friend, your legacy is coming back to haunt me, and I don't particularly relish it.*

Leafing through the Archangel file for a few moments, Greschenko slapped it back down onto her desk.

*This Sheikh has been a thorn in our side for decades.*

She picked up her mobile phone and scrolled through her contact list, pressing the mobile number for Deputy Director Lenov at Directorate S.

Stefania had a difficult time sleeping through the night, tossing and turning most of the time. She lay in bed thinking for hours on end.

*What am I doing? I can't get Thomas out of my mind. And the lies. I lied to him about my religiosity, being Catholic, and for some reason yesterday's mass was inspirational.*

She got out of bed at about 7 o'clock. Dressed in only a black camisole and matching hipsters, she walked to the window, pulling the curtains to one side. Below, a few cars navigated the streets of Santiago. A sunbeam cast a glow from the early morning sun throughout the suite bedroom.

Retreating to the desk, she picked up her phone and texted Rodolfo,

WILL CALL YOU BETWEEN 8 AND 9

She then did some internet research on Thomas. She read his web biography and those of his ancestors with interest. There were past tabloid articles regarding his romantic interests, but nothing salacious.

She then turned to the matter at hand. Her internet research indicated that the signature of the pope she found online matched the signature on the document provided by Father LaCroix. No documentation could be found on the internet containing the Camerlengo's signature. She'd have to revisit the archives. There were also no new photos or gossip of her and Thomas in the tabloids. Maybe the story had blown over.

The night before she'd ordered room service for delivery at 8 o'clock so she undressed and jumped into the shower. They would be leaving for the airport at about 9 o'clock.

After finishing getting ready, Stefania phoned Rodolfo.

"*Pronto*. Good day, Stefania. How does it go?" answered Rodolfo.

"Good day, Rodolfo. Everything is fine. We should be in Rome this afternoon. We'll come to your offices and show you what we have. What's the plan with the Sheikh?"

"Yes, his assistant called me back yesterday. He wants to meet with you and the duke."

"Odd that he knows about his involvement, but I would have wanted Thomas to accompany me nonetheless. What's the schedule then with the Sheikh and the archives?"

"With the Sheikh, you're to dress in a full length *hijab*. I've arranged to have one for you, and you and the duke are to wait in front of Harry's Bar at 1600 to be collected. As to the archives, your pass gets you in whenever you want as long as it's open. You may have to wait until tomorrow. Does that work?"

"Aces," replied Stefania, hesitating for a second, before asking, "I have a little favor to request. How quickly can I get baptized and receive my initiation sacraments in the church?"

Rodolfo laughed.

"A little favor?" he asked. "Hah! I'll call my contacts at the Vatican and see what you'll need to do. Baptism shouldn't be a problem. But communion, confession, and confirmation, that's time-consuming. I'll get back to you. They may expedite it for me. I'll probably have to sponsor you. There will be an expected contribution. Why this all of a sudden?"

Stefania listened to see if Thomas was awake. She walked across to the other side of the room.

"I'd rather not say. I need to be baptized at *Santa Maria della Concezione dei Cappuccini* as soon as possible, and no mention of this in front of the duke."

"I'll see what I can do. I'll see you later. I'm eager to meet this duke of yours. Safe travels."

*41,000 feet above Eastern Spain, June 1*

After the Falcon 8X reached cruising altitude, Stefania reviewed her notes and repeated the facts as she understood them.

"So on September twenty-fifth the Camerlengo met with the pope at his usual time in the morning. Later that day he and Zerkorian met with the pope in the afternoon, which was unusual. Zerkorian carried documents and a blue envelope which LaCroix claims were never found and didn't leave the papal apartments. On the twenty-sixth, twenty-seventh, and twenty-eighth, the Camerlengo meets with the pope in the morning, the same time he does every day. In the afternoon of the twenty-seventh, this Cardinal Siri met with the pope. On the twenty-eighth, the day the pope died, the pope met with Bishop Gonzalvo and later with the Sheikh, the Sheikh being the pope's last visitor from outside the Vatican. That night the pope dies in a locked room. The last person to see him was your aunt."

"Is the key to the inquiry what happened before the pope died or after?" Thomas interrupted.

"I think it's both," Stefania replied. "The pope was discovered the next morning on the twenty-ninth by a nun at about 0530. According to the archives, the pope's body was removed at about 0800, and the papal apartments were sealed at 0830. In that thirty minutes the Camerlengo went through the pope's papers and removed some documents. Later, after the death certificate was issued and dated October 1, 1978, the Camerlengo instructed your aunt to destroy the original death certificate and likewise instructed LaCroix to destroy the consecration of Russia letter and a portion of the letter from Sister Lucia regarding the third secret of Fatima. A new death certificate was created, back-dated, and placed in the official papers in the archives. According to LaCroix, after the visit by Zerkorian on the twenty-fifth, the pope became depressed and, to use his words, 'manic.' The archived records indicate that the Camerlengo routinely met with the pope alone, but LaCroix said he or Zerkorian was with him some of the time. Why couldn't the Camerlengo have removed the documents during one of the routine meetings?"

"If that were the case, why go through the papal apartments for documents after the fact?" Thomas asked. "Was the consecration of Russia and the third secret of Fatima that important? My belief is that there was some connection between the documents the pope was given on the twenty-fifth and the scheduling of the appointments with Gonzalvo and the Sheikh. What about this Cardinal Siri? I think I've heard of him for some reason. Can't place it, though."

Stefania looked through her notes.

"I looked him up this morning briefly. He died in 1989. He was a bishop from Genoa."

"Well, that's a dead end. The Sheikh and Gonzalvo are still alive," noted Thomas.

"Yes, if LaCroix is telling the truth, there's no doubt that there are additional documents which may have some bearing on the matter. If those papers weren't in the papal apartments and weren't given back to the Camerlengo, they were either removed by Siri, who's dead, the Sheikh, or Gonzalvo," responded Stefania.

"Then there's the question, assuming the pope was murdered, it would have had to be a member of the papal household, which Aunt Josephine said was quite unlikely, but if he committed suicide, why?

What was the precipitating factor? I mean, most people don't commit suicide for no reason, and in the church, suicide is a sin. Theoretically, he could have resigned if he didn't want to be pope," said Thomas.

Taking out the missing portion of the third secret of Fatima, Stefania waved it in the air. "What if after he read the third secret, he concluded that he was the false pope, the antipope? Would that be enough to make him suicidal?" she speculated.

"Maybe, but think about it. He was lawfully elected after the prior pope died. There was no controversy about his election. Also, there was no direct connection between the Fatima prophecy and this pope. In history, when there was an antipope, typically there were two claimants to the papacy. You know what? Look up on the internet the prophecy of Saint Malachy for shits and giggles. I'd like to see what it states about the 1978 pontificate."

Stefania pecked a few keys on her laptop.

"Okay, I'm there. Who is Saint Malachy?"

"Saint Malachy was an Irish saint, twelfth century I think. He had a vision where he prophesized all of the popes starting in the twelfth century to the present, including the last pope before the final judgment, whom I recall was named Peter and would destroy the church. No pope has been named Peter since Saint Peter, of course. Scroll down the page to the most recent popes. It should indicate a direct relationship between Saint Malachy's prophecy and the name of each pope."

"Okay, I'm getting there. Here it is. The 109th pope after the prophecy was made is our pope. The prophecy in Latin means 'of the half moon,' but there's no connection between that prophecy and him. Hmm, there's a direct connection for every other pope."

"That's peculiar," Thomas added. "But once again the Fatima prophecy didn't directly identify the pope by name. It was vague."

"Perhaps Rodolfo can make some sense of some of this?" Stefania hypothesized as she picked the death certificate out of her bag.

"The problem for the moment is how am I going to get *this* back into the archives to check it against the original certificate, or at least the Camerlengo's signature? I can't have my phone with me in the archives, and they'll search my bag and coat for documents going in and going out. Either way, if they find the document, we're screwed."

"Correction, Stefania. *You* are screwed; I'll sneak off and grab an espresso!"

Stefania laughed.

"Hilarious, very funny your grace."

Both shared a chuckle.

"What if we photocopy the signature and hide it in your clothing somewhere, maybe your bra or underwear? I mean, the signature is relatively small. It can be copied, cut out, folded. Plus, there must be a loo or something in the archives and you can crumble it up and discard it in the event they search you on your way out so it won't be on your person."

"Your grace has something of a devious mind!" Stefania liked the idea. "So, Thomas, while you've educated me on the sedevacantists and Vatican Two, you've never expressed an opinion on the church. Do you buy in to all the church teachings?"

"Hah, what a loaded question," Thomas responded, raising his voice slightly.

"Are you scared to respond truthfully, your grace?" Stefania, smiling mischievously, queried.

"Of course not. I'm what the Americans would refer to as a 'cafeteria Catholic.' I accept some of the dogma, some of it I don't. I pick and choose, but I'm devoted to the church as an institution."

"Examples, Thomas, examples," Stefania pushed back.

"Well, the church's position on birth control, *in vitro* fertilization, for example, I disagree with. I think priests should marry. Orthodox priests have been marrying for centuries. There's no doctrinal basis for not allowing priests to marry. A perfect compromise would be to permit certain orders of married clergy and other orders of celibate clergy. I don't believe that celibacy is the natural order of things. However, the basis of the church, its foundational teachings of the risen Christ, his resurrection, charity, forgiveness of sin, care for the environment, our earth, and love, are all tenets I embrace."

"How can you be devoted to the church and not all of its teachings? Isn't that an inherent contradiction?"

"The same way you can be devoted to someone you love. You don't agree on everything but agree on the fundamentals, or a political party, for example, or your mother, father, parents. You disagree but love them just the same. The church is an institution which preaches love, forgiveness, and redemption, which cares for

the poor, which educates, provides health care. It's an institution for
good, an institution for positive change. I suppose that's how I
rationalize the contradiction you speak of."

"What about Vatican Two? Do you agree with that?"

"Not particularly. The church could have kept both the Latin
mysticism which had survived in some form for a thousand years, at
least since the Council of Trent, but at the same time allowed the
mass in the vernacular. The progressives wiped the slate clean, so to
speak, and the result, the pews emptied, again, in my view, a product
of failure to compromise between conservatives and progressives;
then came the sexual scandals."

"What does that have to do with it?"

"In my opinion, it lowered the standards for vocations, and
apparently allowed into the priesthood a multitude of paedophiles
and perverts."

"Well, the church's failure to compromise may figure prominently
in our adventure," Stefania added.

"I suppose the lack of compromise in the human element
throughout history has led to the worst in humanity," Thomas
replied.


#


Thomas pushed back in his window seat and peered out the window.
He watched as the jet cut through the thin cirrus clouds high above
the Mediterranean. With his hand over his chin, he contemplated
what he knew.

Thomas realized that the information Stefania had at her disposal
could expose the fact that the pope's death in 1978 was not a natural
death as originally reported by the Vatican. Despite his misgivings,
he concluded he must stay involved to protect the church if need be.

Stefania sat in her seat likewise peering out the portal into the
clouds beyond. He caught a subtle glimpse of her. Their eyes met for
a brief second.

*I've spent more time with Stefania over the last few days than any
other woman in the last five years, save granny,* he thought. *Stefania
is always on my mind. She's in my thoughts, in my dreams, in my
prayers. She's omnipresent.*

94

*My God, I've developed intense feelings as well as an incredible physical desire for a woman who could tear down the labor of my family.*

# Chapter 9
*Seil Island, Scotland, UK, June 1*

The duchess paced through the library of Castle Seil waiting for an expected call.

Her private line rang, and she promptly picked up the receiver.

"You may wish to review the tabloids. Your grandson and this Stefania are being noticed," a man's voice informed.

"No matter," she responded. "I've seen it. The Houghtons had been overlooked by the press and the paparazzi because they were Catholic and didn't fit the mold of the other peers in the UK, some of whom are constantly misbehaving or getting into compromising situations. Divorce, adultery, affairs, seductions, all are commonplace. It was about time someone paid attention to my beloved Thomas, a true and good man. I've seen the reports. There's nothing particularly salacious, just a photo in a scenic locale. The only problem is now the obvious and undeniable association between Thomas and Stefania, especially if Stefania's story ever sees the light of day. Anything else?"

"I could find no evidence of Stefania's baptism at *Santa Maria della Concezione dei Cappuccini*. I can't say she wasn't baptized, but it appeared that it didn't happen there."

"That isn't what I was told," she countered.

"Well then, she lied," was the curt response.

"Please address this and get back to me when you have more certain information."

"Right. I also have my associate working the case. She's less likely to be noticed following them around. I assume you approve."

"Naturally," the duchess responded. "Report back as soon as you learn something new."

She hung up the phone.

As soon as the plane landed at Fiumicino Thomas noticed that his grandmother had tried to call him while he was in the air.

Thomas had previously instructed Emma to reserve his usual hotel suite with a connecting room for Stefania. A chauffeur- driven black BMW X-5 picked them up at the airport.

As soon as they sat in the back seat of the SUV and had their luggage stowed, he placed the call while the driver headed toward the Eternal City.

"Yes, grandmamma, I see you called."

"I question whether Stefania ever properly received the sacraments or was confirmed, and I've seen the tabloid reports. If she's lying about that, what else is she lying about? If you're assisting her, you're complicit in heresy!"

"I'm afraid I don't know what you're talking about," Thomas responded, playing dumb.

"Be careful, Thomas!" the duchess responded with apparent outrage. "I'm having Stefania investigated. I don't want you to be taken advantage of. You're in the tabloids. For God's sake, Thomas, think of your reputation! You need to be more careful."

Thomas didn't respond; he had no choice.

"It's your responsibility to make sure that no damage will come to the church or to your reputation, the family's reputation," the duchess lectured.

"Yes, I fully understand grandmamma. I'm sorry, but I must go," Thomas cut the call short.

*She always gets her way, especially with me, and she can be manipulative.*

Her diatribe had its intended effect. Thomas became anxious and worried. Butterflies danced in his stomach and nausea set in.

*I can't tell Stefania that granny and I had her investigated. I lied to granny, something I never do.*

*I'm literally torn in three because of my love and devotion to granny, my devotion to the church, and now Stefania.*

#

Stefania phoned Rodolfo while Thomas spoke to his grandmother.

"Good day, Rodolfo. We've landed and are on our way. Do you have any news for me?" she asked.

"To become properly initiated in the church, you'll have to go through the right of Christian initiation for adults, a lengthy and somewhat cumbersome process," Rodolfo explained.

"How long will that take?"

"It could be months or more than a year, depending on how much time you could spend on it. Technically, you should be baptized as part of this process. The process could be shortened if you were baptized in any Christian church, but I question whether this would be a good idea if you want to go through the process as a Catholic. I can try to pull some strings and shorten the process, but it typically concludes at Eastertide."

*I'm developing feelings for Thomas and have lied to him and his family. Is it possible that he would forgive me? I'm so guilty. I may have completely and stupidly sabotaged my relationship with him if he finds out the truth, and that's bound to happen. I have to contrive a solution to this dilemma.*

"Aces. I'll see you later."

Stefania finished her call at the same time as Thomas. Her eyes cut to his and she smiled.

"My favorite hotel in Rome is in a quiet area, near the *Parco della Villa Borghese*, close to many of the embassies in Rome, and by coincidence, in close proximity to *The Journal's* offices," Thomas somewhat nervously said, making a clear gulping sound as he swallowed.

Stefania nodded.

"This late spring weather in Rome is delightful," noted Thomas. "Let's check in at the hotel and walk the several blocks to the *Journal's* office down *Via Veneto*."

After check-in they walked by Harry's Bar and *Santa Maria della Concezione dei Cappuccini*, the church where Stefania was allegedly baptized. Now 2 o'clock, they had a little time to discuss the situation with Rodolfo before Stefania had to change into a *hijab* for the rendezvous at 4 o'clock with the Sheikh's car in front of Harry's Bar.

Upon arrival, Thomas and Sofia exchanged pleasantries given their shared heritage. Stefania presented the documents they obtained from LaCroix to Rodolfo and Sofia.

"This is fantastic! I can hardly believe my eyes!" Rodolfo said in obvious distress, gesturing wildly with his hands and arms flailing about as he examined the documents Stefania gave him.

"In my mind," Stefania continued, "the key is to determine whether or not the death certificate from Sister Josephine matched the one in the archives, which would confirm that the death certificate kept by Sister Josephine was genuine. Since the Sheikh was one of the last people to see the pope alive, I'm hopeful he could provide information as to either why he was killed or, if he committed suicide, the reason for it. The next step would be to see what this Bishop Gonzalvo knows."

"I concur with your assessment. Gonzalvo," he quipped, snapping his fingers. He sat at his desk and typed the name onto his computer keyboard. "Now I recall there was a Bishop Affonso Gonzalvo from Brazil. Your Gonzalvo is Affonso. He was the Jesuit Superior in Brazil, a pretty lofty position I would say."

"You'd better get ready," Rodolfo suggested to Stefania. "The Sheikh will be expecting you as well," he said, pointing to Thomas. "Remember, no phones or electronic devices. Leave them here with me. You'll likely be blindfolded for the duration of the drive to the Sheikh's location."

"What do we know about the protocol for this appointment?" Thomas inquired.

"You're to ask no questions about the Sheikh's situation, why he left Egypt, any of that," Rodolfo excitedly explained. "Only questions about the pope are permitted. I tried to meet with the Sheikh for years. Now all of a sudden; very odd. He's eager to speak to you both. His assistant indicated that his people will pick you both up at 1600 in front of Harry's Bar. They'll arrive in a black Maserati Quadroporte. You're to get into the back seat. They'll blindfold you both and drive you to him. My recollection was that he was exiled due to conflict with Egypt National Front and its leaders. He was close with the Coptic Christian community in Egypt."

"So let me get this straight," Stefania asked incredulously. "We're to be blindfolded, driven to an unknown location, then what? This isn't how I thought this would go down."

"You'll interview him," Rodolfo shot back animatedly. "Interview a man who's been in hiding for years, who has a price on his head, to my knowledge has spoken to no one publically, and given no interviews! A man who was once the most influential Muslim leader in the Middle East! This is the chance of a lifetime! I'd go myself, but this is your story. Plus, he may be more at ease with a woman. Who knows?" he asked while chuckling, his palms in the air. "If he's the last person outside the Vatican to have seen the pope alive, he may have an interesting perspective on the pope's state of mind before he died."

Opening the old manila folder where he found the Sheikh's phone number, Rodolfo picked up some old handwritten notes and news articles.

"Ah yes, now I remember. He's a Sufi, an Islamic mystic, a seer," said Rodolfo, now grinning from ear to ear and gesturing wildly with his left hand while holding the folder in his right.

"What does that mean?" Stefania asked.

"It means he prophesizes," answered Rodolfo. "He foretold the fall of the Egyptian National Front during a speech at a mosque. They labeled him an apostate and put a price on his head. There were attempts to kill him in Egypt. I'm not sure if he was as much a heretic as a political liability! He snuck out of Egypt and has been in Rome, but no one knows where he lives as he's been in hiding from the threats on his life made in Egypt. He published opinion pieces on the internet during the crisis in Chechnya, and then wasn't heard from again. He came from a wealthy family, so he probably had funds available to keep a low profile. My notes say that he corresponded with the pope but nothing about meetings."

"This will be dangerous, don't you think?" Stefania queried.

"I shouldn't think so. My guess is the *Carabinieri* know where he lives and he's been under police protection. He probably has bodyguards. He's been able to keep alive this long, so I can't imagine that there will be a problem. Nevertheless, these are the risks us journalists have to endure. Let's put it this way," Rodolfo emphasized, again gesturing wildly with his left hand. "You're in Rome, not Kharkiv."

"I can't imagine this liaison will be fraught with any peril," added Thomas in an obvious attempt to calm Stefania's nerves.

The circumstances surrounding the interview tied Stefania's guts in knots. She hoped Rodolfo or Thomas would assuage her further.

"Why does he want to give an interview now, after all these years?" she asked.

"Excellent question. Who knows? Because it was virtually impossible to obtain an interview, maybe no one asked him to be interviewed regarding the pope, or perhaps he feels safer now after so many years have gone by?" Rodolfo responded, shrugging. "I obtained the *hijab* from Fatimah, a Tunisian woman who works for the *Journal*. Sofia said she was about your size. You can change in the *bagno*."

#

"Not my style, but one compromises style in certain circumstances, I suppose. I'm so out of place," Stefania commented to Thomas as they walked the several blocks from the *Journal's* offices to Harry's Bar on the *Via Veneto*.

In contrast to Stefania, Thomas wore a white shirt, gold tie, blue sports jacket and khaki cotton trousers, comfortable for the warm May day in Rome.

"No offense, but grandmamma will be put off if the tabloids catch a photo of me with a woman in a *hijab*. It might put her over the edge," Thomas said, adding with a chuckle, an obvious attempt at humor to curb Stefania's anxiety.

"No offense taken," Stefania replied with a grin.

Wearing flats as opposed to her usual heels already made Stefania appear shorter than her five feet five inches.

At the appointed time she and Thomas stood in front of the bar in her *hijab* with her shoulder bag and a notebook, since she couldn't carry a phone or electronic devices. Many of the bar's patrons eating *al fresco* gave the couple a look over. Passers-by stared. Some gawked. Stefania perspired, both from nerves and the heat. The black *hijab* seemed to absorb the late day sun like a sponge.

"It is after 1600, and still no car," Stefania blurted.

Abruptly and seemingly out of nowhere, a black Maserati pulled up, screeching to a stop. A man, fiftyish, graying short blond hair, with a thin rye mustache, a large build, a little less than two meters tall, in a dark suit, jumped out of the front passenger seat. He opened the rear passenger door for Thomas and Stefania, and they stepped into the car. The man sat in the rear seat next to Thomas, so things were tight. The driver sped away. The man in the back seat immediately started going through Stefania's bag. Finding only a pad, pen, wallet, makeup, other odds and ends, he gave the bag back.

"Don't be afraid," he said in Italian with what sounded like a German accent. "My name is Wilhelm."

He took out a handheld metal detector and went up and down over both her and Thomas. Apparently discovering only a necklace, earrings, and a bracelet on her and nothing on Thomas, he put the device away. At the intersection of the *Via Veneto* and the *Via Lombardia* the car stopped for a pedestrian crossing. Wilhelm blindfolded them both, and they sped off again.

Vivaldi played on the car audio system.

Stefania's heart rate quickened, and in the warm car interior she started perspiring. She reached over to Thomas' hand and he grasped it, holding it tight.

"Vivaldi," one of my favorites, said Thomas.

"*Ja,*" replied Wilhelm curtly.

Other than the mundane conversation and the music, all Stefania could hear were the thumps of the road and different sounds of the pavement, and finally a cobblestoned street. The car stopped. The driver's window went down, and he started speaking German, a language Stefania knew when she heard it but didn't understand, to someone outside the car.

Wilhelm yelled, "*Raus, macht schnell!*"

The window went back up, the outside sounds ended, and the car lurched forward for maybe fifty feet or so and stopped.

Wilhelm opened the door, clutching Stefania by the arm somewhat roughly, and hurried her quickly through what sounded like a courtyard. The car sped off. There were echoes, the chirping of birds, and the smell of fragrant roses. With the sound of several hard knocks, they came to a door. She heard a shutter open, and Wilhelm spoke to someone inside. The door opened and closed with a loud bang.

*Clearly a large heavy door,* Stefania thought.

Once again the sound of a metal detector going up and down her body, sounds of sniffing and wining; clearly a dog gave her the once over. Someone patted her down.

"*Nichts, ja?*" Wilhelm said reassuringly to the person conducting the search.

"*Nichts!*" he replied.

Wilhelm took off the blindfold. Stefania stood in a small windowless vestibule next to Thomas, whose blindfold had already been removed, behind them a large wooden door with stairs in front of them. The floor and stairway were made of travertine. She noticed a gun holster under Wilhelm's sports jacket. Younger than Wilhelm, the other man had darker hair, and also sported an unconcealed gun holster. A German shepherd dog lay on the cold marble floor panting.

"He's ready for your audience," Wilhelm blurted in accented Italian, guiding the couple up the stairway. Coming to a dark hallway with numerous wooden doors, he knocked on the second door to the right.

"We're here," he said in Italian.

She heard a faint reply, also in Italian, "Enter."

Because the online information and the historic materials on the Sheikh provided by Rodolfo were dated, Stefania didn't know precisely what to expect.

Now inside, she and Thomas were led to two high back brown leather chairs, and in front of them on a sofa sat a distinguished bespectacled elderly man with a short cropped gray beard bedecked in an elaborately embroidered sharkskin *bisht*, with a *kufi* skullcap on his head.

He turned and looked at the two, smiling slightly. The room had windows, but the shutters were drawn, and only thin streams of the Roman summer sun shone through the slits in the shutters which oddly illuminated the man in the skullcap. A calico cat sat next to him on the sofa.

Wilhelm left the room and shut the door behind him. A ceiling fan spun slowly above them, which made the rays of sunlight alternate between bright and dark.

"*Salaam akaikum*, peace be upon you both. Good day, sister, and it's a pleasure to make your acquaintance, Mr. Houghton. Or should I say your grace? Your reputation precedes you," the Sheikh said softly in English, wiping sweat off his forehead with a white handkerchief.

"Thank you, Sheikh. I've heard quite a bit about you as well, and upon you peace," Thomas politely replied.

"Thank you, sir, for agreeing to see me, and *why* are all your guards German?" Stefania asked.

"They're Swiss, not German. You see..." He paused, saying, "I knew you were coming to see me. I foresaw this event." He gestured, palms up. "It was a matter of when it happened. I therefore couldn't refuse your request. You two are meant to be together at this time. You wish to discuss my old friend. Allah be praised."

*Rodolfo said the Sheikh had a second sight, but is he genuine or a crazy old holy man who had lived in isolation with his cat for too long.*

"Well," Stefania continued, saying, "I came across your name in the Vatican archives as someone who was close to the late pope and in fact had met with him several times during his short pontificate and before his death. I'd like to know his mindset before he died, what was discussed that last visit, but why after all these years are you prepared to speak about your relationship with him?"

"The pope was a complex man," he explained, "a man who more than anything wanted peace between the faiths. He understood that the real conflict is between good and evil, between Shaytan, Satan, the devil, and Allah, God, and not between Jews, Muslims, Christians, Hindus, or Buddhists. All people of faith share a common spirituality. The devil exploits the differences. However, what you seek I cannot provide, nor will I speak of anything other than what I'm destined to speak to you by providence. What I can tell you, and I've seen this, is that the answers you seek I cannot provide. You must find them yourself."

"I thought I would have the opportunity to interview you?" Stefania, now confused, asked.

"No," the Sheikh whispered, shaking his head.

"I don't know what answers you're talking about," Stefania replied with incredulity.

Quiet enveloped the room for a moment as the Sheikh sat on his sofa, smiling slightly, petting his cat curled up and lying on his lap purring.

"All in time, all in good time. I've seen where you're to go, and I'm here to tell you how to get there. In the Koran a great deal is devoted to Maryam. Do you know who Maryam is?"

"No sir, I'm not particularly knowledgeable about Islam, nor frankly about the Christian faith, which is why I wasn't thrilled about this assignment at its inception," answered Stefania in a sarcastic tone.

"Do not doubt yourself. You know who Mary was?"

"The Madonna?" she queried.

"Yes. In our faith there's a great devotion to Maryam, the mother of Isa, Jesus. She's one of the most revered women in Islam. The Koran spends a great deal of time speaking of Maryam. In Egypt, both Christians and Muslims alike are devoted to Maryam. Many Muslims go to the shrines of our Coptic brothers and sisters to express their mutual devotion. Maryam is a great intercessor."

The Sheikh pointed to the window with his right hand.

"Here in Rome, on August 5, 358, it miraculously snowed on the Esquiline Hill and, due to that miracle, upon that site was constructed the Major Basilica of Mary, dedicated to the Virgin of the Snows. Maryam uses seers and mystics as her intermediaries on earth, such as in Fatima, Walsingham, Lourdes, Knock, La Salette, Guadalupe, Aparecida, Medjugorie. Many miracles and apparitions have been attributed to her. It's no coincidence, in my mind, apparitions and prophesized secrets took place in Fatima, which in Arabic is Fatimah, the name of the youngest daughter of the Prophet Mohammed."

He paused for a moment, stroking his cat.

"It's through Maryam, Mary, you'll find the way which you seek or will seek. I had a vision of Maryam, the problem solver, as the Catholics call her, the 'untier of knots.' You must seek her intercession and she'll show you the way. Maryam is the mediatrix of all graces. That's all I can tell you, and it's all that I know. I'll speak no more. Your organization has the phone number of my assistant. You can reach me through that number, which can't be traced. Wilhelm, come in."

"Sir, the short story is that I, I mean we, think the pope, your friend, was either killed or committed suicide, and other than the members of the papal household, you were the last person to see him alive. We also think that he became aware of some information at some point which led to his death. Since you were not only one of the last people to see him alive but the only person outside the Vatican who saw him the most in his thirty-three days as pope, we wanted to know if you could shed any light on his mindset before he died?"

The Sheikh wiped sweat off his brow with his handkerchief.

"There's an old saying in Arabic, roughly translated is 'a secret is like a dove. When it leaves my hand, it takes wing,'" he replied, lifting his hands in the air to suggest something flying away.

"It's extremely difficult to believe that you have no inkling, no idea, of what happened given you saw the pope probably eight hours before his death," Stefania countered. "You must know something. Why would you not share what you *do* know?"

"I've told you that providence will lead you to your answer. Maryam, the mediatrix, will guide you. Have faith, and if you have faith, it will lead the way. The Koran teaches that 'It is Allah to leave in error whom He will and to guide whom He pleases.' Allah, God, will guide whom he pleases. You don't need me, sister. At the end of your quest, at such a time you think you have the answer, when one isn't who he is, you must look under the last stone, and when you've uncovered the final stone, which will be in the palm of your hand, please remember another old Arab saying, 'the fruit of silence is tranquility.'"

The Sheikh, holding his cat, stood.

"Good day, and may peace be upon you both. Wilhelm?"

Entering the room, Wilhelm quickly escorted the couple out and down the stairs. The two were blindfolded and guided to the rear seats of the waiting Maserati. The driver waited a moment and the car accelerated onto the street. Wilhelm sat in the front passenger seat for the ride back.

"Did you get that? Try to remember what he said," Thomas whispered to Stefania. "I think it was an enigma of some sort, maybe with clues. Also, he did mention both Fatima and Aparecida."

"Silence!" Wilhelm barked back in Italian.

The car had gone up the street and stopped. At that point Stefania heard at least two loud vehicles going in the other direction toward the Sheikh's residence bouncing down the cobblestoned street. On the way to see the Sheikh Stefania heard no traffic whatsoever on the quiet side-street where she presumed the Sheikh lived.

"*Halt*," Wilhelm commanded the driver and yelled "*Actung, actung, Attentater*!"

Several seconds later the concussion of a huge explosion rocked the car back and forth. Stefania's ears popped and ringing bounced throughout her head like a bell.

Thomas put his arm around Stefania, forcing her to the floor of the car.

"Get down, down, quickly," he directed rather calmly.

Stefania pulled her blindfold down so it hung around her neck.

Thomas grabbed Stefania's arm and hurriedly bounded out of the car with her landing on top of him on the street next to the car.

Stefania, propped herself up off the cobblestones, between the car and the curb, and looked down the street. There, a vehicle had literally blown apart, and charred pieces of it, as well as other glowing debris, were falling onto and around the Maserati like glowing rain. A flaming hulk of what used to be a van sat in front of a gate to a residence, she figured the Sheikh's. Her nostrils burned with thick acrid smoke as flames bellowed from the wreckage.

Amidst the conflagration, somewhat in shock, as if everything moved in slow motion, she watched the driver pop the trunk of the car. Wilhelm jumped out, snatching an assault rifle from the boot.

The driver, now behind the Maserati, also grabbed another gun from the trunk, both now running toward the explosion. Gunfire erupted from a white van toward the residence. Holding her hands to her ears, Stefania watched four men dressed in black with black balaclavas covering their faces, holding assault rifles, emerge from the van. They crouched while walking toward the courtyard, shooting non-stop in that direction.

In seconds of life-shattering terror, the events of the last several days raced through Stefania's mind.

*I thought this wouldn't lead to anything, and now I might not survive.*

"Stay down," Thomas calmly directed.

Thomas left Stefania and crawled to the open trunk. He grabbed another assault rifle, cocked the slide, and started firing in short bursts at the men in black.

The attackers were now caught in a cross-fire between the driver, Wilhelm, and Thomas, and gunfire from inside the courtyard.

On the ground next to the car, Stefania crawled up toward the rear tire to get a better view of Thomas. At that moment Thomas hit one of the attackers with a neck shot. A cloud of crimson blood filled the air next to the wounded man. He immediately collapsed onto the street. The men in black now started returning fire on Thomas, shattering the rear window of the Maserati, showering Stefania with broken glass.

Cowering on the ground, trembling, Stefania tried to shake off the hundreds of pebbles of broken car glass from her now dust-covered hijab.

*I'll have to replace Fatimah's hijab. A strange thought under the circumstances.*

The smell of gunpowder filled the air; the sound of the gunshots echoed up and down the narrow street. The whistle of ricochets reverberated off the nearby buildings. Sirens could be heard fast approaching.

*Thomas don't leave me, please don't leave me to die here,* Stefania pled in her mind.

As if Thomas heard her thoughts, he dropped the gun and grasped her by the forearm.

"Let's go," he calmly shouted.

Heads down, they scampered down the block away from the fray, coughing as they ran. Two police cars, sirens blaring, rushed by them to the chaotic scene, as well as officers on foot with their weapons drawn. Having trouble running in the *hijab*, Stefania stumbled.

Errant shots striking the masonry buildings could be heard up and down the street, as well as the sound of bullets hitting cars and smashing windows. A few shots whistled by Stefania's head. As Stefania and Thomas got farther away, the battle seemed to increase in intensity, and then died out.

Seeing only smoke rising above the rooftops, she and Thomas stopped in a sidewalk *trattoria* for a quick drink of water to clear their throats and catch their breath. Even after taking a drink, the taste of gun smoke, dust, and burning rubber coated her mouth.

Thomas held his hand to his mouth, coughing.

"The Sheikh's guards had loaded AK-47s in the trunk; they meant business," he observed in a raspy voice. "They were certainly not amateurs. My apologies for leaving you like that. My military training took over for a moment. I won't ever do that to you again. Where are we?" he asked.

Stefania looked around.

"I recognize this area. We're close to the *Via Archimede* near the Kuwaiti Embassy."

"Are you alright?" he asked.

"Yes, and you?" she asked. She noticed Thomas's knees were scraped from the fall out of the car. His pants were dirty and torn as he hobbled up the street.

"I'm as right as rain," he replied.

Stefania took stock of herself. Other than her ears ringing, she fared better because she landed on top of Thomas and covered from head to toe with the hijab provided some protection. Still gasping for breath, she brushed off dust, dirt, and some car glass from the now tattered hijab. She tore off the headscarf.

Thomas asked the café owner for the address and used the café's phone to have his driver collect them.

The fog of Stefania's shock had begun to lift. Emerging from the brink of terror, Stefania realized she had survived a life and death event. Tears ran down her cheeks, as she shook uncontrollably.

Stefania hugged Thomas tightly and wouldn't let go, resting her head on his left shoulder.

Thomas pulled away, looking Stefania in the eyes. He ran his hand down the back of her long black tresses. Unexpectedly, they lingered, gazing into each other's eyes. Simultaneously their lips met, a long, passionate kiss.

In that precise moment Thomas was now Stefania's friend, her protector, the one she had come to love but not yet her lover.

#

The two stumbled into Rodolfo's office where Rodolfo and Sofia were glued to the television watching the news reports of the attack near the Kuwaiti Embassy.

Rodolfo looked up and gasped.

"Oh, Madonna, what happened to you two?" he asked.

Stefania struggled to remove the *hijab*, having worn jeans and a blouse underneath.

"Well, we saw the Sheikh. It was relatively uneventful to the point after we left," she explained. "As we drove down the street, the bodyguards saw something, started yelling in German, Swiss, or whatever, and all of a sudden there was an explosion, gunfire. Thomas and I were lucky to get out with our lives."

"The news is saying it was a terrorist attack," chimed in Rodolfo, "but that doesn't register, since it was on a quiet residential side street. My police contacts are telling me that all of the gunmen were killed. I'm also hearing that a former Swiss guard from the Vatican was on the scene and was wounded, which is also coincidental. The police think it was a professional hit, not terrorists. They blew open the gate with an explosive-packed van and rushed through firing, something professional soldiers would do. It wasn't a suicide attack. However, the television reports are not mentioning any of this."

"What about the Sheikh?" asked Stefania.

"There is no mention of the Sheikh. Are you alright?" asked Rodolfo.

"I'm going to need a clean-up, a change of trousers," retorted Thomas, "but I should be alright."

"I hate to sound impertinent, but what did the Sheikh have to say?" Rodolfo queried in reply.

"A riddle of sorts," Thomas explained. "It was clearly a riddle or an enigma of some kind. I've been trying to remember it, and I'd better note it in my phone before I totally lose the thought, something like 'when you reach the end of your quest the answer will be in the palm of your hand,' and there was something else, but with all the commotion it's slipped my mind. I'm sure it'll come back. Do you remember, Stefania?"

"I remember that, and something about when 'you are something,' or when 'one is someone,' I can't phrase it precisely right now," Stefania said, as she finally finished removing the ripped and torn *hijab*. "I'm sorry, I'll buy Fatimah a new *hijab*. The Sheikh said what he wanted to say, then had us escorted out the door."

"What could he have meant, pray?" speculated Thomas. "If I could only recall precisely what he said."

Back at the hotel, Stefania and Thomas lingered for a moment in the common area between their two rooms. She took his hands, held them tight, and gazed into his blue eyes.

"You saved my life today," she said softly.

"And you mine," Thomas, gazing back into hers, replied.

# Chapter 10
*Yasenevo, Russia, June 2*

On this particular Sunday Greschenko sat at her office desk. As she would on a typical weekday morning, she started by swimming several laps in the indoor Olympic-size pool at the SVR headquarters in her skin-tight black spandex high-cut one-piece swimsuit, showered, and dressed in a fashionable black skirt and gray print low-cut blouse.

Once in her office she reviewed foreign press reports while she simultaneously scanned five flat-screen televisions tuned to foreign cable news channels. Greschenko sipped her morning tea as the resurrection of Archangel settled in her mind. It reminded her vividly of Vasily, as if he sat in the chair in front of her.

*He was like a grandfather to me. He nurtured me and taught me everything he knew. But Vasily couldn't teach me to love since he had none in his heart.*

*I can't show weakness; fecklessness fails in the intelligence business. Only the strong of mind and body survive. I've survived, and so far successfully.*

Given the war between Russia and the Ukraine, her Ukrainian background cemented a certain paranoia into her persona. That, combined with her attraction to both women, and of men. Vasily taught Greschenko, however, she's only as good as her last good result. When the time presented itself, her fickle superiors or subordinates would be delighted to lay blame on her. If her dalliances with women became known by her enemies, her days would be numbered.

*Trust no one, love no one, and confide in no one. Always be prepared for the worst.*

Taking this advice to heart, Greschenko recalled her false passports and identification, cash in pounds, Euros, and dollars, as well as weapons, stowed in several locations outside and inside Russia. Keeping a pistol in her office desk at all times, she also carried a silencer enabled

Nagant M1895 revolver in her bag. At a moment's notice, Stefania could dye her hair, change her appearance, and defend herself. If necessary, she could vanish without a trace.

*The fact that Vasily was never purged didn't mean it couldn't happen to me. Vasily said he'd been living on borrowed time, and perhaps he got lucky.*

*My sister and brother and their children prospered in the Ukraine, before they had to flee to Poland during the war. I envy their relatively simple lives in Krakow.*

*I can't imagine giving myself to someone else and trusting that person implicitly. I want a love, but I don't have that kind of trust in me.*

Anatoly walked into her office for the morning intelligence briefing.

"Is there any more news on the agent Zerkorian?" Greschenko, with Archangel on her mind, inquired before Anatoly could start his briefing.

"As a matter of fact there is," Anatoly replied. "First, GRU reports that Zerkorian's MI6 computer file was recently accessed. Second, the MI6 station chief in question made another phone call to London and reported that Zerkorian was a former KGB agent whose last known address was in Baku and was concerned as to why the Britisher duke wanted information on Zerkorian. Apparently MI6 had information connecting Zerkorian to a KGB operation in Armenia in 1991. Here's a transcript of the telephone conversation."

"Is there anything else?" queried Greschenko.

"Yes, I have GRU's report on a terrorist attack, or what GRU believed was a targeted assassination attempt made to look like a terrorist attack, on a Sheikh in Rome. The Sheikh, as we discussed, was also a flagged person in connection with Archangel."

"I see that on the news. Was the attack successful?" asked Greschenko.

"The attempt failed, and the Sheikh wasn't killed. The Sheikh's name is Sheik Ali Salah el-Amin. Apparently this Britisher duke was also inquiring about the Sheikh and was his last visitor before the attack, together with a woman journalist from Rome. All of this is quite coincidental. All the information is in the daily briefing file here—"

Greschenko took the file from Anatoly.

"I'm sorry, I've received an e-mail which requires my immediate attention. Please return in thirty minutes."

Greschenko quickly typed an encrypted e-mail to Deputy Director Anton Lenov of Directorate S of the SVR and to Colonel General Stasevich, the head of GRU, requesting a meeting as soon as they were available. Getting up from her desk, she walked over to her window as she often did when pondering a situation and gazed out to the lush greenery of the park beyond. She leaned on the windowsill in deep thought gazing out as the birds flew by and the trees swayed back and forth in the spring breeze.

"Shit," she said out loud while slamming her right hand against the windowsill.

"Shit, shit, shit!"



The ringtone on her phone indicated an incoming text from Lenov with a coded message to meet at G 1400.

Greschenko knew that cryptic reply meant Assistant Director Lenov of Directorate S and Colonel General Alexei Stasevich of GRU were all available to meet at 1400. As they had done in the past, rather than trust an encrypted conference call or video meeting, they met in person in innocuous random locations far from prying eyes or electronic or other surveillance. Greschenko knew "G" meant Novgorod, at least on that day in June in that year, and specifically outside of the cathedral of Saint Sophia in that ancient Russian city. All three intelligence chiefs separately flew on their state aircraft from wherever they happened to be to Novgorod. The flight from Moscow usually took slightly longer than an hour.

Greschenko expected Stasevich to arrive at Novgorod first with his security detail. His bodyguards would secure the meeting site from prying eyes. Greschenko knew he enjoyed going to "Site G" for their meetings because as a devout Orthodox Christian he would typically arrive early and attend the divine liturgy at the Cathedral of Saint Sophia, or pray and meditate, then emerge for the discussion with his two compatriots.

Greschenko arrived outside the cathedral under partly cloudy skies. Her tan cashmere overcoat offered comfort given the chill in the early June air. Sitting on a park bench, she had her large black Italian leather shoulder bag with her. In it she carried some files, her encrypted tablet, makeup, identification, and her revolver. A custom hidden compartment concealed a false passport as well as a falsified credit card and cash in Euros and dollars. Fair weather clouds flew by on the brisk June breeze.

Lenov, about the same age as Greschenko, and bald by choice, having shaved his head, stood maybe ten meters from Greschenko, admiring the cathedral at a distance. A thin, tall, pale man, Leninesque in appearance, he'd been assistant director of Directorate S for about five years.

Greschenko pulled a note from her bag, thinking long and hard about Vasily's last words to her, about her sexuality. She tapped the note against the bench seat.

"Lenov," she beckoned.

"Yes, Svetlana Sergeyevna," he replied softly as he strode over.

"As I recall you owe me a favor after I took care of an indelicate matter involving your son Ivan."

Lenov's shoulders wiggled nervously. He cleared his throat.

"And?" he asked.

Greschenko handed him a note.

"A name," he mumbled.

"Find out what she has."

He nodded as he folded the note in two and stuffed it into his breast pocket.

A few minutes later Stasevich exited the cathedral and joined Lenov and Greschenko. Stasevich, in his olive drab uniform, short and round, wore wire-rimmed eyeglasses, and although in his fifties, had a thick mane of brown hair which, of course, Greschenko suspected he had colored.

Stasevich's three conspicuous bodyguards kept any curious passersby away from the trio.

"You know, the sung Orthodox liturgy is so powerfully spiritual, I find it—" Stasevich said, before being interrupted.

"Yes, yes, General, please. You've given this academic lecture before," Lenov said, rolling his eyes.

"Well, Svetlana Sergeyevna, why have you gotten us together this time?" asked Stasevich, all the while smiling as if expecting Lenov's interruption.

"Lenov knows some of this, but it's rather complicated, and I'll need some time to explain," Greschenko responded.

"All right," Stasevich replied, "you've thrown out the bait. I'm game, and I've come all this way."

"In the early 1950s the First Directorate KGB devised a plan to marginalize the Catholic Church. It was called Operation Archangel. Only two persons were aware of the full breadth of the operation, the

Chief of the First Directorate, Colonel General Vasily Karpov, and the General Secretary of the CPSU. The chief of the First Directorate reported directly to the general secretary, bypassing the director KGB and other deputies," Greschenko explained.

"Certainly this is the first I've heard of this," observed Stasevich, with a look of surprise.

"Without getting bogged down in details," continued Greschenko, "the operation was successful through 1978. For twenty years, from 1958 to 1978, events at the Vatican were manipulated through Operation Archangel. In 1978 we were unable to control events, and a wet operation was authorized for the then pope, which was successful; so successful in fact that the cause of death could never be traced and wasn't considered suspicious. In any event, the USSR had plausible deniability because the Bulgarians were used for the sanction. A separate sanction was authorized in 1981 which was traced back to the Bulgarians; however, the subject of the sanction, the pope, survived. Even though the sanction was unsuccessful, the full extent of Archangel never came to light. The 1981 sanction was perceived by the west to be a one-time event."

"Mother of God!" exclaimed an excited Stasevich. "Although naturally I'm aware of the attempt on the pope in 1981, the rest is fantastic."

"Well," continued Greschenko in a monotone, explaining, "after the 1981 sanction failed, Archangel was suspended indefinitely. All persons with potential knowledge were flagged in our database. Fast forward to today. KGB is no more, and SVR succeeded First Directorate KGB and therefore took over responsibility for now dormant Archangel. Our friends at MI6 have been inquiring about the person the Bulgarians used to effectuate the 1978 sanction, particularly with regard to his role in the Vatican. He was in deep cover there. That person has valuable knowledge about the sanction."

"This was a phenomenal project, but even if MI6 is making inquiries, I can only guess at the relevance today, but I trust you'll open my eyes, Svetlana Sergeyevna," bellowed Stasevich, somewhat sarcastically.

"As you all know," Greschenko continued, ignoring the interruption, "currently the president is using the Vatican as an intermediary with regard to the great Ukrainian matter, as well as the lifting of sanctions by the UK, and the Vatican has been particularly helpful with our friends in Cuba. There has also been significant cooperation and dialogue involving the Russian Orthodox Church. The patriarch is close with the president and the Vatican, culminating in the joint declaration between the heads of the two churches in Havana in 2016. It's therefore important to the president and the Russian patriarchate that relations with the Vatican remain satisfactory. If the current pope became aware of the 1978 sanction, or worse yet, if the enemies of Russia in the west became aware of Operation Archangel, in the view of the president it would be extremely detrimental to the interests of the Russian Federation."

"Of course, the west could use the information to derail any talks between us, the UK and the Vatican to relieve the UK sanctions in connection with the Ukraine matter," noted Stasevich.

"Are you going to inform Stasevich about our little operation in Rome?" quipped Lenov.

"Yes, I was getting to that," Greschenko noted. "Yesterday, in Rome, at my instigation in an attempt to start tying up loose ends, Directorate S's *Zaslon* special ops unit undertook a classified sanction against a party with potential knowledge of the 1978 wet operation. A sanction order had been issued on this individual during the Second Chechen War. Directorate S made the attempt look like a terrorist attack. Since it didn't succeed, western intelligence will likely trace the sanction back to us, but they won't know why it was authorized. There's also the person, in the former employ of the Bulgarians, who was the agent involved with the 1978 sanction; he's still alive."

Taking out a file from her bag, Greschenko handed it to Stasevich.

"This is the individual. He's currently in Baku. The president has asked that we take all necessary measures to protect the discovery of Archangel. Do you understand?"

"I'm not one to be taken a fool. Of course I understand; I wasn't born yesterday, you know," said Stasevich, clearly antagonized by the question. "We can address this person in Baku, but my gut tells me you have more."

"Oh, she's got more. And you can assume that our friend in Baku will be a problem," Lenov added.

"MI6 was inquiring about our friend in Baku." Greschenko continued, "On behalf of a Britisher duke, a prominent nobleman, the queen's cousin, in fact, and a member of the House of Lords, who it turns out has connections in the Vatican. We have no idea why this duke is asking questions. Directorate S is engaged in surveillance of this Britisher. Because of his rank and position, only the president can authorize a sanction on this person because if anything happens to him MI6 may be able to put the pieces together. You can imagine the consequences. Unless there's irrefutable evidence that this Britisher is in possession of damaging information regarding Archangel or close to obtaining that information, Directorate S is to surveil him and his female friend, a journalist, report on their activities and whereabouts."

"So right now you've got me taking care of an old Bulgarian agent in Baku. Consider it done," Stasevich confirmed. "When do—"

"And I think there's more," Lenov interrupted.

"As soon as practicable," Greschenko answered. "Fortunately, most of those involved in the 1978 sanction are dead and, presumably, all evidence of the 1978 sanction is dead with them. Other than the failed sanction in Rome yesterday, there's another person on the list. Based on intelligence at the time, other than the former agent in Baku and the subject of the sanction in Rome, he's one person alive who may have first-hand knowledge, although he's not an agent. He's elderly, so it should be easy. Here's his file. He's in Brazil."

"GRU has assets in Brazil, so it shouldn't be a problem," observed Stasevich. Looking through the file, he asked, "He's a churchman?"

"Yes, which is why the sanction must appear accidental. We must eliminate any and all potential loose strings in connection with Archangel so that, outside of the three of us and the president, of course, Archangel never existed. These activities cannot be traced to us. Once our problems in Baku and Brazil are resolved with extreme prejudice, the only remaining concern is our problem in Rome, which will be difficult to resolve due to the failure of the *Zaslon* sanction of the other day. Then there's the Britisher and his girlfriend."

"Why don't we terminate the Britisher and his girlfriend?" Stasevich asked. "We can probably effectuate the sanction without it being traced back to us."

"I'm sorry general, but all of your most recent operations, particularly in the UK, seem to have been traced back to us, and the subjects were all Russians!" snapped Greschenko excitedly. "We can't risk assassinating the queen's cousin, a member of parliament with Vatican connections, and have it traced back to us, particularly given present circumstances."

"As far as I'm concerned it's on the table and can't be ruled out," Stasevich countered. "It will make circumstances easier for us, and I frankly am unconcerned with the ramifications."

"Directorate S *will* keep us advised on the status of the Britisher in case we have to go your route," Greschenko responded. Here's the file on the Rome sanction which failed. He's an Egyptian national living in Rome with whom I think you may be already familiar. There are other reasons why his death would be beneficial. It's all in the file. Coincidently, he's a Muslim religious man. Perhaps GRU may have better luck than Directorate S. Other than the three of us, only the president is aware of this operation. All communications to the president are to go through me, but as always, you're free to confirm with him. Let me know the resolution of the situations in Baku and Brazil as soon as they occur. I would suggest we meet confidentially at one of the usual sites to be predetermined by you regularly as needs arise. In the meantime, phone and electronic communications between us should be seldom and sufficiently ambiguous. Also, no substantive material nor communications should be transmitted electronically. The paper files are to be returned to me for destruction after the sanctions are successful."

"Naturally," noted Stasevich. "We're all professionals and have been doing this for some time. So we're to wipe the slate clean on Archangel, so to speak." Looking at the Sheikh's file, Stasevich remarked, "Ah yes, I remember this chap. He was in hiding before. Now who knows? He may be tough to locate."

"Indeed," chimed in Lenov, "indeed."

"Also," Greschenko added, "timing is extremely important. As you know, there's a summit meeting at the Vatican on July first regarding the Ukraine and the UK sanctions. The president and I will both be there. He wants all of Archangel's loose ends tied up by then. That much is imperative."

"I can't make any guarantees," responded Stasevich with a look of concern. "But the biggest problem is the Britisher duke and his girlfriend. Depending on what they know, the trigger may have to be pulled to sanction them before the July first meeting, if not before," he warned.

"Precisely why Directorate OT will hack the Britisher and his girlfriend's electronic and telephonic communications and her journal's communications, bug the journal's offices, so we can monitor them," Greschenko responded.

"Sounds reasonable under the circumstances," agreed Stasevich.

Parting their ways, Greschenko stopped, turned around, and took in the prospect of the towering gold-leafed onion domes of Saint Sophia's gleaming in the June sun as the blue sky above and cotton puff clouds lingered aloft. Getting into the back seat of her black sedan, she rolled down the tinted rear window and glanced again at the cathedral.

*Vasily, you've left me with this miserable problem, rest your soul.*

*Seil Island, Scotland, UK, June 2*

The duchesses' mobile phone rang as she finished her constitutional around the castle grounds following morning mass.

"Yes," she answered demurely, standing on top of a cliff at the edge of the cloud-shrouded Firth of Lorn.

"It's me. I could find no record of Stefania being baptized nor receiving the sacraments at *Santa Maria della Concezione de Cappuccini* in Rome. Also, her parents were divorced, didn't marry in the church, and that their marriage, was, so to say, 'convenient.' I could find no evidence of an annulment."

"So Stefania, whatever her pedigree, is a bastard, as good as a common harlot. She wears that silver and emerald cross around her neck, must be worth a thousand quid if not more, but it's all a lie. Mere window dressing," the duchess responded.

"She's been blatantly disingenuous regarding her background," the man on the phone observed.

"There's only one reason, and one reason only, this could be the case; she's after Thomas' money. Like all the others before her, Stefania is a temptress and a fortune hunter," insisted the duchess.

"Or she's after him for his church contacts," the man said, positing a guess. "Otherwise this Stefania had no scandal in her past. She went to college in the states, had a boyfriend here and there, and works for an Italian journal. Her father is a professor in Rome, and her mother lives in Brazil where her grandfather was a doctor. Her uncle is also a doctor and is a philanthropist of church causes in Brazil."

"Thank you for your report. I'll be back in touch."

Knowing the pair were in Rome, the duchess considered the matter further before confronting Thomas with Stefania's perjury. Stewing on the facts, the duchess' emotions ran the gamut from fury to despair. She intended to confront them both personally.

*What if Thomas doesn't believe my account? What if he doesn't care?*

These questions burdened the duchess' conscience.

*I love Thomas absolutely, and I don't want him to be betrayed. I can't force him to choose, and certainly I don't want to be on the wrong end of*

119

*Thomas' choice. I know Thomas; the more time he spends with Stefania, the more likely he'll develop affections for her. The allure of an attractive young woman could be strong indeed; oft stronger than the ties of blood. I'll have to confront them both, personally.*

She scrolled to the recent calls on her mobile and pressed the call button.

"Yes," he answered.

"I have additional instructions for you," she said.

*Rome, Italy, June 2*

Stefania's project took a back seat on what she expected to be a quiet uneventful Sunday. After they got up and dressed, Thomas suggested, "Let's go out for breakfast, then Sunday mass. I have a surprise for you too."

"Sure, I'm game," responded Stefania. "It looks like it's going to be a beautiful day."

Thomas' car took them to the *Piazza Navona* where they enjoyed a leisurely breakfast *al fresco*, with the gurgling of the nearly empty piazza's fountains in the background. Stefania didn't know where they were going, and Thomas wouldn't tell her.

After they finished eating, Thomas took her hand.

"Come with me," he directed.

Walking hand in hand the short distance to the Church of *San Luigi dei Francesi*, they arrived well before morning mass.

"So we're going to hear mass in Rome in French; that's the surprise?" Stefania inquired with a bite of sarcasm.

"No, not entirely. Patience please." Thomas took her to a side chapel.

"This is known as the Contarelli Chapel, which I consider one of the most spiritual places in Rome. Look at the beauty of this genius, Michelangelo Merisi da Caravaggio's panels dedicated to the life of Saint Matthew."

"I've never been here," noted Stefania. "Your spirituality and depth never ceases to amaze me. You always seem to bear the unexpected, your grace."

Thomas smiled back at Stefania.

They stood in silence, absorbing the subtle light and shadows of Caravaggio's incredible brilliance. The beam of light shining on Saint

Matthew in the *Calling of Saint Matthew* seemed to be reaching out and calling to Stefania as well, her gaze transfixed on the masterpiece.

Sitting and waiting for mass to start, Stefania pondered, *Is this entire project a spiritual journey of sorts, a labor of love, or both? It started as a journalistic assignment but morphed into finding a spirituality I never thought I wanted. Now I'm falling in love with a famous Englishman whom I had never heard of. Am I living a fairy tale? How could my life have changed so much in a mere two weeks?*

"I have another surprise for you," uttered Thomas, breaking the silence with a whisper. "This evening the *Academia Nazionale di Santa Cecilia* is performing among other things *O Fortuna* of the *Carmina Burana* at the *Parco della Musica*. I have tickets for us if you're up to it. It's at half past seven."

"Excellent. That sounds like a pleasant diversion. My papa texted me to have lunch with him. Why don't you join us, then we'll go back to the hotel to get ready for the concert?"

"I'd be delighted," responded Thomas. "Following mass I'll have my driver deliver us to your father's flat."

After mass, Thomas' driver dropped them off at Stefania's father's apartment, and the three went to a nearby restaurant for Sunday afternoon dinner. Thomas and Stefania's father got along extraordinarily well. She picked up some of her clothes at the flat, then the two went back to the hotel, where Stefania and Thomas sat by the pool.

#

As Stefania soaked in the afternoon sun by the pool, Thomas spoke with his assistant Emma on the phone addressing his business affairs and rescheduling appointments, attending to readying his plane for the expected trip to Brazil, as well as scheduling one particularly important appointment the next day. Concluding with Emma, a call came in from Harry, which Thomas immediately took.

"Good afternoon, Thomas," Harry said. "I have information on this Zerkorian of yours."

"Great Harry, so what's the word?" responded Thomas.

"'Zerkorian' is one of this man's several aliases. After 1978 Zerkorian became a KGB agent or an agent of the Bulgarian intelligence service. Either or both, the distinction doesn't matter, with a last known location in Baku, Azerbaijan. What his status was in 1978 was anybody's guess, but no one becomes an eastern bloc agent overnight. In all likelihood, if he ever truly was a priest, it was a deep cover. If he's still alive, consider him dangerous. Also, that Sheikh of yours; someone tried to kill him yesterday in Rome, but I suspect you know that. MI6 knows you visited him yesterday."

"Yes, thanks, Harry. How reliable are your sources?"

"Very." Harry seemed deadly serious. "You should under no circumstances try to seek this Armenian out. Nothing good can come of it."

"Understood. Any word from granny?"

"None. Radio silence," Harry replied. "I've done work for your grandmother for years; you must know what she's capable of. She's asked me to undertake many unsavory tasks to protect your family and its reputation. You shouldn't underestimate her, especially if she's hired one of your father's ex-MI5 chaps and his crew."

"Thanks, Harry," responded Thomas.

Hanging up, Thomas admired Stefania, who appeared the vision of a goddess in her white bikini basking in the afternoon Roman sun on a chaise lounge.

*I desperately want to take the relationship to the next level,* he thought. *But I must maintain control and go slow with Stefania.*

Thomas rubbed his chin. He pondered Stefania's lies and her project which seems to be getting less innocent and more deadly serious with the attack on the Sheikh and revelations about Zerkorian. Also weighed on his mind were the grave implications if the church kept under wraps the suicide, or murder, of the pope.

#

Stefania had been to the *Parco della Musica* in Rome before. Accented by her tan deepened by an afternoon in the sun, Stefania decided to wear a low cut above knee-length one piece black dress, exposing significant cleavage and her bare olive-skinned legs, complemented with black patent leather pumps. Despite the passionate embrace after the attack on the Sheikh, Thomas hadn't made a move on her. Hence, she dressed this evening to get his attention.

Thomas dressed in a dinner tuxedo jacket and tie, and after going through the lengthy admissions process to the venue, she noticed him ever so subtly ogling her.

"Are you checking me out, your grace?" she bluntly asked.

Blushing slightly, Thomas responded with nary a pause.

"My dear, if I caused any offense, I apologize, but I didn't want to be the only male in the lobby not admiring you. It would have been in extremely poor taste, don't you think?"

Stefania laughed.

"Your grace, you have a sense of humor after all. If you don't mind, I must use the *bagno* before the concert."

"No problem at all, but don't be too long. We're tardy as it is and only have a few minutes before we proceed to the *Sala Santa Cecilia*," Thomas responded while checking his watch.

"I'll be but a minute. I have to freshen up."

Stefania entered the ladies room, followed shortly thereafter by a young tall thin blonde woman with shoulder-length hair in a short silver-sequined dress. The lights dimmed on and off. Straightening her hair, Stefania applied some additional ruby red lipstick, rubbed some perfume along her forearms, and also added some gently under her cheek bones. The last of the women in the ladies room departed, leaving only the blonde and Stefania. Out of the corner of her eye she noticed the blonde woman doing something near the door.

"What are you doing?" Stefania asked the woman in Italian as she turned toward her.

The woman didn't have to respond; she took a rubber wedge out of her small silver-sequined purse and jammed it under the bathroom door, then promptly dropped the purse to the floor. The woman, now crouching, reached underneath the pedestaled sink counter and grabbed something from under it.

Her hand gripped a small handgun equipped with a silencer. Smiling at Stefania, the woman seemed transfixed on the necklace Thomas had loaned to her which hung around her neck. She raised the pistol to waist level, approached Stefania, now about two meters away.

All of a sudden, the bombastic beginning of *O Fortuna*, echoed throughout the lobby, drowning out all other sounds. The reverberations of the percussion shook the building.

Stefania, gripped by a rush of adrenaline, grabbed her purse and threw it at the blonde, forcing her to duck. Stefania kicked off her pumps in the direction of the blonde as she fired her handgun. The shot missed, hitting with a "clang" the stainless steel trash receptacle behind Stefania.

The choir continued singing, softer, plodding, quieter but still audible from inside the ladies' room.

Stefania's *capoeira* training instinctually took over. Despite her rather tight skirt, Stefania acrobatically cart-wheeled toward the blonde and kicked the gun out of her hand. The pistol skipped across the *carrara* marble floor and into one of the toilet stalls. The blonde, also clearly trained in martial arts, engaged Stefania, their arms flailing back and forth.

*She's good, but I'm in better shape. I must land a solid kick and get out of this bathroom.*

Stefania backed off to maximize her acrobatic ability. Suddenly the crescendo of the conclusion of *O Fortuna* resounded through the halls.

Someone started pounding at the door.

"Stefania, Stefania!" Thomas yelled outside the door as the concert continued.

Distracted by the pounding at the door, the blonde paused for a fraction of a second. Planting a kick to the head, Stefania knocked the blonde woman off her feet. Her head bounced off the floor, where she lay sprawled and semi-conscious.

Stefania, panting, grabbed her purse, unwedged the door and opened it.

"What's going on?" Thomas asked forcefully as the choir continued with the second movement.

Catching her breath, Stefania pointed to the woman on the bathroom floor.

"She attacked me. She had a gun. I knocked her out. She shot at me but missed. She tried to kill me."

Stefania wiped sweat off her forehead with her arm.

"My God, I can smell the propellant," Thomas exclaimed.

He went in, grabbed a paper towel, and picked up and searched the woman's purse.

"Empty, other than a mobile, which probably contained an e-ticket; certainly no identification," he announced. "The mobile's locked." He stuffed the phone back into the purse, and tossed it onto the woman's chest.

"Let's make haste, straightaway," Thomas insisted, leading Stefania quickly out of the lobby, barefoot, and to the park outside.

"Should we report this to the management here?" asked Stefania.

"I'd rather not, just the same. Let's get you out of here," he responded.

"Agreed," she replied.

The concert continued and no one seemed to notice the commotion in the ladies' room.

"She's become ill," Thomas explained to the door attendants.

"Why would anyone want to kill me?" Stefania asked Thomas.

"I don't know. Maybe it's a case of mistaken identity. Did she say anything? Did she try to rob you?" Thomas asked.

"She said nothing. She stared at my necklace. Her weird smirk haunts me," Stefania replied excitedly with a raised voice.

Arriving back at their hotel, Stefania took a long hot bath, surveyed her bruises, and settled in for the night.

Sore from battle, Stefania slept little, lightly if at all. She stayed in her yoga pants and tank top, typing her notes most of the night.

Stefania finally settled into bed at 3 o'clock. Lying there, on the threshold of sleep, she heard footsteps in the hotel hallway. It sounded like someone slowly approached her door. The locked door latch to her room clicked; someone tried to enter the room. Terrified, she sat up in bed.

*Was it a dream or was it real? Maybe it was Thomas checking the lock.*

She looked toward the door to the common room between her and Thomas'. It was still slightly ajar as she had left it earlier.

Hearing the sound of the television coming from the next room and seeing its flickering light through the crack in the slightly open door, she fell back into a light sleep, satisfied that Thomas was a mere door away and awake.

# Chapter 11
*The Vatican City State, June 3*

Stefania and Thomas arrived at the archives at about 9 o'clock. They had photocopied the Camerlengo's signature, reduced it in size, folded and hid it in Stefania's bra to get it through archives security. Stefania left her phone with Thomas rather than check it with the guard. He agreed he would meet her outside the archives at about 10 o'clock.

Leaving Stefania at the entry point to the archives at 9 o'clock, Thomas hightailed it to the office of the cardinal secretary of state of the Holy See for a scheduled appointment.

The marble floor and elaborate paintings of the cardinal's offices in the Apostolic Palace didn't impress Thomas. He'd been there before. This time Thomas intended to call in a favor, one of maybe a thousand the church owed his family.

The thin old French cardinal, in a white cassock with red piping with a scarlet skullcap on his bald head, stood, his head slightly hunched over, and greeted Thomas from behind his ancient oak desk.

"Good morning, your grace. You're welcomed to sit," said the cardinal in English.

Speaking in the cardinal's native French, Thomas got right to the point.

"Your eminence, the Houghtons have asked little in return for their selfless service to the Holy Roman Church for centuries. Now I have an unusual favor to ask. I'd like my friend Stefania's back-dated baptism and sacramental records on file, despite the fact that she hasn't been baptized or confirmed by the church."

"That's quite an unusual request; however, it will require me to commit a falsehood," the cardinal replied.

"I'm aware," Thomas replied in a stern tone. "If you can't honor my request, please tell me. If you can, I suggest you go to confession after."

The old cardinal seemed to be alarmed by Thomas' indelicate approach.

"Well—" he said.

"If this is addressed to my liking," Thomas interrupted, "my family will donate a substantial sum to renovate one of the ancient Roman churches in desperate need of repair, as well as continued assistance in connection with the issue of sanctions by the UK against Russia, as well as the promise to actually have Stefania baptized and obtain confirmation as soon as reasonably practicable. It's too late to have the record placed in the files of the church of *Santa Maria della Concezione de Cappuccini* in Rome. I would suggest you have the records placed in the files of *Santa Maria della Vittoria*. It should be easy to place the records in that church anyway, because it's your eminence's titular church."

The cardinal secretary of state nodded.

"It will be resolved as you request. In the scheme of questionable matters I've been involved in over the years, this one is rather miniscule, particularly in light of the assistance you can provide. One of my assistants will personally deliver the documents to *Santa Maria della Vittoria* this afternoon."

"Here's the relevant information you'll need," said Thomas, handing the old cardinal an envelope. "Also, your eminence," Thomas queried, "what do you know about the pope's death in 1978?"

"His holiness had a heart attack in the middle of the night and expired. He was found by one of the sisters in attendance in the morning, that's my recollection," the cardinal answered with a puzzled look.

"Weren't you a bishop in the *curia* at the time?" Thomas asked, pressing the matter.

"Yes, but mine was a *curial* position in the congregation for the doctrine of the faith. I wasn't in the papal household," he explained. "Why do you ask?"

Ignoring the question, Thomas looked at his watch.

"I apologize, your eminence. I have to run. Thank you for your assistance."

He quickly left the cardinal's office in the Apostolic Palace and ran to the entrance to the Vatican archives just as Stefania walked out.

"Well?" he asked, catching his breath.

"It took me ten minutes to get through security in and out. They didn't search my person. The signature matched precisely. I flushed the copied signature down the toilet before I reached the security station," Stefania answered with a self-assured smile.

"Excellent work. You're becoming a secret agent; a lovely and beautiful secret agent."

"Flattery will get you everywhere, your grace," Stefania retorted with a grin. "The 1978 material was still in the documents left for me to review. No one seems to have noticed its misplacement."

The two walked out of the Vatican Archives into the morning Roman sun onto the *Vial Vaticano* and up the street, turning onto the *Via Germanico*.

Stefania stopped and glanced at Thomas.

"This means at least they're both genuine. The question is, of course, which certificate is correct?"

"Well, Aunt Josephine and Father LaCroix both said that the first certificate citing the cause of death as an overdose of pentobarbital was genuine," Thomas countered.

"Yes, but all we have is their word. We have no solid proof," insisted Stefania.

"You're correct. That means our next stop is Aparecida. Didn't the Sheikh mention Aparecida?" Thomas recalled.

"Yes, he said something to the effect that we have to follow the Holy Mother, the Madonna," Stefania replied.

"Yes, Aparecida; that would make sense," pondered Thomas. "There's no other reason to go there other than the Shrine to Our Lady."

"And to see this Bishop Gonzalvo," Stefania reminded him.

"Yes, and to see Bishop Gonzalvo," Thomas affirmed.

She turned and planted a big wet kiss on his cheek.

"That means our next stop is Aparecida! You can meet my family in Rio," Stefania replied with glee. "I personally think this Bishop Gonzalvo is the key. The Sheikh wasn't going to give anything up for some reason, certainly without proof. Ultimately the Sheikh may be the one who confirms all the information we obtain. I wish we could remember precisely what the Sheikh told us."

"You're so smart; it's sexy," said Thomas, gazing back at Stefania.

Stefania laughed.

"Again, talk like that will get you anywhere you want, particularly with that accent, your grace."

"Plus, Brazil may be safer than Rome at this point, given what happened yesterday," Thomas added.

Thomas and Stefania made their way to the *Journal's* offices to meet with Rodolfo, where Stefania took the lead.

"The signatures matched, which means one of the death certificates was therefore false, and we're inclined to believe Sister Josephine and Father LaCroix," she explained.

"That's a reasonable deduction," Rodolfo agreed. "The key inquiry is then whether the pope was murdered or committed suicide."

"We believe that both the Sheikh and this retired Bishop Gonzalvo in Brazil probably know the full story behind the pope's death."

"I've tried to phone the Sheikh, but no one would answer," Rodolfo retorted. "I suspect the phone was deactivated as a security measure," he continued. "My sources indicate the Sheikh left in haste during the attack. No one knows where he is. One of his bodyguards was wounded in the attack and later died of his wounds. He was a former member of the Vatican Swiss guard. My sources say all of the Sheikh's security men are former members of the Vatican security service. That poses another question as to what was the connection between the Vatican and the Sheikh that his entire security detail was former Vatican agents. With the Sheikh gone, probably in hiding, I'm inclined to agree this Bishop Gonzalvo is the best bet for any information."

Rubbing his forehead, Rodolfo addressed the two.

"I'm concerned with regard to the attempt on the Sheikh's life. Publically, the *Carabinieri* were saying it was a terrorist attack due to fact that the Sheikh had a price on his head in Egypt. Privately, they're not."

"Why not?" asked Stefania. "We were there. It certainly seemed like a terrorist attack to me. Thomas, don't you agree?"

Thomas, eager to hear Rodolfo's explanation, said nothing.

"None of the assassins were Egyptians," Rodolfo explained. "They were Chechens, and the attack seemed too coordinated for a terrorist attack. The group, clad in body armor, stormed the courtyard. Typically, terrorists want to create public mayhem. To expend substantial assets to target this Sheikh, who had essentially been out of the public eye for decades, isn't logical. Frankly, the Sheikh hadn't even been heard from since the Chechen wars. The team that killed the Sheikh could probably have succeeded in assassinating a major public figure, politician, or celebrity. My contacts in the *Carabinieri* candidly suspect it was a targeted kill. It seemed too coincidental; the release of the records from the 1978 pontificate, and now the attempt on the Sheikh's life. Could they be connected in some way?"

"I should think it's an extraordinary coincidence. We shouldn't jump to conclusions. Thomas and I will be flying out later today for Rio. I shouldn't think we'll contact Gonzalvo in advance, lest we tip him off," commented Stefania.

"I'm sure you're aware, Stefania, depending on what you uncover could make this one of the most pertinent and impactful stories from the twentieth century. This could immediately result in worldwide recognition for you and for the *Journal*," Rodolfo commented. "It's ironic since initially you weren't too enthused in the project."

"I'm now 'all in,' as they say in the states," affirmed Stefania, her eyes cutting to Thomas as she and Rodolfo continued to discuss the assignment.

Thomas caught her glance but, lost in thought, tuned them out.

*I'm invested in Stefania and her project, and having fun in the process. I want to meet her family in Rio,* he thought as he texted Emma to arrange a hotel suite in Rio with separate bedrooms as well as a car rental.

*We've already spent a significant amount of time together, but we'll be spending twelve hours in a plane alone, except for the attendants.*

*Will we become bored with each other? Perhaps we can get some much needed rest. My relationship with Stefania is gaining speed. I desperately want to get physical. I don't know how much longer I can hold out.*

Thomas emerged from his daydream.

"Pardon, I have to phone my grandmother and let her know we're going to Brazil."

Thomas walked to Rodolfo's outer office, closed the door, and phoned granny.

"Grandmamma, I'm flying to Brazil later today to meet Stefania's family."

"Stefania wasn't baptized at the Church of *Santa Maria della Concezione de Cappuccini,* nor did she receive her sacraments there. Moreover, her parents were divorced, they had to get married, and they were never married in a church. I implore you to consider the repercussions given your station in life, the responsibility the family has to both the church and to the crown," the duchess unloaded on Thomas in a surprisingly polite tone.

"Stefania has told me the whole story. I'm aware of it and am not particularly concerned. As to her baptism and sacraments, you should double check your story, because Stefania was initially mistaken. She wasn't baptized and received the sacraments at the Church of *Santa Maria della Concezione de Cappuccini*, but rather at *Santa Maria della Vittoria*, which is in the same area of Rome. She conflated the two churches, you see."

"Dearest," the duchess responded softly, "you know I love you. I thus wish you a safe trip, but don't be under any illusions. I'll have this new story checked out. By the way, I'll be returning to Haverford on the morrow by car."

Uneasiness crept over him, and a throbbing ache invaded his head. The duchess' mind games had their intended effect.

*God, she knows how to get to me.*

As Thomas reentered the office, Rodolfo instructed Stefania, "Please inform me as soon as you make contact with Gonzalvo. You've only been working for me for a short time, but I've no children of my own, and I'm starting to think of you like a daughter. Please be careful. This story seems to be taking on a life of its own and a path that may be dangerous. I never thought—"

"Don't worry, I have Thomas to watch out for me. I'll let you know as soon we meet with Gonzalvo."

Rodolfo smiled.

"All right then, have a good trip, and stay well and stay strong."


*Yasenevo, Russia, June 4*


Arriving at her office following her morning swim, Greschenko noticed lying on her desk a sealed brown envelope addressed to her marked "Top Secret For Your Eyes Only." Not bothering to remove her black cashmere pea coat, Greschenko opened the envelope with her engraved silver letter opener, formerly Vasily's, given to her as a gift. It was Zerkorian's file. Its return by Stasevich meant the sanction occurred as planned. She promptly ran the file through the shredder.

Thirty minutes later Anatoly arrived for his daily intelligence briefing.

"Interesting development overnight," he began. "This Zerkorian, who was flagged in connection with Archangel, was killed in a shootout in Baku with Azerbaijani secret police. The Azerbaijan government is reporting that he was an Armenian agent. During the raid he killed two of them before being riddled with bullets at 0300 in his apartment."

"That's an *interesting development*," Greschenko calmly noted. "So we won't be hearing his name again then."

Greschenko's encrypted cell phone buzzed. She received a coded text from Lenov indicating they were to meet at B 1100.

*Site B is the Gorky Park ice rink*, she thought, quickly calculating how much time to get there.

Anatoly completed his briefing, and Greschenko put her coat back on, summoned her car, and took off for Gorky Park if she wanted to make it there in time. Reaching Gorky Park in about forty minutes, Greschenko walked briskly toward the deserted ice rink area. Lenov and Stasevich were already there waiting.

Rushing up to the two, Greschenko, breathing heavily to catch her breath, blurted, "What's this all about?"

Lenov took his glasses off and rubbed his broad forehead.

"We've got a problem and I thought you should know," Lenov said softly. "The Britisher is on his way to Brazil. Now apparently his journalist friend has family there, but I can't imagine that's the reason for traveling to Brazil. I suspect they're going to see the subject of the sanction in Brazil."

"And what of him?" she inquired.

"He," replied Stasevich as he cleared his throat while taking his military cap off with one hand and sweeping his hair back with the other, "is on holiday, apparently in Brazil because we know he hasn't left the country. His residence is being watched. We tried to find where he went, but no one knows. The sanction will be carried out when he returns. Because of his age, we'll try to make it look accidental or natural."

"We don't have authority to harm the Britisher," Greschenko said with a raised voice. "He must not be hurt nor killed in connection with the sanction, understood? We don't want MI6 poking its nose about."

"Yes, yes, of course, of course. We understood that from last time," responded Stasevich testily. "The Britisher is not to be harmed till we receive authorization from above! Mother of God, I've been following orders for thirty years, but what if the Britisher speaks with the old man before we get to him?"

"Then effectuate the sanction after the Britisher is out of harm's way, then we'll raise the issue of the Britisher with the president."

"Understood," an exasperated Stasevich replied with a huff. "I'll inform you in the usual way when the Brazil sanction is completed."

"Good," Greschenko affirmed. "Then we're all in agreement. Also, by next week we should have bugs in place in the girl's employer's offices in Rome. Hopefully that will keep us ahead of the game."

*41,000 feet above the Atlantic Ocean, June 4*

Leaving Rome at 11 o'clock, Stefania expected to land in Rio early morning Rio time the next day. Her father insisted on taking the couple to dinner in Rome before they left. Not exactly a romantic dinner, but it gave Stefania a little break from being solely with Thomas. After a long Roman dinner, the two packed and left for Fiumicino for the long flight.

After boarding the jet, Stefania declared, "I'm exhausted."

"Let's nap during the flight. I've ordered a light breakfast to be ready for us before we land in Rio but after we pass through the intertropical convergence zone and any turbulence," Thomas replied.

She reclined in her plush leather seat.

Just before sleep arrived, she thought, *I desperately want to get physical with Thomas, but perhaps on a plane, with the two attendants on board, is not the best venue.*

The Falcon 8X took off and the cabin lights dimmed. Stefania fell into a deep sleep.

All of a sudden she felt a slight jolt, then another, a couple more.

*Must be crossing the intertropical convergence zone,* she thought.

Stefania peered out the window at the endless black sea illuminated by the setting crescent moon.

"How far along are we?" she asked Thomas, also now awake.

"We're about two or three hours out from Rio. I'll have breakfast and coffee served."

"Good. I have a new theory and let's brainstorm again over breakfast," she declared.

The attendants started serving breakfast.

"Right. Well what's your new theory?" Thomas asked.

"Is it possible that LaCroix and Sister Josephine, both being sedevacantists, colluded in killing the pope? I apologize. I didn't mean to offend you with the suggestion."

"None taken. It's an interesting theory, but as sedevacantists, they believed the pope wasn't the pope anyway, so why would killing him make a difference? The cardinals would elect a new pope," Thomas replied.

133

"What about the Sheikh?" Thomas continued. "I keep on thinking about what he said. Didn't he say 'when one who isn't whom he is, you'll find the answer in the palm of your hand,' or some such thing?"

"Yes," Stefania agreed. "It was more or less what he said," as she quickly typed it in her notes on her laptop. "What about the third secret of Fatima? What if either people in the Vatican, or the pope himself, thought he was the antipope?"

"But once again," Thomas continued, "unless you believe that Vatican Two undid the church, the pope was duly elected such as all the immediate popes before him. He should have had no reason to believe he wasn't the pope. The only reason the sedevacantists would want him dead would be to elect their own candidate as pope. But the pope's successor continued with the Vatican Two reforms."

"What if their candidate didn't get elected?" Stefania countered.

"I suppose that's a possibility. But it would be so unlikely. Would they really kill the pope on the off chance his successor would scrap Vatican Two? And I thought the new pope was more conservative theologically than his predecessor, anyway. That seems highly unlikely," Thomas responded.

"What about the consecration of Russia to the Holy Mother?" Stefania asked after thinking for a moment. "It was never made public, and the Camerlengo wanted both the last page of the third secret of Fatima and the consecration document destroyed. Would be keeping that secret be a motive, and if so, for whom? Certainly the Camerlengo, since he wanted the documents destroyed, but who else, and why? If the pope was the antipope and the Fatima prophecy was true, was the solution to kill the pope?"

"There are many possibilities here," replied Thomas.

"Well, these are the facts we're dealing with," posited Stefania. "If the first death certificate is correct, the pope either deliberately took a fatal overdose of pentobarbital, or it was administered to him by a member or members of the papal household. The question then becomes why as to either? Hopefully the answer lies with Bishop Gonzalvo."

"Hopefully," Thomas acknowledged. "Let's check in at the hotel in Rio and set out for Aparecida to track down this Bishop Gonzalvo. Says in his web bio he lives there in a residence for retired priests. Then I'd like to visit the Aparecida shrine. Afterward we can come back to Rio and tomorrow visit with your mother, aunt and uncle, whose acquaintance

I'm quite eager to make. I'd also like to visit the statue of Christ the Redeemer in Rio if we have time. Does that work for you?"

"Sounds like a plan," Stefania responded. "One more question. You previously said there would be no pope if the sedevacantists are correct. Why is that? Couldn't they easily elect a new one?"

"Because the pope has to be elected by the college of cardinals. If you believe post-Vatican Two popes aren't true popes, then cardinals created by those popes are not true cardinals. To my knowledge, there are no cardinals still alive who were given their cardinal's hat prior to 1958. That means there's no one under canon law who could elect the pope today. Thus, there could be no valid pope."

"Yikes, as the Americans would say, 'we're skating on thin ice.'"

"Yes, Stefania, very thin ice."

# Chapter 12
*Aparecida, Brazil, June 4*

After the pair landed in Rio, contrary to his usual tactic of having a driver and a car, Thomas leased a Ford Fiesta for the trip.

"Love, would you mind driving?" Thomas asked. "I detest driving on the right side of the road, and I'm likely to get us both killed."

"Not at all. It should take three to four hours to get to Aparecida. But I have some sites I want you to see along the way."

"Terrific, let's go for it. I'd love to see some of the countryside."

Stefania drove Thomas to a lake known as the *Repressa do Funil*, whose hilly and green fields and forested flanks rivaled the vistas of any lake in Europe, and she pointed out the huge dam holding back the lake. Stefania, not wanting to be outdone by the scenery in Scotland, also stopped at the *Parque Nacional do Italiaia*, with its cloud-covered peaks and endless scenic views of wooded mountains, rivers, and meadows. The weather cooperated, as the late fall day was sunny, warm, and balmy for that time of the year. They drove through small villages and large towns. Often they had the road to themselves until they arrived at Aparecida.

"My God, it appears that all of Brazil has converged on Aparecida!" exclaimed Stefania, surprised by all of the activity since she had never actually been there.

"It's a popular spot," said Thomas. "Let's see, the priest's retirement home is in the old section of Aparecida."

The GPS in the car rental directed a right turn here, a left there. The two arrived at the address, a "U" shaped two story white stucco building with an entryway leading to a small cobbled courtyard to which all of the rooms faced. Walking into the courtyard, they encountered a short chunky old woman with gray hair, kerchief on her head, plump round face, wearing a stained white housecoat, sweeping the courtyard.

"She must be the housekeeper," Thomas observed. "Shall I inquire?"

"No, let me," said Stefania, who spoke flawless Brazilian Portuguese. "Excuse me, can you tell us where we might find Bishop Gonzalvo?"

The old lady looked up from her broom.

"The bishop has gone on holiday," she responded, then went back to her sweeping.

"Where did he go? When will he be returning?" Stefania asked.

"He hasn't left forwarding information and is expected back within the next several days," the housekeeper, gesturing wildly with her free hand, answered in a loud surly tone. "He visits parishes in Brazil when a priest is absent for some reason and handles the parochial duties before the priest returns. He could be anywhere. He has a little blue Fiat he drives around in."

"Does he have a mobile phone number?" she asked.

"Hah, you're lucky he even has a phone in his apartment!"

"Can we have his phone number?"

Clearly now bothered, the housekeeper went over to her cleaning closet, looked through a little blue notebook, read the phone number aloud to Stefania, and clearly anticipating her next question blurted, "And his room is 104!"

Somewhat depressed her quarry had eluded them, at least initially, Stefania and Thomas got back into the little Ford and drove to the Aparecida shrine and basilica. Before they left, Stefania noticed a commonly dressed gentleman sitting on a bench across the street from the priest's home reading a newspaper but thought little of it.

The scope and extent of the Aparecida shrine complex overwhelmed Stefania. The monumental Basilica towered over the area. She had difficulty comprehending the vast number of people visiting the shrine.

"I know that October 12th was a state holiday in Brazil devoted to Our Lady of Aparecida, but I didn't realize the extent of the cult surrounding this Marian devotion," Stefania noted.

"Aparecida is the largest Marian shrine in the world," Thomas chimed in. "It's no wonder it's jam-packed with people."

"I'd like to meditate before the statue of Our Lady of Aparecida." Thomas explained, "As legend would have it, three fishermen found the statue, which is now in the shrine, when invoking the name of the Virgin Mary after their nets came back empty. Following the invocation, the fishermen caught many fish. Like the figure of Our Lady of Guadalupe in Mexico, the statue of Our Lady of Aparecida was in the form of an indigenous woman. I believe strongly in the power of prayer, as well as the intercession of the Holy Mother."

Stefania grinned with delight at another of Thomas' impromptu history lessons.

He knelt and prayed in front of the statue for some time.

Stefania, becoming more spiritual as the days went on, also meditated for a moment.

"Since the bishop isn't in Aparecida, let's drive back to Rio, meet with your family, and do some touring the next day," Thomas suggested. "Rather than make the drive again to Aparecida so soon, we can tour the sites in Rio and return to Aparecida two days hence to see if Bishop Gonzalvo has returned."

"That's great," Stefania excitedly replied. "I know this sounds weird, but this place gave me a sense of calm, a sense of inner peace. It's hard to describe,"

Thomas, smiling in response, nodded.

#

Thomas and Stefania arrived in Rio late in the day, both exhausted from both the flight from the night before and the nine hour round trip drive from Rio to Aparecida. They had eaten lunch in Aparecida and dinner at a roadside place on the way back to Rio. The couple embraced and kissed, their lips meeting for a soft and tender moment, and both then retreated to their respective rooms for the night.

Stefania lay awake in her bed.

*How long can I go before making love to Thomas? I desperately want to, but my lies burden me like the weight of an anvil. I can't get to sleep despite my exhaustion.*

Nevertheless, a sense of inner calm permeated her because for the time being her problems were behind her in Europe, and in the room next to her slept the man she had come to love. She reviewed Thomas' internet biography again on her tablet. Slowly, sleep came with the distant hum of traffic from the familiar streets of Rio below echoing in from the open slider to the suite balcony.

The morning seemed to come quickly as Stefania slept in, having to meet at Stefania's uncle's house in the early afternoon. Stefania peeked into the main room of the suite where Thomas apparently sat watching television, drinking espresso, as Stefania entered dressed in a short white robe, leaving little to Thomas' imagination. She kissed him on the cheek and walked to the shower. He caught a glimpse of her naked tan-lined buttocks as she paused for a moment when her robe dropped off as she stepped in to bathe.

*She's the most wonderful woman in the world,* he thought.

Thomas noticed he missed a call from Harry. He phoned Harry while Stefania dried her hair with a blow dryer in her room.

"Harry, old boy, it's Thomas. I see I missed your call?"

"Jesus bloody Christ, Thomas, where the hell are you?"

"Stefania and I are in Brazil tracking a lead on her story. Where are you?" Thomas replied sarcastically.

"I'm in London bloody England, and that bloke Zerkorian of yours is dead."

"Well, that's unfortunate. Despite your admonition, we would have liked to have speaks with him. How long ago did he die?"

"Thomas, he was killed yesterday in Baku in what MI6 is calling a targeted hit," Harry, sounding irritated, replied. "He was living there since 1992 unmolested, and all of a sudden the Azerbaijani authorities claim he's an Armenian agent and he's shot up at 0300. That's a crock. Awfully coincidental, don't you think? You start asking about this chap who might as well not exist, and he's killed in a raid by the Azerbaijani secret police. What is this bloke to you? I don't know what's going on, but you and that bird of yours may be in danger."

"What?" Thomas exclaimed.

"Yes, you heard right. Dead, killed yesterday."

"A few seconds after Stefania and I left the Sheikh's residence in Rome there was that terrorist attack. We barely got out with our lives. Then there was an incident in Rome on Sunday. A woman pulled a gun on Stefania in the loo at the concert hall. We assumed it was a robbery attempt because the woman seemed focused on Stefania's necklace, which is quite valuable, but the woman said nothing to Stefania before taking a shot at her. Fortunately, Stefania is rather adept at defending herself and knocked her out.”

“Thomas, what’s this all about? Did you report the attack on Stefania?”

“It’s rather a long story, and I don’t have time to discuss it now. We didn’t report it. At the time our collective thoughts were to extricate ourselves from the situation. Nevertheless, I need you to see if you can find out what you can about the attack on Stefania in Rome and also what became of the Sheikh. After the attack he disappeared. We’ll want to speak with him again.”

“Thomas, you understand that this Sheikh is a target, and therefore, if you see him, you may become a target as well?” Harry, sounding frustrated, warned. “Stefania may also be a target. Things are getting dangerous.”

“I understand that. We can determine whether to see him if you find out where he is, and more important, how to reach him.”

Seeing Stefania coming out of her room, Thomas hurried to finish the call.

“I’ll be in touch.”

“Who was that?” Stefania curiously asked.

“One of my business associates. Let me get dressed and we’ll be off to your uncle’s place.”

*Leblon, Brazil, June 5*

Wiping sweat from his brow, another warm and sunny but humid day in Rio, Thomas pushed up the air conditioning in the Fiesta to full.

Stefania drove toward Leblon from the hotel in Rio.

“So, what’s the plan for the trip to your uncle’s? Thomas asked.

“We’ll spend today at my uncle’s *casa grande* in Leblon,” Stefania explained. “My mother’s brother, Uncle Mateus, like my grandpapa, is a doctor. Uncle Mateus is fifty-seven and runs a private clinic in Rio. He’s one of the most sought after cosmetic surgeons in Brazil. His reputation spans most of South America, and he regularly sees patients from virtually every country on the continent for various cosmetic procedures, but mostly breast enhancements and a buttock augmentation commonly known as the “Brazilian Butt Lift.”

“That’s quite a resume,” noted Thomas with a raised brow.

"Uncle Mateus also volunteers at many Catholic hospitals to handle cosmetic surgeries for free to children with physical deformities, cleft palates, and the like. My uncle is married to my Aunt Maricel, who will naturally be there as well. My mama, Fernanda, lives in Ipanema, which is nearby but not as prestigious as Leblon," Stefania confided.

"Do you have any cousins?" Thomas asked.

"Oh yes," Stefania replied. "I'm sure my uncle will have everyone over for dinner. He has two daughters, Gabriella, who's twenty-four, and Maria, who's twenty-nine. She's a doctor and works with my uncle at his clinic. His son, Hércules, is twenty-eight and an officer in the Brazilian Navy. I doubt he'll be there however, due to his duties. You would have a lot in common with him. He's a devout Catholic honored by the church in some way, not quite sure."

"That's unfortunate," commented Thomas. "I would have liked to trade service stories with Hércules. I'm always curious about the military in other countries."

"Here's the street," declared Stefania.

On either side of the narrow street were large gated homes surrounded by walls, some with fencing on top. A few parked cars squeezed into spots next to the walls between the driveway gates.

"My, these homes are all rather large by Brazilian standards," said Thomas.

"We are almost there," said Stefania.

Stefania pulled across a sidewalk up to a gate on the right side, almost to the gate itself. She rolled down the window and pressed a code on the keypad. The gate opened. Stefania pulled through and the gate closed behind.

She parked the Fiesta in an interior courtyard in front of one of the four garage doors.

"This is quite a compound," noted Thomas. "If the house weren't three stories I'd say it had a sort of Frank Lloyd Wright influence."

"Yes, it's rather horizontal. Uncle Mateus designed the home himself. He had the two homes located on this spot demolished, and he built this one," replied Stefania.

"It seems quite secure too. The concrete walls surrounding this place must be eight feet at a minimum," said Thomas.

"Yes, the fortunate in Brazil must take necessary precautions."

"Don't you mean the rich in Brazil must take the necessary precautions?" teased Thomas.

"Very funny, your grace."

After climbing stairs to get to the second floor terrace, through the open room wide slider Thomas finally saw what the interior of the place was like. Not a fan of modern architecture, the house was full of clean crisp horizontal lines. The first floor had an open floor plan which extended into a monstrous kitchen, dining room, living area, and television area, with a room wide slider providing access to a terrace and infinity pool overlooking the Atlantic Ocean to the east.

Covering the polished concrete floors were white or black throw rugs, and the white walls were adorned with modern art of various qualities. Other than crucifixes above each exterior doorway, no traditional furnishings or art could be found. Art deco or post-modernist styles littered the place.

Stefania's family, who seemed to be having a drink in the sitting area, all rose to welcome them.

"Ah, you must be Thomas. I am Mateus, Stefania's uncle," said Mateus who greeted him with a handshake. Stefania went directly to hug who Thomas assumed to be her mother and aunt.

"I'm pleased to meet you Mateus. This is an extraordinary home you have here. Quite unique," said Thomas.

"We like to think so," Mateus replied.

Mateus' cell phone rang.

"I apologize. I've got to take this call. I'll be back in a minute."

During the interlude, Thomas took stock of Stefania's family. Thin and handsome, Mateus looked the part of a successful physician, with olive skin and slicked back gray hair. Wearing a white linen suit with a stripped polo shirt.

A striking woman, Fernanda greeted Thomas wearing a Chinese traditional Qipao floral print knee length dress. Fernanda clearly colored her hair blonde, which set off wonderfully her olive-toned skin and curved figure. Thomas learned she had several cosmetic procedures resulting in her looking perhaps ten years younger than her age.

A petite brunette, Stefania's Aunt Maricel appeared equally as striking for a fifty-three year-old woman, deeply tanned from her days by the pool and elegant in the same breath. She wore a short pink v-neck spaghetti strap Bodycon-type dress which accentuated her curves.

Thomas sidled over to Stefania.

"My God, I feel underdressed in a polo shirt and khakis," Thomas whispered to Stefania.

"Don't worry, you look fine," she whispered back. "I suspect they are trying to impress you. It's not every day a duke comes to visit."

"Well at least you look stunning," Thomas replied softly.

"Thanks, your grace," said Stefania softly, putting her hands on her hips. She wore a white patterned dress which appeared to be similar to Maricel's. "Auntie and I are wearing mama's designs."

"I see," said Thomas, giving Stefania a wink.

Mateus put on an elaborate luncheon complete with service one would expect at a fine restaurant.

"Did he bring in this service staff for me?" asked Thomas.

"No, this is his regular staff, and his driver and man servant double as security. Money goes a long way in Brazil," Stefania replied.

"I would say so."

Stefania and Thomas both brought swimsuits and relaxed by the pool with her mother and other relatives, all the while being served with cocktails by her uncle's staff.

From the patio surrounding the salt water pool Thomas took in the breathtaking view of the beach and ocean to their east. After they finished swimming, relaxing in the hot tub with cocktails all afternoon, Stefania and Thomas changed for the anticipated a cocktail party and dinner.

Stefania's entire extended family arrived later in the day, totaling thirty-five people. The party and dinner lasted for hours, and Mateus insisted Thomas and Stefania spend the night and have breakfast with the family in the morning.

The party ended in the wee hours. Thomas, overlooking the street from the pool terrace after dinner, noticed a modest late model hatchback parked down the hilly street with two persons sitting inside.

He wished Stefania a good night, as she shared a room with her cousin Gabriella. Slowly, the staff cleaned up after the party, and the lights in the house went out one by one. Safe inside Mateus' guarded and locked compound, craving sleep, Thomas fell asleep upon hitting the sheets.

*Leblon, Brazil, June 6*

Getting a late start the next morning, Stefania and Thomas stayed through lunch and said goodbyes to many of Stefania's relatives who traveled to see her. Mateus attempted to convince the two to stay again for a more intimate dinner with him, Maricel, and Fernanda. Agreeing there didn't appear to be any urgency with regard to meeting with Bishop Gonzalvo, Stefania acceded to Mateus' request.

Much to his chagrin, Thomas wore his clothes from the previous day. Stefania changed into one of her Cousin Gabriella's outfits. Mateus, Fernanda and Maricel dressed impeccably as the day before.

Mateus walked up to a rather large crucifix on the wall above a small mahogany credenza, took it off the wall, slid it open, produced a key, and unlocked the credenza.  From there he produced a box of cigars and handed one to Thomas.

"Cubans?" Thomas asked.

"The best," replied Mateus, as he lit his cigar with an ornate lighter which he then passed to Thomas.

He then poured two glasses of cognac, handed one to Thomas and headed out to the poolside patio.

"Come with me," he said to Thomas.

Thomas followed, while the ladies stayed inside.

"So how serious are things between you and Thomas?" Fernanda asked Stefania, starting what appeared to be an interrogation.

"We really have only known each other for maybe ten days, but it seems like I've known him my entire life. I think I'm in love with him. His family is prominent in England. He's wealthy. His life is truly incredible. It's been like living a fairy tale flying about the world on his private jet, expensive hotels."

"We checked him out. He's low key, but all over the internet," Fernanda responded matter-of-factly, glass of red wine in hand, "but what does he think about you?"

"Well, he hasn't said how he feels yet. He saved my life in Rome. That has to count for something."

"Have you slept together?" Maricel rather bluntly inquired.

"No, he's been a perfect gentleman, unfortunately," she responded.

"Either that or he's intimidated by you Stefania," Maricel said. "You're gorgeous. Even the most successful men can be put off by a beautiful woman. Sometimes you have to take the initiative."

"I can't imagine that being the case, but there *is* one problem," she cautioned.

"What could that possibly be?" Maricel responded.

"Well, he's from a deeply religious Catholic family. Both he and his grandmother asked if I was properly initiated in the faith, and I lied. I told them I did. Not only that, I told them I was baptized at a church in Rome.

I'm not sure how I'm going to undo these lies. At the time I didn't care; I was in search of my story. Now it matters a great deal. If I tell him the truth he may despise me. His grandmother, the duchess, will surely hate me."

"Darling," Fernanda, trying to console her daughter, softly said, "I'm sorry we never went through the process with you, but you know, your father and I divorced, and you were shuttled from place to place. Neither of us was particularly religious."

"My boss in Rome is looking at getting me through the initiation process in an expedited fashion through his connections with the Vatican. But even so, I think eventually my lies will be exposed. What will I do? I've managed to sidestep getting communion when we go to mass, but eventually I think it will come out, especially if things move to the next step."

"You mustn't give up hope," Fernanda continued. "If this man is worth it to you, we'll assist. Your uncle has connections from his charitable work for the church. I also think one of his cosmetic clients was the niece of a cardinal, and he hardly charged her a *centavos*."

"Do you think Mateus can ask the cardinal for a favor?" Fernanda asked, her eyes cutting to Maricel.

"Oh, I think the cardinal will accept Mateus' phone call. I'll speak with him tonight," Maricel replied.

Stefania hugged and kissed her aunt.

"Thank you, Aunt Maricel, but Thomas must not be aware."

"Of course not, darling."

"In the meantime, my daughter, if you haven't done so already, you must start dressing such that Thomas notices you, if you understand me," Fernanda added.

With that, all three women started laughing.

#

Meanwhile, on the terrace with the lights of Rio glowing in the distance, Mateus and Thomas strolled around the pool.

"Mateus, I must say I feel well underdressed and hopefully I haven't offended you."

"No, no. No offense taken Thomas, the women always like to look their best, especially with Fernanda being a designer. And I'm particular to linen suits," he responded in accented English.

"I must thank you for your incredible hospitality. If this is typical of a Brazilian welcome, I'm short on words."

"So, Thomas, you've been jetting all over the world with my niece. What have you in mind for her?" asked Mateus.

Thomas, startled by Mateus' direct approach, paused before responding. He leaned against the railing overlooking the lights of the city glowing in the night sky with the sea beyond and cleared his throat.

"Mateus, if I may speak freely?"

"Please do."

"You must see, after spending these last ten days or so constantly with Stefania, I've developed an extreme affection, a love for her that's undeniable. I love her with all of my heart. But you must realize, as a man of wealth and position, there are many women out there who are less than pure of heart. Most women I've dated were interested in my wealth, my resources. They were interested in the sixteenth Duke of Radcliffe, not Thomas Houghton. I've been cautious. My grandmother even more so. She wants the best for me. I'm all she has."

"Caution sometimes can be misread by a woman as timidity or disinterest," Mateus noted. "This is particularly so when the man holds the upper hand. You should be direct with her."

"We're devout Catholics," Thomas continued, "and our faith is important not only on a personal spiritual level, but it elevates itself above that due to my position in my country, my service to my sovereign, and my service to my church. I must be careful in choosing a partner. It's helpful that she's Catholic. It seems as if Stefania and I were meant for each other, but I must be sure it's not a passing fancy, and that she, like I, feels a deep connection and chemistry. She's truly the most intelligent, interesting, and charming woman I've ever met. I hope I'm not being impertinent. Do you understand?"

Mateus took a sip of cognac and a puff of his Cuban cigar.

"I understand more than you know," admitted Mateus, gesturing with his cigar. "Maricel and I have been wed for thirty-one years. They haven't all been easy, but what makes it work is that we have a connection. She's best friends with my sister Fernanda. These types of connections, chemistry as you say, make a great deal of difference. We were meant for each other. Oh, we've had tough times, but she was there for me and I was there for her. You must be sure. Stefania is a terrific woman. I can tell you she's pure of heart, she's not superficial. Be advised that I love her as if she were my own daughter. Please don't hurt her."

"I can tell you as we stand here, Mateus, I couldn't think of hurting her. She means so much to me."

Thomas shot down the rest of his cognac.

The men, finished with their cigars and conversation, admired the lights of Rio from the patio and the crescent moon reflecting off the ocean in the distance.

Thomas leaned over the rail and took stock of the street below in front of Mateus' home.

"The street's deserted. The cars are all gone," he said.

Sauntering back to the house from the pool patio went the men, cigars in hand, through the room-wide sliding glass doors.

Mateus and Maricel persuaded the couple, as well as Fernanda, to stay yet another night in Leblon.

# Chapter 13
*Aparecida, Brazil, June 7*

After breakfast with Stefania's mother, aunt, and uncle, Thomas attempted to phone Bishop Gonzalvo in advance to see if he had returned. He didn't answer. Stefania agreed they would again make the four hour drive to Aparecida to see if the bishop had returned. Thomas, having rested two whole days, intended to finally complete the task at hand.

Upon arriving at the priest's retirement home in Aparecida, the couple proceeded to the bishop's apartment. Knocking on the door, they were approached by the same housekeeper as before, who happened to be in the courtyard.

"You've missed him unfortunately. He died last night. I found him this morning in his bed, stiff as a board."

"What?" Thomas, now shocked, excitedly asked, "What happened?"

"What happened?" the housekeeper, repeating Thomas' question, responded incredulously and shrugged. "He was an old man. He died in his sleep in his bed. We should all be so lucky! His funeral mass is at 1000 tomorrow at the *Igreja de São Benedito*."

"Damned peculiar," said Thomas while rubbing his chin. "Can we see his room?" Thomas asked the housekeeper.

"Sure. He didn't have much; he was a Jesuit. It's unlocked, but I'll be back. I have other rooms to clean. His nephew is coming tomorrow from Florianopolis to collect his things."

"Why was his door unlocked?" Stefania, also curious, inquired.

"Hah," the old housekeeper replied with a huff. "The men who live here are all old priests. They don't steal. Most don't have much. They lock their doors when they're away, but when they're at home, not really. Many visit each other regularly. They walk in."

The housekeeper gestured toward the door with her chin.

Entering the small apartment, Thomas flipped on the light switch. The room had white plaster walls with wood ceiling beams, with two windows, one next to the door facing the courtyard and one out the back of the room facing the street, both framed by old white curtains.

An iron frame bed sat to the right with a nightstand next to it underneath the window and a wooden chest of drawers pushed against the wall opposite. Next to the window facing the courtyard stood a small eating table with two chairs in a cozy kitchenette.

The top of the chest of drawers sat some framed photos of the bishop with friends, family, and one photo with the pope, a small erect crucifix, and above the chest hung a lithograph copy of Leonardo di ser Piero Da Vinci's *The Last Supper.* The mattress, stripped bare, had no sheets nor bed covers. On the nightstand a print of the virgin and child sat propped on a little wooden stand. A large crucifix had been affixed to the wall above the bed next to the window.

Thomas opened the nightstand drawer and peered inside.

"There's only a bible, a prayer book, and a set of rosaries," Thomas commented. "This bishop lived a simple life, that's for sure. If Gonzalvo kept things of importance, where might a Jesuit hide something?" he asked Stefania as he gazed around the sparse room. "Where might that be?"

Thomas watched Stefania staring up quizzically at the large crucifix on the wall.

"That crucifix is rather large. Isn't it similar to the one that I saw at your uncle's house?" he queried.

"Yes, it looks to be the same type. Those are somewhat common in Brazil. The top slides off and there are holes in the cross so it becomes a candle holder if you lay it flat on a table. After you slide the top off, there's a compartment inside for the candles. My uncle took the candles out and hides the key to his humidor in there to keep the hired help from pilfering his Cubans."

"A perfect hiding place for things you don't want to be found," Stefania softly murmured just loud enough for Thomas to hear.

She took the crucifix off the wall, slid the top off.

"See?" she said.

Looking in the plenum, Thomas and Stefania observed some old papers, including a folded blue envelope crammed in the crevice, probably ten inches long by an inch wide and an inch or so deep.

"Hmm, what's in here?" Stefania queried.

Removing the papers, she began unfolding them, taking the paper out of the blue envelope. Thomas, now curious, stood next to her to observe the find. Before he could see the documents, Stefania stuffed the papers into her shoulder bag, put the crucifix back together, and hung it back on the wall.

"Let's go, quickly," she ordered.

Thomas followed her out the door. Stefania jumped back at the unexpected appearance of the housekeeper.

"The viewing is at 1400 today. I can give you directions," the housekeeper noted.

"No thank you," Thomas replied and asked, "Why was the bed stripped?"

"Well, you know when someone dies, they relieve themselves. The sheets were soiled."

"Was there any blood?" Thomas inquired. "Did they do an autopsy?"

"No, I found him, didn't see any. Autopsy, hah. You're crazy. He died of old age!"

"Ma'am, other than us, was there anyone who came asking for the bishop lately?"

The housekeeper paused for a moment.

"Well, now that I think of it, the day before you first arrived two gentlemen were asking for the bishop, but I told them what I told you; he was away and I didn't know where he went."

"One more question. Any chance there are any security cameras?" Thomas asked.

"You must be joking," replied the housekeeper with a chuckle.

Thomas and Stefania then quickly turned and walked toward the courtyard gate.

Stefania looked back at the housekeeper.

"Thank you very much for your assistance. Please convey our condolences to the family," she said.

"Who should I say was calling?" the housekeeper yelled back at Thomas and Stefania, now almost out of the courtyard.

Thomas and Stefania didn't respond. The two walked briskly to their car. Stefania jumped into the driver's seat, started the engine, and pressed the gas pedal. The car accelerated with a screech of the tires.

"I'm curious, Thomas. Why all the questions?" she asked.

"Stefania, what are the documents you took?" Thomas responded.

"Let me find a place to pull over and we can look at them together. I think at the least the first page is pertinent."

Driving several miles toward Rio, Stefania pulled over on a quiet side street in the town of Guaratingueta. Sitting in the car, she pulled the folded papers out of her bag and unfolded them. Thomas could see that the first page had the seal of the Holy See on the top, appearing to be a handwritten note in Latin, which Stefania read aloud to Thomas,

"'On this twenty-sixth day of September in the year of our Lord one-thousand nine-hundred and seventy-eight, I, Supreme Pontiff, do hereby bestow the title of Cardinal Priest of the Holy Roman Church to Bishop Affonso Gonzalvo of the Society of Jesus, whom I hold close to my heart.' Signed 'Supreme Pontiff.' So Gonzalvo was the secret cardinal whom LaCroix spoke of. Why was he made a secret cardinal?"

Thomas examined the document.

"Hmm, the 26th was two days before the pope died. This can't be a coincidence. What are the other documents?"

Stefania removed the papers from the blue envelope.

"These seem to be much older; they're in English," she observed.

Thomas looked over from the passenger seat as Stefania digested the document, but he couldn't see it in its entirety. After Stefania finished reading the first page, she quickly flipped to the second, attached to the first page by a rusty staple.

"He killed himself," she whispered, then repeated the phrase louder as she laid the papers on her lap. "He killed himself. He committed suicide! Now it all makes sense. He read the Fatima prophecy about the antipope. After reading this, he didn't think he was pope."

"Well, what *is* it then?" Thomas, incredibly curious, demanded.

Handing the document to Thomas, Stefania stared out the windshield of the car at the street beyond stupefied, as if in shock.

"He killed himself because he didn't think he was the pope," she muttered, speaking softly. "In fact, if this is correct, he wasn't the true pope."

Quickly reviewing the first page, Thomas then flipped the page of the old document.

"MI6? My God, assuming this is genuine, yes." Thomas considered what he had read. "This is so extraordinary, almost unbelievable."

"He made Gonzalvo a secret cardinal because he probably questioned his authority to create a cardinal," Stefania pondered aloud in a solemn tone. "He questioned his authority as pope. He didn't want to rip the church apart. Rather than cause a schism, he committed suicide by overdose. He entrusted Gonzalvo with the information. Why didn't

Gonzalvo destroy these documents, though? The pope's meeting with Siri must have had some significance."

"The Jesuits swear a special vow to obey the pope," Thomas speculated. "So Gonzalvo obeyed who he thought was pope, or maybe the pope he had sworn allegiance to. According to this document, which appears to date from 1958, Cardinal Siri was elected pope in the 1958 Conclave and took the papal name Gregory XVII. If that's the case and he never resigned nor renounced the papacy, then the pope wasn't a true pope, nor was any pope elected after 1958. Even then, if they were elected by cardinals appointed by an antipope, their elections wouldn't be canonically valid. Why was MI6 spying on the conclave of 1958? And how did it get this information?"

Stefania held up the blue envelope.

"This must be the envelope LaCroix was referring to."

Pausing for a moment, Thomas then gasped, slapping his forehead with his right hand.

"My God, I'm recalling it now, the so-called 'Siri Thesis,'" he added.

Stefania narrowed her eyes.

"And what the *hell* is the 'Siri Thesis?'" she asked.

"Well, certain sedevacantist groups believed that Siri was elected pope in 1958. I always thought it was an old wives' tale. In sedevacantist circles it was known as the 'Siri Thesis.' I can't believe I completely forgot about it. I don't remember the specifics, but most of the faithful placed no credence in it. There are alleged factual accounts, but we all assumed they were rubbish."

"Fascinating! There's often some truth behind most rumours," Stefania noted.

"Based on what happened, it's reasonable to assume that the pope believed that the information was true, that Siri was elected pope and didn't renounce the papacy. What transpired when the pope met Siri? We must get back to Rome at once and address this with Rodolfo. See what he can make of it. I don't think we should do it by phone."

"Yes," Stefania agreed, then paused. "No." She paused again. "I mean, I'm sorry we have to stay one more day, or at least through tomorrow morning. I have some important matters to attend to with my aunt and uncle in the morning. We can pack our things and you can stay at my uncle's and handle any business you may have, or you can go riding with my Cousin Maria. She has horses."

"Is it that important?"

"Yes, it is. They wish to spend some private time with me, and I promised them that I would. We had better keep this safe."

Folding the documents, Stefania placed them in a side pocket in her shoulder bag.

Thomas accepted Stefania's explanation without question.

"Well, we'd better get on then," he said.

Starting the car again, Stefania pulled out of the side street toward the main highway toward Rio. After a few miles, the nature of the documents having set in, Thomas leveled with Stefania.

"Stefania, darling, there's something I need to tell you."

"You like me for my sparkling personality?" Stefania light-heartedly responded.

"Well, yes, naturally, among other things, but I fear for our safety. Listen, I had Zerkorian investigated. It appears he was a Bulgarian agent or spy or some such thing. And he was killed the other day in Baku under suspicious circumstances. That, combined with the attack on the Sheikh, the attack on you in Rome, and the death of Bishop Gonzalvo makes me think there's much more to this, and someone wanted to silence these people. I don't want you to be in danger."

"It was nice of you to have Zerkorian investigated for my story. We would have wanted to interview him next. If this is the document Zerkorian gave the pope, I can't imagine the possibilities. However, the document is in English and seems to have come from MI6. We have to sort all this out."

"I suppose. What's your explanation?" Thomas asked.

"The woman who attacked me was obviously staring at my necklace. The attack on the Sheikh was because he'd been targeted for years, and Gonzalvo was old. The housekeeper herself said he died of old age, probably a heart attack, maybe a stroke. If this Zerkorian was a spy or something, he could have been killed for other reasons. Don't you think you're being paranoid?"

"Well, your response isn't what I was expecting, but that's one endearing quality about you, darling; you're somewhat unpredictable. But even paranoids are right once in a while."

Stefania smiled.

"Is my unpredictability something you *love* about me, hmm?" she asked.

Thomas, thinking for a second, gazed at Stefania.

"Yes, yes it is, and by the way, don't you think it's 'our' project by now?"

Turning to Thomas, Stefania blew him a kiss.

"Yes, I suppose it is."

Thomas placed his left hand on her right knee as she drove.

"Also, given what we've discovered," Stefania said, "I'm starting to think LaCroix has more information than he's telling us. As a sedevacantist, he may be holding something back. Maybe we should try to reach out for him again now that we have more information."

"Yes," Thomas agreed, "when we get back."

The late evening sun edged down toward the western horizon. The tangerine sky presaged a quiet night. The warm wind blew wildly through the open car windows blasting Stefania's long black mane about. The sun from the west created a beautiful silhouette of her profile. Thomas gazed at Stefania admiringly before pushing his car seat back, falling asleep, hand on her knee.

*Rio de Janeiro, Brazil, June 8*

Entering the *Igreja de Nossa Senhora do Monte do Carmo da antiga Sé*, Stefania stood and took in the ornate sculpted and gilded woodwork inside the cathedral which gave it a Rococo appearance. A long central aisle led to the brightly lit high altar. The scent of burning candles and faint sense of incense from ceremonies past seemed to permeate the air inside. Although warm and balmy outside, the cool air inside sent goose bumps running up and down Stefania's naked arms. She had never visited this cathedral before but imagined she could as easily have been in Portugal.

An elderly short pithy man clothed in gold hewn chasuble wearing a red skull cap appeared from a side door behind the altar.

Mateus walked up to him.

"Good morning, your eminence. I can't say how much I, and my niece as well, thank you for this incredible favor."

"Mateus, it's the least I can do for you, given all you've done for my family and for the church. If your niece wants to become part of the church that badly, I can't refuse your request."

"May I present my niece and future goddaughter, Stefania, my sister and her mother Fernanda, and my wife Maricel, whom you know, who will be Stefania's godmother. Ladies, I present to you my old friend

Henriques Cardinal Metz, the current Archbishop of Minas Gerais, but maybe pope someday, eh?"

Mateus shared a laugh with the cardinal.

"Your eminence," all three women said, greeting the cardinal more or less in unison.

Stefania understood Mateus arranged to have her initiated into the church that morning, and by the Archbishop of Minas Gerais no less.

#

After arranging the flight back to Rome, Thomas stood on the patio admiring the shimmering ocean under the midday sun from the pool patio. He scrolled through the contacts on his phone, and called Harry.

"Harry, were you able to locate the Sheikh or find out anything about the woman who attacked Stefania in Rome?"

"I have little to report, mate. The Sheikh has literally disappeared, and the attack in the loo at the music hall; well, my sources tell me the *Polizia di Stato* in Rome found a bullet hole in the trash can, a bullet, a forty caliber round, lodged in the wall behind it, and a pair of size eight black patent leather pumps on the floor."

"That's certainly consistent with what I saw," commented Thomas.

"No gun was found," continued Harry. "But there is a CCTV video of a brunette, likely Stefania, entering the bathroom, followed by a blonde bird, then approximately five minutes later a bloke in an evening jacket, that'd be you, mate, with the brunette bird leaving the loo, both looking down, and exiting the hall. Less than five minutes later a somewhat disheveled and roughed up blonde bird departed the loo and the venue with a small purse in hand. They have a more distinct shot of the blonde bird because she looked right at the CCTV camera as she left. Of course, there's no video from inside the loo."

"Is there any way they can identify me or Stefania?" Thomas asked.

"I don't believe so," Harry responded. "The CCTV video is too distant apparently to provide decent identification of all involved, except maybe the blonde bird. The police weren't alerted for some time because the venue staff discovered the bullet hole when cleaning the loo after the concert had concluded. There were no fingerprints in the loo because it had been cleaned thoroughly. The woman's shoes were originally thought to have been left by accident."

155

"How about the pistol? How did she get it into the venue?" Thomas asked Harry.

"The *Polizia* doesn't believe the bird brought the gun to the venue at the time of the event; it would have been discovered during the routine bag search. They believe it was stowed at the venue and retrieved later. The police are questioning the cleaning staff at the hall and anyone else involved but apparently have come up empty, at least at this point. You should consider yourself lucky, old chap."

"Right. Can you check out this Bishop Alfonso Gonzalvo from Aparecida Brazil? We came here to see the bishop and, when we finally got to his apartment, he had died, ostensibly of natural causes. Very odd indeed."

"I'll check Gonzalvo for you, but I'm still concerned for your safety. With all that's happened, his death sounds awfully coincidental. I would once again suggest you hire bodyguards. I can arrange it."

"Let me think about the bodyguards and I'll be back to you. Let me know what you find out about Gonzalvo. For now we're staying at Stefania's uncle's place, and he has security."

"How are you holding up otherwise?" asked Harry.

"It's nice enough here, but I do miss granny, Connie, and the safety of Haverford."

"Right. Stay safe, mate."

Thomas, sweating slightly, thought about Harry's admonition.

*What if we are really in danger? But who could possibly know of what we found other than perhaps LaCroix? Clearly Rodolfo and his wife are beyond suspicion, or were they? And who would result to murder?*

Returning to the house shortly after 2 o'clock, Stefania, Maricel, and Mateus appeared with some shopping bags full of clothes. The group had also eaten lunch. Thomas assumed Stefania's aunt and uncle took her shopping and one last intimate luncheon before she left.

The jet would be ready to leave again for Rome around 4 o'clock, so saying their goodbyes to Mateus and Maricel, they then left for the airport for the long flight back. Expecting to arrive the next morning, Thomas intended to rest on the flight.

#

Before the jet took off, Stefania texted Rodolfo,

A MAJOR FIND IN BRAZIL, COMING BACK TONIGHT, WILL
MEET YOU AT 0900 TOMORROW TO DISCUSS
    She received a text back from Rodolfo,
GREAT SEE YOU AT 9 AT JOURNAL

# Chapter 14
*Rome, Italy, June 8*

Stefania and Thomas slept most of the night on the flight back to Rome, arriving on a warm and sunny Saturday morning. Thomas' car dropped them off at his hotel. After changing clothes, freshening up, and eating lunch at the hotel, they took a short walk to the *Journal's* offices on the *Via Veneto*. A warm breezy day, Stefania wore her hair back in a ponytail.

"See the young slim blonde female tourist? She's been tailing us down the *Via Veneto* from the hotel," Thomas whispered to Stefania.

"Are you sure?" asked Stefania, also now taking note of the woman.

"Is that the woman who attacked you at the concert?"

"I don't think so, but she's too far distant."

Arriving at the *Journal's* offices, Stefania took a quick look at the blonde woman.

"She's a tourist," Stefania asserted. "Look, she's just sitting at the café flipping through her tourist guidebook."

"A bit odd that she chose that coffee house across the street from the *Journal's* offices to plop down for an espresso when we've gone by maybe half a dozen," countered Thomas.

Stefania rolled her eyes.

Stefania, with Thomas in tow, arrived at the *Journal's* empty offices where Rodolfo and Sofia were waiting. Upon entering Rodolfo's offices, Thomas closed the windows and shutters. Rodolfo, looking confused, didn't object.

"Well?" Rodolfo, his hands in the air, with some inflection in his voice, inquired.

"We went to Aparecida to visit the bishop who was on holiday," explained Stefania, "and the housekeeper didn't know when he would return. We then spent a couple of days with my family in Rio, and when they went back to visit the bishop, he had apparently died of natural causes. Thomas had Zerkorian investigated, and Zerkorian was recently killed in Baku under suspicious circumstances. That, coupled with the attack on the Sheikh and the death of the bishop, leads Thomas to believe that all these occurrences are not coincidental."

"I'm sorry, but I'm skeptical that these events are all connected in some way," responded Rodolfo, "but I'm still curious as to what you two turned up in Brazil."

"I tend to agree," said Stefania. "Regrettable coincidences, nothing more."

Deciding against summarizing what they discovered, Stefania took the documents out of her bag and handed them to Rodolfo.

"We found these hidden in the bishop's room. You should read them."

Putting on his reading glasses, Rodolfo began examining the documents, with Sofia reading over his shoulder. After having completed the third page, his hands went limp, nearly dropping the papers onto the wood parquet floor.

"Ah Madonna! If this is true...but how could it be? How could it be kept secret all of these years?" he uttered softly.

He took his eyeglasses off, hands on his head.

Thomas interjected.

"Yes, if this is true, if these are genuine, it could completely rip apart the fabric of the church. It means there hasn't been a legitimate pope since Cardinal Siri died in 1989 and all the named popes after 1958 were antipopes."

"Whether what is contained in the MI6 communiqué is true or not is not at issue," Stefania postulated. "The MI6 communiqué, if read by the pope, combined with the remaining portion of the Fatima prophecy that there would be a false pope, led him to believe that he wasn't the true pope. Even the prophecy of Saint Malachy doesn't allude to this pope. The pope met with Cardinal Siri during this timeframe. If Siri confirmed that he was, in fact, elected and hadn't renounced the papacy, perhaps to save the church the pope committed suicide. That's how I see it."

"But," questioned Rodolfo, "how do you know these documents are genuine?"

"So," answered Stefania, "clearly the MI6 document is dated 1958 and frankly appears to be of that age. The letter of the pope creating Gonzalvo as a cardinal *in pectore* is dated 1978 and can easily be authenticated by checking the handwriting against the pope's. The pope trusted Gonzalvo because of his oath given as a Jesuit, and he was no ordinary Jesuit; he was the provincial superior of Brazil. Nevertheless, as far as we can tell, other than the Sheikh, the only remaining link to all of this is Monsignor LaCroix. Thomas and I don't think he was being entirely truthful, and we want to speak with him again."

"Interestingly enough," Rodolfo, still somewhat solemn, mumbled back in slurred Italian, "I have a brief note the Holy Father wrote to me in September, 1978 commenting on an article which I authored in the *Journal* at that time."

Wandering over to his bookcase, he pulled out his personal bible and unfolded a single sheet of fine woven paper and compared it to the letter from Bishop Gonzalvo's apartment.

"Identical. The letterhead and seal is identical, the paper is identical, and the ink, writing, and signature are identical. May God have mercy on him," Rodolfo said while looking up and somewhat dramatically making the sign of the cross.

"May I see the letter?" Thomas asked.

Rodolfo gently handed it to him, his hand shaking with tremors.

"May I keep this for the time being?"

"You may," Rodolfo quietly consented.

Picking up all of the documents, Stefania folded them and placed them into her shoulder bag.

"We should like to meet again with LaCroix. We also think that the Sheikh knows more, but I can't imagine we'll be hearing from him again soon. Have you heard from him?" she asked.

"No, silence, like he fell off the planet," Rodolfo, clearly distraught, responded in barely audible Abruzzese dialectical Italian. "I shouldn't have you go any further. We should stop now. But if this LaCroix perhaps has information that this is false, that the information in the papers is incorrect, that would resolve a great many things. Even if the pope took his own life, if the content of the papers is incorrect, or the papers themselves are forgeries."

"If the documents are genuine," Thomas added, "the Roman Catholic Church not only is without a true pope, a legitimate pope couldn't be elected because all of the cardinal electors from 1958 are now deceased. Unless, of course, Siri had created cardinals. But who would know whether that occurred? Even so, how many could still be alive or of voting age more than twenty years after his death? And we all thought the sedevacantists were crackpots."

"How will you find LaCroix?" Rodolfo asked while looking at Stefania and Thomas.

"LaCroix has a social media account which he updates remotely and routinely. He apparently is active in sedevacantist circles," Thomas answered. "According to his recent posts he's in Birmingham on a pilgrimage for Saint John Henry Newman, where he's visiting Saint Chad's cathedral and the Birmingham Oratory. Says he'll be out of touch till after vespers tomorrow. We'll fly there today and hopefully catch up with him at the pilgrimage mass at the cathedral tomorrow morning. I'm familiar with both."

"I see," said Rodolfo quietly. "Too bad the Sheikh was not of assistance. I have to imagine he knew what really happened."

"Indeed," added Thomas. "The one thing that I still can't figure out is the Sheikh's riddle. He said something about 'when you find about the one who wasn't who he thought he was,' or some such thing, 'then the answer will be in the palm of your hand.' Assuming that we've now found out that the pope wasn't the true pope, what does the rest of the riddle mean? Perhaps our meeting with LaCroix will shed some light. What's also interesting is that we think the Camerlengo's assistant Zerkorian gave the papers to the pope, but I later found out that Zerkorian was possibly a Bulgarian agent. What would he be doing with MI6 documents?"

"Hmm," Rodolfo solemnly responded, his hand to his forehead.

Sofia rubbed the back of Rodolfo's neck.

"Rodolfo and I will go to holy mass and say a prayer for you both. Hopefully you return with good news," Sofia said.

#

Stefania left the *Journal's* offices walking hand in hand with Thomas back to their hotel.

"Once we get back to the hotel, we'll prepare to leave for Fiumicino in the morning for Birmingham. I'll notify the pilots by text," said Thomas.

"Yes, hopefully we can track down LaCroix," responded Stefania.

Stefania, forgetting briefly the storm of intrigue she had found herself in, stopped underneath the shade of a London Plane Tree in front of *Santa Maria della Concezione dei Cappuccini*, the church where she allegedly received the sacraments.

*I must come clean with Thomas. Tell him the truth about everything.*

"So this is where young Stefania received her confirmation," Thomas teased Stefania.

Stefania countered, "About that—"

Before she could complete the sentence Thomas kissed her passionately. Stefania held his cheeks with her hands. Thomas' hands placed gently on her hips. The sensation of the moment engrossed Stefania. Now in her own private little world, like so many star-crossed lovers in the Eternal City, Stefania avoided making her confession.

# Chapter 15
*Smolensk, Russia, June 8*

Svetlana received a coded text from Stasevich stating F 1100. This meant that Stasevich wanted to meet with Greschenko and Lenov at an unused civilian airstrip south of Smolensk, Russia, known locally as Smolensk South Airport.

Stasevich apparently arrived early and attended the daily liturgy at the Cathedral of the Assumption in Smolensk. Windy and chilly on the deserted tarmac, Greschenko struggled to keep her head scarf on. Lenov, dressed in a traditional *papakha* wool hat and a black leather coat, gave him the look of a Russian Gestapo. They would have to wait for Stasevich.

"Good day Svetlana Sergeyevna," said Lenov.

"Good day Lenov," she replied.

Lenov took a manila envelope out of his jacket and handed it to Greschenko. He turned his back as she opened the flap.

*Photographs.*

A brief glance and she knew.

"She was going to use these to blackmail you," said Lenov looking at the cathedral in the distance.

"What makes you say that?" asked Greschenko.

Lenov turned with a raised brow and a cock of the head.

"I understand that your sexual preferences are your own business Svetlana Sergeyevna but they could come at a price for you and others. If these got into the wrong hands, well, I think you know what would happen to both her and to you. You should be more circumspect with your partners, especially given the president's view of such relations. Hopefully there are not others, are there?"

"Thank you Lenov," Greschenko replied solemnly, knowing that she could not truthfully answer Lenov's question.

"This particular problem has been taken care of. Let's just say we're *now* even."

A black sedan pulled up onto the tarmac and pulled to a stop. A driver in a dark suit got out and opened the rear driver's side door. Stasevich got out in uniform, wearing his *ushanka* fur cap and overcoat. The three stood on the tarmac about one-hundred meters from the neatly parked jets. Stasevich's security detail created a perimeter in case anyone came snooping.

"Well, as you know, we've terminated the Armenian," said Stasevich. "We owe the Azerbaijanis for that one. They lost two secret police in the effort, and the old priest in Brazil was also dispatched. It was made to look like a heart attack or seizure using an overdose injection of propofol. It's virtually untraceable. As far as I know it was assumed to be a natural death. The cause hasn't been questioned."

"For all of our sakes, it had best not be questioned," quipped Greschenko. "What about the Britisher and his girlfriend?"

"Those two came looking for the Brazilian, but he wasn't there, and by the time they returned, he was dead. They didn't speak to him before he died," Stasevich continued.

"Good, and the Egyptian?" queried Greschenko.

"We haven't been able to locate the Sheikh, but we're looking," answered Stasevich. "He's likely still in Italy, or he may have sneaked across to France, in which case he'll be more difficult to find given the large Arab population there. We're making all efforts to find him. It's but two weeks to July first. Are we authorized yet to sanction the Britisher and his female friend?"

"His Excellency directed only if we become aware that they have detrimental information regarding Archangel," Greschenko responded.

"I take it therefore that we have authorization to act in such a circumstance," responded Stasevich.

"I'm in charge of this operation and as far as I'm concerned they're off limits for obvious reasons!" snapped Greschenko.

"That's your opinion," muttered Stasevich.

"What's the status of the Britisher?" asked Greschenko.

"The status of the Britisher?" Lenov asked, seemingly confused. "There were three sanctions; the Egyptian, the Brazilian, and the Armenian. Once the Brazilian and Armenian were liquidated, we stopped following the Britisher in Brazil; no need to expend resources watching him cavort with her relations. We picked him up again when he returned to Rome to see if he leads us to the Egyptian."

"Directorate S was to continue the surveillance at all times," Greschenko curtly shot back.

"We will, as we always do," Lenov replied sternly.

"Well, keep an eye on them. The three sanctions were the persons identified by the Bulgarians in 1978 known to have detrimental knowledge. Our Bulgarian friends sometimes were sloppy, as we all know. There may well be others who have knowledge of aspects of the Archangel plan of whom we're not aware. If the Britisher has any knowledge, he may lead us to them or to the Egyptian."

"Yes, yes, of course, of course, naturally," Lenov responded with a huff.

"I apologize for being tedious, if not somewhat condescending, but the stakes here are high," Greschenko reminded the group.

"Yes, Svetlana Sergeyevna," replied Lenov in a demeaning tone, his eyes moving up from Greschenko's feet to her head. "We're all keenly aware that your thoroughness and attention to detail is what I'm told elevated you to such a lofty position so quickly."

"Good day, gentlemen," said Greschenko.

*Rublyovka, Russia, June 9*

Not at SVR headquarters this Sunday, Greschenko had planned lunch with a female friend, anticipating an afternoon dalliance back at her apartment. Almost out the door, dressed in her sexiest black mini-dress, see-through lace stockings, and revealing silk black top, her cell phone rang.

"Yes, Lenov, any news regarding our special project?"

"Good morning to you too," Lenov replied sarcastically. "Our friends met with their friends in Rome and are leaving. Seems like our friend is going back home. Do you really think it's necessary to continue the surveillance?"

"Yes, I do. We must be absolutely certain," replied Greschenko, perturbed Lenov would question the project based on appearances. "Appearances can be extremely deceiving. The most innocent act could be a front for something much more relevant or sinister. There could be someone out there who might have knowledge which would disclose something. Surveillance has to continue, unless and until we know for sure nothing else exists. As for our Arab friend, he might turn up sooner or later. If he breaks deep cover, we'll find him, and quickly silence him and anyone he came in contact with."

"Thank you for enlightening me Svetlana Sergeyevna, I didn't know these things," Lenov replied sarcastically.

Greschenko ignored his response.

"Directorate S must stay on top of things," she emphasized. "We'll meet later this week I imagine."

"Yes," replied Lenov as the line went silent.

# Chapter 16
*Birmingham, England, UK, June 9*

Nausea filled Stefania's gut as the Falcon 8X bounced up and down, side to side, before finally landing in Birmingham. Upon landing, Stefania let out a sigh of relief.

"Thank God, that's over," she said.

"Yes, I should have warned you, the landings in Birmingham can be rough sometimes. I've arranged for a car to drive us to Saint Chad's. Should take about thirty minutes, and I can't imagine much traffic," Thomas responded. "I want to phone Harry to see if he's found anything new on Gonzalvo."

After they got into the back seat of the Range Rover, Thomas put the call on the speaker.

"I'm sorry, mate, I've not found much that you probably didn't know. Gonzalvo was appointed the provincial superior in Brazil in 1975. Before that he was a translator at the Vatican. He was in Vatican City with the Brazilian entourage for the August 1978 conclave that elected the pope. He stayed in Vatican City to attend to some Jesuit business. He ended up staying for the funeral of the pope a month after his election. He then returned to Brazil where he continued as provincial superior up to his retirement. He lived a quiet life in a priest's retirement community in Aparecida and apparently died a few days ago."

"Thanks, Harry. Let me ask you, is there a test to determine how old a document is?"

"Sure, by content and style of the paper, and ink, which could be chemically tested, a determination could be made of an approximate age or age range. The test isn't precise, but the technology is of recent vintage. I can arrange it. All I would need is a playing-card size piece of the paper. It's an expensive process. This is an odd question, even for you, Thomas."

"I'll be back in touch, Harry, if I need to follow up on the document test. Thanks."

He turned to Stefania.

"Saint Chad's was the first Catholic church constructed after the reformation in England, substantially completed by 1841, and was raised to the status of a cathedral in 1852," noted Thomas. "Saint Chad's isn't as elaborate and stunning as many of the formerly Catholic cathedrals which became Anglican after the reformation, but its red brick Gothic Revival exterior is nonetheless impressive. Its interior, and particularly the apse and high altar, are quite elaborate, with the altar, the apse, and the ceiling decorated in gold leaf, although many of the original historical fittings were purposely removed or defaced after Vatican Two. It's located near the Birmingham city center and a public park. The relics of Saint Chad, rescued by Catholic sympathizers from destruction during the Reformation, were placed in a reliquary above the high altar."

Not paying particular attention to Thomas' history lesson this time, Stefania fiddled with her watch.

"Don't worry," Thomas assured Stefania, "the pilgrimage mass for Saint John Henry Newman starts at 11 o'clock, then there will be a procession from Saint Chad's to the Birmingham Oratory, a little less than two miles away. We should have plenty of time to find LaCroix, if not at Saint Chad's during the procession, at the Oratory."

Arriving at about 10 o'clock, they immediately began searching for LaCroix in the cathedral. Stefania stood in the center aisle. The panoply of color of the cathedral's stained glass windows caught her eye. To her, the place took on a mystical feel as the choir warmed up for mass. Stefania spotted LaCroix kneeling and meditating in the side chapel dedicated to Saint Edward the Confessor. LaCroix wore clerical garb, but not vestments. Stefania would have been politic, particularly in a church, to a priest, but the time for discretion had come and gone.

"Excuse me, Father. Sorry to interrupt," she whispered. "Might we have a word?"

"One moment," he replied, clearly at the tail end of saying a prayer or a novena and wanted to finish.

After a few minutes LaCroix stood and turned to Stefania.

"Since I'm seeing you again, I assume you found something?"

"Let's go outside and talk," suggested Thomas.

They all quietly left the cathedral toward the large park to the side of the cathedral bordering on Shadwell Street. The park started filling with people gathering for the pilgrimage mass. In the park Stefania noticed a thin man who appeared of North African descent with air buds in his ears concentrating on his phone but occasionally raising his eyes, following the threesome about the park. When Stefania made eye contact with him, he looked down.

"Here's the thing," Thomas began. "You must have some idea what the papers were that the pope was given by the Camerlengo and the other assistant Zerkorian, or more particularly, where they came from?"

"What did you find precisely?" LaCroix probed.

Stefania interrupted to get to the point.

"We'd prefer not to be specific. Let's say we think we found the documents, which you think Zerkorian and the Camerlengo gave to the pope. If that's the case, they were clearly given to the pope to make him doubt the legitimacy of his election as pope, regardless as to whether they were genuine or not. Assuming that was the case, why would Zerkorian want to give the documents to the pope?"

"Who had the documents, Bishop Gonzalvo, Cardinal Siri, or the Sheikh?" LaCroix asked. "They're the only ones who could have had it."

"What difference does it make?" Thomas replied.

"I don't think he would have given them to Cardinal Siri. As to the Sheikh, it was a matter of time before they got to him. Whoever got to the Sheikh would get the documents, you see."

"Why did he not trust Siri?" Stefania interjected.

"It wasn't that he didn't trust Cardinal Siri, but it was only after the pope was given the documents did he insist on seeing Siri, so I thought there was some connection. The pope wanted to see Siri in private, and I recall the Camerlengo stopping Siri before he entered the papal apartments and he said something I thought was odd at the time, such as 'remember the oath of secrecy of the conclave.'"

"That does seem odd," Thomas chimed in. "Both the pope and Siri were at the conclave. Even though they swore an oath, they were both present there, and certainly Siri wouldn't be in a position to refuse to discuss it with the pope."

"Unless they weren't talking about the 1978 conclave," Stefania whispered into Thomas' ear.

"I remember it was the day Zerkorian left the documents with the pope that the pope insisted Siri come down to Rome immediately from Genoa. Siri came by train the next day," LaCroix recalled as all three strolled through the park by a few trees.

She then inquired of LaCroix, "Do you know any of the personal details of Zerkorian?"

"He assisted the Camerlengo before I got there. He was about my age. As I said before, he was Armenian, certainly from his name. Like many of us, he spoke several languages, including French, English, Italian, church Latin, Russian, and Armenian. He never talked about his personal life and never spoke of family or relations. I don't think he had any," responded LaCroix, now looking at his watch. "I must be going. I'm concelebrating at mass here today."

Thomas nodded.

"Well, thank you, Father. We certainly appreciate your time. We might as well go to Sunday mass at Saint Chad's," suggested Thomas.

Stefania, taking a seat in a pew with Thomas, observed, but didn't take particular notice of, the North African gentleman who followed them into the church and sat in the back.

She opened the hymnal and began singing the communal hymn "I am the Bread of Life," along with the choir. After receiving communion, she started crying uncontrollably as the choir sung the refrain for the second stanza.

"Are you alright?" Thomas whispered.

Stefania, wiping her eyes dry with a tissue, nodded, mouthed *yes*.

Sitting there, Stefania, who hadn't cared about spirituality or religion for most of her twenty-seven years, had finally come to the realization she had become spiritual. Something woke up inside her. Maybe the Latin mass at Seil Island; perhaps the mass in Santiago or the prayer before Our Lady of Aparecida, or it could have been her baptism and confirmation, the meeting with the mysterious Sufi Sheikh, but faith was now indelibly part of her. She not only had become spiritual but religious.

Just as Thomas filled an amorous void in her life, a spiritual void had been filled. Perhaps she always had faith, and it took a catalyst to open her heart to it.

The choir's singing of the recessional hymn almost put Stefania over the edge with emotion, tears running down her cheeks.

"What is this song? It's so moving," she asked Thomas.

"'All Creatures of Our God and King,' from *The Canticle of the Sun*, a prayer written by Saint Francis of Assisi in 1225," Thomas whispered in response.

Stefania knew in her heart, however, the religion she had recently embraced could be compromised, and she had in her possession information which could destroy it. This internal conflict infected her like a virus.

"I'm eager to see my grandmother, to sleep in my own bed at Haverford, and to see Connie. Nevertheless, I'm concerned and anxious about seeing granny again. She'll have questions, perhaps about you, also about what we've found," Thomas confessed, as they settled into their leather seats of the Falcon 8X for the short flight to Norwich.

"It would be nice if there was a diversion," he continued, "and I haven't yet decided whether to be truthful to granny about what we've discovered."

Stefania, not responding, seemed deep in thought.

While the jet sat on the tarmac awaiting departure, Thomas instinctively phoned Harry.

"Harry, I'd like you to provide me as much information as you can on a Monsignor Francois LaCroix. I'll text you more details."

"Right, I'll investigate him straight away," Harry confirmed.

"I'm famished," Stefania muttered.

"I'm sorry, darling," Thomas responded. "There's nothing on the plane to eat. I fear it will be a short and turbulent flight in any event. Our ravenous stomachs will have to wait to our arrival at Haverford."

"Aces, I'm eager to get to Haverford then, to satisfy my hunger and get through the bumps in the air," Stefania replied.

Both held hands, sitting back in their seats as the plane took off from Birmingham, with Stefania pointing out an obvious disconcerting fact.

"The only reason I could think of that the Camerlengo would tell Siri not to discuss the conclave is if he were speaking of a conclave which took place before, when the pope wasn't a cardinal. There would be no reason for him to adhere to the secrecy oath at a conclave which the pope attended, from a human nature perspective."

"I agree," Thomas retorted. "So that would mean he was referring to the conclaves of 1963 or 1958. This segues with the narrative that Siri was elected at the 1958 conclave. That would certainly be of concern to all three; the pope, Siri, and the Camerlengo."

"But if the Camerlengo was making the pope aware of Siri's election through the documents provided by Zerkorian, why would he not want Siri to speak about the conclave and confirm the information?" Stefania asked. "If that's the case, it's not logical," she opined.

"True. In fact, it's completely illogical," Thomas agreed. "Wouldn't the Camerlengo want Siri to affirm the truth of the document? By reinforcing to him that he should say nothing, Siri would be neither affirming nor denying the truth of it. How does that help the Camerlengo, unless what was reported didn't occur? If that were the case, why wouldn't Siri deny that he was elected pope? That would be easy enough. Making such a concession, which is the official version of events, couldn't violate the secrecy of the conclave. Unless, of course, Siri was in on it."

"Or something happened at one of the conclaves which the Camerlengo didn't want the pope to know about," Stefania added.

"Then there's the issue of the Sheikh's riddle, which continues to haunt me," Thomas posited. "I think we've come to the first part. We've found that the pope was perhaps someone he wasn't supposed to be, but then the answer should be in the palm of our hand. Extraordinarily vexing."

Stefania cuddled next to Thomas as the plane bounced up and down, shimmied, and shook on its descent to Norwich.

"It most certainly is," she agreed, resting her head against Thomas' shoulder as they held hands. "Thomas, I have a confession to make," she whispered.

"It's a little late for confessions, Stefania, don't you think? You should have addressed that while we were in church," Thomas quipped with a smile, trying to assuage Stefania's obvious anxiety.

"I'm deathly afraid of confined spaces, like airplanes. The archives too, for that matter. I hate flying, I'm sorry to say. I try to put on a brave face, but there it is," she confessed with a whisper, holding Thomas closer and tighter.

"I understand, Stefania. I think it's your fear mostly of not being in control. Don't worry, you'll be safe," Thomas whispered back.

As the jet made its final approach to Norwich, Thomas' mind filled with notions.

*Have I lost a certain sense of proportion? Is my affection for Stefania blinding me? I'll lie to granny about Brazil, Bishop Gonzalvo,* he concluded.

The internal dichotomy between the information he knew and his role as a champion of the church weighed heavily as well.

*What we know could destroy an institution my family spent centuries protecting.*

*All of these things are trivial compared to my insane affection for Stefania, stymied and frustrated as it is.*

As she leaned her head on his shoulder he couldn't help but look down her loosely buttoned blouse at her black lace bra.

*I love Stefania and am physically infatuated with her all at the same time, a toxic love concoction. Like Tosca, she makes me forget God.*

*Is that what's happening? I'm blinded by my love for Stefania? I'm forgetting my obligations to my faith?*

As if on script, Stefania turned and looked at him with her green eyes as the jet, bouncing around in the sky, clouds flashing by, descended. As their eyes met, she placed her hands on his cheeks and their lips collided. Thomas's heart now pounded and nearly skipped a beat. The sensation of her warm hands on his cheeks sent shivers up and down his spine, tingling every hair follicle on his body.

*I want Stefania physically and emotionally, but I have to wait. To get physical now, to get engrossed in the emotional progression of a relationship with her, would be devastating.*

#

Strapped in her seat, Stefania prepared for landing. Thoughts cluttered Stefania's mind.

*This short spiritual journey only started a few weeks ago. Now, I'm madly in love with Thomas in a conjugal way. My self-restraint is nearly exhausted.*

*When we kiss, an over-arching warmth permeates my body from head to foot.*

*It's like all of my worries have been left behind and time stands still. I love him, I truly love him, and I can't stand it.*

*I was initially attracted to him because of his status as a duke, his plane, the superficial things and accoutrements which bedecked the man, but after the trip to Brazil and back, the nature of my affection has changed. I want a physical relationship.*

She now suffered from the confusion brought on by a faith she now embraced, the information she had uncovered, and her relationship with Thomas. For the next few blissful minutes as the plane jumped about and the engines whined and squealed, no harm could come to her.

# Chapter 17
*Moscow, Russia, June 9*

Late in the day, Greschenko received a coded text from Lenov. The gang of three, or the "triptych" as she sometimes referred to them, needed to meet quickly. With little advanced notice, they converged again on the deserted Gorky Park ice rink as the sun's last rays were waning on a rather cool day in Moscow.

"So it seems the Britisher and his girlfriend went back to England. We had them followed. They went to Birmingham where they attended a liturgy and met with a French churchman," reported Lenov.

"You interfered with my Sunday night out for this? Mother of God! So maybe they're planning on getting married? So what?" exclaimed Stasevich, voice raised and hands flailing about.

"Let me finish, please. Our agent had a listening device, and although there was a great deal of ambient noise and quite a few people milling about, it was obvious they were talking about our little problem. Our agent found out the identity of this churchman and we had him researched. He was the Armenian's counterpart at the Vatican in 1978, the other assistant to the Camerlengo. The Camerlengo had two assistants; the Armenian was one and this other French churchman, LaCroix, was the other. The Armenian was one of our men inside the Vatican, but LaCroix may have pertinent knowledge." Lenov cut to Greschenko and raised his voice slightly. "Why wasn't this other churchman identified in the file?" he asked.

Greschenko stared back at him.

After a short period of silence, she shot back.

"How in hell should I know? The Bulgarians were often sloppy, as we all know. I inherited the operation from General Karpov, and it had been a dead file for years up to the point when all the flags started popping up. If this LaCroix was in a similar position to Zerkorian, we must assume he's aware of Archangel. Could your agent tell how much the Britisher knew?"

"No, there was too much ambient noise. However, Zerkorian's name was mentioned, as was a reference to a Sheikh, presumably the Egyptian, and a Cardinal Siri, his relevance to this I don't know. We've researched him, and Siri is long dead. But the reference to both Zerkorian and the Sheikh can't be coincidental."

"Then it's settled, as far as I'm concerned," Stasevich piped in. "We must take care of this churchman, the Britisher, *and* his girlfriend—"

Before he could finish, Greschenko interrupted, inquiring of Lenov, "What's the status of this churchman?"

"He's a French priest, a traveler. Not a bishop, patriarch, or metropolitan. We checked him out. He'll not be missed."

"I'll address the matter with His Excellency on the Britisher," Greschenko insisted. "I don't think we've met the president's requirements for a wet operation."

"That's your view, but we all agree the Frenchy priest can be dispatched?" Stasevich asked.

"The priest," Greschenko directed, "should disappear, *but* find out what he knows first. Maybe he knows what the Britisher and his girlfriend know. Once we find out what this LaCroix knows, I can inform the president, then it can be decided what should be done with this Britisher and his bitch. And make this priest's death look like a natural death or an accident, and for God's sake, don't use a nerve agent or polonium! Just make him disappear. His death shouldn't rouse the suspicions of the UK authorities. Agreed?"

"Yes," Stasevich and Lenov replied in unison, the condensation from their collective breaths clearly visible in the cool dry air.

"As head of GRU I can make an independent determination as to the Britisher," snarked Stasevich. "GRU is doing you two a favor by covering your asses on this operation."

"I'm not going to argue the point with you General," snapped back Greschenko. "Operation Archangel is SVR's baby, and I'm therefore in charge."

The lamps popped on in Gorky Park as the sun hovered above the western horizon. In the fading light and coming chill, Greschenko recalled Vasily, her mentor.

*I must do all things possible to clean up Vasily's legacy, Archangel.*

# Chapter 18
*Near Houghton-St. Giles, England, UK, June 9*

Thomas and Stefania arrived at Haverford Hall late, but the duchess waited for them to change and clean up for dinner. Sitting down to eat, the duchess, wearing her black mourning dress, initially engaged in small talk regarding the rough flights and the mass at Saint Chad's, which Thomas explained to her was the purpose for their visit to Birmingham.

*I'll need to use some chicanery to flush the pheasants from the undergrowth,* she thought.

"So Thomas tells me you confused the Santa Marias?" The duchess took a sip of wine, smiling at Stefania from across the table.

"I'm sorry, what's that?" Stefania, with a blank look, asked in return.

"You said you received confirmation at *Santa Maria della Concezione dei Cappuccini?*"

Stefania now looked confused and seemingly strained to remember what she originally told the duchess.

"Yes, that's right," she answered.

"But Thomas told me you actually received the sacrament at *Santa Maria della Vittoria?*" The duchess replied as she cut her roast lamb, matter-of-factly smiling again at Stefania.

*That perplexed expression on Stefania's face speaks volumes.*

Before Stefania could reply, Thomas glared somewhat directly at Stefania.

"I explained to granny that you were incorrect; you conflated the two Santa Marias. You said *Santa Maria della Concezione dei Cappuccini,* but you meant *Santa Maria della Vittoria.* An honest mistake, you see," he calmly and politely pointed out.

"Oh, yes, I had forgotten about saying that," Stefania, evidently picking up on Thomas' cues, retorted.

"I see," the duchess countered with a smile.

*They're both lying,* she thought.

"We've found little additional information. The interview in Spain with LaCroix wasn't helpful, and although Stefania did go back to the Vatican archives, she uncovered nothing new," Thomas offered.

*When the affection of a woman is involved, lying came easily to men, and my dear Thomas has quite readily lied already.*

After dinner, the duchess warmed herself by a small blaze given the cool and windy June evening, sipping brandy. Having an agenda, the duchess only needed to outlast Stefania so that she might speak with Thomas one-on-one. She might not get another opportunity in person for some time. Thomas and Stefania spoke to each other in hushed tones.

After only fifteen minutes, Stefania announced, "I apologize. I have a headache and am exhausted. I'm going to turn in. All of today's activities and the rough flights have taken their toll."

After the twin doors to the salon closed and Stefania made her way up the stairs, the duchess pounced. Looking Thomas straight in the eyes, the duchess inquired, "Thomas David Andrew Pole-Houghton, do you love her, or more precisely, are you in love with her?"

"Yes, I am. I've met her family in Brazil, and they're nice people," Thomas responded, without skipping a beat. "I—"

"I know you both are lying," she interrupted.

The duchess commenced her polite but stern diatribe, which she rehearsed in her mind for days.

"She never was initiated at either of the two churches, at least not till recently. I don't know how you arranged it, but I'll find out. Such actions say a great deal regarding how far you'll go for this woman, so I don't doubt you love her."

"I do love her, grandmamma—" countered Thomas.

"Please do let me finish," the duchess insisted. "The more impertinent inquiry perhaps is does she love you? And if she does, is it because of your wealth, title, and prestige, or is it because of this?"

The duchess pulled up her black dress sleeve and pinched an inch of skin.

"There exists a laundry list of aristocrats who married to 'good matches' only to divorce years later. Divorce is not an option for you. It isn't an option in this family, particularly if there are children involved. Once the honeymoon is over, once the children come, things won't be easy. It's then that marriages are tested and strained. It requires two people on the same page to manage it, and manage it well—"

"But grandmamma—" Thomas attempted to interrupt.

"Please let me finish," she continued her pontification. "Candidly, and this may surprise you, but if she loves you for what's inside and you're in love with her, as long as she's baptized, confirmed, you marry in the church, and she agrees to bring up the children in the faith, I don't care about the rest. But I suggest you address the matter with her because if she's lied to you, that's relevant. If you don't clear up these loose ends, I *will* do it for you. I think you would rather your grandmother not make things uncomfortable for you. How impolitic would that be?"

Picking up her tablet, she handed it to Thomas.

"See this tabloid?" she asked. "It has a photo of you and Stefania walking out of mass at Saint Chad's. The caption reads 'Bachelor Duke and Brazilian Beauty Go to Church.' The tabloids are obviously following you. Despite my relatively monastic existence here in the north country and in Scotland, I still have many connections here and beyond."

"That's only a tabloid, grandmamma. It's harmless drivel," Thomas insisted.

"It connects you to her, and," she added, now raising her voice, "there's the issue of what you and she are working on. I don't know precisely what you've uncovered, but I know you've found something. If the something you've found is detrimental to our church, our faith, the faith that your father and every duke before him has risked life and limb for, the implications are beyond comprehension."

"As I previously explained, it's the best course that I interject myself in Stefania's project," Thomas explained. "In doing so I have some control, grandmamma. We've gone over this before."

"I'm not convinced," she countered.

"I'm sorry, grandmamma, but this is the best way," Thomas responded.

"Rubbish!" she exclaimed. "Let us not forget that this family has served the sovereign and this country as intermediaries with the Vatican for centuries. Are you prepared to engage in an act which I can only describe as sabotage to the faith and would place the position of your family in peril, for this woman?"

"Grandmamma, you must understand that is not what is happening," Thomas interrupted.

"You must think me severely narcissistic. I'm old; I don't care about myself much any longer. I think of only three things; my love for the faith, my duty to this family and my country, and my love of you. All three will never change. However, you have to be well aware of the results of your actions, Thomas," said the duchess, her finger now pointing at Thomas' chest. "Can you live with those consequences? After all is said and done, do you want to be known as the man who imperiled the church, who impeached the faith of one billion souls? I hope you've examined your conscience in that regard. Even complicity in such an act would be sheer insanity. I love you, Thomas, but I'll not countenance this and will do everything in my ability to ensure that it doesn't come to pass. I'll not go to my maker under such circumstances. You were named after Saints Thomas More and Thomas Becket, two great English gentlemen who refused to surrender their faith to temporal influences and who paid for their faith with their lives. I pray to the Lord that you have the strength of conviction of those two men."

The elderly duchess, leaning on her cane, rose from the sofa, Thomas' face illuminated by the flickering blaze.

"I trust in God that I've encouraged you to give your course of action some serious reconsideration."

Thomas stood, speechless. She kissed him on the cheek, walked out of the salon, proceeding up the main stairs for the night.

#

Thomas reclined on the red sofa alone by the fire in the salon with his retriever Connie lying quietly by the fire.

*Was the 1958 MI6 communiqué genuine? Was the 1978 letter in Gonzalvo's possession genuine? Was the Fatima prophecy genuine?*

*I'll have Harry date-test the papers. As to the rest of it, I'll let things play out, then decide how to proceed.*

*If the documents are genuine, I'm in an awful conundrum, with no way out.*

"Connie," he called the black dog up to him. He stroked her long black coat. Between all the thoughts bouncing back and forth in his mind, one peculiar thing kept rising to the top.

*What did the Sheikh's riddle mean? Was it superfluous, or was there something to it?*

Jumping onto the sofa, Connie placed her head on Thomas' lap. In the fireplace in front of them, flames jumped up and down, with the red bed of embers glowing beneath the antique brass andirons.

*The Sheikh said to follow our lady,* he thought. *That's Notre Dame in French, domina notra in Latin, like Nostradamus.*

Drowsing off, and on the edge of sleep, he strangely recalled the famous French seer Michel de Nostredame's prophecy of a pope who was caused to die in the night by his persecutors. Shaking off the coming sleep, he went to his library and pulled Nostradamus' *Les Propheties,* 1557, from the shelf. Century 10, Quatrain 12.

Thomas repeated the original French over and over in his head and translated it to English in his mind.

*My God, centuries ago Nostradamus even predicted the death of a pope in the night due to nefarious reasons.*

Still sleepy, he staggered back to the salon with the book. He sat back on the sofa with Connie in front of the firebox. Pondering the content of the Third Fatima prophecy, the prophecy of the popes of Saint Malachy, and that of Nostradamus, and that his name was a version of "Our Lady" in Latin.

His eyes opened, then closed, opened again, then closed tightly as he drowsed into a slumber on the sofa with his trusted retriever. In those subconscious moments before dreams came, the prophecies and the Sheikh's words burdened his subconscious.

*There are no such things as coincidences, no such things. There is meaning to all occurrences. Prophesies have meaning, even if not self-evident at the time.*

# Chapter 19

*Near Houghton-St. Giles, England, UK, June 10*

"Let's walk the grounds. It seems like a top ten day," Stefania suggested to Thomas as the table was cleared following breakfast.

Thomas looked out the window.

"Alright, it's partly sunny, a bit windy. Nevertheless, better weather than the last several days; a good morning for a constitutional," Thomas responded eagerly.

The couple strode through the park toward the chestnut grove.

"I remembered last night a prophecy by Nostradamus that foretold the suicide of a pope, frightened and led to death at night. Frankly it gave me shivers when I read it," said Thomas.

"Don't you think you might be using the prophecy to justify the conclusion that we've come to, that the pope committed suicide?" Stefania retorted softly.

Thomas sighed.

"Perhaps, but this whole sordid affair is about prophecies, isn't it?" he retorted. "The Sheikh first, then the Fatima prophecy. Saint Malachy and Nostradamus confirm this, and they were legitimate seers."

Stopping, Stefania gazed into Thomas's eyes somewhat adoringly.

"I can't argue with you, Thomas. The pieces of the puzzle seem to fit."

Continuing on their trek throughout the grounds of Haverford Hall, Thomas received a call from Harry.

"Good morning, Harry."

"Thomas, I have information for you on LaCroix, but you should know he's dead."

"What? We were with him yesterday! What happened?" Thomas responded excitedly.

"Apparently following vespers at the Birmingham Oratory last night he was crossing the street and was killed. It was a hit and run. They haven't found the driver or the vehicle. There were no witnesses. It seems like every time you give me a name, the person ends up dead. Not encouraging, my old friend."

"Quite. Well, did you find out anything else?" Thomas replied with concern.

"Yes, LaCroix was an assistant to the Camerlengo at the Vatican up to 1978. After the pope died, the Camerlengo changed, and LaCroix went back to parish life in France, where he became involved in some sedevacantist groups, several of them. While he was a vocal supporter of those groups, it doesn't appear that he was ever a member of any particular one. He then left parish life and sort of became a traveling priest. He bounced around a lot, was active and outspoken on social media in favor of traditionalist Catholic groups. And he died last night. And one more thing, about the blonde bird in Rome. The *Polizia* believe she's an independent contractor, and has about ten aliases. Who hired her is anyone's guess."

"Christ! Listen, can you meet me up here at the Red Lion Pub in Kings Lyn this afternoon? To do that paper test, you indicated you'd need a playing-card size piece of the paper, correct?"

"Sure, I can meet you at Kings Lyn. I'll leave by train later this morning and call or text you when I'm on my way. If there are several different samples, place them separately in plastic bags."

"Right. We'll see you this afternoon."

"What was that all about?" questioned Stefania.

"Apparently our acquaintance Father LaCroix met an unceremonious end last night in Birmingham."

"Oh Madonna, what happened?" exclaimed Stefania.

"He was run down. They don't know who did it, and unfortunately there were no witnesses. I've been pondering for some time whether Harry's earlier warning about our little project was prescient. I mean, you were attacked, the Sheikh was attacked and almost killed, Zerkorian was killed, Gonzalvo died, and now LaCroix is dead. I've asked Harry to meet us at Kings Lyn this afternoon. I'd like to give him a small section of each of the four documents, the Fatima prophecy, the 1958 MI6 communiqué, the 1978 *in pectore* letter, and the pope's letter to Rodolfo, to establish at least whether those documents may be genuine in terms of a date range. Agreed?"

"But," Stefania queried, "wouldn't that test be expensive?"

"Of course, but I'll cover the cost. One other thing, you must realize that I know you didn't receive confirmation at *Santa Maria della*

*Concezione dei Cappuccini.* Granny had you investigated. I told her that there was a mistake and that you actually were baptized at *Santa Maria della Vittoria.*"

"Oh, that explains last night. I was wondering," said Stefania, now blushing. "Things were going so well," she continued stuttering and slipping in and out of Portuguese. "I wanted to fit in. I really like you, and I didn't want to ruin things. I had so little time to think when she asked the question."

"But then you *took* communion at Saint Chads?" Thomas asked.

"While we were in Brazil I told my Aunt Maricel of my predicament, and Uncle Mateus knows the Archbishop of Minas Gerais. That morning we all went to the old cathedral in Rio and I received all of the initiation sacraments," Stefania explained.

"Well, that's a relief," Thomas said, then chuckled. "So you received your sacraments in two places, in Rome and in Rio, so you're covered."

"I don't understand," Stefania, appearing puzzled, remarked.

"It's not important," Thomas replied.

Thomas stood there at the top of the grassy knoll overlooking Haverford Hall. The ancient oaks and elms of the park swayed in the morning breeze. Trees in the distance framed the ruins of an ivy-covered abbey sacked during the Reformation. Stefania's jet black tresses blew about, the June sun glimmering off her shiny locks. Thomas turned to her and swept her hair back.

"You must know, and probably have guessed by now, that I'm madly and passionately in love with you. I can't hold it in any longer. From the minute I saw you at the Vatican that first time I felt it. These last few days have confirmed it in my heart. My heart is yours and will be, now and forever."

Stefania's phone started ringing. Instead of responding to Thomas, she answered the call.

"We're at Thomas' home in the UK," Stefania said, answering the call. Smiling, she turned back to look at Thomas, now perturbed.

"Yes, we met with LaCroix; no, not much, nothing new, except later that night he was hit by a car and killed. Yes, that's true. They don't know who did it."

It was obviously Rodolfo on the phone. Stefania's discussion continued.

Receiving a text from Harry, Thomas showed it to Stefania:

Scampering up to the hall behind Thomas, Stefania finished her conversation with Rodolfo.

Thomas, turning, blurted back at Stefania, "We have little time. We must quickly cut pieces off each of the documents, place each in separate plastic bags, then race off to Kings Lyn to meet Harry. It's a fifteen minute drive."

#

A man had never told Stefania he loved her.

*Should I admit that I love Thomas with all of my heart, which is in fact true? If I do, what would come next? Should I demur to keep his attention and affection affixed and therefore hide my true feelings by 'playing hard to get?' If I concede my love, am I setting myself up for a broken heart? Oh Madonna, I should have discussed such matters with mama and aunty while in Brazil.*

*Unfortunately, Thomas may demand a response before then, although I can't imagine Thomas demanding anything; politely "request" is more his style.*

Stefania's instinctively avoided responding to Thomas's concession of love. Stefania knew her bad instincts could get the better of her.

#

Thomas concentrated on getting to Kings Lyn to meet Harry. Unlike prior occasions, Stefania and Thomas didn't speak as Thomas' driver John sped the black BMW sedan up the country lanes from Haverford Hall to Kings Lyn.

Thomas wondered if he made a huge mistake, pushing matters too quickly with Stefania, and by putting the "L" word out there, did he change the dynamic of their relationship?

As emotions go, love is the ficklest, and Thomas knew it. Many love for money; that's easy enough to obtain. His lust having turned to love; Thomas wanted Stefania's heart; a much more tricky endeavor indeed. His mind and attention distracted, he barely noticed the small white two door following them from Haverford Hall to Kings Lyn.

*Admit it, I'm intimidated by her. Now that I've conceded my love I've lost all control.*

Arriving at the small but crowded Tudor-style Red Lion Pub in Kings Lyn, Thomas spotted Harry sitting at a table with a pint of porter. A tall sixtyish thick hunk of a man with a shaved head wearing a tan slacks, blue shirt, and a tartan vest, Harry looked the part of a private investigator.

"Ah, Thomas. And you must be Stefania," Harry introduced himself, standing briefly.

Thomas and Stefania sat down.

"Here they are," Thomas whispered. "One is marked 'A,' the second is 'B,' the third 'C,' and the fourth is marked 'D.'"

"Thanks, mate. I can have the testing done and the results back to you, at least by phone, in twenty-four to thirty-six hours max."

"Thank you Harry," responded Thomas.

"I can't tell you how bleeding concerned I am," continued Harry. "Every time you drop a name, the name ends up dead! These can't be coincidences. First the Sheikh was nearly killed by what was obviously a trained crew. Then Zerkorian is killed in Baku, where he lived unnoticed in obscurity since 1992. The Azerbaijanis claim they only now discovered he was an Armenian agent, which is rubbish. Stefania is attacked in Rome, Gonzalvo dies of natural causes suddenly in Brazil, this priest LaCroix is strolling home from church without a care in the world and is run down? Christ, Thomas, this smells to high heaven, no pun intended! Do me a favor. Don't drop my name mate."

"But who would want these people dead?" Stefania responded.

"They only have one thing in common," Thomas said relatively softly and somewhat dejectedly. "The three, if Zerkorian ever was truly a priest, were in the Vatican in 1978, and the Sheikh was a close confidant to the pope then. Perhaps we're getting close, too close, to the answer to this little problem for the comfort of some. As we've previously discussed, imagine if we're correct and the pope wasn't the true pope, and in fact none of the popes after 1958 were the true popes. More to the point, the true pope is dead, and there's no way to reestablish the legitimate papacy. The church would be in a permanent state of *sede vacante*. How do you explain that to one billion faithful?"

"I'm not necessarily following all of this, but that would seem to be a motive for the Vatican to want to keep these facts from ever seeing the light of day," Harry said.

"True," Stefania noted, "but why eliminate all of the peripheral players? It would be easy enough to get to Thomas and me, wouldn't it?"

"Perhaps," Harry continued, "someone already tried to do you in, but your death in a robbery attempt, the death of an Armenian in Baku in a police raid, an elderly priest in Brazil due to natural causes, and a nomadic French priest by accident in Birmingham wouldn't arouse suspicion as being connected in any way. Those deaths would largely be assumed to be unrelated."

"What about the Sheikh?" asked Stefania.

"The Sheikh, well, it had to be made to look like a terrorist attack or an assassination, given he's had a price on his head for decades. The random murder of you in the music hall in Rome by a contractor, if made to appear as a robbery, might be unsolvable. Who knows, maybe your necklace was her fee?"

"What do you mean?" Stefania piped in excitedly but in a hushed tone. "The woman who attacked me was a hit-man and the necklace was her payment?"

Harry looked at Thomas. Thomas hadn't shared this tidbit with Stefania. He raised his eyebrows, looking at Harry.

"It's possible that the bird in Rome who attacked you was hired help and the loot from the quarry being the commission for the kill," Harry responded.

"You think that's likely?" inquired Stefania.

"Maybe. I've heard of it before," answered Harry, "but at the end of the day the death of the sixteenth Duke of Radcliffe, the queen's cousin, a member of the House of Lords, well, that would bloody well raise some eyebrows. No stone would be left unturned. And the authorities in the UK don't give a rat's behind about the sensitivities of the Catholic Church. Have you noticed whether you've been followed at all?"

"I've noticed a blonde woman following us in Rome and a car in Rome," observed Thomas, "but she didn't appear to be the same woman whom Stefania took care of in Rome, based on her observation. I thought I saw a couple observing us in Rio, but the next day they were gone."

"When we were at Saint Chad's I noticed a man following us, but he then was at mass, so maybe he was merely a worshipper," Stefania added.

"Hmm, have you noticed anyone trying to gain access to your social media accounts, your phone accounts, anything like that?" asked Harry.

"As a matter of fact," volunteered Stefania, "when I was checking my messages earlier today I noted a message from my e-mail provider indicating that my password was compromised and to go to the link provided and enter my current password and change to another. I ignored it, though, mostly because we had too much going on. I figured I'd get to it later."

"Let me see," Harry insisted, holding out his hand.

Stefania handed her phone to Harry, and he examined the e-mail.

"Don't go to the link," directed Harry. "Delete this notification; it's likely an attempt to compromise your account. Go to your account directly from a laptop on a secure Wi-Fi connection and change your password. Make it complex. At least sixteen characters, letters, and numbers, at least three capital letters, and three or four symbols. Change it weekly. Thomas, you should do the same. Whoever sent this will try to access your account another way. Don't under any circumstances use public Wi-Fi for any purpose. Only communicate with mobile phones."

"Why?" queried Stefania.

"It will be difficult for them to intercept mobile phone calls or text messages, unless of course its MI5 or MI6, in which case you should assume nothing is secure," answered Harry. "Have your phones left your person?"

"No," responded Thomas, "but why do you ask?"

"Someone could have modified the phones to intercept all of your communications. Unless the phones left your person, I wouldn't be concerned about that necessarily. Keep them on you at all times. Don't leave them in hotel rooms or any public place, even for a moment."

"Can you tell who's behind this?" asked Stefania.

"A sophisticated entity. This appears authentic, but it's not. I deal with these types of issues all the time; you know, cyber security. If I hadn't seen this, well, let's say someone or something wants to get into your account. Perhaps they don't know what you know. Whoever it is knows the Sheikh, LaCroix, Gonzalvo, and Zerkorian knew things. They don't know what you know, but they want to know. Or at least they want to make sure they know before, well, Thomas, I suggest you get bodyguards, protection. I can arrange it."

Thomas rubbed his cheek with his right hand for a few seconds.

"Let me think on it, Harry. We'll get back to you." Turning to Stefania, he asked, "What do you think?"

"I don't know what to think."

Harry got up from the table, guzzling down the rest of his beer.

"I also brought you a gift," said Harry.

Taking out a small black electronic device, Harry slid it across the table to Thomas.

"This is a jamming device. Keep it with you at all times and keep it turned on. It will prevent electronic eavesdropping on you during conversations. Here's the recharger. I've had it on the whole time we were talking. Now, I must be getting back to London. My train should be pulling up to the platform any minute now. I'll be in touch. Please do call me if you want me to arrange for security."

Snatching up the glassine envelopes, Harry put them into a brown leather satchel under the table, grabbed it, and hurriedly departed, walking out the pub door, up the street in the direction of the train station.

Thomas and Stefania left for Haverford, but Thomas, fearing rejection, didn't dare raise the issue of his affection for Stefania.

# Chapter 20
*Peredelkino, Russia, June 10*

At Lenov's request, Greschenko converged quickly for an early morning meeting at the southwest Moscow suburb of Peredelkino, the location of the former summer *dacha* of the Russian writer Boris Pasternak, who was persecuted by Greschenko's mentor, General Vasily Karpov. Greschenko knew that Karpov had visited Pasternak at the dacha in 1958 to cajole him to renounce the Nobel Prize for literature. Pasternak's dacha had since become a museum. Vasily gifted to Greschenko a signed copy of Pasternak's masterpiece, *Doctor Zhivago*, which he obtained from the author on that fateful visit in 1958. One of her most prized possessions, Greschenko read it often.

Greschenko, Stasevich, and Lenov took a stroll on a path through the nearby dark pine forest. Greschenko thought the cloudy day and dark forest presaged a sense of misfortune. As the three walked, the mist from their collective breaths wafted through the damp pine-scented June air.

"Well?" asked Stasevich.

Lenov uncharacteristically waivered before answering.

"Yes, well?" Greschenko pressed during the interlude.

"The French priest LaCroix is dead," Lenov reported.

Stasevich, shaking in his olive overcoat, took his military muskrat fur *ushanka* off his head, stopped walking and turned toward Lenov in obvious anger.

"What?" he shouted. "You know GRU was approved to carry out the sanction. This was GRU's wet operation. You were to engage in surveillance and advise! This is an outrageous breach of protocol!"

Lenov, in a suit and tie, black leather overcoat with his trademark *papakha*, himself now obviously agitated, addressed Stasevich excitedly, waving his index finger in Stasevich's direction.

"General, please control yourself! Remember to whom you're speaking. Our agents were following the priest after he left church last evening. They were going to snatch him, shoot him up with scopolamine, and find out what he knew. After we were done with him, he would be handed over to your agents for disposal. He wouldn't have been missed. Then out of nowhere, as I understand it, at dusk a small white car sped down the street and hit the old man head on, killing him instantly."

"Were there any witnesses?" asked Greschenko.

"As far as we know, our agents were the only ones who witnessed the event. It happened so suddenly they weren't even able to see the vehicle number or the make and model of the auto."

An unusual silence hung over the three. The only sounds were that of the forest; birds chirping, crickets, a soft breeze whistling through the pine needles, and the creaking of the trees swaying back and forth. As they walked, pine cones and needles cracked under foot. Stasevich's three-man security detail followed closely.

Greschenko, in her black cashmere overcoat and black Italian leather riding-type boots, wearing a black sable *ushanka,* hung her head in dejection.

"Ugh! Well, a hit do you think?"

"We have no idea. As far as we can tell, the local police have no clue either. They're treating it as a hit and run," Lenov retorted, looking at Stasevich as if he had an answer to the conundrum.

"I apologize for my outburst, but it seems too coincidental for it to be anything other than a sanction; MI6 perhaps? Who else would want this priest dead? Do you think the Britisher pulled some strings and had him bumped off?"

"Why would the English care?" Greschenko answered. "The only entity other than Russia who would want to silence this LaCroix would be, well, the Vatican. The Britisher is well connected to the Vatican."

"Nay, nay, nay," replied Stasevich, bending over and drawing on the ground with a stick he found. "The Vatican isn't in the business of assassinations, at least as far as we know. All of that talk is fiction. I've never heard of it, and I've heard of a lot of strange things. The Vatican is too incompetent. Look how it handled the sex scandals and how easily we infiltrated it for years. But I can't help but believe this was no coincidence. For the killing to have been successful while we were observing the Frenchy is both brazen and brilliant."

"Maybe the Americans?" inquired Greschenko, thinking out loud while looking at the other two.

"Unlikely, but possible," pondered Lenov. "However, the only connection with this man and Archangel is the Britisher. MI6 or a private hit would make the most sense. One last thing, and also curious, this morning our agents observed the Britisher and his lover meeting with an unknown man who arrived and left by train to London. We've not yet determined who that person is, but they had a jamming device so their conversation couldn't be monitored electronically. Let's put it this way. If the Britisher had this priest murdered, he's much more dangerous than we've been led to believe. Since he had a jamming device, he's aware his communications may be compromised. But why kill the Frenchy?"

"For the same reasons we wanted him dead," stated a frustrated Greschenko, shrugging. "This aristocrat is loyal to the Vatican. Perhaps he wanted the priest dead to keep him quiet. Maybe this unknown man was the contact for the hit. Of course, that doesn't bode well for his girlfriend. If she intends to tell what she knows, she may get hit by a car next!"

All three shared a laugh at the thought.

"But this doesn't solve our problem," Greschenko continued. "Sure, the Frenchy is dead, but we don't know what he knew, and Directorate OT hasn't been able to hack the girlfriend's e-mail. OT has hacked the e-mail of the girlfriend's journal in Rome and also bugged their offices. We've managed to bug the Britisher's landline phone to his estate. I haven't received a report yet, but we'll see what they know. I understand we've intercepted phone calls involving the Britisher's grandmother. Nothing from him yet."

"July first is two weeks hence!" Stasevich, now standing, exclaimed animatedly. "I have the authority to dispatch both of them, the nobleman and the girl. Who cares how it appears. Let the British authorities speculate all they want. We'll use a nerve agent, polonium, or a thallium derivative, quick and deadly. That will tie up all the loose ends and we can be rid of this little distraction. That's my solution and recommendation. Let's be done with this!"

Greschenko shook her head.

"No," she tersely insisted. "I'd still like to know what they know before we pull the trigger. We also need to find out why the Frenchman was a target, and if so, who handled it."

"We'll follow up on that," said Lenov, kicking a pine cone through the woods.

"You are playing with fire Greschenko," Stasevich retorted with a huff. "And when you play with fire you get burned, and I for one don't like getting burned. I'll inform His Excellency of my recommendation to be rid of the Britisher once and for all."

Greschenko scoffed.

"You don't like taking orders from a woman," Greschenko responded snidely with a raised voice.

Stasevich responded with a scoff.

Greschenko emerged from the pine-scented aroma of the forest among the ancient dachas from the Soviet era. The wind picked up and blew through her as if naked. At this moment Greschenko, dejected, cold, and vulnerable, saw herself taunted by Lenov, under assault by Stasevich, and beguiled by Thomas Houghton.

Reminded of Vasily's admiration for Pasternak, Greschenko stopped for a moment to gaze admiringly at Boris Pasternak's brown and white clapboard dacha.

"So from here genius rose."

# Chapter 21

*Near Houghton-St. Giles, England, UK, June 10*

Thomas and Stefania spoke little during the ride back to Haverford. Upon arrival, Thomas declared, "Dearest, I have to address various business matters with Emma, so I fear I'll be occupied the rest of the day in my study. You're welcomed to anything you should like. I apologize, but due to all of this traveling I've neglected my business affairs."

"I don't mind at all, Thomas. I'd like to type my notes, get them organized so that ultimately, when this is concluded, I can publish the article in the *Journal*. I also want to check in with mama in Brazil. So I'll be hold up in my room. Please fetch me for dinner."

"Of course. I'll collect you prior to dinner for cocktails, say at 7 o'clock?"

"Great, I'll be ready then."

Thomas lightly kissed Stefania on the lips and walked toward his study.

Stefania, upon reaching her room, first tried calling her mother, who didn't pick up, as well as her aunt. She would try them again after dinner. Settling in, she began typing her notes on her laptop on the desk facing out the window.

Stefania noticed the fine weather had turned since morning, and clouds and wind were rolling in. Gray clouds shed water over the distant hills, and raindrops started pelting her bedroom window.

#

In his study, Thomas received an unexpected phone call on his mobile.

"Thomas, this is James."

"James, are you and Catarina in residence?"

"No, we're returning from a trip to Portugal, and we heard you were at Haverford. Frankly, we've seen your photos in the tabloids and are eager to meet your new female friend, if that's not too presumptuous. Catarina is excited. The tabloids say she's Brazilian."

"Of course, you and Catarina should join us for cocktails and dinner tonight. I've actually been thinking of you; I'd like you and Catarina to meet Stefania."

"That will work perfectly as we have all our luggage, and we'll be by Haverford by six."

"You can dress and freshen up here. A terrific surprise. Granny will be delighted to see you as well. Cocktails are at seven."

Dinner time came quickly, and Thomas collected Stefania from her room.

Stefania had dressed in a sleeveless low cut black lace dress showing plenty of cleavage, also accentuating her long tanned legs.

"You look absolutely heavenly. I must say, you're the picture of perfection. The most beautiful woman I've ever known."

"Thank you, Thomas."

Stefania kissed him briefly on lips.

Stopping in the hall for a moment, Thomas cautioned, "I think we should be on guard and tell grandmamma as little as possible."

"I concur," agreed Stefania. "Everything, the death of LaCroix, the attack at the concert, attempt to breach my e-mail account, as well as Harry's admonition, has left me quite spooked."

"There's a surprise for dinner," Thomas said with some elation.

"Oh, what surprise?" Stefania queried.

"A good friend and his wife will be joining us," Thomas responded. "Actually, my Cousin James and his wife Catarina, the ninth earl and countess Layton, will be nipping by on their way back to his family estate twenty miles to the north. James and I went to Sandhurst together. Other than Artie, the Duke of Shopshire, James is my closest friend. We were raised as brothers and I was best man at his wedding. The earls Layton are also Houghtons, a cadet branch of my family, and other than grandmamma, James as a distant cousin is my closest living relation on my father's side of the family. James had actually been introduced to his wife Catarina through granny's connections."

"What's Catarina's background?" asked Stefania.

Thomas smiled. "You and Catarina may have some things in common. I think you might hit it off. Catarina is five years younger than James, about your age, and is from a prominent Portuguese family. They spend about half their time in Portugal and half in the UK."

"This is quite a surprise. I'm eager to meet them both. Won't your grandmother object?"

"I can't imagine. James is always welcomed in this house, and my grandmother is his godmother. Also, the additional company will give us cover if granny tries to interrogate us."

As they filed into the library before dinner, Thomas couldn't help but notice that both the earl and countess seemed to be carbon copies of Thomas and Stefania.

The dinner conversation centered around Thomas and Stefania's time in Brazil, the earl and countess' recent stay on the Portuguese coast, and other relatively mundane dinner conversation. Thomas observed Stefania and the countess hitting it off, speaking to each other in Portuguese, to the obvious irritation of the duchess, who didn't understand the language.

After dinner, Thomas and James reminisced quietly about their days growing up, their time at Sandhurst, and in the service. Stefania and Catarina huddled by the fire, speaking in Portuguese. Thomas could understand Stefania describing favorably her trip to Scotland.

All the time the duchess sat isolated in the corner with a small glass of port in hand. The duchess seemed resigned to wait everyone out, but it appeared her age and lack of fortitude got the best of her. She turned in by 11 o'clock.

The other two couples sat, drank, and talked for another two hours or so.

"James and Catarina, you must stay the night. You both have had too much to drink and the rain is coming down in buckets," Thomas implored.

"Thomas, we can't impose," James responded.

"Don't be preposterous. You can, you will, and we'll enjoy your company. You have your luggage here from your trip. You already have a room, for God's sake."

James looked at Catarina, nodding.

"Okay, you've convinced us."

"Tomorrow the ladies can go into Norwich. You and I can ride through the park," said Thomas.

"Of course, you and your horses, Thomas," responded James.

The four left the salon, and Thomas accompanied Stefania to her room.

At the threshold to her room, Thomas leaned in and kissed Stefania. They continued for a few minutes, Thomas' hand caressing Stefania's back. Thomas, recognizing he still had no response from his entreaty to Stefania, slowly pulled away. Stefania seemed to want to linger in the embrace.

"I'm so glad to meet your friends, and the time with James and Catarina really made the evening," said Stefania.

"Have a good night, darling."

"Same to you," Stefania replied as she closed the door to her room.

#

Once in her room, Stefania immediately picked up her phone. Her mother had called while downstairs at dinner.

*I'm drunk and tired. The call to mama can wait.*

She stripped off her dress, stepped out of it as it hit the floor, threw her bra onto the chair, and fell into bed wearing only a black lace camisole and matching briefs. Heavy rain and wind rattled the leaded glass window, helping glide Stefania to a deep sleep, neglecting, for the time being, the troubles at hand.

*Norwich, England, UK, June 11*

After breakfast, James and Thomas went riding throughout the park. Stefania and Catarina took off to Norwich so they could peruse the market and shop at the Royal Arcade and Jerrold's.

The weather cleared, and rays of sunlight shone through the few clouds over the countryside as the morning mist rose from the fields.

*I love my alone time with Thomas, but this is a nice change of pace,* thought Stefania.

After shopping, the ladies took luncheon in Norwich.

*I've yet to speak to mama for advice. Perhaps Catarina can help. But can she be trusted?*

Stefania noticed a blondish, trendily dressed twenty-something woman who had followed them to the exclusive restaurant but disappeared.

"This is James' favorite place, and mine. He has an account here, so lunch is on him," Catarina bragged in Portuguese followed with a laugh as the two were seated for luncheon.

After drinking some wine, Stefania relaxed.

196

"So Stefania, what's the nature of your relationship with Thomas? Is it love, a friend with benefits, friends, what?" Catarina asked again in Portuguese.

"He told me, in the most romantic, polite, and endearing way, that he loves me," Stefania responded.

"What did you tell him?"

"Well, we were interrupted, and I never gave him an answer, I never told him how I feel."

"How do you feel?"

"I love him. Who wouldn't? He's perfect. I've never been told before by a man that he loves me. Frankly, I don't know how to respond, the timing of it. Should I play hard to get? Should I concede my love? Then, of course, where will it go from here?"

"But are you *in love* with him?"

"Yes, with all of my heart. Maybe it's my first time, but I've never felt this way about someone. I wanted to discuss it with my mama in Brazil but haven't been able to reach her. Do you have any advice?"

Grinning, Catarina took a sip of red wine, patting her lips down with her white linen napkin.

"In my experience, playing hard to get works with some men, but with men of accomplishment, success, and privilege, it's a waste of time. Men like Thomas and James can get any woman they want, and they know it, and if they don't realize it, shame on them. They're extremely cautious for fortune hunters, blackmailers, and thieves. Unless Thomas and James are cut from a different cloth, and they aren't, once a profession of love is made, if it's unrequited, he'll move on. If he lingers, it will be to his detriment. Thomas obviously has concluded that, on a deep level, he loves you. On a superficial level, you're gorgeous, there's no doubt about that. If he wanted, he could have swept you off your feet, flown you to Ibiza for a weekend romp, and you would never hear from him again, not that Thomas is that type."

"How can you be so sure of this, Catarina?" Stefania asked.

"It's easy," Catarina responded. "Men like Thomas and James crave stability and practicality, at least for the time being, and that means they're one-woman men. If Thomas is anything like James, he'll put his heart and soul into you, put you on a pedestal. He also wants a teammate, because being the sixteenth duke of Radcliffe is a tough job to do alone, and the duchess won't be around forever. Mutual support, intellectual, emotional and physical is what he wants. He wants to be your rock and his yours. Hold back your love at your peril, girlfriend. If he senses that you're wavering, he'll cut you off, he'll ghost you. Remember, he's practical about life and love."

"Sounds like you've got it all figured out," noted Stefania.

"Yep. So, have you shagged?"

"Not yet, but I think we both want to."

"That's because Thomas is in love with you. If he wasn't, believe me, you'd be a member of the mile high club three or four times over by now. There's also the religious aspect. It wasn't an issue with James and me, but Thomas is devout, which is rare these days. He sees you as someone who'll complement him. My guess is he believes your chance meeting at the Vatican was no coincidence. James wooed me and jetted me around, but I was coy, not too hard to get. He got enough that he fell in love with me, and after that it was all downhill."

"To concede my feelings to Thomas goes against my better instincts," noted Stefania. "I might get hurt. You're telling me it sounds like I'll get hurt if I don't respond. I certainly don't want to lose Thomas. Do you love James?"

"Of course. I must say I kind of thought he was a tosser when I first met him, but after our first long dinner I fell hard. We were introduced through Thomas' grandmother's connections. She knew my father somehow through the Fatima pilgrimage. The toughest part was waiting for James to concede his love. The woman should never profess love first, but once James did, well, and don't get me wrong, we're very happy. My family loves him. His English family takes getting used to, but we spend about half the time in Portugal, and he's getting used to the better weather and much better cuisine!"

Catarina and Stefania both shared a laugh.

"Remember," Catarina continued, "if you marry, you'll be marrying a package. You marry not only Thomas, but the duchess, the Radcliffe title, and all of its upsides and pitfalls. You'll have to go to state occasions; your life won't entirely be your own. Because of Thomas' position, you'll have to be on your best behavior. And there will be children, but you'll be able to afford governesses so that you can keep that spark alive because, believe me, children will sap the energy out of most of the best marriages. We had our first last year, Eduardo, and he's at home with his grandmother and the governess, and I'm here with you, having a great time drinking copious amounts of a rather delightful Bordeaux from Medoc."

The two women lifted their glasses to toast.

"It would be great if you could get him to split time between England and maybe Rome or Brazil," Catarina pondered.

"As it is now, he spends a significant amount of time in Rome, and he seemed to enjoy spending time with papa in Rome and with mama's family in Rio."

"What's not to like about Rio?" Catarina laughed. "I sealed the deal with James on a trip to Brazil when I wore a thong bikini at Ipanema Beach! And a candid piece of advice; have a child, preferably a boy, as soon as possible. All Thomas' titles, lands, money, pass through the male line. If he dies and there are no children, his title and wealth goes to, well, I actually think to James; James, as a second cousin, is Thomas' heir if there are no children. If you have a boy, he'll take care of you. You'll need a spare in case. Otherwise, if Thomas passes, you might be left with your journalism job and little else. I hate to be morbid, but those are the facts, at least as I understand them."

"Good to know. That's very good to know."

"If you marry, your life will be completely different, if you choose so. You won't have to work. Everything will be done for you," Catarina said, followed with a grin. "You'll never have to fly commercial again."

"Let me ask, how did the religion thing come into play with you and James?"

"James was Church of England, not particularly devout, and his mother wasn't either, although I think she's a Catholic hater. So we compromised. We got married in an Anglican church. As a matter of fact, we married here in Norwich, at St. Peter's. My son, Eduardo, was baptized Catholic, and it was agreed we would raise all of our children Catholic. My parents were insistent and wouldn't have it any other way. James has since converted to Catholicism under the Ordinariate; he had some assistance from Thomas' grandmother, as you can imagine. As to the children, my mother-in-law has little say in the matter. You can certainly expect that you'll have to raise the children Catholic. I assume you are?"

"Well, I wasn't Catholic, I was sort of...nothing. Agnostic or atheist I suppose. But during the course of an article I'm working on which involves the church, I became more interested in it. I've become more spiritual. Ultimately I received confirmation in Brazil during our recent visit."

"And this had nothing to do with your relationship with Thomas?"

Stefania smiled, held up her thumb and index fingers next to each other, and replied, "Just a little."

"Please don't become a teetotaler, then I won't have anyone to speak Portuguese to and get drunk with in Norwich!"

"Have you ever known a Brazilian to be a teetotaler?"

Both women laughed.

Catarina regaled Stefania with the joys and disasters of pregnancy and motherhood. The luncheon continued through late afternoon. A little tipsy afterward, Stefania phoned John, the driver, who picked the giggling ladies and their shopping bags up in front of the restaurant for the forty minute drive back to Haverford Hall. Stefania barely noticed the blonde woman sitting on a sidewalk bench outside the restaurant.

The duke's driver drove the black BMW four door sedan through the rolling countryside toward Haverford. Green fields and hedgerows flew by on the narrow country lane.

Stefania looked back.

"I think a small white car is following us," she said.

"He's following us all right," John, the duke's driver, confirmed, "since we left Norwich."

Stefania turned around and looked out the rear window.

The white car accelerated, seemingly attempting to hit the BMW from behind. John accelerated, the BMW's speed and agility apparently no match for the smaller car, avoiding a potential crash.

"He's still following us," Stefania said, then laughed. "I think that blonde woman I saw outside the restaurant is in the passenger seat, but I can't be sure. What could she want?"

"I see it," John replied, looking in the rear view mirror. "Fortunately, I suspect I know these country lanes much better than they do. I'll put some distance between us."

The BMW accelerated with a lurch forward.

"There's another car following the white car; a black SUV," John noted. His eyes narrowed as he looked into the rear view mirror.

"Probably some local brigands or drunks," Catarina blurted.

Stefania also laughed.

"He's closing distance again. Hold on!" John asserted loudly, peering back into the rear view mirror.

The BMW again took off.

"That was close. They nearly hit us," Stefania exclaimed.

"There's a split in the lane ahead. I can get back to Haverford either way, but I'll wait to the last minute to make the turn. Hold on," John instructed.

"We're bouncing around like we're on a carnival ride," Catarina said, laughing again.

Stefania joined in the laughter as the two bounced about the back seat.

Stefania heard a loud screeching of tires from behind, and the two turned around to look. The SUV had apparently driven the white car off the road into a shallow ditch bounded by a hedgerow.

"Hold on. Here's where we make our move," cautioned John.

John took a quick right at the split in the road.

Stefania and Catarina leaned to the right as the car made the jerky turn, then looked back. The SUV continued down the other fork in the road.

"Must have been a row between the two cars," John theorized.

"Yes, must have," Stefania agreed, accepting that explanation, settling back for the rest of the ride to Haverford with Catarina.

#

Following arrival back at Haverford, the two ladies freshened up for dinner.

After dinner, the couples made their way to the salon.

"John told me you had a bit of a fright on the way back from Norwich. Someone tried to run you off the road?" Thomas whispered into Stefania's ear.

Stefania put her red glossy lips right next to Thomas's left ear after nibbling on his lobe for a second.

"Darling, I think it was a bout between the two cars behind," she whispered.

"But dearest, I heard there was a blonde woman in the car. Was it the same woman from Rome, do you think? If so, this might be much more serious," whispered Thomas, now smiling due to Stefania's little nibble.

Stefania, now thoroughly drunk and eager to get to the salon and enjoy an after dinner cocktail with Catarina and James, ran her tongue along Thomas' ear.

"I couldn't tell if it was the same woman, but I don't think it was. If she were after me, why did the other car run them off the road then disappear?" she whispered in reply.

"Good point. Why indeed," Thomas replied.

Stefania took his chin in her left hand and planted a long, deep, passionate kiss on his mouth with a slight thrust of her tongue, while at the same time grasping Thomas' buttock with her right hand, pulling their bodies together.

Stepping back, Stefania walked in the direction of the salon and turned to Thomas.

"Satisfied?"

"I suppose so, yes," he replied, grinning from ear to ear, wiping the lipstick from his mouth with a handkerchief.

#

After post-dinner drinks and conversation, the women turned in for the night, both content to leave the men alone to commiserate after dinner. Stefania had hit it off with Catarina. Frowning much of the time, the duchess also turned in for the night.

*I still want to speak with mama, but it's too late and I'm tired*, she rationalized postponing the call yet again.

Upon reaching her room, Stefania stood at the window overlooking the moonlit countryside with clouds passing here and there in front of the waxing moon. From her room she could make out the vast park before her and pondered the fact if she and Thomas married, Haverford Hall with all of its enormity and beauty would be her new home. In the distance she noticed a pair of headlamps on the country lane. A lone car slowly lingered at the gate to Haverford Hall before it drove off. She drew the draperies closed, kicked off her red patent leather pumps, stripped, and settled in for the night.

*Near Houghton St. Giles, England, UK, June 12*

With Stefania and Catarina gone to a spa in Norwich, Thomas, as well as James, occupied their time in Thomas' study responding to e-mails and phone calls.

Thomas sat at his desk intently reviewing Harry's invoices for services rendered.

"So how serious is it with Stefania?" James asked.

"Pardon?" responded Thomas, startled by the abrupt interruption to the relative quiet of the study.

"I'm sorry, Thomas, but I don't mean to be impolitic, but what's the status of your relationship with Stefania?" James repeated. "I'm curious naturally, but I should probably know before Catarina and I take our leave. She may know more than I, depending, of course, on what Stefania explained."

"I'm not sure," Thomas sheepishly responded.

"Ah, what do you mean, man, you're not sure?" James asked, surprise in his voice.

"The other day we were up on the knoll in the park and I told her I loved her," Thomas revealed, now pacing back and forth.

"Good God, man, what was her response?"

"She didn't respond; well, it wasn't so much she didn't respond as we were interrupted. She took a call and it was never raised again. I fear I've cocked up. How did it go with you and Catarina when, you know, you got serious?"

"I fear I'm not going to be much help. Catarina got me all hot and bothered wearing a thong bikini on Ipanema Beach. We then went for drinks in our hotel bar, I told her I loved her. She responded, 'I know,' and laid a long deep snog on me that I'll never forget, grabbed me by my knob, and led me up to our hotel room. After an hour of the best shagging I've ever had, she got up from the bed as I lay there exhausted, and as she walked into the bathroom naked as the day she was born, she matter-of-factly turned back to me and remarked, in Portuguese of course, 'Oh, by the way, I love you too.'"

"You make it sound so romantic," said Thomas.

"Sorry. Told you I wasn't going to be much assistance, and I really don't have any advice for you either," James apologized. "This is uncharted territory for me at least. One thing I can tell you, and I know you, Thomas; as soon as you shag, you'll be in for the long haul."

"I may be a neophyte in the love department, but I know that much. She's the first woman I've really fallen in love with. Unlike the others, she has no expectations and demands nothing. Nevertheless, I've resisted her charms with all my might, you can be rest assured."

"I can only imagine; she's insanely beautiful, with all due respect, old boy."

"No offense taken. Let's keep this between us, James," Thomas replied softly. "I'm quite embarrassed by the whole thing. Frankly, I'm being ripped apart at the seams as well. Stefania's project has taken a life of its own and could have serious implications for the church, and for our family. If granny knew all the facts, Christ only knows what she'd do. I have to consider its impact on me as well. Fortunately having you and Catarina here has been a welcome diversion."

"Is there anything you'd wish to share?"

"No, I'd rather not, just the same, but the fewer who know, the better," responded Thomas in a sterner tone while rubbing his chin with his right hand. "And there are quite a few blokes involved in our little project who seem to have been bumped off lately, one by one."

"Well then, I'd rather not be bumped off," responded James with a laugh.

Thomas grinned, but he knew it was no laughing matter.

# Chapter 22
*Sergiev Posad (Zagorsk), Russia, June 12*

The encrypted text she received from Lenov meant a meeting in Sergiev Posad, a small city approximately seventy-five kilometers northeast of Moscow, typically a ninety minute drive from her office.

The cool morning air jolted Greschenko as she stepped out of her bodyguard driven car. She walked toward the orchard and a small park outside of the monastery complex in Sergiev Posad. Greschenko meandered through the park, never losing sight of Lenov, both waiting for Stasevich to emerge. Finally, Stasevich materialized with his bodyguards from the whitewashed Assumption Cathedral and joined the other two.

"This is one of my favorite places. The cathedral with the famous icon of the Last Supper by Simon Ushakov makes it the most beautiful church in all of the Russias—"

Greschenko, while always curious about the place, didn't care one way or the other.

"Can we get to why we're here?" she interrupted, staring at Lenov, her brows raised.

"Well, what do we have?" Stasevich followed in an unusually good mood, also looking at Lenov.

"Apparently this Britisher and his girlfriend are in no rush to do anything," said Lenov. "As far as we can tell, they're enjoying time off with some friends, another British nobleman and his wife, at the duke's manor house. The girlfriend and the other woman were speaking another language together, probably Portuguese, so our agent couldn't understand them or get close enough to record the conversation, unfortunately. However, they went shopping, had some lunch. Nothing unusual. They've been there since Sunday. The men go horseback riding as far as we can tell. When they're not out on the town, they're in the manor house doing whatever."

"So that's all we have is a social update?" Stasevich asked incredulously.

Lenov smiled mischievously.

"No, someone appeared to deliberately try to run the girl off the road," Lenov countered. "Fortunately she had a good driver and a fast car. Our agents were following and ran the other car off the road. Maybe we should've let them get to the girl?"

"Are you certain?" Greschenko asked.

"Let's put it this way. Our agents doubled back, but by the time they reached the car, it managed to leave the scene," Lenov replied. "Could have been a case of mistaken identity, but it certainly appeared that the driver was attempting to force the girl off the road."

Greschenko turned and stared at Stasevich.

He scoffed.

"Then your agents did their job. The girl's death now, before we know what she knows, would be unfortunate. I have something more," Greschenko interjected. "Directorate OT was able to bug the offices of the woman's publication in Rome. On Monday she phoned her office and reported that the Frenchy had died. She indicated that they didn't know who did it. Other than that, there was small talk regarding scheduling, their location, and so on. However, the girl did seem to indicate they had made contact with the Frenchy. That seemed relevant and important. It's clear that there was something significant about the Frenchman because they clearly and deliberately met with him in Birmingham. So far nothing has turned up on the *Journal's* e-mails. The fact that we now have access through the *Journal* is helpful."

"What about the editor? Let's interrogate him," Stasevich insisted.

"We've considered taking the *Journal's* editor in and interrogating him," replied Lenov. "But that's too risky. Again, this editor is a high profile individual with contacts at the Vatican and in the Italian government and police. He would be missed. Hopefully, something will turn up in his e-mails, or the Britisher's girlfriend will call him again and we'll get more detailed information. We haven't been able to intercept their cell phone calls from the Britisher's estate. The house is too far distant from anyplace where an inconspicuous mobile intercept could be set up."

Greschenko looked Stasevich's way.

"And I've spoken to the president and he agrees with my opinion that the Britisher's high profile could cause problems for us," said

Greschenko. Moreover, if we go after the girl, the Britisher will likely use his contacts in the government to address her disappearance. We've already seen it appears as if he's working with MI6. If others are trying to kill her, they must be stopped, at least until we know what the two of them know, seize any evidence, and, of course, the president authorizes the sanction."

"And I've also spoken to His Excellency," snapped Stasevich back at Greschenko. "It seems rumours of certain sexual indiscretions by you have reached his ear. For your sake, I hope they are untrue, or at the very least are unverifiable. If they are, your role in this operation may therefore be short-lived."

Greschenko's eyes shifted to Stasevich.

"I have many enemies. They would like nothing more to bring me down with unbridled innuendo," Greschenko replied calmly. "You can be rest assured that a rumour is all that it is."

"It's your skin Greschenko," Stasevich retorted in a serious tone. "You'd best take care. All things considered, despite our disagreements, I'd rather be working with you than the alternatives. Resolving this matter in a favorable manner may save your skin, if it's on the hook."

"I have something else," Lenov interrupted.

Lenov pulled a manila file from his jacket and showed it to the other two. All three huddled together, looking at the open portfolio.

"An interesting development from Directorate OT's surveillance of the Britisher's estate's land line," reported Lenov. "It appears his grandmother is, shall we say, involved in some interesting activities."

Greschenko reviewed the file with Stasevich looking over her shoulder. Lenov paced in the background.

Stasevich broke the silence.

"I suggest we pull an Oswald with this chap."

With that, all three laughed in unison.

Greschenko examined the file in detail and looked up at the other two. Lenov stared back and raised his eyebrows.

"Hmm. I need little convincing," she said. "Excellent idea. Go with it."

"We're also investigating the financing of these activities," said Lenov pointing to the file.

"Excellent. Now we have to sit tight for the time being and be patient," replied Greschenko. "I'd love to know what the Britisher or the girl knows, but time is starting to run out."

Stasevich rolled his eyes and let out a breath of air while staring at the cloudy June sky.

"No shit," snarked Stasevich. "We may not have that luxury."

As Greschenko's black sedan sped back toward Moscow through the pine forests, pastures, and emerald fields of Moscow Oblast's countryside, angst gripped her. Her stomach fluttered with jitters and her mind flew in different directions. She instinctively checked the secret compartment in her bag for her fake passport and Euros.

*If proof of my relationship with Katya gets to the president, I'll be sacked or worse. Christ, I hope Lenov did his job.*

Greschenko, settling into the back seat, pulled her tablet out of her bag and began viewing the SVR's electronic file on Thomas.

*Men. Their competitive spirit is too overt. I'm more competitive and self-assured than the lot of them. That combined with their obvious weaknesses, makes me even more dangerous.*

Cocking her head to one side, she pondered over Thomas' photo.

*He's handsome and rich, to be sure.*

*I don't like this Stefania. Who is this mysterious Britisher nobleman? I should like to meet him, or at least perhaps engage in surveillance personally.*

She knew in her business, being a stalker always helped.

*Yes, I must engage personally in surveillance of this Thomas Houghton.*

# Chapter 23



Thomas and Stefania arrived back at Haverford Hall late in the afternoon after a boisterous lunch with James and Catarina. Between the four of them, many cocktails, and three bottles of wine, plenty of jocularity went around. James and Catarina left directly from Norwich.

"I'm going to my room. I'd like to call my mama," Stefania said.

"That's fine. I'll be in my study," replied Thomas.

Thomas walked into his study to check his e-mails and attend to some business matters left over from the morning when he received a call on his mobile phone; it was Harry. Thomas promptly picked up the call.

"Thomas, the papers were tested; I have the results. I can provide a hard copy of the report when we meet next. I don't want to e-mail them to you."

"Right. What have you, Harry?"

"The paper in envelope 'A' dates from the early 1940s. The content indicates that it was manufactured on the continent, probably southern Europe, but given the war, probably in a neutral or nonaligned state, such as Spain or Portugal. It was a common paper, could have been note paper, readily available. It's not a copy. The paper in envelope 'B' dates from the late 1950s or early 1960s and clearly from southern Europe, probably Italy. Not particularly high quality but of the type used in the photocopying, teletypes, or mimeographs by governmental agencies or academia of the time. Based on chemical analysis, it's a copy made in the 1950s or early 1960s. Copying or printing chemicals are present on the paper. The paper in envelope 'C' dates from the late 1970s or early 1980s. It's the highest quality paper of the lot. It has a significant quantity of cotton fiber and would have been used only in the highest governmental or business circles. The expert opined it was likely the stationary of a high government or business official, of someone of substantial wealth or influence. Unlike the others, the small piece you provided contained a portion of a watermark, which would have indicated that it was manufactured, in all likelihood, in western Germany, Switzerland, or Austria, a German-speaking country. The expert indicated he wouldn't be surprised if the paper was embossed with a letterhead or a coat of arms, some such thing. The paper in envelope 'D' was an exact match to the paper in envelope 'C.' Does any of this make sense to you?"

"Great news. Let me put it this way, Harry. We were told that the first paper was from 1943, the second from 1958, and the third from 1978. We knew for sure that the fourth paper was from 1978 and the same source purportedly as the third. I think you confirmed what we were led to believe is true. The only thing is the second document we thought was from the UK, not Italy. That throws a wrench into the works. The first paper we have reason to believe was from Portugal, and the third was from Italy, but that doesn't mean it wasn't manufactured in another part of Europe. Let me pose a question to you, hypothetically, of course. Who in 1958 or thereabouts would be in possession of intercepted written MI6 intelligence reports from western Europe?"

"That's an easy answer; the Soviets or Warsaw Pact agents. Certainly, Western Europe was full of Soviet and eastern bloc spies, others, sympathizers for hire, or blackmail. The only question is whether they were double agents or not."

"That's logical, given Zerkorian's Soviet connection. If the Soviets, say again hypothetically in 1958, intercepted an MI6 intelligence report, how would it be, you know, distributed internally by them?"

"Well, the communication couldn't have been purloined wholesale as it would be missed. It would be either photographed or copied on location and the film or copy transmitted typically by the KGB resident back to Moscow via diplomatic pouch. Most times MI6 didn't know its intelligence had been compromised unless it was too late or they captured the agent. There were many agents who either died of natural causes or went back to Russia without the full extent of their deception ever being known by MI6. Plus, some intercepts weren't particularly earth-shattering, perhaps mundane, and even if MI6 knew they were compromised, they wouldn't tip the Soviets off by taking out the source because they knew they had a double agent in their midst."

"Let's say the Soviets intercepted an MI6 intelligence report in 1958 in Italy. Would it be likely to have been copied in Italy, on Italian paper, and sent back to Russia?"

"Certainly, yes, or photographed and then printed on the paper and sent back."

Thomas considered the matter for a few moments, resulting in a lengthy pause.

"Thomas, are you there?" Harry questioned with a bark.

"Yes, sorry; just thinking. Would the Soviets ever create a false MI6 intelligence report and leak it to third sources?"

"Maybe. It depends on the circumstances. Tough to say. Why all of these questions?"

"Let's say, again hypothetically, that the 1958 document purported to be a MI6 report, on Italian paper, but transmitted in 1978, so that means either it's a copy of the MI6 report made in Italy, or it's a false report, also created in Italy, correct?"

"True, but keep in mind that I doubt the Soviets, in creating a false report in 1978 back dated to 1958, would have been paying much attention to the paper used. I mean, it could be a coincidence or not. This technology is relatively new."

"I see. Let me put it this way. I have reason to believe that this 1958 document was in the possession of Zerkorian in 1978. If the document was false, why would he use the original copy from 1958?"

"He wouldn't. If it was meant to create a false impression, it would more likely than not have been created contemporaneously in 1978. I would say it's a safe bet that the 1958 document is genuine."

"Interesting notion. Based on what you've told me, I'd have to say I agree with your assessment."

Thomas again paused on the line as he considered the matter.

"Have you found the Sheikh?" asked Thomas.

"No. It's like he's fallen off the face of the earth, and my contacts at MI6 won't assist. My guess either they know and aren't saying, or they don't know and want to find out. Oh, and they know for sure you were the last person to see the Sheikh before he literally almost got blown up. MI6 may come calling."

"Hmm, about the Rome incident; anything additional turn up?" inquired Thomas.

"Another negative," responded Harry. "And by the way, I still haven't been able to identify the investigator hired by your grandmother, but it may be Nigel Houston, not a particularly savory character; a bastard really, and he's no plod. He's ex-MI5 and employs a crew, all ex-MI5.

His specialty is making deaths look accidental. Have you given thought to bodyguards?"

"I have," Thomas countered, "but I'm thinking it would draw more attention to us. Stefania and James' wife Catarina were on their way back to Haverford from Norwich and someone attempted to run them off the road. That car was then run off the road by another pursuer. Stefania and my driver John seem to think it was a row between the two cars. I'm not so sure. What do you think?"

"I think you ought to get a bloody bodyguard; maybe two would suffice. That's what I think, mate."

"I'll take it under advisement."

"So how are things with Stefania?"

"I, I don't really know. In a fit of insanity I told her I loved her."

"Well, what did she say?"

"She didn't, and hasn't said anything about it."

"Why did you say it, man? Bloody hell!"

"We were on the top of the knoll at Haverford. It was an incredible day. It seemed right. That's how I feel, or felt."

"I can't say whether you did right or wrong bloke," offered Harry. "My success with women is limited to paying for toms."

"Harry, I thank you for all of your assistance. I'd like to have the hard copy of the report from the paper expert. When can you get it to me?"

"I can come up tomorrow morning. This time I'll drive up to Haverford. As you know, I've got some business in Walsingham for you in the afternoon. I'll leave first thing, probably be there for luncheon if you'd oblige."

"Naturally, please do. We look forward to seeing you. Until tomorrow then."

Thomas hung up and reclined in his leather desk chair which creaked slightly as he did so.

"I really don't want to be alone with Stefania at this point. Granny would be at dinner at least," he said to no one in particular.

*I don't know what to do. I can't focus on anything but Stefania and my intense love for her. I won't confront her regarding the issue.*

*If granny presses me for information, I'll be evasive,* he concluded.

#

Stefania finally managed to reach her mother by phone.

"Mama, Thomas professed his love to me in the most amazing romantic way. I haven't responded. What should I do?"

"You love him, yes?" Fernanda responded.

"Yes, but my instincts tell me not to give in, true?"

"My darling, when love is involved, your instincts can lead you astray. I've been in at least one situation where I sincerely regret not expressing my affection for a man who loved me. His pride was offended, and I never heard from him again. I lost him."

"But how do you think I should respond to Thomas?" Stefania asked.

"Men are proud beings, especially those like Thomas. If you don't love him, you should be honest with him. If you love him, you should tell him, particularly since he obviously loves you. I must say I think he's a terrific catch, and he would make any woman happy. The question is whether he would make *you* happy. Based on my observations when you were here and the fact that you went through the entire initiation process for him, I would suggest to you that you concede your love. God has given us only one life upon this earth. It's best to make it as happy as one is able. Being happily in love is one of the delightful states of affairs I can ever imagine."

"Thank you, mama. Thank you so much."

"I'm so pleased you've found love, my child. My life has been improvised, and true love has eluded me."

"There's also the problem of the project I'm working on; it could have dire consequences for Thomas and his family. It weighs on my heart like lead."

"Since I don't know the specifics, all I can tell you is to follow your heart."

"Thank you, mama, for your help, but I have to decide how to address my feelings to Thomas. The time and circumstances have to be right."

"Don't wait too long, Stefania, my sweet daughter. Good luck, and I love you."

"Love you too, mama."

#

Arriving in the drawing room for pre-dinner cocktails before Thomas, Stefania deliberately dressed provocatively in a sleeveless skin tight above the knee red dress Catarina picked out while shopping.

The duchess, already there, cornered Stefania near the red cushioned sofa.

"Please do sit down."

"Thank you, duchess."

"My dear, you've been spending a lot of time with my grandson, and you must understand that I love him very much. What are your intentions?"

"What are my intentions?" Stefania yelped, shocked at the question.

"Yes, what are your intentions with regard to Thomas? How do you feel?"

"Duchess, I don't wish to be impolitic, but you're asking about my feelings, my intentions, which are my own and which I'm under no obligation to share. I would suggest you consult with your grandson as to his intentions. My views, my feelings, are for the benefit of myself. I have nothing else to say on the matter."

The duchess' face evinced distress at the impertinence of Stefania.

"This conversation has concluded, but you haven't heard the last from me," the duchess blurted. "Blasted upstart!"

#

Arriving before dinner, Thomas noticed the lack of discussion in the drawing room. While eating dinner, after several glasses of wine and some small talk about their time with James and Catarina, the duchess launched again.

"I know you were in Birmingham in connection with this project of hers. What did you uncover?"

"We went to Saint Chad's for the pilgrimage to the Birmingham Oratory for Saint John Henry Newman, nothing more," Thomas replied.

"You lie to me, Thomas? Blatant recalcitrance; this is not the end of the matter as far as I'm concerned. This row is not resolved."

The duchess threw her napkin down onto her chair, left before she finished dinner, and went presumably to her room.

Retiring back to the drawing room where a small fire warmed the elaborate white marble hearth, Stefania sat next to Thomas on the red cushioned sofa facing the fire, drinking *vino sancti*. Connie lay in front of the hearth with just the flickering flames providing an orange glow in the otherwise dark room. The late spring sun had set on the dells, and darkness had enveloped Haverford Hall like a blanket.

"Haverford Hall is a fantastical place, but you must know that," Stefania noted.

"I'm aware, but it pleases me very much that it's grown on you," replied Thomas with a smile. "I've heard from Harry regarding the document test."

"Great. So what were the results?"

"All the pieces fit, except the only hitch was the second document, which we thought was from the UK. It's likely a contemporaneous copy made in 1958 of an original. So that means if that document was given by Zerkorian to the pope in 1978, it's genuine. If Zerkorian was a Soviet or Bulgarian agent, it's probably an original copy from 1958 of a Soviet intercept of a MI6 communication. There would be no reason for Zerkorian to provide a false document from 1978 on pedestrian paper from 1958 when the science to date the paper hadn't been invented yet, at least not to pinpoint the date of manufacture as precisely as we can today. Harry will be driving up for luncheon tomorrow with the written report from the paper expert."

Stefania placed her wine down on the end table, turned to Thomas.

"So that means that what we have is actually the missing portion of the third secret of Fatima, a copy of an original MI6 communiqué from 1958 indicating that Cardinal Siri had been elected pope, and an original letter from the pope himself creating Gonzalvo a cardinal *in pectore*. We've already concluded that the pope's signature is genuine."

"Yes, I think that more or less precisely sums it up. The question, of course, is whether Siri had actually been elected pope. It certainly appears that Zerkorian and the Camerlengo used the MI6 document and the Fatima prophecy to influence the pope to either resign or commit suicide. The MI6 report could still be a fraud, maybe to feed the Soviets false information, but I should think that wouldn't be the case. Why would MI6 want the Soviets to think that Siri was elected pope? The report is dated the second day of the 1958 conclave. Surely the Soviets would know the answer as to who was elected pope in a day or two. Did MI6 want to give the Soviets heartburn for a couple of days? I suppose so, but can't imagine it—"

Interrupting, Stefania bristled.

"I'm sorry. I think all of the pieces do fit perfectly. The narrative is that persons within the Vatican, perhaps a cabal, certainly the Camerlengo was involved, devised a sinister plot to stop the pope from rolling back the reforms of Vatican Two. The church had held back a portion of the third secret of Fatima for obvious reasons."

"I agree that the pope had to be aware of the prophecies of Fatima, Saint Malachy, and he didn't fit in anywhere," Thomas interjected.

"Yes, and the MI6 communiqué was the last straw," continued Stefania. "The pope summoned Siri for a meeting. Siri either refused to answer questions based on the secrecy of the conclave or actually confirmed he had been elected. The pope was left holding an empty bag. All of the evidence supported the proposition that he wasn't the pope, illegitimate, or at least there was a competing papacy. Perhaps it was too much for him to bear. To resign conceding there was a second papacy since 1958 would convulse a great scandal. If the cabal's objective was to have the pope commit suicide, it succeeded."

"But was, in fact, Siri elected pope? I don't know how we answer that question. If the MI6 document came from Zerkorian, who was an eastern bloc agent, we can assume the source was likely the Soviets. They might know the answer, or MI6, if there are any files around from almost sixty years ago. Of course, the likelihood of obtaining that information is infinitesimal."

"What difference does any of that make? The key was creating the perception that the pope was illegitimate. As an aside, Nostradamus' prophecy also supports the theory that the Pope was killed deliberately, which supports my version of events!"

"I suppose that's a sensible interpretation." Thomas paused. "I agree that the pope would have had to know about the prophesies of Saint Malachy and Fatima. But there's another thing that continues to weigh on my mind, an enigma which has been burdening me for some time. What exactly did the Sheikh say when we met him?"

Picking up his phone, Thomas scrolled through his notes.

"Something about when you find out someone who isn't who he said he was 'you'll find the answer in the palm of your hand.' Now what the bloody hell does that mean?"

Stefania focused on what Thomas said.

"Well, what do you hold in the palm of your hand? What do you hold in the palm of your hand?" she repeated.

Stefania looked at Thomas holding his phone scrolling through his notes.

"Your phone. You hold your phone in the palm of your hand," she said.

"True, true, but what on my phone? Well, my phone has little information regarding what we did other than the meeting with the Sheikh I attended. What about your phone? You were at the archives. A lot of your notes are on your phone. Is there anything on your phone?"

Taking her phone out, Stefania sat next to Thomas on the sofa and scrolled through her notes which she had transcribed electronically from her written notes. They had reviewed most of this before meetings between the pope, the Sheikh, Bishop Gonzalvo, the Camerlengo, and Cardinal Siri.

"It's all the same material."

Stefania paused.

"Oh Madonna, there is one thing I completely forgot."

She began scrolling through her photographs and found it.

"I thought this document was innocuous, but given what we've found since, it may be relevant."

Stefania showed it to Thomas.

"What is this?" Thomas asked, looking at her phone. "It's in church Latin. You can read Latin much better than I. It's small type on the phone and difficult to read. E-mail it to me and we'll look at a blow-up on my laptop."

Stefania e-mailed the photo to Thomas.

"When I was at the archives the first time, my time was almost up so I took a photo of the document, but I didn't think it was pertinent since it dated from well before the pope's papacy in 1978 and seemed to be about a meeting of cardinals," she explained.

"Let's have a look," said Thomas.

Stefania pulled up a chair, and they sat side by side looking at his computer screen. Logging onto his laptop, Thomas downloaded and enlarged the photograph, then switched seats with Stefania.

"Well, what does it say?" he inquired, looking over her shoulder.

Stefania began reading the document and immediately became dumbstruck, more so than when she read the documents they recovered from Gonzalvo's room. She turned to Thomas.

"This was no ordinary meeting," she said in a solemn and serious tone. "This document is a request directed to certain cardinals to attend a *conclave*."

"Right. Well, which conclave, 1958, 1963, or 1978?"

"This document is a request by the Camerlengo to attend a conclave in the Sistine Chapel commencing on November 27, 1970."

Thomas scratched his head.

"What? That makes no sense, no sense at all. There was no conclave in 1970."

"According to this document, the conclave was called due to creation of a *sede vacante* as a result of the resignation of Pope Gregory XVII. The conclave was called by the then Camerlengo, who was the Archbishop of Erongo."

"Oh my God. Do you think the document is genuine?" Thomas asked.

"Let me put it this way. It was with the documents from 1978 which were produced in error by the Vatican archives. We have to assume it's genuine."

"Let me search the pastoral visits of Pope Paul VI in 1970."

Thomas leaned over and pecked the laptop keyboard.

"Hmm, on November 27, 1970 Paul VI was in Iran. He then visited a number of countries, culminating in Ceylon on December 5th. He wasn't in Vatican City from November 26 through December 5, 1970. Does the document list the cardinals?"

"Yes," responded Stefania.

"Please get your laptop," he ordered.

Complying, Stefania returned a few minutes later.

"Give me your laptop and read to me the name of each cardinal identified."

Stefania read each name one by one; there were twenty-one of them. As she did so, Thomas searched each one on the internet.

"As far as I can tell, the names on the list were cardinals who were created prior to 1958 by Pius XII who were still alive in 1970. None of these cardinals were created by John XXIII, Paul VI, or by anyone else for that matter. All of these people are long dead. Interestingly, Siri is not among the names of the cardinals invited, so that means he was likely Gregory XVII. The Archbishop who signed this is long dead. Are there any other names mentioned?"

Stefania, examining the document, scrolled down to the bottom.

"It references the vice-Camerlengo who witnessed the document."

"Well, who is it? What's his name?"

"I actually know this man! This is the man who gave me the initiation sacraments in Rio. It says here Monsignor Henriques Metz. He's now the Archbishop of Minas Gerais and a cardinal. My Uncle Mateus is friends with him."

Getting up, Thomas began pacing back and forth in his study.

"All of this is so farfetched as to be unfathomable, insane. I must be going mad. If all this is true, there were two lines of the papacy. The split probably happened in 1958."

"If that's the case," replied Stefania, "does it still exist, and if so, which cardinals and bishops are aligned with which pope? Who is the real pope? My God, we have to speak with Cardinal Metz!"

Stefania quickly printed a copy of the photo of the document.

"Do you think the pope was made aware of this before his death in 1978?"

"Hard to say," answered Thomas. "I'll text Emma to have the jet ready for tomorrow afternoon to fly to Rio. We'll leave for Brazil tomorrow after we meet with Harry. Do you want to see if we can stay with your uncle and if he can get us an audience with Cardinal Metz? You can tell him that I'd like to meet him in connection with a potential contribution to the Brazilian church or something of that nature. Offers of cash always get one an audience."

"I'm phoning Uncle Mateus and Aunt Maricel now. I'm sure it won't be a problem staying there. The problem may be getting to see Metz."

Stefania put the call on speaker.

"Hello," Mateus answered.

"Yes, Uncle Mateus," said Stefania.

"My dear niece, nice to hear from you," Mateus replied.

"Yes, Thomas needs to meet with Archbishop Metz to discuss some church matters, maybe a contribution to the Brazilian church due to his assistance on my confirmation. Do you think you could arrange an audience as soon as possible?"

"I'll phone him right now and get back to you. You know I'm always glad to assist you, my dear. You're welcomed to stay with us if you return to Brazil."

"Thanks, uncle. I'll wait to hear back from you. Love you. Goodbye."

"If we're able to confirm with Metz the document that you saw at the archives is legitimate," noted Thomas, "perhaps Metz would elaborate and fill in the details. That's a big 'if;' it all depends on Metz's cooperation. I've been anxious about this whole project. This new discovery has turned everything sideways. The fear of the unknown or what has yet to come."

"Agreed," Stefania responded in Italian, "and I too am nervous about what we may find out from Metz."

"It sounds more dramatic in Italian," Thomas remarked with a smile.

Walking Stefania up to her room, Thomas hugged her briefly as they shared a long kiss outside her door.

"Until tomorrow, my love," Thomas whispered into her ear in Italian.

Smiling, Stefania took a little tug of Thomas's earlobe.

"Yes, until tomorrow," she whispered in Italian, her lips touching his ear.

# Chapter 24
*Rublyovka, Russia, June 13*

Svetlana's mobile phone rang; the time, 0203, and the caller ID, "Lenov."

Formerly sound asleep, now groggy in her apartment Greschenko answered the call. A head with long braded blonde hair and blue eyes peaked out from under the comforter next to her and then hit the pillow again.

"Our subject is on the move again, back to Brazil. He leaves this afternoon," Lenov blurted.

Wearing only a pink tank top and matching pink briefs, Greschenko sat up in bed thinking for a moment.

"Please have your agents and the GRU attaché prepared to meet me at the consulate in Leblon tomorrow after I land. I'll ask to have my plane ready to go in an hour. I'd like to see what's going on with my own eyes. Let Stasevich know what's happening. I'll provide details once I land."

"I disagree with you going to Brazil, but I assume I can't dissuade you," Lenov insisted.

"No, I'm going to Brazil; you'll hear from me when I get there."

"Understood," he responded, hanging up.

Greschenko scrolled through her contacts and phoned Anatoly.

"Have my jet readied for a flight to Rio to leave as soon as possible. I'll drive to Kubinka myself, no time for the car. Meet me there. Alert the consulate in Leblon that I'll be there later today and have a room at my usual hotel reserved," she ordered and hung up.

She bent over and kissed her liaison on the lips.

"You can let yourself out in the morning," she directed the blonde in her bed.

A high pitched "yes" was heard and a rustling of sheets.

The couple sat in the leather seats of the Falcon 8X on the taxiway at Norwich airport, waiting for takeoff clearance.

Stefania's phone rang, the caller ID, Uncle Mateus. Stefania put the call on the speaker.

"I've made contact with Metz, but he isn't in Rio. Cardinal Metz is at the *Basilica Nossa Senhora do Pilar* in Ouro Preto in Minas Gerais, where he is to say mass on Sunday. The cardinal would be willing to meet with you and Thomas in Minas Gerais; otherwise, you'll have to wait until he returns to Rio the following Tuesday or—"

"We can't wait until Tuesday next," Thomas said, interrupting. "My recollection is that Minas Gerais is a little farther in the air than Rio, and we'll fly there directly rather than drive from Rio. I'll inform the pilot. We should have sufficient fuel for the trip. What's the closest airport to Ouro Preto?"

"The closest major airport is at Tancredo Neves," replied Mateus, "and if you're looking for a place to stay in that area, the best hotels are in Belo Horizonte. Obviously, you can fly back to Rio and stay with us."

"Thank you, Mateus. We'll see you in Brazil at some point. Please inform the cardinal we'll see him tomorrow in Ouro Preto."

"Yes, looking forward to seeing you both."

After putting his seat belt on, Thomas fiddled with his phone and briefed Stefania.

"I've texted Emma to book us a car rental at the airport at Tancredo Neves. From the airport you'll have to drive us to Ouro Preto. Hopefully we won't need to stay the night, and we can fly back to Rio and stay with your aunt and uncle."

The jet's engines roared. It began its takeoff roll. Stefania, sitting next to Thomas, held his hand tightly. The plane reached take-off velocity quickly and flew aloft into the sullen overcast Norfolk sky. The jet bounced up and down as it cleared the low clouds breaking through to the few remaining wisps of sunlight above. Stefania and Thomas settled next to each other for their long flight. The setting sun shone through the porthole from the west onto Stefania's face.

Stefania, with her hair in a ponytail, wore black yoga pants and a spandex sports top. While she dressed for comfort for the flight, her outfit left little to the imagination, and she knew it.

Stefania wanted to wait for the right moment, but she worried that with every minute that went by the risk of her losing Thomas increased. Thomas impulsively kissed her on the lips; they kissed intensely for several minutes.

Stefania, breaking off the embrace, gazed into Thomas' piercing blue eyes, holding his hands in hers.

"I wanted the time to be right, but this is about as right as it gets. I don't want to wait any longer. Thomas, I love you with all of my heart. You caught me by surprise the other day, but these past few weeks...I can't fathom being without you. I care for you so much. Your love has filled a hole in my heart."

Thomas looked back into Stefania's eyes.

"You, dearest," Thomas whispered, "have made me the happiest man alive. You're the love of my life."

Their lips met again. Stefania threw her legs over Thomas'. The couple then embraced as the plane gained altitude and sliced through the thin cold air high above the clouds. Both, tangled together like a spider's web, faded to drowsiness and ultimately a sleepy flight. Relieved for that moment anyway, there were only good thoughts for the night ahead.

*40,000 feet above the Atlantic Ocean, June 13*

Sipping a tumbler of vodka on ice, other than the flight attendants and her assistant Anatoly, Greschenko sat alone in her government jet as it hurled toward Rio, 40,000 feet above the Atlantic Ocean about 1,500 nautical miles southwest of Thomas' plane. Passing the time, Greschenko re-read Thomas and Stefania's electronic files on her encrypted tablet.

The more she read about Thomas, the more intrigued she became.

*What is he like? What is it like to be the girlfriend of a British duke? Why is he so religious? Why is he attracted to this ne'er-do-well?*

The more she learned about Thomas, the more she envied Stefania.

*I despise this Stefania; he's too good for her.*

*This duke is an honest and religious man, perhaps one of the few men who could be trusted in a relationship*, she mused.

The vodka having its desired effect, Greschenko's eyelids weakened and finally closed. She slowly drifted into a light sleep.

# Chapter 25
*Minas Gerais, Brazil, June 14*

Thomas and Stefania landed at Tancredo Neves and set out by rental car to Ouro Preto for their visit to the archbishop.

"As I recall there are several interesting churches in Ouro Preto. The *Basilica Nossa Senhora do Pilar* is arguably the finest baroque church in the region, its altar meticulously adorned with gold leaf, the ceiling of its nave decorated with paintings and frescoes," Thomas explained to Stefania. "Despite our meeting with the archbishop, I'm frankly excited to visit the place, as I've heard anecdotally much of the area's natural beauty."

"You always have a history or geography lesson," quipped Stefania. "It's known as one of the loveliest areas in Brazil. I've never been there but always wanted to go."

"Do you think it will be safe?" Thomas asked.

"As long as you're with a local like me," Stefania replied confidently.

"We've already seen you can defend yourself rather well," Thomas quipped.

On their way to Oura Preto Stefania drove through the thick green forests of the Serra do Gandarela National Park, confirming Stefania's accounts of the natural beauty of the area. The bright Brazilian sunshine provided a pleasant diversion from the dreary day they had left behind.

During the drive, Stefania thought long and hard about how to address the archbishop when they finally met.

"Thomas, if you wouldn't mind, let me be the lead with the cardinal," she quipped. "As a Brazilian woman, I may be able to have better luck getting him to talk. I have a plan in any event. I think you'll know when to jump in."

"Right," Thomas agreed, nodding. "With pleasure love, I look forward to seeing you work your magic, although my guess is I'm only going to catch bits and pieces due to my rather subpar Portuguese."

Upon reaching Ouro Preto, Thomas observed in amazement, "This is much like a small city in Portugal or Spain," pointing with his finger. "Look, most of the buildings are stucco, either white-washed or painted in bright colors, with marble, sandstone, or brightly painted surrounds, and the windows are covered with ornate shutters and the roofs tiled. All of the roads are cobbled or brick, like one would see maybe in a small village in the Pyrenees. How absolutely wonderful!"

Palm trees and flowering vines dotted the landscape. Many windows along the streets had elaborate railings, flower boxes, and balconies. The narrow side streets offered little available parking. Fortunately Stefania, excellent at parallel parking, particularly on the narrow and hilly cobbled side streets of Ouro Preto, found a spot.

"The air here smells sickly sweet, like honey," observed Stefania. "Must be all of the flowering vines."

After Stefania parked the car, the two headed up a hilly narrow cobbled street to the basilica. They arrived at two huge bronze doors with a green patina from exposure to the elements over the years. The sand-colored church stood on a small square with its two bell towers looming over the small shops and homes lining the narrow streets beyond.

The opulence of the church didn't disappoint.

"Who would have thought we'd find such spectacular but intimate artwork of this small church in this obscure town in interior Brazil," Stefania noted.

"This rivals anything I've seen in Europe," Thomas observed.

The two stood in the middle of the church's apse, taking in the sublime breath of the place. They took little notice of several old women praying the rosary, a couple of tourists milling about in the side chapels and lighting votive candles which flickered in the dim light of the interior. Stefania lost track of time, and after about twenty minutes of wandering throughout the church realized they had best find the archbishop.

As in many churches, a thin little old man who seemed to be a caretaker sat behind a desk next to the door.

"Sir, where may we find the cardinal?" Stefania politely inquired.

"The archbishop is either in the vestry or at the rectory," the old man indicated. "I'll check. Whom should I say is calling?"

"Stefania DiMaggio. He's expecting me and my friend Thomas."

A few minutes later the man reappeared.

"Go to the house next door. The archbishop will receive you there," he said.

They walked outside in the bright tropical sun, turned the corner, and went to the door of a street-side home a few steps from the small basilica. After ringing the bell, they were met by a short older chunky woman wearing a floral pattern apron who looked like a housekeeper. After taking their names, she invited them in, where they waited in a small parlor decorated in traditional country Brazilian style, with light wood paneling, dark wood floor and furnishings, and wood-beamed ceiling.

The cardinal entered a few minutes later. He wore a white cassock with scarlet piping and buttons.

"Ah, Stefania, I thought I might see you again but not so soon," he said in Portuguese. "It's wonderful you visit. And your grace, it's a pleasure to make your acquaintance. Your reputation, and your family's reputation for its contribution to the church and to the faith, is certainly well known. I'm hesitant to hazard a guess as to why you wanted to visit with me here in the Brazilian interior, *pre cana* perhaps? Planning on tying the knot?" he asked with a friendly chuckle.

Stefania blushed at the reference. Obviously the cardinal had no idea why Thomas and Stefania wanted an audience.

"Thank you, your eminence. No *pre cana* yet, although maybe at some point, but the matter we've come to see you about is quite delicate."

The cardinal, looking slightly confused, still smiled.

"I can't imagine what that could be, but I'm happy to assist in any way. Certainly I'm grateful to your uncle for all his assistance and I'd be hard pressed to deny the duke my ear. Let's all sit. Would you like something to drink?"

"No, thank you," replied Stefania.

Removing from her bag the printed invitation to the conclave in 1970, Stefania handed it to the cardinal.

"We wanted to discuss this with you."

He pushed his reading glasses to the bottom of his nose. Immediately the color drained from his face, leaving it ashen.

"May I ask where did you get this?" he asked in a serious and much more hushed tone, his face now expressionless.

"The source of the document is immaterial," responded Stefania, "except that I obtained it from a reputable source, and we have no reason to belief it's not genuine. Your eminence, that *is* your signature, isn't it? It matches your signatures on my initiation documents from Rio."

The old cardinal, obviously now emotionally distraught and caught by surprise, didn't respond. Silence permeated the room. He continued staring at the document, his hands shaking with a slight tremor of age. Beads of perspiration formed on his forehead. The cardinal remained dumbstruck.

Stefania pulled out a copy of the MI6 communiqué from 1958 and handed it to the cardinal.

"Here's something else. Can you shed any light on this?"

The cardinal eagerly took the new document as if it offered some respite from Stefania's first request. He placed the first document on his lap. The second document clearly caused the old man even more consternation. His breathing became labored and quickened. Stefania knew he could read and write English.

"My God," he blurted. His trembling hands lowered the document and placed it on top of the first. "So you know; so you know everything."

The old cardinal, now nervous and stunned, couldn't match Stefania's wily wits. Intending to bluff her way to the truth, Stefania played the bad cop, while Thomas, the ever polite English gentleman, observed; a carefully choreographed "good cop" and "bad cop" routine.

"Yes, we know. Siri was elected in 1958. He resigned in 1970, and a conclave was held. There were two separate lines of the papacy. A pope and an anti-pope. The 'Siri Thesis' is fact, not fiction."

The old man rubbed his cheeks in exasperation.

"It was assumed this would never come to light. After 1970 when Pope Gregory, I mean Siri, resigned and the conclave elected Paul VI pope, it was thought that would right the wrong. After the 1970 conclave, the papacy was joined again. Most of those involved died, but they kept their secrets. Only those at the 1958 Conclave knew of the split. All documents were to be destroyed, except these, I guess, which were not. I've never seen this English document. All of Siri's fifteen cardinals were confirmed by Paul VI at the March 1973 consistory, solving that problem."

Stefania quickly processed this new information.

"So what you're saying is that other than those at the 1958 conclave, none of the other cardinals knew of the split?"

"There were Siri's fifteen cardinals, but assuming everyone kept their word, and I have no reason to believe otherwise, I can't imagine that any of the other cardinals knew. This is the first time the matter has been raised to me since 1970."

"What about the pope? He was made cardinal in 1973. Was he one of Siri's cardinals?"

"No. He was conservative, but he would never have tolerated a split in the papacy. He couldn't know. In fact, if he knew, I would have been aware. There were fifteen others; they've all gone to heaven, bless them. They were made cardinals by Paul VI so that, after the excommunications, they all were brought back to the fold and all the bishops consecrated by them, and all the priests ordained by the bishops would be legitimate. In full communion, the excommunications were lifted. This is why the next two popes would be conservatives. The only problem, of course, were the sacramental acts performed by the cardinals, bishops, and priests when they were excommunicates. Those issues were never resolved before Paul VI died. He became irrational in his later years."

*I've learned a lot through my time on this project but now I need assistance.*

She winked at Thomas.

Thomas jumped in, as if on cue. "Your Eminence, excuse me, you and Stefania have your facts straight, but I'm having trouble following as my Portuguese is not that fluent. So John excommunicated Siri after his election?" he asked.

"There were mutual excommunications," the cardinal answered, now in English. "After Siri was elected, there was a revolt, mostly by the French, Belgian, Dutch, German cardinals, and liberal Italians in the *curia*. As I understand it, they refused to accept Siri's election. They claimed their lives and the lives of their families were in danger, that there would be repression in the Soviet bloc against Catholics. They would be blackmailed due to sex and other scandals."

"Well, did Siri not accept the papacy?" Thomas inquired.

Metz's voice crackled and he coughed, quickly pouring himself a glass of water from a nearby pitcher.

"After a significant period of argument they kept on voting, although Siri never resigned nor renounced the papacy. John was ultimately elected," he explained. "When Siri and his remaining supporters refused to recognize John, John excommunicated them and anyone who was affiliated with them. Siri then excommunicated John and the cardinals who voted for John, which included some who voted for Siri the first time. None of this was ever made public due to the sanctity of the conclave and the fact that John knew that, under canon law, Siri was properly elected, hadn't renounced the papacy, and had chosen his regnal name."

"So they both acted as pope?" asked Stefania.

"Although there were mutual excommunications, both sides acted like nothing had happened. Siri went back to Genoa as archbishop but otherwise acted if he had papal authority. Both John and Gregory created bishops and ordained priests. Neither recognized by the other side. Most of the priests and bishops who were ordained or created by Siri had no idea; the cardinals did, though. The canonical status of the consecrations and ordinations was solved by the lifting of the mutual excommunications at the time of the 1970 conclave, but the issue was to whether the sacraments and actions of these men while they were excommunicates was never resolved. So thousands, perhaps millions of marriages, last rites, baptisms, vocations, confirmations, confessions, initiations between 1958 and 1970 were all called into question, regardless as to whether you believe Gregory or John was pope. This would include the funeral rites of the United States President in 1963. Due to the schism, the Second Vatican Council which concluded in 1965 and was finally implemented in 1969, was of dubious efficacy. To make sure that the 1970 conclave was legitimate under canon law, only those cardinals created prior to the 1958 conclave participated."

"Unbelievable. The sedevacantists were right all along," blurted Thomas.

"But they didn't know," commented Metz. "If the sedevacantists got word of what had actually happened, as many of them surmised but had no proof, it would have gone public and therefore created a public schism in the church, as there was, and still is, a significant sedevacantist movement. It was agreed that the conclave would occur while Paul was on a prolonged trip. Pursuant to the Apostolic Constitution and canon law, the conclave had to take place in the Sistine Chapel. That was the only way to effectuate a legitimate papal election. Paul VI wasn't a cardinal in 1958 so he couldn't participate anyway."

"But what about the 1963 Conclave?" he asked.

"Gregory hadn't made any cardinals yet, but he and his supporters attended, and they all voted for Siri, claiming he was the rightful pope, not recognizing any of the cardinals made by John XXIII. Naturally, Siri lost due to the fact that John created cardinals who attended the conclave, including Paul VI, who became pope."

"Why was there this schism?" Thomas queried.

"You don't understand. They wanted to, and did, remove the cope, our vestments, made the priests wear sheets like druids. Churches were sanitized. They replaced the high altar with a table. They destroyed the magisterium, the mysticism of the church. The mass in Latin was enchanting, and they replaced it with boredom. They took away our feast days, Saint Christopher, Our Lady of Sorrows, all went by the wayside. What came after was liberation theology, and the dictatorship of relativism in the church. Many were upset; many didn't want change. Siri wanted a compromise. The mass would be offered both in Latin and in the vernacular. The vestments, the liturgical calendar would remain."

"Why wasn't there any objection, any push-back to these changes if they were so controversial?" asked Thomas.

"John was obstinate and cruel. He threatened anyone who objected with excommunication. And I suspect there were cardinals who had secrets, who could be blackmailed, and John knew this. Those who opposed stood with Gregory to the point the new mass was inevitable, when there was no choice and it made no difference. Even today every time there's a Latin Rite mass with the priests dressed as priests, not as druids, the crowds pour in. The new mass destroyed the church, vocations and baptisms plummeted, church attendance in Europe and North America went down precipitously, then there were the sex scandals, so many. Vocations dropped, so they took anyone into the priesthood, including apparently many degenerates, and then they covered for their sins. That's the legacy of Vatican Two."

"What happened to the ballots from the 1970 conclave?" Thomas asked.

"I kept them. We couldn't burn them in the Sistine Chapel; there was no stove. I took the ballots attached to the string, stuffed them into my bag, and brought them back to Brazil. There was only one vote, and we all knew what the result would be."

The cardinal placed his head in his hands, looking down.

"You understand the information and documents you have at your disposal will upend the Catholic world," he said. "It will be a great convulsion. Thousands of marriages, baptisms, funerals would be placed in doubt. It might create another schism. The sedevacantists would finally succeed in splitting the church."

Like a huge weight had been thrust again upon his shoulders, the cardinal seemed inconsolable.

"Go. You must leave," he directed, pointing to the door while staring down at the wooden plank floor. "Please go."

They left him sitting alone in the room with his head in his hands, tears running down his cheeks.

Thomas and Stefania quietly left, walking to a small park-like space to the left of the basilica, where they found a bench under a tree and sat down to talk.

Stefania, exasperated, took a deep breath.

"Of course the cardinal didn't know that there was more," she noted. "The pope committed suicide in 1978 because he didn't think he was the true pope, but in fact, due to the 1970 conclave, he was, in fact, the true pope. He committed suicide under a false illusion."

"Incredible indeed," whispered Thomas. "This whole thing is an insane story, bordering on the bizarre. You've uncovered perhaps the greatest story out of the twentieth century. It's almost unbelievable; it's fantastic. We should fly back to Rio today rather than stay the night in Belo Horizonte, visit with your family for appearances sake, then get back to Rome. It would be nice to obtain the ballots, but I don't think that's an option at this point."

"Yes, we'll stay the night in Leblon with my aunt and uncle and be off tomorrow morning to Rome."

The two stood and walked hand in hand toward their car under the wonderful warm Brazilian sun.

*Leblon, Brazil, June 14*

In a wood-paneled conference room on the third floor of the Russian Consulate, Greschenko sat waiting for Directorate S's agents to drive her to the surveillance location of Stefania and Thomas.

Greschenko stood with both her hands on the granite conference table.

"What do you mean, you've lost them?" she screamed at the speaker phone to the agents of Directorate S on the other end.

She rarely lost her composure, but she had.

"How do you lose an airplane? Did they fly to Brazil? Are they in the Atlantic Ocean?"

"The Britisher didn't follow his flight plan," she was told. "We're working with the Brazilian Air Force to find out where they landed."

"Well, find them, and don't call back until you've done so. I want to know precisely where they are, even if it's at the bottom of the sea!"

She pressed the red button on the speaker phone ending the call.

Not in control, something Greschenko despised, she stepped out onto the balcony with the tropical breeze blowing the white curtains about. Toward the palm-shaded white sandy beaches of Ipanema, speaking to Vasily Karpov as if he were there, she whispered, "If they died accidentally, that solves all of our problems, my dear Vasily."

Pausing for a moment, biting her lower lip, she continued, "But in such a case I shall never meet this incredible Britisher duke."

#

Arriving at Mateus and Maricel's home in Leblon in time for a late dinner, Stefania and Thomas pulled through the gate in their rental car and unloaded their luggage under cover of dusk for a one night stay. From the terrace Thomas glanced down the street. A couple of occupied cars sat across from Mateus' residence.

*Who is after us wouldn't know we were in Brazil, and I can't imagine they'd follow us all the way here. Plus, Mateus has security guards,* Thomas assured himself.

After dinner the group enjoyed drink and conversation by the pool and settled in for the night.

#

Sitting up in bed in her hotel room, Greschenko perused Thomas's file on her encrypted tablet.

Her mobile phone rang.

"The Britisher and the girl turned up at her uncle's home in Leblon," the voice on the other end blurted.

"Pick me up in front of the hotel in five minutes," Greschenko barked back.

Clambering out of bed wearing nothing but a silk nightshirt, Greschenko threw on yoga pants, a gray tank top, a black hoodie, and black knee high boots. She grabbed her bag and took the elevator to the lobby. Outside, a car waited.

*I must now attend to the task at hand, to locate, observe, follow, and if necessary, protect the duke and his girlfriend, at least until the president orders a sanction.*

Left off at the SVR agent's car on the street close to the gate to Mateus' home, shortly thereafter Greschenko curiously observed through the rear view mirror the arrival of an additional car parked ten meters behind hers. Bathed in a cloak of darkness the narrow street was silent, except for the occasional feral cat walking across or a dog barking in the distance. All the lights in Mateus' house were now dark.

*Leblon, Brazil, June 15*

At first light Thomas awoke early by excited talking and raised voices. He stumbled out of his room to determine the cause of the ruckus, where he met Stefania in the hallway. They followed the voices to the sitting room.

"He's dead, he's dead," Mateus, still in his red silk bathrobe, yelled, flailing his arms in the air as he paced back and forth in front of the sitting room television, a large flat screen. Maricel stood in her matching silk red bathrobe sobbing.

"Who's dead?" asked Stefania, still in pink sports shorts and a matching tank top she had slept in.

"The archbishop, the cardinal! Metz!" Mateus shouted excitedly.

"There must be some mistake," declared Thomas, wearing his white robe.

"No, see?" Mateus insisted, pointing to the television.

The four stood, watching the news report for a few moments.

Stefania translated the news report from Portuguese for Thomas.

"She's saying sometime the previous night the cardinal, clothed in his full choir dress, climbed to the top of one of the bell towers of the basilica *Nossa Senhora do Pilar* and jumped to his death with his pastoral staff in hand. His lifeless body, his right hand still clutching his staff, lay on the cobbled square below through the morning hours when he was found in a pool of blood by some pilgrims, his miter lying on the ground a few feet away."

"My God, it sounds like he committed suicide!" Maricel exclaimed.

Thomas turned to Stefania.

"Or he was pushed," he whispered.

"When did you leave him?" Mateus asked excitedly.

"In the afternoon," Stefania responded. "We drove back to Belo Horizonte, flew out in late afternoon. He was alone when we left him. He seemed fine."

Mateus switched channels back and forth. All of the channels were carrying the same story.

"In most countries the peculiar death of a Catholic prelate wouldn't attract much attention," Thomas softly said to Stefania. "In the states or UK it wouldn't even make the evening news or the front page of a news website, but it must be because Brazil is a predominantly and devout Catholic country this is *big* news."

"Oh Madonna! What should we do?" Stefania whispered back.

"Dearest, go back to your room, collect your things as quickly as possible. Let's plan to leave here within the half-hour. I'll notify the pilots we'll be flying out within the hour. If the authorities find out we met with Metz yesterday, we will be questioned, possibly detained."

Stefania, nodding in agreement, kissed Thomas on the cheek and went to her room.

In less than thirty minutes the couple gave some quick goodbyes, hugs, and kisses and took their luggage down to their white Ford Fiesta rental.

"I'll load the boot. Please hit the switch to open the gate," Thomas directed Stefania.

Stefania walked over the wall next to the gate and bent over, pressing the automatic gate switch. In doing so a round compact from her makeup kit fell out of her shoulder bag and rolled down the driveway by the now open gate onto the sidewalk.

Stefania ran down to retrieve it.

A black hatchback sped from down the street up onto the sidewalk toward her.

Rushing down the driveway to the street, Thomas yelled, "Stefania, Stefania!"

Now both on the sidewalk in the crosshairs of the oncoming car, a white four door sedan, screeching as it accelerated, pulled across the street into the path of the black hatchback, forcing it against a wall with a crash.

Steam from the hatchback's radiator escaped into the air with a hiss and glass from its headlights littered the sidewalk. The hatchback now sat there, wedged against the wall to Mateus's compound. The car's masked driver frantically attempted to get out of the car, but the front door seemed jammed.

"Quick, let's get the hell out of here," Thomas shouted to Stefania.

Jumping into their Fiesta, Thomas and Stefania headed out in the other direction. As they careened past the opened gate out of the driveway, Thomas, sitting in the passenger's seat, stared back at the female passenger in the white car which saved them. Looking back, he saw the woman and man in a dark coat get out of their car. Thomas made eye contact with her, a fortyish attractive brunette in black yoga pants and a black hoodie. She held a silencer-equipped pistol, raised it, and pumped two bullets into the head of the man at the wheel of the hatchback who attempted to run them down.

"They dispatched the driver! They bloody knocked him off," Thomas exclaimed. "Make haste to the airport. Don't worry about dropping off the rental!"


#


*41,000 feet above the Atlantic Ocean, June 15*


"The death of the cardinal and subsequent obvious attempt on our lives means we're in real danger," Thomas concluded. "The only reason anyone would want to harm us has to do with the story and its implications. Also, there's the interference of the woman who saved our lives. I can't imagine who that was."

"Maybe you have a guardian angel," Stefania suggested to Thomas, although, as a woman, she harbored a subconscious jealousy that a woman other than herself had saved Thomas. "If it weren't so deadly serious, it might be humorous that you, my darling Thomas, saved my life and now some unknown woman returned the favor and saved ours. We should address our findings with Rodolfo tomorrow morning. I e-mailed him before we took off and suggested we meet at the *Journal's* offices at 0900. He confirmed by return e-mail."

"Yes, we can clean up at the hotel, catch a quick breakfast, and walk down the *Via Veneto* to the *Journal's* offices. Tomorrow being a Sunday, we shall be able to meet with Rodolfo in complete privacy."

The fog of love disappeared from Stefania's mind.

*Things have taken a serious turn. While love conquers many obstacles, it can't stop a car hurtling down a street or a bullet shot from a pistol.*

The two held hands and snuggled next to each other under a blanket.

Out the cabin window, lightning lit the skies from nearby thunderstorms typical of the intertropical convergence zone. After twenty minutes or so, the storms were behind them. The vast darkness of the Atlantic Ocean on a starry moonless night stretched to the horizon.

*What we've discovered will destroy my new found faith, as well as Thomas in the process. For now, at least, I'm with my dearest Thomas, safe, almost eight miles above the Atlantic Ocean.*

#

Some two-hundred nautical miles behind Stefania and Thomas, Greschenko's jet flew through the night sky toward Rome. She thought about the day's events and looked forward to landing, planning the next day out in her mind.

"I'll continue directly to the embassy where a full report on Thomas and Stefania's goings on in Brazil will await," she said to Anatoly.

"I made the arrangements before we departed," Anatoly responded. "Also Deputy Director Lenov and General Stasevich have been notified. They will be meeting us in Rome."

"Excellent," Greschenko replied. "Their first move will to go to her journal's offices, which fortunately we are aware of due to the fact that we've bugged the office and now have access to the journal's e-mail account."

"Good old fashioned intelligence gathering," affirmed Anatoly.

"Yes. Hopefully we'll be in Rome in ample time to listen to the conversation in real time. Unlike us, the duke and his girlfriend will be held up in customs upon arrival, and the meeting isn't until 0900," she noted.

As much as she tried, she couldn't purge Thomas from her thoughts.

*His eyes betrayed a sense of terror and curiosity. He didn't know who I am but wanted to know. I want to know Thomas.*

*My life has been lonely, a life which I've dedicated to the Russian Federation. All my lovers try to blackmail me.*

*A wealthy man like Thomas could relieve me of all of my obligations; he could hide me, protect me. He could whisk me away; he could love me. Maybe as a man of faith, he has a kind and trusting heart. A man who could be trusted. Imagine that.*

Nursing some vodka on ice, she closed her eyes and settled in for the long flight. The flashes of lightning from outside the plane lit up the now dark cabin. She presciently assumed that the next day would be hectic.

# Chapter 26
*Rome, Italy, June 16*

"Instead of walking down to Rodolfo's, we'll take the car today. I'm thoroughly paranoid," Thomas said to Stefania as they left their hotel suite. "I've already ordered the car."

"Sounds like a good idea given the circumstances," Stefania responded, seeming distracted.

As the car proceeded down the *Via Veneto*, Thomas, now suspicious, noted, "I think those two motor scooters are following us. Blast, I left the electronic jamming device Harry gave us in the hotel room. It doesn't matter; I forgot to recharge the bloody thing."

Stefania didn't respond.

The car dropped them off at the *Journal's* offices. Thomas' senses were alight for things out of the ordinary. At the curb Thomas looked up and down the grand avenue. A leggy blonde woman examined a tourist map at an espresso bar across the street. Several tables down along the sidewalk an Italian gentleman took in the Sunday morning news on his tablet. The bells from the nearby churches in Rome called the faithful to Sunday mass.

Arriving at Rodolfo's offices a little after 0900, Stefania began the briefing, speaking in Italian.

"Let me start from the beginning in terms of why we went back to Brazil. Thomas and I kept on thinking about what the Sheikh had told us. I realized there was an innocuous document which was actually more relevant than we thought."

Picking a copy of the document out of her bag, she presented it to Rodolfo. Quietly he reviewed the document while Sophie read it over his shoulder.

"The document calls for a conclave in November 1970 due to the resignation of Pope Gregory XVII," Stefania explained as Rodolfo examined the document. "It's signed by the Camerlengo, who is long deceased, but the vice-Camerlengo who witnessed the document, a monsignor then, is, I mean was, a cardinal and Archbishop of Minas Gerais, Bishop Metz, and was a friend of my uncle. I compared the signature on this document with his signature on my sacramental documents, and it matched. We went to Brazil to question him about this."

"Oh Madonna," said an obviously exasperated Rodolfo, his brows raised and his eyeglasses perched on the edge of his nose.

"There's one last twist, she noted. "It's likely that the newly elected pope in 1978 knew that Siri was elected pope in 1958. However, we don't think he knew about the 1970 conclave. Since Siri was still alive in 1978, the pope probably presumed he was illegitimate, which precipitated his suicide."

"What?" asked Rodolfo incredulously also in Italian. "So you're saying the pope committed suicide under false pretenses?"

"In his mind," Stefania continued, "the pope in 1978 was left with three unenviable choices, he could continue as pope, believing that he wasn't the true pope, or he could admit the dual papacy and resign in favor of Siri, but that would send the church into a tailspin. It would have torn it asunder, possibly creating a schism between the modernists and the traditionalists, or he could commit suicide and let the chips fall where they may after his death. He chose suicide."

"But why would that be the best option. I'm still not comprehending?" asked Rodolfo.

"The various prophecies, those of Saint Malachy, and the missing portion of the Third Secret of Fatima certainly implied that he was illegitimate. In retrospect, the two prior popes, at least until 1970, were illegitimate. The original death certificate indicates the pope died in 1978 from a barbiturate overdose. The MI6 document was likely given to him by his Camerlengo's assistant, this Father Zerkorian, who died in Baku ten days ago in a gunfight. We think the MI6 document was given to the pope to precipitate suicide, or resignation, at the very least to destabilize the church and convince him of his illegitimacy."

"We also learned from Metz that there were mutual excommunications by Siri and John XXIII," added Thomas.

Rodolfo and Sofia sat there without speaking. Minutes slipped by.

"Of course, there's also the Nostradamus prophesy of a pope who commits suicide in the night," she added.

Stefania sipped some water out of a bottle from her ever-present shoulder bag.

"There were rumours that the pope was going to steer the church in a more conservative direction and that he was a staunch anti-communist," Stefania continued.

"Of course, there's all the mysterious deaths surrounding this story," interjected Thomas.

"Yes, Father LaCroix, who provided some important documentation and information, was killed in a hit and run accident in Birmingham a few days ago. The culprit wasn't caught. Then yesterday Bishop Metz, who confirmed many of these facts, jumped off, or was pushed off, a bell tower of his basilica in Brazil to his death. Bishop Gonzalvo, who had met with the pope prior to his suicide, died suddenly, but we found the MI6 document in his room. Also yesterday someone tried to run down Thomas and me outside my uncle's home in Rio. Let's not forget that someone also tried to kill the Sheikh. We never told you about the attempt on my life at the *Parco della Musica*. There are dark forces surrounding this investigation. I'm frankly not sure in what direction to go. This is an incredible story, but Thomas and I now believe our lives are in danger. Someone doesn't want this story getting out. We don't know who; it could be the Vatican itself or other actors. We have sufficient documentation to support the story, and Thomas and I can corroborate events."

Rodolfo finally woke up from his daze.

"My devotion to the church and my journalistic duties are conflicted. I have no idea what to do!" he exclaimed.

Rodolfo placed his hands on his forehead. He stood and paced about his office.

"If this is all true, the papacy was in a perpetual state of *sede vacante* or schism from 1958 to 1970. The popes during that time were illegitimate, and Siri wasn't the Bishop of Rome. He was never installed officially as pope, never acted as such publically, and was arguably an excommunicate. The Second Vatican Council itself could be illegitimate."

Silence permeated the room. Rodolfo heaved a sigh.

"Write the story," Rodolfo solemnly directed. "Write the goddamned story. When it's finished, we can consider what to do. In the meantime, be careful." Thinking aloud, he said, "This could be the story of the century, at least in the Catholic world. It would be explosive in Italy particularly, as well as in South America. It could also further damage a church beset by scandals from the financial to the sexual. It might be the final nail in the coffin, particularly in western Europe and North America, where the church has many enemies and scandals."

"Understood," replied Stefania.

"Perhaps the *Journal* could present the story in a manner in the best light," he theorized, "but that's pie in the sky thinking. The clear inference is that the attempt to cajole the pope to commit suicide or resign was an inside job at the Vatican. There can be no debating that fact. Only church actors would want to put a lid on the story today."

Rodolfo paused as he paced about his office before continuing his speech.

"Saint John of the Cross once said, 'If a man wishes to be sure of the road he treads on, he must close his eyes and walk in the dark.' I suggest we all close our eyes, surrender ourselves to God, and ponder the events we're about to set in motion. Now you must excuse us. Sofia and I will be going to Sunday mass."

"Do you mind if we accompany you?" Thomas queried. "I think we could all use some divine guidance."

"Not at all," Rodolfo responded.

Walking up the *Via Veneto* under the shade of the London Plane trees lining the boulevard to the 10 o'clock mass at *Santa Maria della Concezione dei Cappuccini*, it didn't escape Thomas' notice that they were followed a short distance behind by the leggy blonde tourist from the sidewalk cafe and the Italian man with his tablet.

#

Several blocks away in a conference room filled with electronics at the embassy of the Russian Federation, Greschenko met with Anatoly, as well as Stasevich and Lenov. Lenov and Stasevich had flown in for the event, waiting to hear in real time what Thomas and Stefania reported to Rodolfo. The entire group could hear the discussion via speaker.

"We know that Stefania and Thomas met with the cardinal in Oura Preto before his untimely death," Greschenko noted. "However, nothing in the cardinal's background seems to raise any connection with Archangel. You've all read the file on the contractor. He had to be dispatched; otherwise, he would have likely killed the Britisher and the woman, and we'd never know what they've discovered."

Lenov and Stasevich nodded in agreement.

"Yes, nice job, Greschenko. A bullet to the head is worth its price in gold," said Stasevich.

Settling in their seats, they listened to the conversation in Rodolfo's office.

Greschenko, fluent in Italian, immediately understood the tenor of conversation and recognized the potential ramifications.

"This situation is much more complicated than we anticipated. Archangel opened up a pig sty. We *may* be able to use the pig shit to our advantage, like fertilizer."

"How so?" Lenov inquired.

Greschenko stood and walked about the room.

"What if?" she said to herself but loud enough for all to hear. Picking up her tablet, she quickly reviewed Thomas' electronic file and the file on the assassin who was killed in Leblon. "Yes, I know what we need to do."

Greschenko's newfound obsession with Thomas lingering in the back of her mind made her more determined to resolve the situation in a manner which suited her personal and professional objectives.

"If all of the pieces neatly fall in place, well then, we must phone the president immediately. I'll explain during the call."

The gears in Greschenko's mind worked fast on a solution. She had a creative one, but the president would have to approve it. She, Lenov, and Stasevich took the elevator to the embassy's secure basement conference room for a video telephone conference with the president. She closed the door to the windowless wood-paneled room as Lenov and Stasevich sat at the long Italian marble conference table.

#

Returned from mass, Thomas, in a contemplative mood, sat on the balcony at the hotel overlooking the Roman skyline, dominated by the dome of Saint Peter's Basilica. He watched as low dark clouds rolled in. Stefania sat at the desk in the suite intensely engrossed in drafting the story on her laptop.

Thomas' phone rang.

"Yes Emma," he answered.

"The secretary of state of the Holy See requests your presence at a meeting in the Apostolic Palace in Vatican City at 5 o'clock," blurted Emma in a somewhat panicked voice. "Stefania is also expected to attend. You're instructed to inform no one of this meeting. The call came from the usual number at the Vatican and was from the secretary's assistant, whose voice I recognized."

"Were you given an explanation as to the purpose of this meeting?"

"None. Only that you're to inform no one about this meeting."

"Right," he said ending the call.

"My assistant Emma called. The secretary of state of the Holy See wants an audience with us at 5 o'clock, specifically with both of us."

"Aces, but why do they want to meet with *us*?" she asked.

"I think you can assume that Rodolfo has spoken to his contacts and we're being called to task. He'll probably try to pressure you not to release the story. They indicated we're to inform no one. So no need to let Rodolfo know, although I suspect he already does; he might even be there. If we're going to make this meeting, we must away with all possible dispatch. I would suggest we keep with us all of the documents and your computer. Don't risk leaving anything here. It could be a ploy to get us away from the hotel."

"What if it *is* a trick?"

"Then we'll know when we get to the gate. We have to assume it's not."

Stefania and Thomas quickly changed into more presentable clothes, although, due to the time limitation, Thomas didn't deem themselves appropriately attired. Stefania managed a red stylish loose-fitting frock, the only dress she had with a hemline below the knees and a button down sweater to cover her shoulders. Thomas managed a blue blazer, a button down with a red rep tie, and gray gabardine trousers.

The driver picked the two up in front of the hotel for the ten or fifteen minute drive to the Vatican City State in Thomas' usual car, a Black BMW X-5.

"It looks like rain is coming," Thomas observed, seeing the clouds had lowered and a steady rain had started to fall.

The day turned gray and gloomy, and the typically picturesque drive up the grand boulevard of the *Via della Conciliazione* lost its luster. The SUV cruised by marble veneered Roman buildings with ceramic tile roofs, including one of Thomas' favorite small churches, the *Chiesa di Santa Maria di Transpontina,* with its incredible vaulted ceiling. The large lamps of the great concourse flew by every few seconds. In the distance Saint Peter's Square, grasped like open palms on each side by Bernini's Colonnade, grew closer. Thomas held Stefania's hand, but she said little.

"I'm always greeted well at the Vatican given my wealth and his family's contributions to the church, but I imagine the reception this time might be frosty given the practical impact of the facts of what we've uncovered," he said.

*Much is in jeopardy; my position with the church, my family's reputation and position in the UK, granny's hopes, dreams, and desires. I may have to ultimately choose between all of these things and the love of my life. To this point, I've unequivocally chosen Stefania over all else. These other considerations didn't seem as important as her love, affection, devotion, and the mad intoxicating physical attraction I have for her,* he thought.

Thomas' belly jumped with anxiety, and a slight nausea set in.

Thomas looked up through the car's sunroof at the gray cloud-shrouded sky as if seeking divine intervention.

*This quick change in the weather harbors something ominous.*

#

Stefania's stomach also tied in knots, she fiddled with her hair.

*I've put so much of myself into the story, I've discovered love in Thomas, and faith found me. But my story will impugn the faith I've embraced and, in the process, the man I loved. I've never been in love before. I've never been flown all over the world, slept in castles and mansions, bonded with Thomas, my best friend, companion, and protector.*

She looked up at the raindrops landing on the glass sunroof of the SUV and the clouds overhead. A flash of lightning lit the sky, and a clap of thunder reverberated through the streets like an echo in a canyon. With the flash of lightning, dread filled her.

#

Thomas knew the pope was away at *Castel Gandolfo,* so Saint Peter's Square was relatively deserted given the rainy weather. At Saint Peter's Square, the driver made a quick right and drove through the *Piazza Papa Pio XII,* then a quick left through the gate to the Vatican City State on the *Via di Porta Angelica* where they were greeted by Gendarmes, who upon reviewing their passports waved them forward onto the *Via Sant' Anna* where the car drove through an aperture into one of the interior courtyards of the grand Apostolic Palace.

Upon arrival in the interior courtyard, their sedan pulled up to the bronze doors to the palace. An assistant to the secretary of state held an umbrella over the two and escorted them to the entrance doors.

Thomas noticed two black four-door sedans neatly parked a few feet away in the courtyard with flags of state mounted on the front quarter panels. Now underneath the *porte cochere,* the attendant guided the two up a large staircase and down a long corridor trimmed in the pink and green hues of Italian marble. Having been to the Apostolic Palace before, Thomas knew precisely where they were going.

"The cardinal secretary of state is a crafty man, and much of what he does is for dramatic effect," he whispered to Stefania. "I surmise that the meeting will occur in one of the elaborately frescoed Raphael Rooms. While most of the public is familiar with the tremendous frescoes of the Sistine Chapel, the frescoes of the Raphael Rooms are equally as striking, if not more intricate, and provide more proportion to the adorned spaces. I'll wager we're being led to the *Stanza della Segnatura,* or the Room of the Signatura."

Stefania nodded in acknowledgement, her mind clearly preoccupied. Thomas took her heavy shoulder bag, which contained all of her papers and her laptop.

"Incredible," Thomas whispered, pointing. "The frescoes were all painted by Raffaello Sanzio da Urbino. That one is the Disputation of the Holy Sacrament."

Stefania stopped and stood still. She seemed transfixed on the great fresco.

Thomas, however, immediately noticed the others in the room and the seating arrangements. There were chairs arranged in a semi-circle with a larger chair facing all the others with a large knee-high table between. Stefania and Thomas took the empty two chairs. Across from them sat several others, including an Orthodox bishop, a diplomat wearing his sash of office, a Russian general in uniform, a thin bald man in an ill-fitting suit and tie, and a beautiful woman whom Thomas recognized from Rio, the one who saved their lives. She was his, as Stefania put it, "guardian angel."

Complete silence shrouded the room, and the mere rustling of papers, whisper, or moving of a chair reverberated throughout the chamber. Thomas, now curious about this woman, couldn't help glancing at her. She responded with a smile and nod of recognition. Thomas' intrigue grew, much like when he first met Stefania. The Russian woman wore a black silk skirt which covered her athletic legs, and a red patterned silk blouse buttoned appropriately almost to the neckline.

*Who is this mysterious woman?*

Thunder again could be heard rumbling outside, and the sound seemed to ricochet off the buildings in Vatican City and through the halls of the Apostolic Palace.

Double wood doors leading to the room opened with a loud thud, the sound rattling throughout the room, and the old cardinal secretary of state emerged wearing a simple cardinal's cassock, white with red trim and buttons, with his scarlet *zucchetto* skullcap on his head, followed by his assistant, a bishop, in his black cassock with purple trim. Their footsteps echoed throughout the grand room.

"I introduce his grace, the Duke of Radcliffe, his companion, Stefania DiMaggio of the *Italian Monthly Journal*. Here we have Metropolitan Alexei," said the cardinal in English. "He's Russian Orthodox Metropolitan Bishop of Borodino, its legate to the Holy See. Next to him is His Excellency, the Ambassador Nikov, the Ambassador to the Holy See of the Russian Federation, as well as Colonel General Stasevich of the Russian Army, and Deputy Directors Greschenko and Lenov, of Russia's Foreign Intelligence Service."

"I'm sure you two are questioning why I brought you here," said the cardinal, glancing at Thomas and Stefania. "For the answer to this question, I'm going to let Deputy Director Greschenko explain."

Greschenko, smiling slightly, remained seated, re-crossed her legs and began speaking in accent-less American English.

"Thank you, your eminence."

Now staring at Thomas and apparently deliberately ignoring Stefania, she started with what appeared to be a contrived narrative.

"I'm Svetlana Greschenko with Russian intelligence. We became aware of various matters when an Armenian agent, Emil Zerkorian, was killed in Baku by the Azerbaijani authorities. Files were found, names, *et cetera*, dealing with his time here at the Vatican. The Russian Federation, the Russian Orthodox Church, and the Holy See have entered into a period of *détente*, so to speak. Thus, we immediately brought this information to the attention of Metropolitan Alexi here. We continued to work the matter and determined that someone had hired *this* man."

Greschenko proceeded to place several photos of the same person on the table so everyone could see.

"His name is Nigel Houston," she explained after a brief pause. "He or his associates killed a Bishop Gonzalvo in Aparecida, a Father LaCroix in Birmingham, and Cardinal Metz in Ouro Preto, and was probably involved in the attempted assassination of the former Grand Mufti of Alexandria here in Rome, which wasn't successful. We determined that Mr. Houston was a former MI5 agent who was a professional hit man. So the question has arisen, who would want all of these people dead?"

Greschenko paused again, looking Thomas in the eyes as she took some additional papers from a file next to her chair.

"Mr. Houston was paid the sum of two-hundred thousand pounds sterling on June first which was wired to his bank account on the Isle of Man, a notorious tax haven. We traced the funds to the account of the Baron of *Eilean Seil* held in a Cook Island Trust. He's your uncle, yes?" she asked, looking at Thomas. "Here are the details of the financial transactions."

She placed papers on the table in front of Thomas, which he picked up and began examining.

"You'll find if you do your own investigation that there are two-hundred thousand pounds sterling missing from the baron's accounts. The records are indisputable. Moreover, an associate of Houston attempted to dispatch Ms. DiMaggio in the washroom of a concert hall here in Rome and on a back country lane near the duke's home in England. It's likely that the same person who hired Mr. Houston to kill all these people, and to attempt the murder of Ms. DiMaggio in Rome, hired him to run you and Ms. DiMaggio down in Leblon. Houston died in the process of that attempt. Our understanding is that the only person who could have authorized the transfer of the funds to Houston would be your grandmother, the dowager duchess, because your uncle, the baron, is not of sound mind and is institutionalized."

She paused again, as if for dramatic effect.

"Naturally," she continued, raising her voice slightly, "if it became public that the Duchess of Radcliffe had hired a hit man to target and kill a bishop, a cardinal, an elderly priest, a Sheikh, her own grandson the Duke of Radcliffe, not to mention a journalist, well, it would be an incredible and salacious scandal."

Thomas, in a state of disbelief, feverishly continued reviewing the financial documents given to him.

"This can't be true. You must be mad! You don't know what you're bloody talking about."

"As I said," Greschenko calmly retorted, "I think you'll find that the funds are missing from the baron's account, and they were transferred surreptitiously to Houston's account. It's all quite clear. In my experience there are two prime motivators in the human experience, love and faith. Both are dangerous emotions and fickle. Love can turn to hate with little warning. Your grandmother had to make a choice, and she chose her faith over you. Unfortunate, but the facts don't lie. With you dead, your heirs would be your distant Cousin James, the current Earl Layton, and his children. He's Catholic and his child is being raised Catholic, correct?"

"That's it?" Thomas, now incredulous, asked. "You brought us here to tell me that my grandmother is a murderer? And that she wanted me dead?"

"Not quite," responded the cardinal, shifting in his chair, turning toward Thomas. "There's the matter of your planned article and the documents and information you possess."

"What of it?" Thomas asked.

"Our Russian friends," continued the cardinal after a pause, "uncovered much of this in the process of tracking down Houston. You see, if the information you have gets out, if it's made public, of course the whole matter of Houston will then come out, who paid him, what he did. While your story about the church will embolden its enemies, particularly in the United States, Europe, and the UK, the church will survive in some form, as it always has. The paradoxical question is will you and your grandmother survive the scandal that ensues? You'll still have money and titles, but would it be worth it? You know there are elements in the UK who would delight to see you embroiled in scandal. Everyone has enemies, even you, even inside the church. Your grandmother could not only be prosecuted in the UK but in Italy and Brazil for contract murder and attempted murder. Is that how you want your web biography to read in twenty, forty, sixty, one-hundred years?"

"So what are you saying?" Thomas queried.

The cardinal cleared his throat.

"What I'm saying is that I would request that you leave all the documents in your possession, as well as Ms. DiMaggio's computer, and your phones, with us here. I understand that the Russians will be able to find any material you've stored remotely on the cloud or some such thing. While you might still have a story, there will be no way to prove it. Everyone with first-hand knowledge is dead. And, of course, if the story gets out, there's the subtext of your grandmother's hiring of Mr. Houston, which I'm sure you'd rather keep from public consumption, will come out. No story, no subtext. It's not particularly complicated."

"This is blackmail!" Stefania yelled. "Blackmail pure and simple!"

"I prefer to call it a *quid pro quo*," the cardinal replied with a smirk. "Newton's Third Law states that 'For every action there is an equal and opposite reaction.' It's a fundamental tenet of life." Thomas considered the dialogue.

*Not everyone with knowledge is dead. The Sheikh is still alive and out there somewhere. Also, there were the ballots from the 1970 conclave sitting in a file or box somewhere in the archbishop's residence in Minas Gerais. Maybe the invitation to the 1970 conclave was still in the archives, if it hadn't been discovered.*

After a lengthy pause and complete silence, Greschenko took out a large brown envelope and threw it onto the table in front of Stefania. It landed with a thud. While doing so, Greschenko bent over ever so slightly staring into Thomas' eyes.

*Those eyes*, he thought, *are emotionless; black as coal, as if piercing my soul.*

"Ms. DiMaggio, this should compensate you amply for the loss of your computer, phone, and perhaps the loss of your story," said Greschenko.

Thomas snatched up the envelope, opening it.

"It's packed with crisp one-hundred euro notes," he exclaimed. "A bribe; it's a bloody bribe."

"Not a bribe; a generous payment of five-hundred thousand Euros by the Russian Federation on behalf of the Holy See to Ms. DiMaggio for her services as a journalist," said the cardinal. "Not too different from your graces' request regarding Ms. DiMaggio's sacramental documents, which were perjured by me for a promise in return."

Greschenko nodded in agreement.

"Yes," Greschenko said. "Thank you for your story, to which the Holy See now will hold all rights. Ms. DiMaggio, consider this your compensation. Here's a contract which you will sign transferring all rights, title, and interest in the story to the Holy See. It also contains a non-disclosure clause. You'll find that it's all quite in order. You'll have to pay taxes on the funds, of course, which will be reported to the Italian revenue authorities."

"Don't judge me too harshly, your grace," the cardinal remarked. "I wear the scarlet hat of a cardinal of the church, which means I've sworn an oath to give my life to protect the faith. The existence of a *sede vacante,* or however you want to describe it, between 1958 and 1970 can never be made public. It would provide the sedevacantist movement with the legitimacy it has long craved, result in a permanent schism, and perhaps lead to the destruction of the church."

"I won't do it, I won't!" Stefania shouted, looking at Thomas.

Several minutes passed, although they could easily have been hours. Thomas looked through the documentation of the financial transfers and reviewed the contract the Russians had prepared.

At that moment he remembered the Sheikh's final words to them both, "The fruit of silence is tranquility."

He pondered the Sheikh's advice and turned to Stefania.

"Unfortunately, you must," he said. "It's all here. There's no choice. This will destroy me, my reputation, my family, destroy my grandmother, and let's not forget the massive devastation it will heap upon the church." Empathizing with Stefania, Thomas urged her to accept the money, whispering, "Money doesn't heal all wounds, but it makes them less painful."

"I appreciate your attempt to convince me, but I'm not consoled. This *is* the most money I've ever seen," Stefania quietly whispered back to Thomas.

No one spoke as Stefania counted the money, apparently thinking long and hard during the interlude.

"I will accept. I'll accept this deal. I don't wish to harm Thomas or his family," she affirmed as she quickly signed the document presented to her, throwing the pen back onto the table, which slid off onto the floor at Greschenko's feet.

"Your eminence, neither the Holy Father nor anyone else in the Vatican is aware of this story or what you've orchestrated here today. Am I correct?" Thomas inquired in the cardinal's native French.

"You have your secrets, your grace, and I have mine. We all have secrets," the cardinal responded, also in French.

The cardinal got up to show Stefania and Thomas out, Stefania now carrying only her shoulder bag now empty save for some personal items and the package of Euros.

"Now that wasn't so hard, was it? May God bless you both for your sacrifice today. We'll be in touch with you soon, your grace. Our Russian friends would like you to work with us in connection with the ongoing dialogue regarding the lifting of economic sanctions by the UK."

Walking out of the elaborate room and down the halls of the Apostolic Palace, Thomas could hear the church bells tolling at a small abbey in Vatican City, calling the cloistered sisters there to prayer. After a few seconds, the chanting of the opening prayers of vespers could be faintly heard, the sweet angelic voices of the nuns wafting through the air between the now distant rumbles of thunder.

*"Deu, in adjutorium meum intende. Domine, ad adiuvandum me festina. Gloria Patrie, et Filio, et Spiritui Sancto. Sicut erat in prinicpio, et nunc et simper, et in saecula saeculorum. Amen. Alleluia."*

"Oh yes, oh Lord, please make haste to help me," Thomas muttered.

Through a driving rain they drove back to the hotel.

"Your supposedly pious grandmother tried to have us both killed!" Stefania blurted, breaking the tense silence with the obvious. "How ironic. That's crazy! What if she tries again? You were prepared to sweep this under the rug to protect your backside. I'm going to collect my things at the hotel and go back to my father's flat."

"I'm truly sorry, but you must understand the circumstances."

"Oh I understand, believe me. My eyes are wide open."

"I think you should tell Rodolfo what transpired and why the story can't run. I suspect he'll be relieved."

"I suppose he will be, now that you mention it. With no proof, the story can't be written, and he and the *Journal* will be off the hook."

At the hotel Thomas waited by the BMW while Stefania packed upstairs. After she came down he helped her stow her suitcases. Standing by the SUV in the pouring rain, Thomas kissed her on the forehead. She ran her hand along his rain-soaked cheek, removed from her neck the silver and emerald cross Thomas loaned her on the road from Glasgow, and placed it in Thomas's open palm, then she closed his fingers around it.

"Will I see you again?" he inquired.

"I've got some thinking to do," Stefania replied, looking at the ground.

"You know, there will always be a place in my heart for you," Thomas whispered back.

Stefania gazed back at Thomas, their eyes meeting ever so briefly. She swept her now wet tresses back.

"Again, there's a hole in my heart," she said as she wiped tears from her face with her sweater sleeve. After one last glance at Thomas, she stepped into the BMW, shut the door, and it sped away through the drenching downpour.

Walking back into the hotel, he sat at the bar and ordered a gin and tonic. The emotional roller coaster of the last several weeks, the traveling back and forth across the ocean, left him drained, physically and emotionally.

#

On their way back to the Russian Embassy, Svetlana, Lenov, and Stasevich sat in the back seats of one of the embassy's two black limousines. The metropolitan and Russian ambassador took the second limousine.

"Congratulations are in order, Svetlana Sergeyevna," commended Lenov. "This was one of the best conceived plans. They all bought the story, including the lies, and the benefits to our government are incalculable."

"Yes, thank you," pondered Greschenko softly with a sense of absence. "Thank you. Everything fell into place perfectly," she muttered, her mind in another place.

"Well, if it wasn't my insistence that we hire the old duchess' contractor, this Nigel Houston fellow, who couldn't be traced back to us, this wouldn't have gone so well," Stasevich bragged. "Houston never knew he was working for us. He assumed he was working for the old British lady, and us, whomever we were, were paying him more, so he did what we wanted. It was genius for us to foil his attempt in Rio. Absolute genius. Too bad we can't get the five-hundred thousand euros back we paid to the dead contractor. That's left a big hole in my overseas budget."

"I thought it was *my* idea," Lenov opined. "Anyway, we *will* try to get the money back somehow. Consider we also now have the duke's girlfriend essentially taking a bribe and have implicated the duke's family in a murder for hire plot."

"Excellent point," piped in Stasevich.

"Something tells me with those little tidbits we can call on the duke for assistance in the future," noted Lenov.

"Let's not forget the best part," said Stasevich. "We controlled activities in the Vatican until 1978 without them even knowing it. Then there's the former MI5 agent, a paid hit man by the duke's grandmother, we can link to at least two deaths to keep the secret from coming out."

"We didn't know of this schism, which was created by Archangel, but now that we have not only all of the facts, the documents, computers, and resolved the matter, Russia is in the clear," added Lenov. "We saved the Ukraine negotiations and the Vatican in one fell swoop. The irony here is so thick you could cut it with a knife."

"Yes," Greschenko agreed softly, still distracted. "Irony at its epic best."

"Greschenko, this would make a great novel if the girlfriend actually knew the whole story and lived to publish it," said Lenov.

"And all resolved before the July first summit between the pope, the prime minister, and the president," Stasevich added slapping his knee. "The president owes us a hundred-fold for this success. Even if the rumours of your sexuality *are* true, I'm sure the president will *now* look the other way."

Greschenko's eyes cut to Stasevich and frowned. About to lay into him, her phone rang. She picked it up.

"Where is he?" she asked.

"He's at the *Grand Hotel Parco Borghese*, sitting at the bar to the left of the reception desk."

"You may cease your surveillance of him. I'll take over from here."

"Acknowledged," said the voice on the other end.

"Drop me off a block from the *Grand Hotel Parco Borghese*," she barked to the driver.

"There is the one loose string, the Sheikh," noted Stasevich. "He'll turn up eventually, and when he does, we'll take care of him."

Detouring from the route to the embassy, the driver dropped Greschenko off. She got out, walked a block, and entered the foyer of the hotel. The bar was to the oblique left. She strode in. Thomas sat by himself nursing a cocktail. Sitting directly next to him, Greschenko purposely invaded his personal space.

"Sir, I'll have vodka on the rocks please," she instructed the bartender in perfect Italian.

"You. I'm not sure whether to thank you or hate you."

"I prefer thanks. In that case, you're welcome. We haven't been properly introduced. I'm Svetlana."

"I'm Thomas, but of course you know that. One question; how did Zerkorian lead you to Houston? That part doesn't make sense to me."

Greschenko took a sip of her vodka, the ice cubes clinking against the glass.

"That, your grace, is a Russian state secret, and we go to great lengths to protect our state secrets."

"Zerkorian was no Armenian, was he? He was a Russian agent. His death in Baku was related to this, wasn't it?"

"You're asking about more state secrets again," Greschenko, smiling, replied.

"This is quite coincidental, you being at the hotel," Thomas noted.

Greschenko again smiled.

"It's no coincidence."

"Of course not. In any event, however, you became involved. I do owe you a debt of gratitude for saving my life and the life of my friend Stefania."

"Do you love her?" Greschenko inquired.

"Yes, yes I do, with all of my heart," Thomas quietly replied.

"And where *is* this Stefania?" she asked.

"She's left for her father's flat here in Rome. As you can imagine, things have unfortunately become rather complicated. My guess is that I'll not be seeing her for some time. Things have to be sorted out. She did say you were my 'guardian angel' for saving my life."

"You chose your faith over love. That's admirable."

"Was it Dorothy Day, I think it was, who famously chose God over man, but I didn't do so for such a noble reason," Thomas responded, after finishing a sip of his cocktail. "I also chose my own wellbeing and wealth, and that of my family over love. That's *not* particularly admirable, is it? Uncontrollable fate hounds me like a plague."

"Fate plagues all of us in its own way, but isn't it what we make of our fate that matters?" asked Greschenko.

"It doesn't seem so, does it now," responded Thomas.

"Don't be so hard on yourself. Life offers many choices, some savory but most not particularly so," Greschenko noted. Grinning she raised her glass of vodka for a toast. "Well, here's to guardian angels then. We all need at least one. We can agree to that, yes?"

Thomas raised his glass and touched it to hers with a faint smile.

"Yes, here's to guardian angels."

*Rome, Italy, June 17*

Dutifully reporting to work, as much as she didn't want to do so, Stefania tepidly entered Rodolfo's office, closing the door.

His eyes looking over his reading glasses, Rodolfo asked in a fatherly kind of way, "Anything new to report, my child?"

Sitting down, Stefania looked Rodolfo in the eyes.

"How solemn your inquiry is, almost like you know that whatever answer I provide won't be correct," she softly replied.

"For me, Stefania, what you discovered, there exists no adequate resolution," he responded quietly.

"We were summoned to the Vatican," Stefania noted almost matter-of-factly, assuming Rodolfo knew anyway.

"You were what?" Rodolfo asked with a sense of disbelief and surprise. He stood from his desk. "Well, what happened?"

"Oh, and the Russians were there. They said that Thomas' grandmother attempted to have us killed in Brazil, and that the man she hired killed LaCroix, Gonzalvo, and Metz. They had evidence of the money transfers, and if we didn't give up all of our information, electronic and otherwise, they would out Thomas and his grandmother."

Walking out from behind his desk, Rodolfo exclaimed, "Oh Madonna!"

"So we agreed. Thomas's arm didn't have to be twisted much." Stefania, standing, opened her shoulder bag and threw the wrapped euro notes onto Rodolfo's desk. "They gave me this to purchase my silence. The story is gone, you see. You should be satisfied."

"And what of Thomas?" Rodolfo asked, staring at the Euros.

"What of Thomas?" Stefania stuttered. Tears welling in her eyes, she replied, "Thomas," shaking her head. Biting her lip, she wiped her eyes with her hand.

Rodolfo and Stefania embraced, and he stroked her hair as she wept on his shoulder.

"There's an old Italian saying," he whispered into her ear, "'Love is like a dove. It's beautiful when it's there, but it can fly away when you don't want it to.' My dear, the heart is the most fragile of the human organs. Only time, my child, heals the heart. I can provide no solace. I'm afraid it will be a long time. Only when you're prepared to forgive him will it be healed."

*Several Months Later*
*Rome, Italy, November 1*

Stefania returned to the Contarelli Chapel at the Church of *San Luigi dei Francesi*, a spot in Rome that had become sentimental to her, for mass on All Saints Day. After mass she sat and meditated in front of Caravaggio's *Calling of Saint Matthew*.

Her eyes shut, she knelt and prayed for nothing in particular except happiness, an emotion which had eluded her for months. The great masterpiece amazed her as it always had. A ray of sun, illuminated the subtle shadows of the painting, called to Matthew. A tear emerged from the edge of her eye, meandered down the crevice between her nose and cheek, bounced off her lips, slid to her chin, and dropped to the floor. She wiped her chin dry with her baggy sweater sleeve, looked at her phone.

Standing, she took one last glance at the painting. A cool and dreary day in Rome, she slipped her gray wool jacket over her wool sweater, adjusted her neck scarf, snatched up her shoulder bag, and made her way out of the church. Looking down, checking the messages on her phone as she reached the grand church doors, Stefania bumped into a man. Her shoulder bag dropped to the floor and its contents spilled, scattering about.

Her attention turned to her bag on the floor in the entryway to the church.

"Excuse me, miss, I'm so sorry. Please let me assist you," said the man in Italian.

Stefania looked up.

"Thomas?" she exclaimed.

Her heart fluttered, like it skipped a beat. Joy overcame her. Her body tingled from head to toe.

"Stefania, what a surprise," Thomas responded as he gathered the odds and ends from her bag from the floor. "How are you?"

"I'm well. I'm just leaving after mass, and you?" she asked.

"I'm fine," responded Thomas. "It's All Saints Day, and I thought I'd come in and admire Caravaggio and meditate. When I'm in Rome and have time, I often stop in here."

The two paused awkwardly for a moment, but to Stefania it seemed like a year. She hadn't seen Thomas since she left him at the hotel on that rainy day in June. He seemed genuinely happy to see her.

Thomas broke the silence.

"Do you have an appointment? Do you have to be anywhere?" he asked.

"Right now, no, not at all. Why?" Stefania replied.

"Well, I thought if you had a few minutes we could grab an espresso or early lunch and catch up if you're interested?" Thomas inquired.

"I'd like that," Stefania responded with a smile. "I'd like that very much."

###